THE BOSTONIANS

Henry James

The Bostonians

A Novel

Introduction by

IRVING HOWE

Professor of English

Hunter College

THE MODERN LIBRARY · *New York*

THE MODERN LIBRARY

is published by RANDOM HOUSE, INC.

Manufactured in the United States of America

Introduction

BY IRVING HOWE

In the year 1886 Henry James, by then a writer of acknowledged rank, published two lavishly composed novels, *The Bostonians* and *The Princess Casamassima*. Taken together they mark a distinct phase in his career, for not only do they constitute an impressive portion of the work he accomplished during his "middle period"—that high plateau of creativeness which begins with *The Portrait of a Lady* and ends with *The Awkward Age*—but they also share a community of subject matter and literary method that sets them somewhat apart from the bulk of James' fiction.

Both novels deal ambitiously, though also rather furtively, with the public world, with the fluid contours of society and the tempting dangers of politics. Rich and supple in style, they are written with an assurance which suggests a master's growing awareness that, come what may and be his fortune what it will, he *is* a master. In both novels James negotiates that risky transition from public to private experience which is the sure sign of a writer sensitive to the nature of society and convinced, however little he may say so, that it has a reality of its own which cannot be grasped simply by observing its members individually. And in both novels no distinction can finally be made between public and private experience, so that the deformations of the one soon become the deformations of the other. Yet James does not rest there, for he knows that the private deformations will react upon the public, causing those tragedies, absurdities and spent heroisms with which the novels are filled.

Neither the reviewers nor the public were very friendly to the two books when they first appeared. Today it is a little hard to understand why, since quite apart from any deeper or more recondite significance that may be assigned to these novels, one supposes they would have delighted readers simply through their surface vivacity, *The Princess Casamassima* by its boldness in seizing upon European anarchism for its locale, *The Bostonians* by its marvellously dry wit in satirizing New England society.

The explanation for their failure is to be found—if one can be found at all—in the quality of American culture during the 1880's. Wit and the talent it implies for self-criticism were not greatly cherished in the America of seventy years ago; an age of complacence, as we have reason to know, prefers that its writers avoid the satiric and astringent. *The Bostonians* wounded the self-regard of earnest middle-class readers, for it took a dim view of the New England reforming tradition which, by then, had been comfortably aligned with the national appetite for self-congratulation. In a tone of biting cleverness that must have bewildered many of his readers, James had called into question the persistent fondness of Americans for thinking of themselves as the salt of the earth—the newest salt and the best salt. Nor has time softened the force of his attack. If *The Bostonians* is read with a full awareness, which means a readiness to admit that it jars many of our fondest opinions, it becomes clear that the book is a deep-going and, thereby, radical criticism of American life.

The public failure of *The Bostonians* and *The Princess Casamassima* hurt and bewildered James. Nor was he so vain as to pretend indifference. "I have entered upon evil days," he wrote to William Dean Howells in 1888, "I am still staggering a good deal under the mysterious and (to me) inexplicable damage wrought—apparently—upon my situation by my last two novels . . ."

To some extent this disappointment may have hastened his turn from the social novel, which meant, as he knew, to forego his earlier ambition to become the American Balzac. But for all his surface tenderness, James was not the man to be deflected from his path because reviewers were obtuse and readers apathetic. What decided him in abandoning the public themes of these two novels (he wrote to his brother) was his "sense of knowing terribly little about the kind of life I have attempted to describe." Though essentially true for *The Princess Casamassima,* this was not at all true for *The Bostonians*—which may help explain why the first is an absorbing failure and the second a masterpiece. Nonetheless, James' remark contains a shrewd self-criticism, for despite lucky hits and clever guesses he lacked that passionate absorption in the worlds of business and politics which a social novelist must have.

II

Yet it would be a mistake to suppose that these novels constitute a mere sport in James' career. Both in the writing of nineteenth-century America and in James' own novels one can see the slow growth of a literary tradition that will reach a climax in *The Bostonians*. Those areas of native experience which an American Balzac would have had to exhaust, James had already begun to outline in his early novels. Especially noteworthy as a forerunner of *The Bos-*

tonians is that brilliant short novel *The Europeans,* in which James struck the "New England tone" at its fine thin best, a New England tone he brought into ambiguous but finally triumphant relation with the more sumptuous tones of Europe. New England is the setting of both novels, but in *The Europeans* it is notable for its moral refinement while in *The Bostonians* it has declined into a mean and eccentric shabbiness. Between the "worlds" of the two novels there falls the shadow of the Civil War.

The roots of *The Bostonians* extend, of course, beyond James' own work. A heavy line of intellectual and literary influence can be traced from Hawthorne to James, visibly so in *The Bostonians,* deeply buried but still to be felt in such novels as *The Golden Bowl.* Both writers face problems that clearly place them as sensitive Americans living in the nineteenth century. In Hawthorne the moral sense has been largely detached from its earlier context of orthodox faith, but it has found little else in which to thrive, certainly no buoying social vision—which may explain why Hawthorne turned to allegory, the one literary mode in which it might seem possible to sustain the moral sense as an independent force. In James the moral sense is at least as acute and troublesome as in Hawthorne, but James has learned how to embody and test it through portrayals of social manners and relations. Yet the themes of the two writers are quite similar. Both are obsessed by the problem of integrity: how, they repeatedly ask, can a human being, involved as he must be in limiting and treacherous social relationships, yet maintain something of his personal uniqueness? The great sin in Hawthorne's novels, which is the presumption of taking into one's hands the destiny of another person, is also the great sin in James' novels. Both writers are concerned with the emergence and survival of personality, and both see this problem as particularly difficult in a culture where the idea, not to mention the fact, of experience is morally suspect. No portrait of Hawthorne, wrote James, "is at all exact which fails to insist upon the constant struggle which must have gone on between his shyness and his desire to know something of life; between what may be called his evasive and inquisitive tendencies." This sentence is one of the most important ever written about American literature, and not least because it is as true for James as for Hawthorne.

When Hawthorne came to write *The Blithedale Romance,* a novel that is in many ways a forerunner of *The Bostonians,* he tried to relate the problem of experience to the idealistic and sentimental reformers who had swarmed over New England in the decades before the Civil War. James' complaint that the book lacked the wounding edge of satire, that it let "the author's fellow-communists . . . off so easily," is accurate yet hardly to the point, for James failed to see that no matter what Hawthorne said about his fellow-colonists at Brook Farm they held for him the attraction of abundant and savored experience. The sexually magnificent Zenobia and even the fanatical reformer Hollingsworth are the figures in *The Blithedale Romance* through whom the blood of life pulses, while the "positive" characters are prim, dry, bleached.

Hawthorne looked upon the enthusiasm, if not the ideas, of the reformers as a temptation, and temptations can seldom serve as the object of satire. James, however, had taken a step beyond temptation: his reformers no longer have the capacity for a large irregular experience, they have declined into eccentric chatter. When he wrote that *The Blithedale Romance* was too mild he was not really telling us very much about the book; he was anticipating the assumptions from which *The Bostonians* would later be written.

But in another criticism of *The Blithedale Romance* James was far more acute:

> As the action advances in *The Blithedale Romance* we get too much out of reality . . . I should have liked to see the story concern itself more with the little community in which its earlier scenes are laid . . .

This seems exactly right—yet, one may wonder, isn't it also true for *The Bostonians,* a novel in which the first 150 pages treat brilliantly of the world of Boston reform and the remainder narrows down to a personal struggle between Olive Chancellor, the bitter feminist, and Basil Ransom, the Southern conservative? I hope to show that it is not true. For James, whether knowingly or not, had found a way of avoiding the weakness that had beset Hawthorne when he tried to deal with an American political theme and would beset most other American novelists when they confronted American politics. In almost every nineteenth-century American novel which touches, no matter how gingerly, on the life of politics, one comes up against the despairing cry: *It is too late, there is no place for the sensitive and thoughtful man, perhaps there never was.*

This cry is heard most sharply in Henry Adams' *Democracy,* a novel published seven years before *The Bostonians;* it is heard, even if dimly and muffled, in *The Blithedale Romance.* James, who had fewer hopes or illusions than most American writers, shared in this feeling, yet he found a way of avoiding its literary price; he found a way of avoiding that surrender to the "evasive tendency," that withdrawal from the urgencies of the subject matter, which occurs about midway through so many American novels dealing with the life of politics.

III

James generally started a novel with a clear sketch in mind of his essential themes and structure. In a notebook entry for 1883 he wrote concerning the relationship of Olive Chancellor and Verena Tarrant that it "should be a study of one of those friendships between women which are so common in New England." After remarking that the idea for the book had been suggested to him by Daudet's *Évangéliste,* he goes on to say:

If I could only do something with that *pictorial* quality. At any rate, the subject is very national, very typical. I wished to write a very *American* tale, a tale very characteristic of our social conditions, and I asked myself what was the most salient and peculiar point in our social life. The answer was: the situation of women, the decline of the sentiment of sex, the agitation on their behalf.

What is more, the device through which James generally works out a disciplined relation to his material—the strict confinement of a novel's "point of view" to one or two observing characters—does not seem to interest him very much in *The Bostonians*. Judged by narrowly "Jamesian" standards, *The Bostonians* might even be said to suffer from an undisciplined pictorial looseness. But if so, we have every reason to be grateful. Much of its charm, even some of its wit, comes from James' affectionate rendering of places and scenes. The elegance of Olive Chancellor's drawing room, the dinginess of the Cambridge street in which the Tarrants live, the glimmering mildness of Cape Cod in the summer— these are among the permanent values of the book. The musty mumbling circle of reformers meeting, and sagging, in Miss Birdseye's rooms, the wonderful and gently satirized Miss Birdseye as she summons the heroic past of Abolitionism, the moment when Ransom and Verena stand gravely before the scroll of the dead in Memorial Hall, the brutal clash between Ransom and Olive at Verena's New York debut—these scenes, etched with a dry sharp clarity, stay fresh and alive in one's mind.

But even in terms of strict loyalty to his theme, James was entirely right in turning to the pictorial method. The dramatic concentration that is gained from seeing an action through the eyes of one or two sensitive observers is sometimes possible in *The Bostonians,* and then the camera narrows down to the blighted vision of Olive Chancellor or Basil Ransom. But such a narrowing is not always desirable. For *The Bostonians* as conceived, and its first 150 pages as written, it is essential that we gain a sense of the larger workings and rhythms of society, which in most of James' novels, confined as they are to private dramas, he can afford to skimp. One of the ways, for example, in which James suggests that the glories of Abolitionism and the Boston reform movements are a thing of the past is by showing us the slowly accumulating seediness of the city itself as it stumbles into the factory age:

> [From Olive Chancellor's window one could see] a few chimneys and steeples, straight, sordid tubes of factories and engine-shops, or spare, heavenward finger of the New England meeting house. There was something inexorable in the poverty of the scene, shameful in the meanness of its details, which gave a collective impression of boards and tins and frozen earth, sheds and rotting piles, railway-lines striding flat across a thoroughfare of puddles . . . loose fences, vacant lots, mounds of refuse, yards bestrewn with iron pipes, telegraph poles and bare wooden backs of places.

Apart from such superb descriptive passages, James' yielding to the pictorial impulse makes possible a treatment of character that sets *The Bostonians* apart from most of his other novels. James' excessive identification with the weakness and deprivations of his more vulnerable characters—which mars such books as *Roderick Hudson, The Portrait of a Lady* and *The Princess Casamassima*—is here no problem at all. There are no "poor shabby gentlemen" in *The Bostonians* over whom James can quiver and softly moan, no brave American girls trapped in the moral pits of Europe. The luxury of renunciation, one of the few to which James was ever susceptible, does not tempt him in *The Bostonians,* for the characters of this novel do try to live by their desires. In *The Bostonians* James keeps his distance, often a quite cool and hostile distance, from almost all of his characters; he is not, in any damaging sense, involved with their destinies.

But James' concern with the pictorial does something even more remarkable for *The Bostonians*. It allows him a free and happy release of aggressive feelings such as he seldom ventures in his other novels: he needn't, in *The Bostonians,* "consider" his characters too tenderly, they are fair game, at times mere objects of satire—and it would be sanctimonious to deny that James finds a distinct pleasure, or that we share it, in swooping down on the frauds and quacks of Boston. When we first meet Olive Chancellor, we are told that a smile playing about her lips "might have been likened to a thin ray of moonlight resting upon the walls of a prison." Selah Tarrant, mesmerist father of Verena, "looked like the priest of a religion that was passing through the stage of miracles"; Matthias Pardon, the poisonous reporter, "regarded the mission of mankind upon earth as a perpetual evolution of telegrams." In such sentences, and in the passages from which they are drawn, the prose races forward with a spontaneous sharpness and thrust, it breathes an assurance that permits James to risk, and control, the broadest touches of burlesque.

The qualities I have related to James' striving for pictorial effects are central to the book, and all of them contribute to its underlying tone or attitude. *The Bostonians* is infused with skepticism, not only in regard to New England reformers but also to the claims and pretensions of American society as a whole. The idea of social reform is treated less with hostility—for it isn't ideas as such that form his main target—than with cool and ironic misgivings. This may be offensive to our liberal or radical pieties, but there, as James might say, it is. Nor is the offense to conservative pieties any the less, for it is precisely the conservative mood of the book that brings it into a certain conflict with conservative doctrine.

James' skepticism is that of a man who is living, and knows he is living, in the backwash of a great historical moment. It is the skepticism of a man who in his own life has known something about the reformers of yesterday (many of them friends of his father, Henry James, Sr., himself one of the more attractive figures of the Emersonian Age) and who wants little to do with them, except perhaps to honor their memories. Though entirely nonpolitical in the ordinary sense, James had been a warm partisan of the North during the

Civil War, and the fact that the years of sacrifice and consecration had been followed by a time in which mediocrity and downright venality dominated national life, had left a scar upon his consciousness. James, to be sure, felt none of the frustration at having been brushed aside by the politics of his time that ate into the heart of Henry Adams, but he understood—or sensed—the nature of the social and moral changes that were brushing aside people like Adams. The bitterness that rises from every page of Adams' *Democracy* is a far more intense emotion than the skepticism of *The Bostonians,* but given the differences in temperament, character and ambition of the two men, they still share many implicit attitudes toward the America of the 1870's and 1880's. Both stand on the margin of American society, estranged from its dominant powers, helpless before the drift toward a world of industry and finance, money and impersonality. Only, Adams grows heartsick watching the death of the earlier America to which he is emotionally pledged, while James finds a kind of solace, to say nothing of a remarkable fulfillment, in the practice of his art.

IV

The Bostonians charts the parallel disarrangement, sometimes verging on a derangement, of public and private, political and sexual life. James was bold enough to see that the two spheres of experience could not be kept apart, and that it would be a fatal error for a novelist if he tried to. He was even bolder in supposing that the ideological obsessions which form so constant a peril for public life will leave their mark, not merely on social behavior, but also on the most intimate areas of private experience.

This boldness of observation is beautifully mirrored in James' prose. Because he is so thoroughly in command of the relation between public and private experience, James can allow himself an epigrammatic swiftness and "hardness" of style that is rare in both his earlier and his later work. For he is writing on the secure assumption that the social surface can be made to yield the necessary clues as to what is happening beneath it—and this may help explain why in *The Bostonians* James is so much less concerned than in his other novels with getting to the "essence" of characters and situations, why he places a higher value on the outer grain and texture of experience. It is for similar reasons that neither Olive Chancellor nor Basil Ransom changes very much in the course of the novel, or that no revelation is made of previously unseen depths in their characters. Both are essentially the same at the end that they were at the beginning, except that one has triumphed and the other has been defeated; and it is precisely to the clash leading to the triumph and the defeat that our main attention is directed. We are concerned here primarily with the terms of their struggle, and concerned on the assumption that, in the hands of a writer like James, this will tell us all we need to know.

In seeing how ideology—the systematized hardening of ideas—can penetrate even the most private areas of experience, James anticipated one of the great insights of psychoanalytic theory: that the price of a complex civilization is often the complex diminution of pleasure. And he understood, as well, that civilization seems to take a malicious delight in exacting this price from those most intent on reforming it. All the major characters in *The Bostonians*—Olive Chancellor, through her need to reject both the masculine and feminine modes of life, Verena Tarrant, through her need to believe in the wisdom of those who make demands on her, Basil Ransom, through his need to proclaim his masculinity as if it were a manifesto—are victims not only of each other but also of themselves. Olive Chancellor is an open enemy of the pleasure principle, because she knows it cannot be reconciled with her peculiar brand of feminism; Verena Tarrant is a befuddled enemy, because she has "bad lecture-blood in her veins"; and even Basil Ransom, the one character ready to invoke the pleasure principle, does not and cannot really live by it.

The Bostonians, said James, was to be concerned with

"the decline in the sentiment of sex"—a phrase that can be read in at least two ways. One of them would point to the problematic status of women in modern society, the other to the equally problematic relation between pleasure and civilization. Not one of the people in *The Bostonians* has a secure sense—so secure, that is, as to require neither affirmation nor discussion—of what his culture expects from him in his sexual role. All of them are displaced persons, floating vaguely in the large social spaces of America.

What one notices first is the extent to which a breakdown has occurred in the traditional role of women—a role that is more exalted in national legend than in actuality. And while Basil Ransom is ready to talk about the proper place of women, who are for him the solacing and decorative sex, James is far too much a realist to suggest that they can or ever will again assume this place: even Ransom's lady relatives in Mississippi, deprived of their darkies, have been reduced to hard work. If Ransom is expressing James' views at all, it is in a style so deliberately inflated as to carry the heaviest ironic stress. In the hidden depths of the novel there may be some notion of what a harmonious relationship between the sexes should be, but it is not the relationship Ransom advocates and, except for vague intimations of a comely conservatism, it is not a relationship James could easily have specified. Nor was there any reason why he should have. It was enough that he so brilliantly observed the dislocations of sentiment and status which create, in almost all the characters of the novel, a nagging, distinctly "modern" anxiety.

Part of the humor in *The Bostonians*—at times, it must be admitted, a rather hard-spirited humor—comes from James' quickness at seizing upon those large glaring elements of the ridiculous that were inherent in the feminist movement and, for that matter, in the whole feminine effort to find new modes of social conduct. Yet James is fair enough to grant that feminism cannot be understood as if it were a mere sport of the New England mind. That such a movement could hardly avoid neurotic and morbid contaminations seems obvious enough: no social movement can. But this fact would hardly be very interesting if James did not also see feminism as inseparable from the conditions of American culture, as emblematic of a social and moral malaise. James understood that, while his immediate task was to focus on whatever might be strange and eccentric in his subject, his final aim could only be to present a critical vision of American life.

Far from indulging any notions about "eternal" wars between the sexes—Olive Chancellor and Basil Ransom can hardly be said to represent the sexes!—James established his drama in the actualities of late nineteenth-century American life. The form, the tone, the quality of feminism in *The Bostonians* is not to be imagined as existing anywhere and at any time but those specified by James—which is to say that it is part of the vast uprooting of American life which begins after the Civil War and has not yet come to an end.*

If, then, *The Bostonians* is concerned with dramatizing a parallel disarrangement of social and sexual life, what are we to make of the underlying view of society or, if you wish, of human behavior from which the book is written?

Part of the answer, I think, has already been suggested. James writes from a conservative skepticism that is more readily understood as a cultural value than as an explicit politics. This conservative skepticism is a remnant of politics, not his own, but that of his family and tradition, which James is perhaps repudiating but more likely shedding. Like many writers who appear after an age in which politics has

---

* The disposition to speak of society in metaphors drawn from personal life was to remain with James throughout his life. Some 20 years after *The Bostonians,* he wrote of devastated Richmond:

The feminization is there just to promote for us some eloquent antithesis; just to make us say that whereas the ancient order was masculine, fierce and mustachioed, the present is at most a sort of sick lionness who has so visibly parted with her teeth and claws that we may patronizingly walk around her.

been important, James registers a certain impatience with the idea or the need for politics. And like the good innocent American that on one side of himself he was to remain throughout his life, James is also registering an uneasy contempt for the very idea of "public life," which for him would always be at odds with private values.

At times this comes rather close to being an esthetic (perhaps even an esthete's) reaction to the life of politics, a judgment of one area of experience in terms of another, which is almost always a dangerous kind of judgment to make. One of the few times that James relaxes his hostility to Olive Chancellor is the moment she draws back from the feminists because they offend, not her moral sense, but her fastidious sensibility. Throughout the book there are occasions in which James seems to be applying small measures to large matters, judging difficult social and moral issues by esthetic criteria a little too neat for the job.

But both his conservative skepticism and his occasional estheticism are secondary to the perception that lies at the heart of the novel: that somehow, for reasons he cannot quite grasp, the proportions and rhythms of life in America have gone askew. In the mass industrial society that was coming into existence toward the end of the nineteenth century, the role of the sexes with regard to one another was no longer clear, the centers of authority and affection had become blurred, the continuity of family culture was threatened, but most important of all: the idea of what it meant to be human had come into question. All that we have since associated with industrial society was moving into sight—call it depersonalization or *anomie,* the sapping of individuality or the loss of tradition. James could not quite meet this problem through a frontal attack, but in *The Bostonians* he approached it in his own way. He did not specify the social coordinates, the fundamental causes, of the problem, but he dramatized and elaborated it with a critical sharpness that no American novelist has yet surpassed. Basil Ransom, the recalcitrant Southerner, was a convenient device for mar-

shalling the possibilities of opposition to things as they were:
he appealed to James' sense of complaint and his sense of
humor; but it went no further, James' irony spared him no
less than it spared anyone else in *The Bostonians*.

V

For a writer who is often said to shy away from physical
experience, James, in *The Bostonians,* seems remarkably
aware of the female body. It is an awareness that comes into
play somewhat negatively, since he is presenting a singularly
unattractive group of women; but his acute and witty apprehension of their sexlessness or their sexual distortions would
be quite impossible if he did not have in reserve a sense of
the possibilities of human sexuality.

Mrs. Luna's "hair was in clusters of curls, like bunches of
grapes; her tight bodice seemed to crack with vivacity."
Verena Tarrant, predictably, has "a flat young chest" and
Miss Birdseye "no more outline than a bundle of hay." Dr.
Prance is "spare, dry, hard, . . . If she had been a boy
she would have borne some relation to a girl, whereas Dr.
Prance appeared to bear none whatever." Olive Chancellor's
appearance is deliberately left vague, except for the clue
given our sense of catastrophe when we learn, upon her first
meeting with Ransom, of "the vague compassion which [her]
figure excited in his mind."

Not only do these descriptions quiver with a life of their
own, they also point to the social relations and complications
that James is trying to illuminate. The disarrangements of
society, as sometimes the obsessions of politics, are embodied
in the often deformed and grotesque sexual lives of the characters, and particularly the women.

Mrs. Luna, that bound and bulging female, claims to command the traditional resources of her sex, but the claim is so
preposterous as to become a subject for comic by-play. She
seems always to have just emerged from the armory of her
boudoir, wielding the weapons of sexual calculation with so
absurd a belief in their power that they quite obliterate her

personal sex. ("Mrs. Luna was drawing on her gloves; Ransom had never seen any that were so long; they reminded him of stockings, and he wondered how she managed without garters at the elbows.") Yet she is at least as far as any woman in the novel from the norm of womanliness James seems to have intended, for her sexuality has turned rancid, it has been corrupted into a strategy for social acquisition.

For all the moral and psychological differences between them, Mrs. Luna and Olive Chancellor occupy symmetrical points of distance from their society: it is hardly an accident that James imagined them as sisters who despise one another. Olive Chancellor regards the sexual impulse as an enemy of her purpose, Mrs. Luna employs it as a convenience of her ego. In Olive the sexual impulse has been starved by her radical fanaticism, in Mrs. Luna it has been debased by her conservative parasitism. Olive feels nothing but aggression toward society, Mrs. Luna wishes merely to appropriate its comforts. Nonetheless, Olive's rejection of the feminine role and Mrs. Luna's exploitation of it have many elements in common. Both are self-betrayed in their life as women, the one through the grandeur of ideology and the other through the paltriness of vanity. Neither really "belongs" anywhere, Olive keeping a finicky distance from the reformers with whose cause she identifies, Mrs. Luna being unable to break into the elegant social circles to which she aspires. And in both women the waste of sexual power is paralleled by a social malaise that seeps into their very souls, leaving one of them embittered and the other petulant.

Except for the still impressionable Verena, all the women in the novel seem, by intent, off-center and abnormal, lacking in womanliness or femininity. Dr. Prance, for example, represents an extreme possibility of feminism; she is a comic grotesque, rather likable for her blunt common sense but also frightening in her disciplined incapacity for emotion. She is a *reductio,* though hardly *ad absurdum,* of feminism, a warning of what it could become if driven to its extreme.

For she has done what Olive Chancellor would like to do but cannot quite manage: she has totally denied her life as a woman. This, James seems to be saying, is how you may yet prance, dear ladies—like the good and terrible Mary Prance.

But James was too shrewd an observer, and too skilled a novelist, to set off against this grim specter of feminism an ideal or idealized figure of feminine loveliness. Verena Tarrant has little but her promise, and her promise consists of little but her malleability. If all the other characters are seen in their activity, she alone is treated in terms of her "essence," so that no matter how much her outer, social being has been tarnished by the quackery of Boston there remains a pure feminine center, available to none but Basil Ransom.

If James meant Verena as the one "positive" moral force, the one figure toward whom our response should be more sympathetic than ironic, he failed; for she is unable—she simply is not interesting enough—to assume so crucial a role. But if she is intended mainly as a charming creature over whose imperilled innocence a violent battle of ideologies is being fought, he brilliantly succeeded. For seen in this way Verena need exert no active power, she need only be more attractive and receptive than the other women—which, in the circumstances, is not very difficult.

Still, James is not given to romantic idealizations in *The Bostonians* and even toward Verena, one of its few attractive figures, he can show a healthy disrespect. In a chilling passage toward the end of the novel, he proves himself quite aware that even at its most apparently innocent the feminine character can have a biting malice of its own and an aggressiveness that is almost as great a threat to male assurance as the open assaults of the feminists. When Verena asks Ransom, "Why don't you write out your ideas?", James remarks with a stress that is unmistakable: "This touched again upon the matter of his failure; it was curious how she couldn't keep off it, hit it every time." And this, we may surmise, will be Verena's role in the future; to "hit it off every time" her all too normal contribution to the felicities of domestic life in America.*

But it is through Olive Chancellor that James registers the full and terrible price that is paid by a first-rate intelligence as it is ravaged by social disorder and psychological obsession. Her condition is analyzed with so fine a touch that for a time it almost seems true, as some critics have argued, that she is merely the sum of her symptoms. Finally, however, it is not at all true, for precisely the ruthlessness in James' treatment of Olive, his refusal, except perhaps at the very end, to offer her a shred of sympathy, drives him to the most intense dramatization of her predicament. Were he sympathetic to Olive, James could risk a number of literary short cuts, but being hostile he must, for persuasion's sake, depict and penetrate and comment with a particular fullness.

Conceiving of herself as a St. Theresa of Beacon Hill, Olive is afflicted with a yearning for martyrdom that can find no satisfactory release, if only because she cannot bear to acknowledge the private and contaminated sources of this yearning. Her rejection of femininity goes far beyond a distaste for the traditional status of women: it is part of her fundamental impatience with the elementary conditions of human life. ("It was the usual things of life that filled her with silent rage; which was natural enough inasmuch as, to her vision, almost everything that was usual was iniquitous.") She rejects the idea of "the natural," either as fact or category. Olive's sexual ambiguity, like her social rootlessness,

---

* The idea that passive femininity can subdue male energy as aggressive feminism cannot is another link between *The Blithedale Romance* and *The Bostonians*. In Hawthorne's novel the saturnine reformer, Hollingsworth, is finally captured and tamed by Priscilla, a pale New England maiden who, like Verena, has been involved in mesmerist exercises. Toward the Priscilla-Verena figure and all that she stands for Hawthorne betrays a deeper, if more cautious, hostility than James: he had more at stake.

is in part due to her fastidious incapacity for accepting any of the available modes of life. It would be a gross error to see her feminist ideas simply as a rationalization for her private condition, since part of what she says—it might be remembered—happens to be true. Partly her rebellion *is* against society, but her mistake is to suppose it entirely against society; she does not see—how can she bear to see? —that it is also against herself, and not merely against that which, by accident or luck, is misshapen in herself but against all that is biologically "given" or conditioned in human life.

Olive's lesbianism becomes both cause and emblem of her social incapacity. Though James hardly presents heterosexual relations in any ideal light, he implies that they at least make possible sustained and regular communication between human beings, thereby becoming one of the tacit means by which society is knit together. Olive's lesbianism, however —partly because it is antipathetic to society, partly because it is suppressed—cuts her off from everyone, except for a time Verena, and renders her incapable of genuine communication in either public or private life. Only in light of this fact can one grasp how overwhelming, indeed almost shocking a humiliation James imposes upon her in the final scene where she is forced to placate an audience roaring with impatience to hear her lost and beloved Verena.

Seen from one point of view, Olive is a descendant of Hawthorne's villains—but with this crucial difference, that James realizes she commits the great sin of manipulating human beings not from some sourceless malignity but from her own clearly specified sickness and vulnerability. Actually, she is the most vulnerable figure in the book and toward the end James allows not merely an awareness of how painful her defeat is (for she is never even granted a confrontation, she is simply run away from) but also a sense that in defeat she achieves a gloomy sort of magnificence.

Her symptoms are presented with a remarkable directness:

persistent hysteria, a will to power that is inseparable from a will to prostration, an unqualified aggression toward men.* Her activities always demand analysis in terms of something other than their apparent meaning. When she talks about politics, we think of sex; when she talks about love, we think of the urge to power; when she talks about history, we think of humiliation. Yet, as James keeps insisting, she is a woman of attainment and rectitude—were she not at least the intellectual equal of Basil Ransom, her defeat would hardly matter. Her fanaticism is a function of a gnarled and impoverished psyche; her destructive will, the means by which ideology is transformed into hysteria. Both as a person in her own right and as the agent of a mean and narrowing culture, she is lost.

VI

In opposition to this disordered world Basil Ransom stands for—for what? It is a temptation to see him as the representative of masculine strength, traditional order, conservative wit. Thus, one critic:

> Of first-rate intelligence, completely "unreconstructed," holding "unprogressive" ideas of manliness, courage and chivalry, Basil Ransom . . . has a set of civilized principles to fall back upon . . .

Another critic:

> By choosing a Southerner for his hero, James gained an immediate and immeasurable advantage . . . When he involved the femininist movement with even a late adumbration of the immense tragic struggle between North and South, he made it plain that his story had to do with a cultural crisis . . .
> James conceived Ransom as if he were the leading, ideal intelligence of the group of gifted men who, a half-century

---

* It is sometimes asked whether James "really knew" how thoroughly he had drawn a lesbian type. The question is relevant only if we suppose that because people of an earlier age did not use our vocabulary they necessarily understood less than we do.

later, were to rise in the South and to muster in its defense whatever force may be available to an intelligent romantic conservatism . . .

[Ransom] has the courage of the collateral British line of romantic conservatives—he is akin to Yeats, Lawrence and Eliot in that he experiences his cultural fears in the most personal way possible, translating them into sexual fear, the apprehension of the loss of manhood.

These remarks seem to me an instance of how critics can be "taken in" by a character who did not for a moment delude his creator. From the very moment we see him, Basil Ransom—an opinionated provincial ("he had read Comte, he had read everything")—is treated by James with a cool and detached irony. Ransom *does* have a considerable attractiveness, if only because he is trying, by the force of his will, to extricate himself from defeat. But he can lay claim to none but personal powers; his cultural tradition is smashed and no one knows this better than he. It is true that he is free from the small shabbiness of the New England mind in its decline, but neither does he command anything resembling its original power; for him, writes James, vice was "purely a species of special cases of explicable accidents." And while he lays claim to a disenchanted realism, he reveals more than a touch, as James meant he should, of the sentimental and callow. He considered that women "were essentially inferior to men and infinitely tiresome when they refused to accept the lot which men had made for them"—an example, no doubt, of the "civilized principles" upon which he can fall back.

James' tone is unmistakable. Ransom's appearance, he writes, "might have indicated that he was to be a great American statesman; or, on the other hand, [it] might simply prove that he came from Carolina or Alabama." A little later James remarks of Ransom that "he had an immense desire for success," thereby noting that side of the Southern conservative which, if given half the chance, will out-Northern the Northerners. Still later, James writes that Ransom's

"scruples were doubtless begotten of a false pride, a sentiment in which there was a thread of moral tinsel, as there
was in the Southern idea of chivalry . . ."

But most remarkable of all is the incident in which Ransom solemnly declares himself ready for both marriage and
the future on the extraordinary ground that one of his essays
has finally been accepted by "The Rational Review," a jour-
nal of which the title sufficiently suggests both its circulation
and influence. If nothing else, this would be enough to convince us that Ransom is as naïvely and thoroughly, if not
as unattractively, the victim of a fanatical obsession as Olive
Chancellor—this characteristic delusion of the ideologue
(the pathos of which is one of the few things that makes
poor Ransom endearing) that if only his precious words
once appear in print, the world will embrace his wisdom
and all will be well.

Were Ransom an "ideal intelligence," the novel would be
hopelessly unbalanced. For what possible drama or significance could there be in a clash between so exalted a figure
as he would then be and so wretched an antagonist as Olive
Chancellor? The truth, I would suggest, is that in his way
Ransom is as deeply entangled with his ideology as Olive
with hers, and that the clash between styles of culture which
is supposed to be reflected in their struggle is actually a rather
harsh comedy in which both sides, even if to unequal degrees,
are scored off by James.

Nowhere is this truer than in Ransom's presumed "apprehension of the loss of manhood." For while it is a common
assumption of our culture that the "biological" is the most
profound and fundamental variety of experience, before
which all else must seem pale and unreal, it is worth remembering that the biological, or the sense of it, can also become
imbued with ideology. In the case of Ransom, his "apprehension of the loss of manhood," in addition to being an
authentic personal emotion, is frequently part of his rhetoric
of moral and intellectual aggrandizement.

This, indeed, is the great stroke of *The Bostonians:* that

everything, even aspects of private experience supposedly inviolable, is shown to be infected with ideology. When Ransom, in his Central Park speech, appeals to Verena to break from Olive, he does so not merely in the name of his personal love but also through the catch-words of politics, and curiously enough one that is closer to New England radicalism than to Southern conservatism: he urges her to stand forth in the name of *personal freedom*. When Olive and Verena listen to Beethoven, "symphonies and fugues only stimulated their convictions, excited their revolutionary passion . . ." —the very music becomes a medium of ideology. Everything is touched by it, from politics to sex, from music to love.

That being so, we are in a better position to judge the complaint often made about *The Bostonians,* that there is a loss of certainty and brilliance midway through the book. It is true that *The Bostonians* does falter about halfway, but only because James is not quite sure how to manage one of the boldest and most brilliant transitions of his entire work. The first 150 pages of the novel present directly a world of contention and decline; there follows a somewhat hesitant section, set mainly in New York—and then the struggle is resumed, more bitterly, more fiercely, more poisonously, on the face of it a struggle of love but in its depths a struggle of politics.

Ransom wins. Despite all of James' qualifications in regard to Ransom, he grants him certain attractions and powers. Ransom is no poor shabby gentleman watching life glide away; he is a man of energy and will, as hard as Olive and less frenetic. And for James, always a little uneasy before the more direct forms of masculine energy, there is a fascination in seeing this energy exert itself. But the logic of the book itself demands that Ransom win. For if the struggle between Ransom and Olive over Verena is a struggle between competing ideologies over a passive agent of the natural and the human, then it is a struggle between ideologies that are not equally in opposition to the natural and the human. When she is finally driven to her choice, Verena chooses in accordance with those rhythms of life which Olive bluntly violates but Ransom merely exploits. In a dazzling final sentence James writes that "It is to be feared that with the union, so far from brilliant, into which she was about to enter, these [tears] were not the last she was destined to shed." What James thought of Ransom's pretensions, what he made of the whole affair, how thoroughly he maintained the critical and ironic tone throughout the book, is suggested in this hint that Ransom and Verena, married at last, would live unhappily ever after.

Book First

I

"Olive will come down in about ten minutes; she told me to tell you that. About ten; that is exactly like Olive. Neither five nor fifteen, and yet not ten exactly, but either nine or eleven. She didn't tell me to say she was glad to see you, because she doesn't know whether she is or not, and she wouldn't for the world expose herself to telling a fib. She is very honest, is Olive Chancellor; she is full of rectitude. Nobody tells fibs in Boston; I don't know what to make of them all. Well, I am very glad to see you, at any rate."

These words were spoken with much volubility by a fair, plump, smiling woman who entered a narrow drawing room in which a visitor, kept waiting for a few moments, was already absorbed in a book. The gentleman had not even needed to sit down to become interested: apparently he had

3

taken up the volume from a table as soon as he came in, and, standing there, after a single glance round the apartment, had lost himself in its pages. He threw it down at the approach of Mrs. Luna, laughed, shook hands with her, and said in answer to her last remark, "You imply that you do tell fibs. Perhaps that is one."

"Oh no; there is nothing wonderful in my being glad to see you," Mrs. Luna rejoined, "when I tell you that I have been three long weeks in this unprevaricating city."

"That has an unflattering sound for me," said the young man. "I pretend not to prevaricate."

"Dear me, what's the good of being a Southerner?" the lady asked. "Olive told me to tell you she hoped you will stay to dinner. And if she said it, she does really hope it. She is willing to risk that."

"Just as I am?" the visitor inquired, presenting himself with rather a work-a-day aspect.

Mrs. Luna glanced at him from head to foot, and gave a little smiling sigh, as if he had been a long sum in addition. And, indeed, he was very long, Basil Ransom, and he even looked a little hard and discouraging, like a column of figures, in spite of the friendly face which he bent upon his hostess's deputy, and which, in its thinness, had a deep dry line, a sort of premature wrinkle, on either side of the mouth. He was tall and lean, and dressed throughout in black; his shirt collar was low and wide, and the triangle of linen, a little crumpled, exhibited by the opening of his waistcoat, was adorned by a pin containing a small red stone. In spite of this decoration the young man looked poor—as poor as a young man could look who had such a fine head and such magnificent eyes. Those of Basil Ransom were dark, deep, and glowing; his head had a character of elevation which fairly added to his stature; it was a head to be seen above the level of a crowd, on some judicial bench or political platform, or even on a bronze medal. His forehead was high and broad, and his thick black hair, perfectly straight and glossy, and without any division, rolled back from it in a leonine

4

manner. These things, the eyes especially, with their smouldering fire, might have indicated that he was to be a great American statesman; or, on the other hand, they might simply have proved that he came from Carolina or Alabama. He came, in fact, from Mississippi, and he spoke very perceptibly with the accent of that country. It is not in my power to reproduce by any combination of characters this charming dialect; but the initiated reader will have no difficulty in evoking the sound, which is to be associated in the present instance with nothing vulgar or vain. This lean, pale, sallow, shabby, striking young man, with his superior head, his sedentary shoulders, his expression of bright grimness and hard enthusiasm, his provincial, distinguished appearance, is, as a representative of his sex, the most important personage in my narrative; he played a very active part in the events I have undertaken in some degree to set forth. And yet the reader who likes a complete image, who desires to read with the senses as well as with the reason, is entreated not to forget that he prolonged his consonants and swallowed his vowels, that he was guilty of elisions and interpolations which were equally unexpected, and that his discourse was pervaded by something sultry and vast, something almost African in its rich, basking tone, something that suggested the teeming expanse of the cotton field. Mrs. Luna looked up at all this, but saw only a part of it; otherwise she would not have replied in a bantering manner, in answer to his inquiry: "Are you ever different from this?" Mrs. Luna was familiar—intolerably familiar.

Basil Ransom colored a little. Then he said: "Oh yes; when I dine out I usually carry a six-shooter and a bowie knife." And he took up his hat vaguely—a soft black hat with a low crown and an immense straight brim. Mrs. Luna wanted to know what he was doing. She made him sit down; she assured him that her sister quite expected him, would feel as sorry as she could ever feel for anything—for she was a kind of fatalist, anyhow—if he didn't stay to dinner. It was an immense pity—she herself was going out; in Boston you must jump at invitations. Olive, too, was going somewhere after dinner, but he mustn't mind that; perhaps he would like to go with her. It wasn't a party—Olive didn't go to parties; it was one of those weird meetings she was so fond of.

"What kind of meetings do you refer to? You speak as if it were a rendezvous of witches on the Brocken."

"Well, so it is; they are all witches and wizards, mediums, and spirit-rappers, and roaring radicals."

Basil Ransom stared; the yellow light in his brown eyes deepened. "Do you mean to say your sister's a roaring radical?"

"A radical? She's a female Jacobin—she's a nihilist. Whatever is, is wrong, and all that sort of thing. If you are going to dine with her, you had better know it."

"Oh, murder!" murmured the young man vaguely, sinking back in his chair with his arms folded. He looked at Mrs. Luna with intelligent incredulity. She was sufficiently pretty; her hair was in clusters of curls, like bunches of grapes; her tight bodice seemed to crack with her vivacity; and from beneath the stiff little plaits of her petticoat a small fat foot protruded, resting upon a stilted heel. She was attractive and impertinent, especially the latter. He seemed to think it was a great pity, what she had told him; but he lost himself in this consideration, or, at any rate, said nothing for some time, while his eyes wandered over Mrs. Luna, and he probably wondered what body of doctrine *she* represented, little as she might partake of the nature of her sister. Many things were strange to Basil Ransom; Boston especially was strewn with surprises, and he was a man who liked to understand. Mrs. Luna was drawing on her gloves; Ransom had never seen any that were so long; they reminded him of stockings, and he wondered how she managed without garters above the elbow. "Well, I suppose I might have known that," he continued, at last.

"You might have known what?"

"Well, that Miss Chancellor would be all that you say. She was brought up in the city of reform."

"Oh, it isn't the city; it's just Olive Chancellor. She would reform the solar system if she could get hold of it. She'll reform you, if you don't look out. That's the way I found her when I returned from Europe."

"Have you been in Europe?" Ransom asked.

"Mercy, yes! Haven't you?"

"No, I haven't been anywhere. Has your sister?"

"Yes; but she stayed only an hour or two. She hates it; she would like to abolish it. Didn't you know I had been to Europe?" Mrs. Luna went on, in the slightly aggrieved tone of a woman who discovers the limits of her reputation.

Ransom reflected he might answer her that until five minutes ago he didn't know she existed; but he remembered that this was not the way in which a Southern gentleman spoke to ladies, and he contented himself with saying that he must condone his Boeotian ignorance (he was fond of an elegant phrase); that he lived in a part of the country where they didn't think much about Europe, and that he had always supposed she was domiciled in New York. This last remark he made at a venture, for he had, naturally, not devoted any supposition whatever to Mrs. Luna. His dishonesty, however, only exposed him the more.

"If you thought I lived in New York, why in the world didn't you come and see me?" the lady inquired.

"Well, you see, I don't go out much, except to the courts."

"Do you mean the law-courts? Everyone has got some profession over here! Are you very ambitious? You look as if you were."

"Yes, very," Basil Ransom replied, with a smile, and the curious feminine softness with which Southern gentlemen enunciate that adverb.

Mrs. Luna explained that she had been living in Europe for several years—ever since her husband died—but had come home a month before, come home with her little boy,

7

the only thing she had in the world, and was paying a visit to her sister, who, of course, was the nearest thing after the child. "But it isn't the same," she said. "Olive and I disagree so much."

"While you and your little boy don't," the young man remarked.

"Oh no, I never differ from Newton!" And Mrs. Luna added that now she was back she didn't know what she should do. That was the worst of coming back; it was like being born again, at one's age—one had to begin life afresh. One didn't even know what one had come back for. There were people who wanted one to spend the winter in Boston; but she couldn't stand that—she knew, at least, what she had not come back for. Perhaps she should take a house in Washington; did he ever hear of that little place? They had invented it while she was away. Besides, Olive didn't want her in Boston, and didn't go through the form of saying so. That was one comfort with Olive; she never went through any forms.

Basil Ransom had got up just as Mrs. Luna made this last declaration; for a young lady had glided into the room, who stopped short as it fell upon her ears. She stood there looking, consciously and rather seriously, at Mr. Ransom; a smile of exceeding faintness played about her lips—it was just perceptible enough to light up the native gravity of her face. It might have been likened to a thin ray of moonlight resting upon the wall of a prison.

"If that were true," she said, "I shouldn't tell you that I am very sorry to have kept you waiting."

Her voice was low and agreeable—a cultivated voice—and she extended a slender white hand to her visitor, who remarked with some solemnity (he felt a certain guilt of participation in Mrs. Luna's indiscretion) that he was intensely happy to make her acquaintance. He observed that Miss Chancellor's hand was at once cold and limp; she merely placed it in his, without exerting the smallest pressure. Mrs. Luna explained to her sister that her freedom of speech was caused by his being a relation—though, indeed, he didn't seem to know much about them. She didn't believe he had ever heard of her, Mrs. Luna, though he pretended, with his Southern chivalry, that he had. She must be off to her dinner now, she saw the carriage was there, and in her absence Olive might give any version of her she chose.

"I have told him you are a radical, and you may tell him, if you like, that I am a painted Jezebel. Try to reform him; a person from Mississippi is sure to be all wrong. I shall be back very late; we are going to a theatre-party; that's why we dine so early. Good-bye, Mr. Ransom," Mrs. Luna continued, gathering up the feathery white shawl which added to the volume of her fairness. "I hope you are going to stay a little, so that you may judge us for yourself. I should like you to see Newton, too; he is a noble little nature, and I want some advice about him. You only stay to-morrow? Why, what's the use of that? Well, mind you come and see me in New York; I shall be sure to be part of the winter there. I shall send you a card; I won't let you off. Don't come out; my sister has the first claim. Olive, why don't you take him to your female convention?" Mrs. Luna's familiarity extended even to her sister; she remarked to Miss Chancellor that she looked as if she were got up for a sea-voyage. "I am glad I haven't opinions that prevent my dressing in the evening!" she declared from the doorway. "The amount of thought they give to their clothing, the people who are afraid of looking frivolous!"

2

Whether much or little consideration had been directed to
the result, Miss Chancellor certainly would not have incurred this reproach. She was habited in a plain dark dress,
without any ornaments, and her smooth, colorless hair was
confined as carefully as that of her sister was encouraged to
stray. She had instantly seated herself, and while Mrs. Luna
talked she kept her eyes on the ground, glancing even less
toward Basil Ransom than toward that woman of many
words. The young man was therefore free to look at her; a
contemplation which showed him that she was agitated and
trying to conceal it. He wondered why she was agitated, not
foreseeing that he was destined to discover, later, that her
nature was like a skiff in a stormy sea. Even after her sister
had passed out of the room she sat there with her eyes
turned away, as if there had been a spell upon her which
forbade her to raise them. Miss Olive Chancellor, it may be
confided to the reader, to whom in the course of our history
I shall be under the necessity of imparting much occult information, was subject to fits of tragic shyness, during which
she was unable to meet even her own eyes in the mirror.
One of these fits had suddenly seized her now, without any
obvious cause, though, indeed, Mrs. Luna had made it worse
by becoming instantly so personal. There was nothing in the
world so personal as Mrs. Luna; her sister could have hated
her for it if she had not forbidden herself this emotion as
directed to individuals. Basil Ransom was a young man of

first-rate intelligence, but conscious of the narrow range, as yet, of his experience. He was on his guard against generalizations which might be hasty; but he had arrived at two or three that were of value to a gentleman lately admitted to the New York bar and looking out for clients. One of them was to the effect that the simplest division it is possible to make of the human race is into the people who take things hard and the people who take them easy. He perceived very quickly that Miss Chancellor belonged to the former class. This was written so intensely in her delicate face that he felt an unformulated pity for her before they had exchanged twenty words. He himself, by nature, took things easy; if he had put on the screw of late, it was after reflection, and because circumstances pressed him close. But this pale girl, with her light-green eyes, her pointed features and nervous manner, was visibly morbid; it was as plain as day that she was morbid. Poor Ransom announced this fact to himself as if he had made a great discovery; but in reality he had never been so "Boeotian" as at that moment. It proved nothing of any importance, with regard to Miss Chancellor, to say that she was morbid; any sufficient account of her would lie very much to the rear of that. Why was she morbid, and why was her morbidness typical? Ransom might have exulted if he had gone back far enough to explain that mystery. The women he had hitherto known had been mainly of his own soft clime, and it was not often they exhibited the tendency he detected (and cursorily deplored) in Mrs. Luna's sister. That was the way he liked them—not to think too much; not to feel any responsibility for the government of the world, such as he was sure Miss Chancellor felt. If they would only be private and passive, and have no feeling but for that, and leave publicity to the sex of tougher hide! Ransom was pleased with the vision of that remedy; it must be repeated that he was very provincial.

These considerations were not present to him as definitely as I have written them here; they were summed up in the vague compassion which his cousin's figure excited in his mind, and which was yet accompanied with a sensible reluctance to know her better, obvious as it was that with such a face as that she must be remarkable. He was sorry for her, but he saw in a flash that no one could help her: that was what made her tragic. He had not, seeking his fortune, come away from the blighted South, which weighed upon his heart, to look out for tragedies; at least he didn't want them outside of his office in Pine Street. He broke the silence ensuing upon Mrs. Luna's departure by one of the courteous speeches to which blighted regions may still encourage a tendency, and presently found himself talking comfortably enough with his hostess. Though he had said to himself that no one could help her, the effect of his tone was to dispel her shyness; it was her great advantage (for the career she had proposed to herself) that in certain conditions she was liable suddenly to become bold. She was reassured at finding that her visitor was peculiar; the way he spoke told her that it was no wonder he had fought on the Southern side. She had never yet encountered a personage so exotic, and she always felt more at her ease in the presence of anything strange. It was the usual things of life that filled her with silent rage; which was natural enough, inasmuch as, to her vision, almost everything that was usual was iniquitous. She had no difficulty in asking him now whether he would not stay to dinner—she hoped Adeline had given him her message. It had been when she was upstairs with Adeline, as his card was brought up, a sudden and very abnormal inspiration to offer him this (for her) really ultimate favor; nothing could be further from her common habit than to entertain alone, at any repast, a gentleman she had never seen.

It was the same sort of impulse that had moved her to write to Basil Ransom, in the spring, after hearing accidentally that he had come to the North and intended, in New York, to practise his profession. It was her nature to look out for duties, to appeal to her conscience for tasks. This attentive organ, earnestly consulted, had represented to her that he was an offshoot of the old slave-holding oligarchy which, within her own vivid remembrance, had plunged the country into blood and tears, and that, as associated with such abominations, he was not a worthy object of patronage for a person whose two brothers—her only ones—had given up life for the Northern cause. It reminded her, however, on the other hand, that he too had been much bereaved, and, moreover, that he had fought and offered his own life, even if it had not been taken. She could not defend herself against a rich admiration—a kind of tenderness of envy—of any one who had been so happy as to have that opportunity. The most secret, the most sacred hope of her nature was that she might some day have such a chance, that she might be a martyr and die for something. Basil Ransom had lived, but she knew he had lived to see bitter hours. His family was ruined; they had lost their slaves, their property, their friends and relations, their home; had tasted of all the cruelty of defeat. He had tried for a while to carry on the plantation himself, but he had a millstone of debt round his neck, and he longed for some work which would transport him to the haunts of men. The State of Mississippi seemed to him the state of despair; so he surrendered the remnants of his patrimony to his mother and sisters, and, at nearly thirty years of age, alighted for the first time in New York, in the costume of his province, with fifty dollars in his pocket and a gnawing hunger in his heart.

That this incident had revealed to the young man his ignorance of many things—only, however, to make him say to himself, after the first angry blush, that here he would enter the game and here he would win it—so much Olive Chancellor could not know; what was sufficient for her was that he had rallied, as the French say, had accepted the accomplished fact, had admitted that North and South were a single, indivisible political organism. Their cousinship—that of Chancellors and Ransoms—was not very close; it was the kind of thing that one might take up or leave alone, as one pleased. It was "in the female line," as Basil Ransom had written, in answering her letter with a good deal of form and

13

flourish; he spoke as if they had been royal houses. Her mother had wished to take it up; it was only the fear of seeming patronizing to people in misfortune that had prevented her from writing to Mississippi. If it had been possible to send Mrs. Ransom money, or even clothes, she would have liked that; but she had no means of ascertaining how such an offering would be taken. By the time Basil came to the North—making advances, as it were—Mrs. Chancellor had passed away; so it was for Olive, left alone in the little house in Charles Street (Adeline being in Europe), to decide.

She knew what her mother would have done, and that helped her decision; for her mother always chose the positive course. Olive had a fear of everything, but her greatest fear was of being afraid. She wished immensely to be generous, and how could one be generous unless one ran a risk? She had erected it into a sort of rule of conduct that whenever she saw a risk she was to take it; and she had frequent humiliations at finding herself safe after all. She was perfectly safe after writing to Basil Ransom; and, indeed, it was difficult to see what he could have done to her except thank her (he was only exceptionally superlative) for her letter, and assure her that he would come and see her the first time his business (he was beginning to get a little) should take him to Boston. He had now come, in redemption of his grateful vow, and even this did not make Miss Chancellor feel that she had courted danger. She saw (when once she had looked at him) that he would not put those worldly interpretations on things which, with her, it was both an impulse and a principle to defy. He was too simple—too Mississippian—for that; she was almost disappointed. She certainly had not hoped that she might have struck him as making unwomanly overtures (Miss Chancellor hated this epithet almost as much as she hated its opposite); but she had a presentiment that he would be too good-natured, primitive to that degree. Of all things in the world contention was most sweet to her (though why it is hard to imagine, for it always cost her tears, headaches, a day or two in bed, acute emotion), and it was very possible Basil Ransom would not care to contend. Nothing could be more displeasing than this indifference when people didn't agree with you. That he should agree she did not in the least expect of him; how could a Mississippian agree? If she had supposed he would agree, she would not have written to him.

3

When he had told her that if she would take him as he was he should be very happy to dine with her, she excused herself a moment and went to give an order in the dining room. The young man, left alone, looked about the parlor—the two parlors which, in their prolonged, adjacent narrowness, formed evidently one apartment—and wandered to the windows at the back, where there was a view of the water; Miss Chancellor having the good fortune to dwell on that side of Charles Street toward which, in the rear, the afternoon sun slants redly, from an horizon indented at empty intervals with wooden spires, the masts of lonely boats, the chimneys of dirty "works," over a brackish expanse of anomalous character, which is too big for a river and too small for a bay. The view seemed to him very picturesque, though in the gathered dusk little was left of it save a cold yellow streak in the west, a gleam of brown water, and the reflection of the lights that had begun to show themselves in a row of houses, impressive to Ransom in their extreme modernness, which overlooked the same lagoon from a long embankment on the left, constructed of stones roughly piled. He thought this prospect, from a city-house, almost romantic; and he turned from it back to the interior (illuminated now by a lamp which the parlor-maid had placed on a table while he stood at the window) as to something still more genial and interesting. The artistic sense in Basil Ransom had not been highly cultivated; neither (though he had passed his early years as the son of a rich man) was his conception of material comfort very definite; it consisted mainly of the vision of plenty of cigars and brandy and water and newspapers, and a cane-bottomed armchair of the right inclination, from which he could stretch his legs. Nevertheless it seemed to him he had never seen an interior that was so much an interior as this queer corridor-shaped drawing room of his new-found kinswoman; he had never felt himself in the presence of so much organized privacy or of so many objects that spoke of habits and tastes. Most of the people he had hitherto known had no tastes; they had a few habits, but these were not of a sort that required much upholstery. He had not as yet been in many houses in New York, and he had never before seen so many accessories. The general character of the place struck him as Bostonian; this was, in fact, very much what he had supposed Boston to be. He had always heard Boston was a city of culture, and now there was culture in Miss Chancellor's tables and sofas, in the books that were everywhere, on little shelves like brackets (as if a book were a statuette), in the photographs and watercolors that covered the walls, in the curtains that were festooned rather stiffly in the doorways. He looked at some of the books and saw that his cousin read German; and his impression of the importance of this (as a symptom of superiority) was not diminished by the fact that he himself had mastered the tongue (knowing it contained a large literature of jurisprudence) during a long, empty, deadly summer on the plantation. It is a curious proof of a certain crude modesty inherent in Basil Ransom that the main effect of his observing his cousin's German books was

to give him an idea of the natural energy of Northerners. He
had noticed it often before; he had already told himself that
he must count with it. It was only after much experience he
made the discovery that few Northerners were, in their secret soul, so energetic as he. Many other persons had made
it before that. He knew very little about Miss Chancellor;
he had come to see her only because she wrote to him; he
would never have thought of looking her up, and since then
there had been no one in New York he might ask about her.
Therefore he could only guess that she was a rich young
woman; such a house, inhabited in such a way by a quiet
spinster, implied a considerable income. How much? he
asked himself; five thousand, ten thousand, fifteen thousand
a year? There was richness to our panting young man in the
smallest of these figures. He was not of a mercenary spirit,
but he had an immense desire for success, and he had more
than once reflected that a moderate capital was an aid to
achievement. He had seen in his younger years one of the
biggest failures that history commemorates, an immense national *fiasco,* and it had implanted in his mind a deep aversion to the ineffectual. It came over him, while he waited for
his hostess to reappear, that she was unmarried as well as
rich, that she was sociable (her letter answered for that) as
well as single; and he had for a moment a whimsical vision
of becoming a partner in so flourishing a firm. He ground his
teeth a little as he thought of the contrasts of the human lot;
this cushioned feminine nest made him feel unhoused and
underfed. Such a mood, however, could only be momentary,
for he was conscious at bottom of a bigger stomach than all
the culture of Charles Street could fill.

Afterwards, when his cousin had come back and they had
gone down to dinner together, where he sat facing her at a
little table decorated in the middle with flowers, a position
from which he had another view, through a window where
the curtain remained undrawn by her direction (she called
his attention to this—it was for his benefit), of the dusky,
empty river, spotted with points of light—at this period, I

say, it was very easy for him to remark to himself that nothing would induce him to make love to such a type as that. Several months later, in New York, in conversation with Mrs. Luna, of whom he was destined to see a good deal, he alluded by chance to this repast, to the way her sister had placed him at table, and to the remark with which she had pointed out the advantage of his seat.

"That's what they call in Boston being very 'thoughtful,'" Mrs. Luna said, "giving you the Back Bay (don't you hate the name?) to look at, and then taking credit for it."

This, however, was in the future; what Basil Ransom actually perceived was that Miss Chancellor was a signal old maid. That was her quality, her destiny; nothing could be more distinctly written. There are women who are unmarried by accident, and others who are unmarried by option; but Olive Chancellor was unmarried by every implication of her being. She was a spinster as Shelley was a lyric poet, or as the month of August is sultry. She was so essentially a celibate that Ransom found himself thinking of her as old, though when he came to look at her (as he said to himself) it was apparent that her years were fewer than his own. He did not dislike her, she had been so friendly; but, little by little, she gave him an uneasy feeling—the sense that you could never be safe with a person who took things so hard. It came over him that it was because she took things hard she had sought his acquaintance; it had been because she was strenuous, not because she was genial; she had had in her eye—and what an extraordinary eye it was!—not a pleasure, but a duty. She would expect him to be strenuous in return; but he couldn't—in private life, he couldn't; privacy for Basil Ransom consisted entirely in what he called "laying off." She was not so plain on further acquaintance as she had seemed to him at first; even the young Mississippian had culture enough to see that she was refined. Her white skin had a singular look of being drawn tightly across her face; but her features, though sharp and irregular, were delicate in a fashion that suggested good breeding. Their line was perverse, but it was not poor. The curious tint of her eyes was a living color; when she turned it upon you, you thought vaguely of the glitter of green ice. She had absolutely no figure, and presented a certain appearance of feeling cold. With all this, there was something very modern and highly developed in her aspect; she had the advantages as well as the drawbacks of a nervous organization. She smiled constantly at her guest, but from the beginning to the end of dinner, though he made several remarks that he thought might prove amusing, she never once laughed. Later, he saw that she was a woman without laughter; exhilaration, if it ever visited her, was dumb. Once only, in the course of his subsequent acquaintance with her, did it find a voice; and then the sound remained in Ransom's ear as one of the strangest he had heard.

She asked him a great many questions, and made no comment on his answers, which only served to suggest to her fresh inquiries. Her shyness had quite left her, it did not come back; she had confidence enough to wish him to see that she took a great interest in him. Why should she? he wondered. He couldn't believe he was one of *her* kind; he was conscious of much Bohemianism—he drank beer, in New York, in cellars, knew no ladies, and was familiar with a "variety" actress. Certainly, as she knew him better, she would disapprove of him, though, of course, he would never mention the actress, nor even, if necessary, the beer. Ransom's conception of vice was purely as a series of special cases, of explicable accidents. Not that he cared; if it were a part of the Boston character to be inquiring, he would be to the last a courteous Mississippian. He would tell her about Mississippi as much as she liked; he didn't care how much he told her that the old ideas in the South were played out. She would not understand him any the better for that; she would not know how little his own views could be gathered from such a limited admission. What her sister imparted to him about her mania for "reform" had left in his mouth a kind of unpleasant after-taste; he felt, at any rate, that if she had

19

the religion of humanity—Basil Ransom had read Comte, he had read everything—she would never understand him. He, too, had a private vision of reform, but the first principle of it was to reform the reformers. As they drew to the close of a meal which, in spite of all latent incompatibilities, had gone off brilliantly, she said to him that she should have to leave him after dinner, unless perhaps he should be inclined to accompany her. She was going to a small gathering at the house of a friend who had asked a few people, "interested in new ideas," to meet Mrs. Farrinder.

"Oh, thank you," said Basil Ransom. "Is it a party? I haven't been to a party since Mississippi seceded."

"No, Miss Birdseye doesn't give parties. She's an ascetic."

"Oh, well, we have had our dinner," Ransom rejoined, laughing.

His hostess sat silent a moment, with her eyes on the ground; she looked at such times as if she were hesitating greatly between several things she might say, all so important that it was difficult to choose.

"I think it might interest you," she remarked presently. "You will hear some discussion, if you are fond of that. Perhaps you wouldn't agree," she added, resting her strange eyes on him.

"Perhaps I shouldn't—I don't agree with everything," he said, smiling and stroking his leg.

"Don't you care for human progress?" Miss Chancellor went on.

"I don't know—I never saw any. Are you going to show me some?"

"I can show you an earnest effort toward it. That's the most one can be sure of. But I am not sure you are worthy."

"Is it something very Bostonian? I should like to see that," said Basil Ransom.

"There are movements in other cities. Mrs. Farrinder goes everywhere; she may speak tonight."

"Mrs. Farrinder, the celebrated——?"

"Yes, the celebrated; the great apostle of the emancipation of women. She is a great friend of Miss Birdseye."

"And who is Miss Birdseye?"

"She is one of our celebrities. She is the woman in the world, I suppose, who has labored most for every wise reform. I think I ought to tell you," Miss Chancellor went on in a moment, "she was one of the earliest, one of the most passionate, of the old Abolitionists."

She had thought, indeed, she ought to tell him that, and it threw her into a little tremor of excitement to do so. Yet, if she had been afraid he would show some irritation at this news, she was disappointed at the geniality with which he exclaimed:

"Why, poor old lady—she must be quite mature!"

It was therefore with some severity that she rejoined:

"She will never be old. She is the youngest spirit I know. But if you are not in sympathy, perhaps you had better not come," she went on.

"In sympathy with what, dear madam?" Basil Ransom asked, failing still, to her perception, to catch the tone of real seriousness. "If, as you say, there is to be a discussion, there will be different sides, and of course one can't sympathize with both."

"Yes, but every one will, in his way—or in her way—plead the cause of the new truths. If you don't care for them, you won't go with us."

"I tell you I haven't the least idea what they are! I have never yet encountered in the world any but old truths—as old as the sun and moon. How can I know? But *do* take me; it's such a chance to see Boston."

"It isn't Boston—it's humanity!" Miss Chancellor, as she made this remark, rose from her chair, and her movement seemed to say that she consented. But before she quitted her kinsman to get ready, she observed to him that she was sure he knew what she meant; he was only pretending he didn't.

"Well, perhaps, after all, I have a general idea," he confessed; "but don't you see how this little reunion will give me a chance to fix it?"

She lingered an instant, with her anxious face. "Mrs. Farrinder will fix it!" she said; and she went to prepare herself.

It was in this poor young lady's nature to be anxious, to have scruple within scruple and to forecast the consequences of things. She returned in ten minutes, in her bonnet, which she had apparently assumed in recognition of Miss Birdseye's asceticism. As she stood there drawing on her gloves—her visitor had fortified himself against Mrs. Farrinder by another glass of wine—she declared to him that she quite repented of having proposed to him to go; something told her that he would be an unfavorable element.

"Why, is it going to be a spiritual *séance?*" Basil Ransom asked.

"Well, I have heard at Miss Birdseye's some inspirational speaking." Olive Chancellor was determined to look him straight in the face as she said this; her sense of the way it might strike him operated as a cogent, not as a deterrent, reason.

"Why, Miss Olive, it's just got up on purpose for me!" cried the young Mississippian, radiant, and clasping his hands. She thought him very handsome as he said this, but reflected that unfortunately men didn't care for the truth, especially the new kinds, in proportion as they were good-looking. She had, however, a moral resource that she could always fall back upon; it had already been a comfort to her, on occasions of acute feeling, that she hated men, as a class, anyway. "And I want so much to see an old Abolitionist; I have never laid eyes on one," Basil Ransom added.

"Of course you couldn't see one in the South; you were too afraid of them to let them come there!" She was now trying to think of something she might say that would be sufficiently disagreeable to make him cease to insist on accompanying her; for, strange to record—if anything, in a person of that intense sensibility, be stranger than any other —her second thought with regard to having asked him had deepened with the elapsing moments into an unreasoned terror of the effect of his presence. "Perhaps Miss Birdseye won't like you," she went on, as they waited for the carriage.

"I don't know; I reckon she will," said Basil Ransom good-humoredly. He evidently had no intention of giving up his opportunity.

From the window of the dining room, at that moment, they heard the carriage drive up. Miss Birdseye lived at the South End; the distance was considerable, and Miss Chancellor had ordered a hackney coach, it being one of the advantages of living in Charles Street that stables were near. The logic of her conduct was none of the clearest; for if she had been alone she would have proceeded to her destination by the aid of the streetcar; not from economy (for she had the good fortune not to be obliged to consult it to that degree), and not from any love of wandering about Boston at night (a kind of exposure she greatly disliked), but by reason of a theory she devotedly nursed, a theory which bade her put off invidious differences and mingle in the common life. She would have gone on foot to Boylston Street, and there she would have taken the public conveyance (in her heart she loathed it) to the South End. Boston was full of poor girls who had to walk about at night and to squeeze into horsecars in which every sense was displeased; and why should she hold herself superior to these? Olive Chancellor regulated her conduct on lofty principles, and this is why, having tonight the advantage of a gentleman's protection, she sent for a carriage to obliterate that patronage. If they had gone together in the common way she would have seemed to owe it to him that she should be so daring, and he belonged to a sex to which she wished to be under no obligations. Months before, when she wrote to him, it had been with the sense, rather, of putting *him* in debt. As they rolled toward the South End, side by side, in a good deal of silence, bouncing and bumping over the railway tracks very little less, after all, than if their wheels had been fitted to them, and looking out on either side at rows of red houses, dusky in the lamplight, with protuberant fronts, approached by ladders of stone; as they proceeded, with these contemplative undulations, Miss Chancellor said to her companion, with a concentrated desire to defy him, as a punishment for having thrown her (she couldn't tell why) into such a tremor:

"Don't you believe, then, in the coming of a better day—in its being possible to do something for the human race?"

Poor Ransom perceived the defiance, and he felt rather bewildered; he wondered what type, after all, he *had* got hold of, and what game was being played with him. Why had she made advances, if she wanted to pinch him this way? However, he was good for any game—that one as well as another—and he saw that he was "in" for something of which he had long desired to have a nearer view. "Well, Miss Olive," he answered, putting on again his big hat, which he had been holding in his lap, "what strikes me most is that the human race has got to bear its troubles."

"That's what men say to women, to make them patient in the position they have made for them."

"Oh, the position of women!" Basil Ransom exclaimed. "The position of women is to make fools of men. I would change my position for yours any day," he went on. "That's what I said to myself as I sat there in your elegant home."

He could not see, in the dimness of the carriage, that she had flushed quickly, and he did not know that she disliked to be reminded of certain things which, for her, were mitigations of the hard feminine lot. But the passionate quaver with which, a moment later, she answered him sufficiently assured him that he had touched her at a tender point.

"Do you make it a reproach to me that I happen to have a little money? The dearest wish of my heart is to do something with it for others—for the miserable."

Basil Ransom might have greeted this last declaration with the sympathy it deserved, might have commended the noble aspirations of his kinswoman. But what struck him, rather, was the oddity of so sudden a sharpness of pitch in an intercourse which, an hour or two before, had begun in perfect amity, and he burst once more into an irrepressible laugh. This made his companion feel, with intensity, how little she was joking. "I don't know why I should care what you think," she said.

"Don't care—don't care. What does it matter? It is not of the slightest importance."

He might say that, but it was not true; she felt that there were reasons why she should care. She had brought him into her life, and she should have to pay for it. But she wished to know the worst at once. "Are you against our emancipation?" she asked, turning a white face on him in the momentary radiance of a street lamp.

"Do you mean your voting and preaching and all that sort of thing?" He made this inquiry, but seeing how seriously she would take his answer, he was almost frightened, and hung fire. "I will tell you when I have heard Mrs. Farrinder."

They had arrived at the address given by Miss Chancellor to the coachman, and their vehicle stopped with a lurch. Basil Ransom got out; he stood at the door with an extended hand, to assist the young lady. But she seemed to hesitate; she sat there with her spectral face. "You hate it!" she exclaimed, in a low tone.

"Miss Birdseye will convert me," said Ransom, with intention; for he had grown very curious, and he was afraid that now, at the last, Miss Chancellor would prevent his entering the house. She alighted without his help, and behind her he ascended the high steps of Miss Birdseye's residence. He had grown very curious, and among the things he wanted to know was why in the world this ticklish spinster had written to him.

4

She had told him before they started that they should be
early; she wished to see Miss Birdseye alone, before the
arrival of anyone else. This was just for the pleasure of
seeing her—it was an opportunity; she was always so taken
up with others. She received Miss Chancellor in the hall of
the mansion, which had a salient front, an enormous and
very high number—756—painted in gilt on the glass light
above the door, a tin sign bearing the name of a doctress
(Mary J. Prance) suspended from one of the windows of
the basement, and a peculiar look of being both new and
faded—a kind of modern fatigue—like certain articles of
commerce which are sold at a reduction as shopworn. The
hall was very narrow; a considerable part of it was occupied
by a large hat tree, from which several coats and shawls already depended; the rest offered space for certain lateral
demonstrations on Miss Birdseye's part. She sidled about
her visitors, and at last went round to open for them a door
of further admission, which happened to be locked inside.
She was a little old lady, with an enormous head; that was
the first thing Ransom noticed—the vast, fair, protuberant,
candid, ungarnished brow, surmounting a pair of weak,
kind, tired-looking eyes, and ineffectually balanced in the
rear by a cap which had the air of falling backward, and
which Miss Birdseye suddenly felt for while she talked, with
unsuccessful irrelevant movements. She had a sad, soft, pale
face, which (and it was the effect of her whole head) looked

as if it had been soaked, blurred, and made vague by exposure to some slow dissolvent. The long practice of philanthropy had not given accent to her features; it had rubbed out their transitions, their meanings. The waves of sympathy, of enthusiasm, had wrought upon them in the same way in which the waves of time finally modify the surface of old marble busts, gradually washing away their sharpness, their details. In her large countenance her dim little smile scarcely showed. It was a mere sketch of a smile, a kind of installment, or payment on account; it seemed to say that she would smile more if she had time, but that you could see, without this, that she was gentle and easy to beguile.

She always dressed in the same way: she wore a loose black jacket, with deep pockets, which were stuffed with papers, memoranda of a voluminous correspondence; and from beneath her jacket depended a short stuff dress. The brevity of this simple garment was the one device by which Miss Birdseye managed to suggest that she was a woman of business, that she wished to be free for action. She belonged to the Short-Skirts League, as a matter of course; for she belonged to any and every league that had been founded for almost any purpose whatever. This did not prevent her being a confused, entangled, inconsequent, discursive old woman, whose charity began at home and ended nowhere, whose credulity kept pace with it, and who knew less about her fellow-creatures, if possible, after fifty years of humanitary zeal, than on the day she had gone into the field to testify against the iniquity of most arrangements. Basil Ransom knew very little about such a life as hers, but she seemed to him a revelation of a class, and a multitude of socialistic figures, of names and episodes that he had heard of, grouped themselves behind her. She looked as if she had spent her life on platforms, in audiences, in conventions, in phalansteries, in *séances;* in her faded face there was a kind of reflection of ugly lecture lamps; with its habit of an upward angle, it seemed turned toward a public speaker, with an effort of respiration in the thick air in which social reforms are usually discussed. She talked continually, in a voice of which the spring seemed broken, like that of an over-worked bell-wire; and when Miss Chancellor explained that she had brought Mr. Ransom because he was so anxious to meet Mrs. Farrinder, she gave the young man a delicate, dirty, democratic little hand, looking at him kindly, as she could not help doing, but without the smallest discrimination as against others who might not have the good fortune (which involved, possibly, an injustice) to be present on such an interesting occasion. She struck him as very poor, but it was only afterward that he learned she had never had a penny in her life. No one had an idea how she lived; whenever money was given her she gave it away to a negro or a refugee. No woman could be less invidious, but on the whole she preferred these two classes of the human race. Since the Civil War much of her occupation was gone; for before that her best hours had been spent in fancying that she was helping some Southern slave to escape. It would have been a nice question whether, in her heart of hearts, for the sake of this excitement, she did not sometimes wish the blacks back in bondage. She had suffered in the same way by the relaxation of many European despotisms, for in former years much of the romance of her life had been in smoothing the pillow of exile for banished conspirators. Her refugees had been very precious to her; she was always trying to raise money for some cadaverous Pole, to obtain lessons for some shirtless Italian. There was a legend that an Hungarian had once possessed himself of her affections, and had disappeared after robbing her of everything she possessed. This, however, was very apocryphal, for she had never possessed anything, and it was open to grave doubt that she could have entertained a sentiment so personal. She was in love, even in those days, only with causes, and she languished only for emancipations. But they had been the happiest days, for when causes were embodied in foreigners (what else were the Africans?), they were certainly more appealing.

She had just come down to see Doctor Prance—to see

whether she wouldn't like to come up. But she wasn't in her room, and Miss Birdseye guessed she had gone out to her supper; she got her supper at a boarding table about two blocks off. Miss Birdseye expressed the hope that Miss Chancellor had had hers; she would have had plenty of time to take it, for no one had come in yet; she didn't know what made them all so late. Ransom perceived that the garments suspended to the hat rack were not a sign that Miss Birdseye's friends had assembled; if he had gone a little further still he would have recognized the house as one of those in which mysterious articles of clothing are always hooked to something in the hall. Miss Birdseye's visitors, those of Doctor Prance, and of other tenants—for Number 756 was the common residence of several persons, among whom there prevailed much vagueness of boundary—used to leave things to be called for; many of them went about with satchels and reticules, for which they were always looking for places of deposit. What completed the character of this interior was Miss Birdseye's own apartment, into which her guests presently made their way, and where they were joined by various other members of the good lady's circle. Indeed, it completed Miss Birdseye herself, if anything could be said to render that office to this essentially formless old woman, who had no more outline than a bundle of hay. But the bareness of her long, loose, empty parlor (it was shaped exactly like Miss Chancellor's) told that she had never had any needs but moral needs, and that all her history had been that of her sympathies. The place was lighted by a small hot glare of gas, which made it look white and featureless. It struck even Basil Ransom with its flatness, and he said to himself that his cousin must have a very big bee in her bonnet to make her like such a house. He did not know then, and he never knew, that she mortally disliked it, and that in a career in which she was constantly exposing herself to offense and laceration, her most poignant suffering came from the injury of her taste. She had tried to kill that nerve, to persuade herself that taste was only frivolity in the disguise of knowledge; but her susceptibility was constantly blooming afresh and making her wonder whether an absence of nice arrangements were a necessary part of the enthusiasm of humanity. Miss Birdseye was always trying to obtain employment, lessons in drawing, orders for portraits, for poor foreign artists, as to the greatness of whose talent she pledged herself without reserve; but in point of fact she had not the faintest sense of the scenic or plastic side of life.

Toward nine o'clock the light of her hissing burners smote the majestic person of Mrs. Farrinder, who might have contributed to answer that question of Miss Chancellor's in the negative. She was a copious, handsome woman, in whom angularity had been corrected by the air of success; she had a rustling dress (it was evident what *she* thought about taste), abundant hair of a glossy blackness, a pair of folded arms, the expression of which seemed to say that rest, in such a career as hers, was as sweet as it was brief, and a terrible regularity of feature. I apply that adjective to her fine placid mask because she seemed to face you with a question of which the answer was preordained, to ask you how a countenance could fail to be noble of which the measurements were so correct. You would contest neither the measurements nor the nobleness, and had to feel that Mrs. Farrinder imposed herself. There was a lithographic smoothness about her, and a mixture of the American matron and the public character. There was something public in her eye, which was large, cold, and quiet; it had acquired a sort of exposed reticence from the habit of looking down from a lecture desk, over a sea of heads, while its distinguished owner was eulogized by a leading citizen. Mrs. Farrinder, at almost any time, had the air of being introduced by a few remarks. She talked with great slowness and distinctness, and evidently a high sense of responsibility; she pronounced every syllable of every word and insisted on being explicit. If, in conversation with her, you attempted to take anything for granted, or to jump two or three steps at a time, she paused, looking at you with a cold patience, as if she knew that trick, and then went on at her own measured pace. She lectured on temperance and the rights of women; the ends she labored for were to give the ballot to every woman in the country and to take the flowing bowl from every man. She was held to have a very fine manner, and to embody the domestic virtues and the graces of the drawing room; to be a shining proof, in short, that the forum, for ladies, is not necessarily hostile to the fireside. She had a husband, and his name was Amariah.

Doctor Prance had come back from supper and made her appearance in response to an invitation that Miss Birdseye's relaxed voice had tinkled down to her from the hall over the banisters, with much repetition, to secure attention. She was a plain, spare young woman, with short hair and an eyeglass; she looked about her with a kind of nearsighted deprecation, and seemed to hope that she should not be expected to generalize in any way, or supposed to have come up for any purpose more social than to see what Miss Birdseye wanted this time. By nine o'clock twenty other persons had arrived, and had placed themselves in the chairs that were ranged along the sides of the long, bald room, in which they ended by producing the similitude of an enormous streetcar. The apartment contained little else but these chairs, many of which had a borrowed aspect, an implication of bare bedrooms in the upper regions; a table or two with a discolored marble top, a few books, and a collection of newspapers piled up in corners. Ransom could see for himself that the occasion was not crudely festive; there was a want of convivial movement, and, among most of the visitors, even of mutual recognition. They sat there as if they were waiting for something; they looked obliquely and silently at Mrs. Farrinder, and were plainly under the impression that, fortunately, they were not there to amuse themselves. The ladies, who were much the more numerous, wore their bonnets, like Miss Chancellor; the men were in the garb of toil, many of them in weary-looking overcoats. Two or three had retained their overshoes, and

as you approached them the odor of the india rubber was
perceptible. It was not, however, that Miss Birdseye ever
noticed anything of that sort; she neither knew what she
smelled nor tasted what she ate. Most of her friends had
an anxious, haggard look, though there were sundry exceptions—half a dozen placid, florid faces. Basil Ransom
wondered who they all were; he had a general idea they
were mediums, communists, vegetarians. It was not, either,
that Miss Birdseye failed to wander about among them with
repetitions of inquiry and friendly absences of attention; she
sat down near most of them in turn, saying "Yes, yes,"
vaguely and kindly, to remarks they made to her, feeling for
the papers in the pockets of her loosened bodice, recovering
her cap and sacrificing her spectacles, wondering most of all
what had been her idea in convoking these people. Then
she remembered that it had been connected in some way
with Mrs. Farrinder; that this eloquent woman had promised
to favor the company with a few reminiscences of her last
campaign; to sketch even, perhaps, the lines on which she
intended to operate during the coming winter. This was
what Olive Chancellor had come to hear; this would be the
attraction for the dark-eyed young man (he looked like a
genius) she had brought with her. Miss Birdseye made her
way back to the great lecturess, who was bending an indul-
gent attention on Miss Chancellor; the latter compressed into
a small space, to be near her, and sitting with clasped hands
and a concentration of inquiry which by contrast made Mrs.
Farrinder's manner seem large and free. In her transit, however, the hostess was checked by the arrival of fresh pil-
grims; she had no idea she had mentioned the occasion to so
many people—she only remembered, as it were, those she
had forgotten—and it was certainly a proof of the interest
felt in Mrs. Farrinder's work. The people who had just come
in were Doctor and Mrs. Tarrant and their daughter Verena;
he was a mesmeric healer and she was of old Abolitionist
stock. Miss Birdseye rested her dim, dry smile upon the
daughter, who was new to her, and it floated before her

that she would probably be remarkable as a genius; her parentage was an implication of that. There was a genius for Miss Birdseye in every bush. Selah Tarrant had effected wonderful cures; she knew so many people—if they would only try him. His wife was a daughter of Abraham Greenstreet; she had kept a runaway slave in her house for thirty days. That was years before, when this girl must have been a child; but hadn't it thrown a kind of rainbow over her cradle, and wouldn't she naturally have some gift? The girl was very pretty, though she had red hair.

5

Mrs. Farrinder, meanwhile, was not eager to address the assembly. She confessed as much to Olive Chancellor, with a smile which asked that a temporary lapse of promptness might not be too harshly judged. She had addressed so many assemblies, and she wanted to hear what other people had to say. Miss Chancellor herself had thought so much on the vital subject; would not she make a few remarks and give them some of her experiences? How did the ladies on Beacon Street feel about the ballot? Perhaps she could speak for *them* more than for some others. That was a branch of the question on which, it might be, the leaders had not information enough; but they wanted to take in everything, and why shouldn't Miss Chancellor just make that field her own? Mrs. Farrinder spoke in the tone of one who took views so wide that they might easily, at first, before you could see how she worked round, look almost meretricious;

she was conscious of a scope that exceeded the first flight of your imagination. She urged upon her companion the idea of laboring in the world of fashion, appeared to attribute to her familiar relations with that mysterious realm, and wanted to know why she shouldn't stir up some of her friends down there on the Mill-dam?

Olive Chancellor received this appeal with peculiar feelings. With her immense sympathy for reform, she found herself so often wishing that reformers were a little different. There was something grand about Mrs. Farrinder; it lifted one up to be with her: but there was a false note when she spoke to her young friend about the ladies in Beacon Street. Olive hated to hear that fine avenue talked about as if it were such a remarkable place, and to live there were a proof of worldly glory. All sorts of inferior people lived there, and so brilliant a woman as Mrs. Farrinder, who lived at Roxbury, ought not to mix things up. It was, of course, very wretched to be irritated by such mistakes; but this was not the first time Miss Chancellor had observed that the possession of nerves was not by itself a reason for embracing the new truths. She knew her place in the Boston hierarchy, and it was not what Mrs. Farrinder supposed; so that there was a want of perspective in talking to her as if she had been a representative of the aristocracy. Nothing could be weaker, she knew very well, than (in the United States) to apply that term too literally; nevertheless, it would represent a reality if one were to say that, by distinction, the Chancellors belonged to the *bourgeoisie*—the oldest and best. They might care for such a position or not (as it happened, they were very proud of it), but there they were, and it made Mrs. Farrinder seem provincial (there was something provincial, after all, in the way she did her hair too) not to understand. When Miss Birdseye spoke as if one were a "leader of society," Olive could forgive her even that odious expression, because, of course, one never pretended that she, poor dear, had the smallest sense of the real.

She was heroic, she was sublime, the whole moral history of Boston was reflected in her displaced spectacles; but it was a part of her originality, as it were, that she was deliciously provincial. Olive Chancellor seemed to herself to have privileges enough without being affiliated to the exclusive set and having invitations to the smaller parties, which were the real test; it was a mercy for her that she had not that added immorality on her conscience. The ladies Mrs. Farrinder meant (it was to be supposed she meant some particular ones) might speak for themselves. She wished to work in another field; she had long been preoccupied with the romance of the people. She had an immense desire to know intimately some *very* poor girl. This might seem one of the most accessible of pleasures; but, in point of fact, she had not found it so. There were two or three pale shop-maidens whose acquaintance she had sought; but they had seemed afraid of her, and the attempt had come to nothing. She took them more tragically than they took themselves; they couldn't make out what she wanted them to do, and they always ended by being odiously mixed up with Charlie. Charlie was a young man in a white overcoat and a paper collar; it was for him, in the last analysis, that they cared much the most. They cared far more about Charlie than about the ballot. Olive Chancellor wondered how Mrs. Farrinder would treat that branch of the question. In her researches among her young townswomen she had always found this obtrusive swain planted in her path, and she grew at last to dislike him extremely. It filled her with exasperation to think that he should be necessary to the happiness of his victims (she had learned that whatever they might talk about with her, it was of him and him only that they discoursed among themselves), and one of the main recommendations of the evening club for her fatigued, underpaid sisters, which it had long been her dream to establish, was that it would in some degree undermine his position—distinct as her prevision might be that he would be in waiting at the door. She hardly knew what to say to Mrs. Farrinder when this momentarily misdirected woman, still preoccupied with the Mill-dam, returned to the charge.

"We want laborers in that field, though I know two or three lovely women—sweet *home-women*—moving in circles that are for the most part closed to every new voice, who are doing their best to help on the fight. I have several names that might surprise you, names well known on State Street. But we can't have too many recruits, especially among those whose refinement is generally acknowledged. If it be necessary, we are prepared to take certain steps to conciliate the shrinking. Our movement is for all—it appeals to the most delicate ladies. Raise the standard among them, and bring me a thousand names. I know several that I should like to have. I look after the details as well as the big currents," Mrs. Farrinder added, in a tone as explanatory as could be expected of such a woman, and with a smile of which the sweetness was thrilling to her listener.

"I can't talk to those people, I can't!" said Olive Chancellor, with a face which seemed to plead for a remission of responsibility. "I want to give myself up to others; I want to know everything that lies beneath and out of sight, don't you know? I want to enter into the lives of women who are lonely, who are piteous. I want to be near to them—to help them. I want to do something—oh, I should like so to speak!"

"We should be glad to have you make a few remarks at present," Mrs. Farrinder declared, with a punctuality which revealed the faculty of presiding.

"Oh dear, no, I can't speak; I have none of that sort of talent. I have no self-possession, no eloquence; I can't put three words together. But I do want to contribute."

"What *have* you got?" Mrs. Farrinder inquired, looking at her interlocutress, up and down, with the eye of business, in which there was a certain chill. "Have you got money?"

Olive was so agitated for the moment with the hope that this great woman would approve of her on the financial side that she took no time to reflect that some other quality might, in courtesy, have been suggested. But she confessed to possessing a certain capital, and the tone seemed rich and deep in which Mrs. Farrinder said to her, "Then contribute that!" She was so good as to develop this idea, and her picture of the part Miss Chancellor might play by making liberal donations to a fund for the diffusion among the women of America of a more adequate conception of their public and private rights—a fund her adviser had herself lately inaugurated—this bold, rapid sketch had the vividness which characterized the speaker's most successful public efforts. It placed Olive under the spell; it made her feel almost inspired. If her life struck others in that way—especially a woman like Mrs. Farrinder, whose horizon was so full—then there must be something for her to do. It was one thing to choose for herself, but now the great representative of the enfranchisement of their sex (from every form of bondage) had chosen for her.

The barren, gas-lighted room grew richer and richer to her earnest eyes; it seemed to expand, to open itself to the great life of humanity. The serious, tired people, in their bonnets and overcoats, began to glow like a company of heroes. Yes, she would do something, Olive Chancellor said to herself; she would do something to brighten the darkness of that dreadful image that was always before her, and against which it seemed to her at times that she had been born to lead a crusade—the image of the unhappiness of women. The unhappiness of women! The voice of their silent suffering was always in her ears, the ocean of tears that they had shed from the beginning of time seemed to pour through her own eyes. Ages of oppression had rolled over them; uncounted millions had lived only to be tortured, to be crucified. They were her sisters, they were her own, and the day of their delivery had dawned. This was the only sacred cause; this was the great, the just revolution. It must triumph, it must sweep everything before it; it must exact from the other, the brutal, blood-stained, ravening race, the last particle of expiation! It would be the greatest change the world had seen; it would be a new era for the human family, and the names of those who had helped to show the way and lead the squadrons would be the brightest in the tables of fame. They would be names of women weak, insulted, persecuted, but devoted in every pulse to their being to the cause, and asking no better fate than to die for it. It was not clear to this interesting girl in what manner such a sacrifice (as this last) would be required of her, but she saw the matter through a kind of sunrise-mist of emotion which made danger as rosy as success. When Miss Birdseye approached, it transfigured her familiar, her comical shape, and made the poor little humanity hack seem already a martyr. Olive Chancellor looked at her with love, remembered that she had never, in her long, unrewarded, weary life, had a thought or an impulse for herself. She had been consumed by the passion of sympathy; it had crumpled her into as many creases as an old glazed, distended glove. She had been laughed at, but she never knew it; she was treated as a bore, but she never cared. She had nothing in the world but the clothes on her back, and when she should go down into the grave she would leave nothing behind her but her grotesque, undistinguished, pathetic little name. And yet people said that women were vain, that they were personal, that they were interested! While Miss Birdseye stood there, asking Mrs. Farrinder if she wouldn't say something, Olive Chancellor tenderly fastened a small battered brooch which confined her collar and which had half detached itself.

6

"Oh, thank you," said Miss Birdseye, "I shouldn't like to
lose it; it was given me by Mirandola!" He had been one of
her refugees in the old time, when two or three of her
friends, acquainted with the limits of his resources, wondered how he had come into possession of the trinket. She
had been diverted again, after her greeting with Doctor
and Mrs. Tarrant, by stopping to introduce the tall, dark
young man whom Miss Chancellor had brought with her to
Doctor Prance. She had become conscious of his somewhat
somber figure, uplifted against the wall, near the door; he
was leaning there in solitude, unacquainted with opportunities which Miss Birdseye felt to be, collectively, of value,
and which were really, of course, what strangers came to
Boston for. It did not occur to her to ask herself why Miss
Chancellor didn't talk to him, since she had brought him;
Miss Birdseye was incapable of a speculation of this kind.
Olive, in fact, had remained vividly conscious of her kinsman's isolation until the moment when Mrs. Farrinder lifted
her, with a word, to a higher plane. She watched him across
the room; she saw that he might be bored. But she proposed
to herself not to mind that; she had asked him, after all, not
to come. Then he was no worse off than others; he was
only waiting, like the rest; and before they left she would
introduce him to Mrs. Farrinder. She might tell that lady
who he was first; it was not every one that would care to
know a person who had borne such a part in the Southern

disloyalty. It came over our young lady that when she sought the acquaintance of her distant kinsman she had indeed done a more complicated thing than she suspected. The sudden uneasiness that he flung over her in the carriage had not left her, though she felt it less now she was with others, and especially that she was close to Mrs. Farrinder, who was such a fountain of strength. At any rate, if he was bored, he could speak to someone; there were excellent people near him, even if they *were* ardent reformers. He could speak to that pretty girl who had just come in—the one with red hair—if he liked; Southerners were supposed to be so chivalrous!

Miss Birdseye reasoned much less, and did not offer to introduce him to Verena Tarrant, who was apparently being presented by her parents to a group of friends at the other end of the room. It came back to Miss Birdseye, in this connection, that, sure enough, Verena had been away for a long time—for nearly a year; had been on a visit to friends in the West, and would therefore naturally be a stranger to most of the Boston circle. Doctor Prance was looking at her —at Miss Birdseye—with little, sharp, fixed pupils; and the good lady wondered whether she were angry at having been induced to come up. She had a general impression that when genius was original its temper was high, and all this would be the case with Doctor Prance. She wanted to say to her that she could go down again if she liked; but even to Miss Birdseye's unsophisticated mind this scarcely appeared, as regards a guest, an adequate formula of dismissal. She tried to bring the young Southerner out; she said to him that she presumed they would have some entertainment soon—Mrs. Farrinder could be interesting when she tried! And then she bethought herself to introduce him to Doctor Prance; it might serve as a reason for having brought her up. Moreover, it would do her good to break up her work now and then; she pursued her medical studies far into the night, and Miss Birdseye, who was nothing of a sleeper (Mary Prance, precisely, had wanted to treat her for it), had heard her, in the stillness of the small hours, with her open windows (she had fresh air on the brain), sharpening instruments (it was Miss Birdseye's mild belief that she dissected), in a little physiological laboratory which she had set up in her back room, the room which, if she hadn't been a doctor, might have been her "chamber," and perhaps was, even with the dissecting, Miss Birdseye didn't know! She explained her young friends to each other, a trifle incoherently, perhaps, and then went to stir up Mrs. Farrinder.

Basil Ransom had already noticed Doctor Prance; he had not been at all bored, and had observed everyone in the room, arriving at all sorts of ingenious inductions. The little medical lady struck him as a perfect example of the "Yankee female"—the figure which, in the unregenerate imagination of the children of the cotton states, was produced by the New England school system, the Puritan code, the ungenial climate, the absence of chivalry. Spare, dry, hard, without a curve, an inflection or a grace, she seemed to ask no odds in the battle of life and to be prepared to give none. But Ransom could see that she was not an enthusiast, and after his contact with his cousin's enthusiasm this was rather a relief to him. She looked like a boy, and not even like a good boy. It was evident that if she had been a boy, she would have "cut" school, to try private experiments in mechanics or to make researches in natural history. It was true that if she had been a boy she would have borne some relation to a girl, whereas Doctor Prance appeared to bear none whatever. Except her intelligent eye, she had no features to speak of. Ransom asked her if she were acquainted with the lioness, and on her staring at him, without response, explained that he meant the renowned Mrs. Farrinder.

"Well, I don't know as I ought to say that I'm acquainted with her; but I've heard her on the platform. I have paid my half-dollar," the doctor added, with a certain grimness.

"Well, did she convince you?" Ransom inquired.

"Convince me of what, sir?"

"That women are so superior to men."

"Oh, deary me!" said Doctor Prance, with a little impatient sigh; "I guess I know more about women than she does."

"And that isn't your opinion, I hope," said Ransom, laughing.

"Men and women are all the same to me," Doctor Prance remarked. "I don't see any difference. There is room for improvement in both sexes. Neither of them is up to the standard." And on Ransom's asking her what the standard appeared to her to be, she said, "Well, they ought to live better; that's what they ought to do." And she went on to declare, further, that she thought they all talked too much. This had so long been Ransom's conviction that his heart quite warmed to Doctor Prance, and he paid homage to her wisdom in the manner of Mississippi—with a richness of compliment that made her turn her acute, suspicious eye upon him. This checked him; she was capable of thinking that *he* talked too much—she herself having, apparently, no general conversation. It was german to the matter, at any rate, for him to observe that he believed they were to have a lecture from Mrs. Farrinder—he didn't know why she didn't begin. "Yes," said Doctor Prance, rather drily, "I suppose that's what Miss Birdseye called me up for. She seemed to think I wouldn't want to miss that."

"Whereas, I infer, you could console yourself for the loss of the oration," Ransom suggested.

"Well, I've got some work. I don't want any one to teach me what a woman can do!" Doctor Prance declared. "She can find out some things, if she tries. Besides, I am familiar with Mrs. Farrinder's system; I know all she has got to say."

"Well, what is it, then, since she continues to remain silent?"

"Well, what it amounts to is just that women want to have a better time. That's what it comes to in the end. I am aware of that, without her telling me."

"And don't you sympathize with such an aspiration?"

"Well, I don't know as I cultivate the sentimental side," said Doctor Prance. "There's plenty of sympathy without mine. If they want to have a better time, I suppose it's natural; so do men too, I suppose. But I don't know as it appeals to me—to make sacrifices for it; it ain't such a wonderful time—the best you *can* have!"

This little lady was tough and technical; she evidently didn't care for great movements; she became more and more interesting to Basil Ransom, who, it is to be feared, had a fund of cynicism. He asked her if she knew his cousin, Miss Chancellor, whom he indicated, beside Mrs. Farrinder; *she* believed, on the contrary, in wonderful times (she thought they were coming); she had plenty of sympathy, and he was sure she was willing to make sacrifices.

Doctor Prance looked at her across the room for a moment; then she said she didn't know her, but she guessed she knew others like her—she went to see them when they were sick. "She's having a private lecture to herself," Ransom remarked; whereupon Doctor Prance rejoined, "Well, I guess she'll have to pay for it!" She appeared to regret her own half-dollar, and to be vaguely impatient of the behavior of her sex. Ransom became so sensible of this that he felt it was indelicate to allude further to the cause of woman, and, for a change, endeavored to elicit from his companion some information about the gentlemen present. He had given her a chance, vainly, to start some topic herself; but he could see that she had no interests beyond the researches from which, this evening, she had been torn, and was incapable of asking him a personal question. She knew two or three of the gentlemen; she had seen them before at Miss Birdseye's. Of course she knew principally ladies; the time hadn't come when a lady-doctor was sent for by a gentleman, and she hoped it never would, though some people seemed to think that this was what lady-doctors were working for. She knew Mr. Pardon; that was the young man with the "side-whiskers" and the white hair; he was a kind of editor, and he wrote, too, "over his signature"—perhaps

Basil had read some of his works; he was under thirty, in spite of his white hair. He was a great deal thought of in magazine circles. She believed he was very bright—but she hadn't read anything. She didn't read much—not for amusement; only the "Transcript." She believed Mr. Pardon sometimes wrote in the "Transcript"; well, she supposed he *was* very bright. The other that she knew—only she didn't know him (she supposed Basil would think that queer)—was the tall, pale gentleman, with the black mustache and the eyeglass. She knew him because she had met him in society; but she didn't know him—well, because she didn't want to. If he should come and speak to her—and he looked as if he were going to work round that way—she should just say to him, "Yes, sir," or "No, sir," very coldly. She couldn't help it if he did think her dry; if *he* were a little more dry, it might be better for him. What was the matter with him? Oh, she thought she had mentioned that; he was a mesmeric healer, he made miraculous cures. She didn't believe in his system or disbelieve in it, one way or the other; she only knew that she had been called to see ladies he had worked on, and she found that he had made them lose a lot of valuable time. He talked to them—well, as if he didn't know what he was saying. She guessed he was quite ignorant of physiology, and she didn't think he ought to go round taking responsibilities. She didn't want to be narrow, but she thought a person ought to know something. She supposed Basil would think her very uplifted; but he had put the question to her, as she might say. All she could say was she didn't want him to be laying his hands on any of *her* folks; it was all done with the hands—what wasn't done with the tongue! Basil could see that Doctor Prance was irritated; that this extreme candor of allusion to her neighbor was probably not habitual to her, as a member of a society in which the casual expression of strong opinion generally produced waves of silence. But he blessed her irritation, for him it was so illuminating; and to draw further profit from it he asked her who the young lady was with the red hair—

the pretty one, whom he had only noticed during the last ten minutes. She was Miss Tarrant, the daughter of the healer; hadn't she mentioned his name? Selah Tarrant; if he wanted to send for him. Doctor Prance wasn't acquainted with her, beyond knowing that she was the mesmerist's only child, and having heard something about her having some gift—she couldn't remember which it was. Oh, if she was his child, she would be sure to have some gift—if it was only the gift of the g——well, she didn't mean to say that; but a talent for conversation. Perhaps she could die and come to life again; perhaps she would show them her gift, as no one seemed inclined to do anything. Yes, she was pretty-appearing, but there was a certain indication of anemia, and Doctor Prance would be surprised if she didn't eat too much candy. Basil thought she had an engaging exterior; it was his private reflection, colored doubtless by "sectional" prejudice, that she was the first pretty girl he had seen in Boston. She was talking with some ladies at the other end of the room; and she had a large red fan, which she kept constantly in movement. She was not a quiet girl; she fidgeted, was restless, while she talked, and had the air of a person who, whatever she might be doing, would wish to be doing something else. If people watched her a good deal, she also returned their contemplation, and her charming eyes had several times encountered those of Basil Ransom. But they wandered mainly in the direction of Mrs. Farrinder—they lingered upon the serene solidity of the great oratress. It was easy to see that the girl admired this beneficent woman, and felt it a privilege to be near her. It was apparent, indeed, that she was excited by the company in which she found herself; a fact to be explained by a reference to that recent period of exile in the West, of which we have had a hint, and in consequence of which the present occasion may have seemed to her a return to intellectual life. Ransom secretly wished that his cousin—since fate was to reserve for him a cousin in Boston—had been more like that.

By this time a certain agitation was perceptible; several

ladies, impatient of vain delay, had left their places, to appeal personally to Mrs. Farrinder, who was presently surrounded with sympathetic remonstrants. Miss Birdseye had given her up; it had been enough for Miss Birdseye that she should have said, when pressed (so far as her hostess, muffled in laxity, could press) on the subject of the general expectation, that she could only deliver her message to an audience which she felt to be partially hostile. There was no hostility there; they were all only too much in sympathy. "I don't require sympathy," she said, with a tranquil smile, to Olive Chancellor; "I am only myself, I only rise to the occasion, when I see prejudice, when I see bigotry, when I see injustice, when I see conservatism, massed before me like an army. Then I feel—I feel as I imagine Napoleon Bonaparte to have felt on the eve of one of his great victories. I *must* have unfriendly elements—I like to win them over."

Olive thought of Basil Ransom, and wondered whether he would do for an unfriendly element. She mentioned him to Mrs. Farrinder, who expressed an earnest hope that if he were opposed to the principles which were so dear to the rest of them, he might be induced to take the floor and testify on his own account. "I should be so happy to answer him," said Mrs. Farrinder, with supreme softness. "I should be so glad, at any rate, to exchange ideas with him." Olive felt a deep alarm at the idea of a public dispute between these two vigorous people (she had a perception that Ransom would be vigorous), not because she doubted of the happy issue, but because she herself would be in a false position, as having brought the offensive young man, and she had a horror of false positions. Miss Birdseye was incapable of resentment; she had invited forty people to hear Mrs. Farrinder speak, and now Mrs. Farrinder wouldn't speak. But she had such a beautiful reason for it! There was something martial and heroic in her pretext, and, besides, it was so characteristic, so free, that Miss Birdseye was quite consoled, and wandered away, looking at her other guests vaguely, as if she didn't know them from each other, while she mentioned to them, at a venture, the excuse for their disappointment, confident, evidently, that they would agree with her it was very fine. "But we can't pretend to be on the other side, just to start her up, can we?" she asked of Mr. Tarrant, who sat there beside his wife with a rather conscious but by no means complacent air of isolation from the rest of the company.

"Well, I don't know—I guess we are all solid here," this gentleman replied, looking round him with a slow, deliberate smile, which made his mouth enormous, developed two wrinkles, as long as the wings of a bat, on either side of it, and showed a set of big, even, carnivorous teeth.

"Selah," said his wife, laying her hand on the sleeve of his waterproof, "I wonder whether Miss Birdseye would be interested to hear Verena."

"Well, if you mean she sings, it's a shame I haven't got a piano," Miss Birdseye took upon herself to respond. It came back to her that the girl had a gift.

"She doesn't want a piano—she doesn't want anything," Selah remarked, giving no apparent attention to his wife. It was a part of his attitude in life never to appear to be indebted to another person for a suggestion, never to be surprised or unprepared.

"Well, I don't know that the interest in singing is so general," said Miss Birdseye, quite unconscious of any slackness in preparing a substitute for the entertainment that had failed her.

"It isn't singing, you'll see," Mrs. Tarrant declared.

"What is it, then?"

Mr. Tarrant unfurled his wrinkles, showed his back teeth. "It's inspirational."

Miss Birdseye gave a small, vague, unskeptical laugh. "Well, if you can guarantee that——"

"I think it would be acceptable," said Mrs. Tarrant; and putting up a half-gloved, familiar hand, she drew Miss Birdseye down to her, and the pair explained in alternation what it was their child could do.

Meanwhile, Basil Ransom confessed to Doctor Prance that he was, after all, rather disappointed. He had expected more of a program; he wanted to hear some of the new truths. Mrs. Farrinder, as he said, remained within her tent, and he had hoped not only to see these distinguished people but also to listen to them.

"Well, *I* ain't disappointed," the sturdy little doctress replied. "If any question had been opened, I suppose I should have had to stay."

"But I presume you don't propose to retire."

"Well, I've got to pursue my studies sometime. I don't want the gentlemen-doctors to get ahead of me."

"Oh, no one will ever get ahead of you, I'm very sure. And there is that pretty young lady going over to speak to Mrs. Farrinder. She's going to beg her for a speech—Mrs. Farrinder can't resist that."

"Well, then, I'll just trickle out before she begins. Good night, sir," said Doctor Prance, who by this time had begun to appear to Ransom more susceptible of domestication, as if she had been a small forest creature, a catamount or a ruffled doe, that had learned to stand still while you stroked it, or even to extend a paw. She ministered to health, and she was healthy herself; if his cousin could have been even of this type Basil would have felt himself more fortunate.

"Good night, Doctor," he replied. "You haven't told me, after all, your opinion of the capacity of the ladies."

"Capacity for what?" said Doctor Prance. "They've got a capacity for making people waste time. All I know is that I don't want any one to tell *me* what a lady can do!" And she edged away from him softly, as if she had been traversing a hospital ward, and presently he saw her reach the door, which, with the arrival of the later comers, had remained open. She stood there an instant, turning over the whole assembly a glance like the flash of a watchman's bull's-eye, and then quickly passed out. Ransom could see that she was impatient of the general question and bored with being reminded, even for the sake of her rights, that she was a woman—a detail that she was in the habit of forgetting, having as many rights as she had time for. It was certain that whatever might become of the movement at large, Doctor Prance's own little revolution was a success.

7

She had no sooner left him than Olive Chancellor came toward him with eyes that seemed to say, "I don't care whether you are here now or not—I'm all right!" But what her lips said was much more gracious; she asked him if she mightn't have the pleasure of introducing him to Mrs. Farrinder. Ransom consented, with a little of his Southern flourish, and in a moment the lady got up to receive him from the midst of the circle that now surrounded her. It was an occasion for her to justify her reputation of an elegant manner, and it must be impartially related that she struck Ransom as having a dignity in conversation and a command of the noble style which could not have been surpassed by a daughter—one of the most accomplished, most far-descended daughters—of his own latitude. It was as if she had known that he was not eager for the changes she advocated, and wished to show him that, especially to a Southerner who had bitten the dust, her sex could be magnanimous. This knowledge of his secret heresy seemed to him to be also in the faces of the other ladies, whose circumspect glances, however (for he had not been introduced), treated it as a pity rather than as a shame. He was conscious of all these middle-aged feminine eyes, conscious of curls, rather limp, that depended from dusky bonnets, of heads poked forward, as if with a waiting, listening, familiar habit, of no one being very bright or gay—no one, at least, but that girl he had noticed before, who had a brilliant head, and who now hovered on the edge of the conclave. He met her eye again; she was watching him too. It had been in his thoughts that Mrs. Farrinder, to whom his cousin might have betrayed or misrepresented him, would perhaps defy him to combat, and he wondered whether he could pull himself together (he was extremely embarrassed) sufficiently to do honor to such a challenge. If she would fling down the glove on the temperance question, it seemed to him that it would be in him to pick it up; for the idea of a meddling legislation on this subject filled him with rage; the taste of liquor being good to him, and his conviction strong that civilization itself would be in danger if it should fall into the power of a herd of vociferating women (I am but the reporter of his angry *formulæ*) to prevent a gentleman from taking his glass. Mrs. Farrinder proved to him that she had not the eagerness of insecurity; she asked him if he wouldn't like to give the company some account of the social and political condition of the South. He begged to be excused, expressing at the same time a high sense of the honor done him by such a request, while he smiled to himself at the idea of his extemporizing a lecture. He smiled even while he suspected the meaning of the look Miss Chancellor gave him: "Well, you are not of much account after all!" To talk to those people about the South—if they could have guessed how little he cared to do it! He had a passionate tenderness for his own country, and a sense of intimate connection with it which would have made it as impossible for him to take a roomful of Northern fanatics into his confidence as to read aloud his mother's or his mistress's letters. To be quiet about the Southern land, not to touch her with vulgar hands, to leave her alone with her wounds and her memories, not prating in the market place either of her troubles or her hopes, but waiting as a man should wait, for the slow process, the sensible beneficence, of time—this was the desire of Ransom's heart, and he was aware of how little it could minister to the entertainment of Miss Birdseye's guests.

"We know so little about the women of the South; they are very voiceless," Mrs. Farrinder remarked. "How much can we count upon them? in what numbers would they flock to our standard? I have been recommended not to lecture in the Southern cities."

"Ah, madam, that was very cruel advice—for us!" Basil Ransom exclaimed, with gallantry.

"*I* had a magnificent audience last spring in St. Louis," a fresh young voice announced, over the heads of the gathered group—a voice which, on Basil's turning, like everyone else, for an explanation, appeared to have proceeded from the pretty girl with red hair. She had colored a little with the effort of making this declaration, and she stood there smiling at her listeners.

Mrs. Farrinder bent a benignant brow upon her, in spite of her being, evidently, rather a surprise. "Oh, indeed; and your subject, my dear young lady?"

"The past history, the present condition, and the future prospects of our sex."

"Oh, well, St. Louis—that's scarcely the South," said one of the ladies.

"I'm sure the young lady would have had equal success at Charleston or New Orleans," Basil Ransom interposed.

"Well, I wanted to go farther," the girl continued, "but I had no friends. I have friends in St. Louis."

"You oughtn't to want for them anywhere," said Mrs. Farrinder, in a manner which, by this time, had quite explained her reputation. "I am acquainted with the loyalty of St. Louis."

"Well, after that, you must let me introduce Miss Tarrant; she's perfectly dying to know you, Mrs. Farrinder." These words emanated from one of the gentlemen, the young man with white hair, who had been mentioned to Ransom by Doctor Prance as a celebrated magazinist. He, too, up to this moment, had hovered in the background, but he now gently clove the assembly (several of the ladies made way for him), leading in the daughter of the mesmerist.

She laughed and continued to blush—her blush was the faintest pink; she looked very young and slim and fair as Mrs. Farrinder made way for her on the sofa which Olive Chancellor had quitted. "I *have* wanted to know you; I admire you so much; I hoped so you would speak tonight. It's too lovely to see you, Mrs. Farrinder." So she expressed herself, while the company watched the encounter with a look of refreshed inanition. "You don't know who I am, of course; I'm just a girl who wants to thank you for all you have done for us. For you have spoken for us girls, just as much as—just as much as——" She hesitated now, looking about with enthusiastic eyes at the rest of the group, and meeting once more the gaze of Basil Ransom.

"Just as much as for the old women," said Mrs. Farrinder, genially. "You seem very well able to speak for yourself."

"She speaks so beautifully—if she would only make a little address," the young man who had introduced her remarked. "It's a new style, quite original," he added. He stood there with folded arms, looking down at his work, the conjunction of the two ladies, with a smile; and Basil Ransom, remembering what Miss Prance had told him, and enlightened by his observation in New York of some of the sources from which newspapers are fed, was immediately touched by the conviction that he perceived in it the material of a paragraph.

"My dear child, if you'll take the floor, I'll call the meeting to order," said Mrs. Farrinder.

The girl looked at her with extraordinary candor and confidence. "If I could only hear you first—just to give me an atmosphere."

"I've got no atmosphere; there's very little of the Indian summer about *me!* I deal with facts—hard facts," Mrs. Farrinder replied. "Have you ever heard me? If so, you know how crisp I am."

"Heard you? I've lived on you! It's so much to me to see you. Ask mother if it isn't!" She had expressed herself, from the first word she uttered, with a promptness and assurance which gave almost the impression of a lesson rehearsed in advance. And yet there was a strange spontaneity in her manner, and an air of artless enthusiasm, of personal purity. If she was theatrical, she was naturally theatrical. She looked up at Mrs. Farrinder with all her emotion in her smiling eyes. This lady had been the object of many ovations; it was familiar to her that the collective heart of her sex had gone forth to her; but, visibly, she was puzzled by this unforeseen embodiment of gratitude and fluency, and her eyes wandered over the girl with a certain reserve, while, within the depth of her eminently public manner, she asked herself whether Miss Tarrant were a remarkable young woman or only a forward minx. She found a response which committed her to neither view; she only said, "We want the young—of course we want the young!"

"Who is that charming creature?" Basil Ransom heard his cousin ask, in a grave, lowered tone, of Matthias Pardon, the young man who had brought Miss Tarrant forward. He didn't know whether Miss Chancellor knew him, or whether her curiosity had pushed her to boldness. Ransom was near the pair, and had the benefit of Mr. Pardon's answer.

"The daughter of Doctor Tarrant, the mesmeric healer —Miss Verena. She's a high-class speaker."

"What do you mean?" Olive asked. "Does she give public addresses?"

"Oh yes, she has had quite a career in the West. I heard her last spring at Topeka. They call it inspirational. I don't know what it is—only it's exquisite; so fresh and poetical. She has to have her father to start her up. It seems to pass into her." And Mr. Pardon indulged in a gesture intended to signify the passage.

Olive Chancellor made no rejoinder save a low, impatient sigh; she transferred her attention to the girl, who now held Mrs. Farrinder's hand in both her own, and was pleading with her just to prelude a little. "I want a starting-point—I want to know where I am," she said. "Just two or three of your grand old thoughts."

Basil stepped nearer to his cousin; he remarked to her that Miss Verena was very pretty. She turned an instant, glanced at him, and then said, "Do you think so?" An instant later she added, "How you must hate this place!"

"Oh, not now, we are going to have some fun," Ransom replied good-humoredly, if a trifle coarsely; and the declaration had a point, for Miss Birdseye at this moment reappeared, followed by the mesmeric healer and his wife.

"Ah, well, I see you are drawing her out," said Miss Birdseye to Mrs. Farrinder; and at the idea that this process had been necessary Basil Ransom broke into a smothered hilarity, a spasm which indicated that, for him, the fun had already begun, and procured him another grave glance from Miss Chancellor. Miss Verena seemed to him as far "out" as a young woman could be. "Here's her father, Doctor Tarrant—he has a wonderful gift—and her mother—she was a daughter of Abraham Greenstreet." Miss Birdseye presented her companion; she was sure Mrs. Farrinder would be interested; she wouldn't want to lose an opportunity, even if for herself the conditions were not favorable. And then Miss Birdseye addressed herself to the company more at large, widening the circle so as to take in the most scattered guests, and evidently feeling that after all it was a relief that one happened to have an obscurely inspired maiden on the premises when greater celebrities had betrayed the whimsicality of genius. It was a part of this whimsicality that Mrs. Farrinder—the reader may find it difficult to keep pace with her variations—appeared now to have decided to utter a few of her thoughts, so that her hostess could elicit a general response to the remark that it would be delightful to have both the old school and the new.

"Well, perhaps you'll be disappointed in Verena," said

Mrs. Tarrant, with an air of dolorous resignation to any event, and seating herself, with her gathered mantle, on the edge of a chair, as if she, at least, were ready, whoever else might keep on talking.

"It isn't *me,* mother," Verena rejoined, with soft gravity, rather detached now from Mrs. Farrinder, and sitting with her eyes fixed thoughtfully on the ground. With deference to Mrs Tarrant, a little more talk was necessary, for the young lady had as yet been insufficiently explained. Miss Birdseye felt this, but she was rather helpless about it, and delivered herself, with her universal familiarity, which embraced everyone and everything, of a wandering, amiable tale, in which Abraham Greenstreet kept reappearing, in which Doctor Tarrant's miraculous cures were specified, with all the facts wanting, and in which Verena's successes in the West were related, not with emphasis or hyperbole, in which Miss Birdseye never indulged, but as accepted and recognized wonders, natural in an age of new revelations. She had heard of these things in detail only ten minutes before, from the girl's parents, but her hospitable soul had needed but a moment to swallow and assimilate them. If her account of them was not very lucid, it should be said in excuse for her that it was impossible to have any idea of Verena Tarrant unless one had heard her, and therefore still more impossible to give an idea to others. Mrs. Farrinder was perceptibly irritated; she appeared to have made up her mind, after her first hesitation, that the Tarrant family were fantastical and compromising. She had bent an eye of coldness on Selah and his wife—she might have regarded them all as a company of mountebanks.

"Stand up and tell us what you have to say," she remarked, with some sternness, to Verena, who only raised her eyes to her, silently now, with the same sweetness, and then rested them on her father. This gentleman seemed to respond to an irresistible appeal; he looked round at the company with all his teeth, and said that these flattering allusions were not so embarrassing as they might otherwise be, inasmuch as any success that he and his daughter might have had was so thoroughly impersonal: he insisted on that word. They had just heard her say, "It is not *me,* mother," and he and Mrs. Tarrant and the girl herself were all equally aware it was not she. It was some power outside—it seemed to flow through her; he couldn't pretend to say why his daughter should be called, more than any one else. But it seemed as if she *was* called. When he just calmed her down by laying his hand on her a few moments, it seemed to come. It so happened that in the West it had taken the form of a considerable eloquence. She had certainly spoken with great facility to cultivated and high-minded audiences. She had long followed with sympathy the movement for the liberation of her sex from every sort of bondage; it had been her principal interest even as a child (he might mention that at the age of nine she had christened her favorite doll Eliza P. Moseley, in memory of a great precursor whom they all reverenced), and now the inspiration, if he might call it so, seemed just to flow in that channel. The voice that spoke from her lips seemed to want to take that form. It didn't seem as if it *could* take any other. She let it come out just as it would—she didn't pretend to have any control. They could judge for themselves whether the whole thing was not quite unique. That was why he was willing to talk about his own child that way, before a gathering of ladies and gentlemen; it was because they took no credit—they felt it was a power outside. If Verena felt she was going to be stimulated that evening, he was pretty sure they would be interested. Only he should have to request a few moments' silence, while she listened for the voice.

Several of the ladies declared that they should be delighted —they hoped that Miss Tarrant was in good trim; whereupon they were corrected by others, who reminded them that it wasn't *her*—she had nothing to do with it—so her trim didn't matter; and a gentleman added that he guessed there were many present who had conversed with Eliza P. Moseley. Meanwhile Verena, more and more withdrawn into herself, but perfectly undisturbed by the public discussion of her mystic faculty, turned yet again, very prettily, to Mrs. Farrinder, and asked her if she wouldn't strike out—just to give her courage. By this time Mrs. Farrinder was in a condition of overhanging gloom; she greeted the charming suppliant with the frown of Juno. She disapproved completely of Doctor Tarrant's little speech, and she had less and less disposition to be associated with a miracle-monger. Abraham Greenstreet was very well, but Abraham Greenstreet was in his grave; and Eliza P. Moseley, after, all, had been very tepid. Basil Ransom wondered whether it were effrontery or innocence that enabled Miss Tarrant to meet with such complacency the aloofness of the elder lady. At this moment he heard Olive Chancellor, at his elbow, with the tremor of excitement in her tone, suddenly exclaim: "Please begin, please begin! A voice, a human voice, is what we want."

"I'll speak after you, and if you're a humbug, I'll expose you!" Mrs. Farrinder said. She was more majestic than facetious.

"I'm sure we are all solid, as Doctor Tarrant says. I suppose we want to be quiet," Miss Birdseye remarked.

8

Verena Tarrant got up and went to her father in the middle of the room; Olive Chancellor crossed and resumed her place beside Mrs. Farrinder on the sofa the girl had quitted; and Miss Birdseye's visitors, for the rest, settled themselves attentively in chairs or leaned against the bare sides of the parlor. Verena took her father's hands, held them for a moment, while she stood before him, not looking at him, with her eyes toward the company; then, after an instant, her mother, rising, pushed forward, with an interesting sigh, the chair on which she had been sitting. Mrs. Tarrant was provided with another seat, and Verena, relinquishing her father's grasp, placed herself in the chair, which Tarrant put in position for her. She sat there with closed eyes, and her father now rested his long, lean hands upon her head. Basil Ransom watched these proceedings with much interest, for the girl amused and pleased him. She had far more color than any one there, for whatever brightness was to be found in Miss Birdseye's rather faded and dingy human collection had gathered itself into this attractive but ambiguous young person. There was nothing ambiguous, by the way, about her confederate; Ransom simply loathed him, from the moment he opened his mouth; he was intensely familiar—that is, his type was; he was simply the detested carpetbagger. He was false, cunning, vulgar, ignoble; the cheapest kind of human product. That he should be the father of a delicate, pretty girl, who was apparently clever too, whether she had a gift or no, this was an annoying, disconcerting fact. The white, puffy mother, with the high forehead, in the corner there, looked more like a lady; but if she were one, it was all the more shame to her to have mated with such a varlet, Ransom said to himself, making use, as he did generally, of terms of opprobrium extracted from the older English literature. He had seen Tarrant, or his equivalent, often before; he had "whipped" him, as he believed, controversially, again and again, at political meetings in blighted Southern towns, during the horrible period of reconstruction. If Mrs. Farrinder had looked at Verena Tarrant as if she were a mountebank, there was some excuse for it, inasmuch as the girl made much the same impression on Basil Ransom. He had never seen such an odd mixture of elements; she had the sweetest, most unworldly face, and yet, with it, an air of being on exhibition, of belonging to a troupe, of living in the gaslight, which pervaded even the details of her dress, fashioned evidently with an attempt at the histrionic. If she had produced a pair of castanets or a tambourine, he felt that such accessories would have been quite in keeping.

Little Doctor Prance, with her hard good sense, had noted that she was anemic, and had intimated that she was a deceiver. The value of her performance was yet to be proved, but she was certainly very pale, white as women are who have that shade of red hair; they look as if their blood had gone into it. There was, however, something rich in the fairness of this young lady; she was strong and supple, there was color in her lips and eyes, and her tresses, gathered into a complicated coil, seemed to glow with the brightness of her nature. She had curious, radiant, liquid eyes (their smile was a sort of reflection, like the glisten of a gem), and though she was not tall, she appeared to spring up, and carried her head as if it reached rather high. Ransom would have thought she looked like an Oriental, if it were not that Orientals are dark; and if she had only had a goat she would have resembled Esmeralda, though he had but a vague recollection of who Esmeralda had been. She wore a light-brown dress, of a shape that struck him as fantastic, a yellow petticoat, and a large crimson sash fastened at the side; while round her neck, and falling low upon her flat young chest, she had a double chain of amber beads. It must be added that, in spite of her melodramatic appearance, there was no symptom that her performance, whatever it was, would be of a melodramatic character. She was very quiet now, at least (she had folded her big fan), and her father continued the mysterious process of calming her down. Ransom wondered whether he wouldn't put her to sleep; for some minutes her eyes had remained closed; he heard a lady near him, apparently familiar with phenomena of this class, remark that she was going off. As yet the exhibition was not exciting, though it was certainly pleasant to have such a pretty girl placed there before one, like a moving statue. Doctor Tarrant looked at no one as he stroked and soothed his daughter; his eyes wandered round the cornice of the room, and he grinned upward, as if at an imaginary gallery. "Quietly—quietly," he murmured, from time to time. "It will come, my good child, it will come. Just let it work—just let it gather. The spirit, you know; you've got to let the spirit come out when it will." He threw up his arms at moments, to rid himself of the wings of his long waterproof, which fell forward over his hands. Basil Ransom noticed all these things, and noticed also, opposite, the waiting face of his cousin, fixed, from her sofa, upon the closed eyes of the young prophetess. He grew more impatient at last, not of the delay of the edifying voice (though some time had elapsed), but of Tarrant's grotesque manipulations, which he resented as much as if he himself had felt their touch, and which seemed a dishonor to the passive maiden. They made him nervous, they made him angry, and it was only afterwards that he asked himself wherein they concerned him, and whether even a carpetbagger hadn't a right to do what he pleased with his daughter. It was a relief to him when Verena got up from her chair, with a movement which made Tarrant drop into the background as if his part were now over. She stood there with a quiet face, serious and sightless; then, after a short further delay, she began to speak.

She began incoherently, almost inaudibly, as if she were talking in a dream. Ransom could not understand her; he thought it very queer, and wondered what Doctor Prance would have said. "She's just arranging her ideas, and trying to get in report; she'll come out all right." This remark he heard dropped in a low tone by the mesmeric healer; "in report" was apparently Tarrant's version of *en rapport*. His prophecy was verified, and Verena did come out, after a little; she came out with a great deal of sweetness—with a very quaint and peculiar effect. She proceeded slowly, cautiously, as if she were listening for the prompter, catching, one by one, certain phrases that were whispered to her a great distance off, behind the scenes of the world. Then memory, or inspiration, returned to her, and presently she was in possession of her part. She played it with extraordinary simplicity and grace; at the end of ten minutes Ransom became aware that the whole audience—Mrs. Farrinder, Miss Chancellor, and the tough subject from Mississippi— were under the charm. I speak of ten minutes, but to tell the truth the young man lost all sense of time. He wondered afterwards how long she had spoken; then he counted that her strange, sweet, crude, absurd, enchanting improvisation must have lasted half an hour. It was not what she said; he didn't care for that, he scarcely understood it; he could only see that it was all about the gentleness and goodness of women, and how, during the long ages of history, they had been trampled under the iron heel of man. It was about their equality—perhaps even (he was not definitely conscious) about their superiority. It was about their day having come at last, about the universal sisterhood, about their duty to themselves and to each other. It was about such matters as these, and Basil Ransom was delighted to observe that such matters as these didn't spoil it. The effect was not in what she said, though she said some such pretty things, but in the picture and figure of the half-bedizened damsel (playing, now again, with her red fan), the visible freshness and purity of the little effort. When she had gained confidence she opened her eyes, and their shining softness was half the effect of her discourse. It was full of schoolgirl phrases, of patches of remembered eloquence, of childish lapses of logic, of flights of fancy which might indeed have had success at Topeka; but Ransom thought that if it had been much worse it would have been quite as good, for the argument, the doctrine, had absolutely nothing to do with it. It was simply an intensely personal exhibition, and the person making it happened to be fascinating. She might have offended the taste of certain people—Ransom could imagine that there were other Boston circles in which she would be thought pert; but for himself all he could feel was that to *his* starved senses she irresistibly appealed. He was the stiffest of conservatives, and his mind was steeled against the inanities she uttered—the rights and wrongs of women, the equality of the sexes, the hysterics of conventions, the further stultification of the suffrage, the prospect of conscript mothers in the national Senate. It made no difference; she didn't mean it, she didn't know what she meant, she had been stuffed with this trash by her father, and she was neither more nor less willing to say it than to say anything else; for the necessity of her nature was not to make converts to a ridiculous cause, but to emit those charming notes of her voice, to stand in those free young attitudes, to shake her braided locks like a naiad rising from the waves, to please every one who came near her, and to be happy that she pleased. I know not whether Ransom was aware of the bearings of this interpretation, which attributed to Miss Tarrant a singular hollowness of character; he contented himself with believing that she was as innocent as she was lovely, and with regarding her as a vocalist of exquisite faculty, condemned to sing bad music. How prettily, indeed, she made some of it sound!

"Of course I only speak to women—to my own dear sisters; I don't speak to men, for I don't expect them to like what I say. They pretend to admire us very much, but I should like them to admire us a little less and to trust us a little more. I don't know what we have ever done to them that they should keep us out of everything. We have trusted *them* too much, and I think the time has come now for us to judge them, and say that by keeping us out we don't think they have done so well. When I look around me at the world, and at the state that men have brought it to, I confess I say to myself, 'Well, if women had fixed it this way I should like to know what they would think of it!' When I see the dreadful misery of mankind and think of the suffering of which at any hour, at any moment, the world is full, I say that if this is the best they can do by themselves, they had better let us come in a little and see what *we* can do. We couldn't possibly make it worse, could we? If we had done only this, we shouldn't boast of it. Poverty, and ignorance, and crime; disease, and wickedness, and wars! Wars, always more wars, and always more and more. Blood, blood—the world is drenched with blood! To kill each other, with all sorts of expensive and perfected instruments, that is the most brilliant thing they have been able to invent. It seems to me that we might stop it, we might invent something better. The cruelty—the cruelty; there is so much, so much! Why shouldn't tenderness come in? Why should our woman's hearts be so full of it, and all so wasted and withered, while armies and prisons and helpless miseries grow greater all the while? I am only a girl, a simple American girl, and of course I haven't seen much, and there is a great deal of life that I don't know anything about. But there are some things I feel—it seems to me as if I had been born to feel them; they are in my ears in the stillness of the night and before my face in the visions of the darkness. It is what the great sisterhood of women might do if they should all join hands, and lift up their voices above the brutal uproar of the world, in which it is so hard for the plea of mercy or of justice, the moan of weakness and suffering, to be heard. We should quench it, we should make it still, and the sound of our lips would become the voice of universal peace! For this we must trust one another, we must be true and gentle and kind. We must remember that the world is ours too, ours —little as we have ever had to say about anything!—and that the question is *not* yet definitely settled whether it shall be a place of injustice or a place of love!"

It was with this that the young lady finished her harangue, which was not followed by her sinking exhausted into her chair or by any of the traces of a labored climax. She only turned away slowly towards her mother, smiling over her shoulder at the whole room, as if it had been a single person, without a flush in her whiteness, or the need of drawing a longer breath. The performance had evidently been very easy to her, and there might have been a kind of impertinence in her air of not having suffered from an exertion which had wrought so powerfully on every one else. Ransom broke into a genial laugh, which he instantly swallowed again, at the sweet grotesqueness of this virginal creature's standing up before a company of middle-aged people to talk to them about "love," the note on which she had closed her harangue. It was the most charming touch in the whole thing, and the most vivid proof of her innocence. She had had immense success, and Mrs. Tarrant, as she took her into her arms and kissed her, was certainly able to feel that the audience was not disappointed. They were exceedingly affected; they broke into exclamations and murmurs. Selah Tarrant went on conversing ostentatiously with his neighbors, slowly twirling his long thumbs and looking up at the cornice again, as if there could be nothing in the brilliant manner in which his daughter had acquitted herself to surprise *him,* who had heard her when she was still more remarkable, and who, moreover, remembered that the affair was so impersonal. Miss Birdseye looked round at the company with dim exultation; her large mild cheeks were shining with unwiped tears. Young Mr. Pardon remarked, in Ransom's hearing, that he knew parties who, if they had been present, would want to engage Miss Verena at a high figure for the winter campaign. And Ransom heard him add in a lower tone: "There's money for some one in that girl; you see if she don't have quite a run!" As for our Mississippian he kept his agreeable sensation for himself, only wondering whether he might not ask Miss Birdseye to present him to the heroine of the evening. Not immediately, of course, for the young man mingled with his Southern pride a shyness which often served all the purpose of humility. He was aware how much he was an outsider in such a house as that, and he was ready to wait for his coveted satisfaction till the others, who all hung together, should have given her the assurance of an approval which she would value, naturally, more than anything he could say to her. This episode had imparted animation to the assembly; a certain gaiety, even, expressed in a higher pitch of conversation, seemed to float in the heated air. People circulated more freely, and Verena Tarrant was presently hidden from Ransom's sight by the close-pressed ranks of the new friends she had made. "Well, I never heard it put *that* way!" Ransom heard one of the ladies exclaim; to which another replied that she wondered one of their bright women hadn't thought of it before. "Well, it *is* a gift, and no mistake," and "Well, they may call it what they please, it's a pleasure to listen to it"—these genial tributes fell from the lips of a pair of ruminating gentlemen. It was affirmed within Ransom's hearing that if they had a few more like that the matter would soon be fixed; and it was rejoined that they couldn't expect to have a great many—the style was so peculiar. It was generally admitted that the style was peculiar, but Miss Tarrant's peculiarity was the explanation of her success.

9

Ransom approached Mrs. Farrinder again, who had remained on her sofa with Olive Chancellor; and as she turned her face to him he saw that she had felt the universal contagion. Her keen eye sparkled, there was a flush on her matronly cheek, and she had evidently made up her mind what line to take. Olive Chancellor sat motionless; her eyes were fixed on the floor with the rigid, alarmed expression of her moments of nervous diffidence; she gave no sign of observing her kinsman's approach. He said something to Mrs. Farrinder, something that imperfectly represented his admiration of Verena; and this lady replied with dignity that it was no wonder the girl spoke so well—she spoke in such a good cause. "She is very graceful, has a fine command of language; her father says it's a natural gift." Ransom saw that he should not in the least discover Mrs. Farrinder's real opinion, and her dissimulation added to his impression that she was a woman with a policy. It was none of his business whether in her heart she thought Verena a parrot or a genius; it was perceptible to him that she saw she would be effective, would help the cause. He stood almost appalled for a moment, as he said to himself that she would take her up and the girl would be ruined, would force her note and become a screamer. But he quickly dodged this vision, taking refuge in a mechanical appeal to his cousin, of whom he inquired how she liked Miss Verena. Olive made no answer; her head remained averted, she bored the carpet with her conscious eyes. Mrs. Farrinder glanced at her askance, and then said to Ransom serenely:

"You praise the grace of your Southern ladies, but you have had to come North to see a human gazelle. Miss Tarrant is of the best New England stock—what *I* call the best!"

"I'm sure from what I have seen of the Boston ladies, no manifestation of grace can excite my surprise," Ransom rejoined, looking, with his smile, at his cousin.

"She has been powerfully affected," Mrs. Farrinder explained, very slightly dropping her voice, as Olive, apparently, still remained deaf.

Miss Birdseye drew near at this moment; she wanted to know if Mrs. Farrinder didn't want to express some acknowledgment, on the part of the company at large, for the real stimulus Miss Tarrant had given them. Mrs. Farrinder said: Oh yes, she would speak now with pleasure; only she must have a glass of water first. Miss Birdseye replied that there was some coming in a moment; one of the ladies had asked for it, and Mr. Pardon had just stepped down to draw some. Basil took advantage of this intermission to ask Miss Birdseye if she would give him the great privilege of an introduction to Miss Verena. "Mrs. Farrinder will thank her for the company," he said, laughing, "but she won't thank her for me."

Miss Birdseye manifested the greatest disposition to oblige him; she was so glad he had been impressed. She was proceeding to lead him toward Miss Tarrant when Olive Chancellor rose abruptly from her chair and laid her hand, with an arresting movement, on the arm of the hostess. She explained to her that she must go, that she was not very well, that her carriage was there; also that she hoped Miss Birdseye, if it was not asking too much, would accompany her to the door.

"Well, you are impressed too," said Miss Birdseye, looking at her philosophically. "It seems as if no one had escaped."

Ransom was disappointed; he saw he was going to be taken away, and, before he could suppress it, an exclamation burst from his lips—the first exclamation he could think of that would perhaps check his cousin's retreat: "Ah, Miss Olive, are you going to give up Mrs. Farrinder?"

At this Miss Olive looked at him, showed him an extraordinary face, a face he scarcely understood or even recognized. It was portentously grave, the eyes were enlarged, there was a red spot in each of the cheeks, and as directed to him, a quick, piercing question, a kind of leaping challenge, in the whole expression. He could only answer this sudden gleam with a stare, and wonder afresh what trick his Northern kinswoman was destined to play him. Impressed too? He should think he had been! Mrs. Farrinder, who was decidedly a woman of the world, came to his assistance, or to Miss Chancellor's, and said she hoped very much Olive wouldn't stay—she felt these things too much. "If you stay, I won't speak," she added; "I should upset you altogether." And then she continued, tenderly, for so preponderantly intellectual a nature: "When women feel as you do, how can I doubt that we shall come out all right?"

"Oh, we shall come out all right, I guess," murmured Miss Birdseye.

"But you must remember Beacon Street," Mrs. Farrinder subjoined. "You must take advantage of your position —you must wake up the Back Bay!"

"I'm sick of the Back Bay!" said Olive fiercely; and she passed to the door with Miss Birdseye, bidding good-by to no one. She was so agitated that, evidently, she could not trust herself, and there was nothing for Ransom but to follow. At the door of the room, however, he was checked by a sudden pause on the part of the two ladies: Olive stopped and stood there hesitating. She looked round the room and spied out Verena, where she sat with her mother, the center of a gratified group; then, throwing back her head with an air of decision, she crossed over to her. Ransom said to himself that now, perhaps, was his chance, and he quickly accompanied Miss Chancellor. The little knot of reformers watched her as she arrived; their faces expressed a suspicion of her social importance, mingled with conscientious scruples as to whether it were right to recognize it. Verena Tarrant saw that she was the object of this manifestation, and she got up to meet the lady whose approach was so full of point. Ransom perceived, however, or thought he perceived, that she recognized nothing; she had no suspicions of social importance. Yet she smiled with all her radiance, as she looked from Miss Chancellor to him; smiled because she liked to smile, to please, to feel her success—or was it because she was a perfect little actress, and this was part of her training? She took the hand that Olive put out to her; the others, rather solemnly, sat looking up from their chairs.

"You don't know me, but I want to know you," Olive said. "I can thank you now. Will you come and see me?"

"Oh yes; where do you live?" Verena answered, in the tone of a girl for whom an invitation (she hadn't so many) was always an invitation.

Miss Chancellor syllabled her address, and Mrs. Tarrant came forward, smiling. "I know about you, Miss Chancellor. I guess your father knew my father—Mr. Greenstreet.

Verena will be very glad to visit you. We shall be very happy to see you in *our* home."

Basil Ransom, while the mother spoke, wanted to say something to the daughter, who stood there so near him, but he could think of nothing that would do; certain words that came to him, his Mississippi phrases, seemed patronizing and ponderous. Besides, he didn't wish to assent to what she had said; he wished simply to tell her she was delightful, and it was difficult to mark that difference. So he only smiled at her in silence, and she smiled back at him—a smile that seemed to him quite for himself.

"Where do you live?" Olive asked; and Mrs. Tarrant replied that they lived at Cambridge, and that the horsecars passed just near their door. Whereupon Olive insisted "Will you come very soon?" and Verena said, Oh yes, she would come very soon, and repeated the number in Charles Street, to show that she had taken heed of it. This was done with childlike good faith. Ransom saw that she would come and see anyone who would ask her like that, and he regretted for a minute that he was not a Boston lady, so that he might extend to her such an invitation. Olive Chancellor held her hand a moment longer, looked at her in farewell, and then, saying, "Come, Mr. Ransom," drew him out of the room. In the hall they met Mr. Pardon, coming up from the lower regions with a jug of water and a tumbler. Miss Chancellor's hackney coach was there, and when Basil had put her into it she said to him that she wouldn't trouble him to drive with her—his hotel was not near Charles Street. He had so little desire to sit by her side—he wanted to smoke—that it was only after the vehicle had rolled off that he reflected upon her coolness, and asked himself why the deuce she had brought him away. She *was* a very odd cousin, was this Boston cousin of his. He stood there a moment, looking at the light in Miss Birdseye's windows and greatly minded to re-enter the house, now he might speak to the girl. But he contented himself with the memory of her smile, and turned away with a sense of relief, after all, at having got out of such wild company, as well as with (in a different order) a vulgar consciousness of being very thirsty.

10

Verena Tarrant came in the very next day from Cambridge to Charles Street; that quarter of Boston is in direct communication with the academic suburb. It hardly seemed direct to poor Verena, perhaps, who, in the crowded streetcar which deposited her finally at Miss Chancellor's door, had to stand up all the way, half suspended by a leathern strap from the glazed roof of the stifling vehicle, like some blooming cluster dangling in a hothouse. She was used, however, to these perpendicular journeys, and though, as we have seen, she was not inclined to accept without question the social arrangements of her time, it never would have occurred to her to criticize the railways of her native land. The promptness of her visit to Olive Chancellor had been an idea of her mother's, and Verena listened open-eyed while this lady, in the seclusion of the little house in Cambridge, while Selah Tarrant was "off," as they said, with his patients, sketched out a line of conduct for her. The girl was both submissive and unworldly, and she listened to her mother's enumeration of the possible advantages of an intimacy with Miss Chancellor as she would have listened to any other fairy tale. It was still a part of the fairy tale when this zealous parent put on with her own hands Verena's smart hat and feather, buttoned her little jacket (the buttons were immense and gilt), and presented her with twenty cents to pay her carfare.

There was never any knowing in advance how Mrs. Tarrant would take a thing, and even Verena, who, filially, was much less argumentative than in her civic and, as it were, public capacity, had a perception that her mother was queer. She was queer, indeed—a flaccid, relaxed, unhealthy, whimsical woman, who still had a capacity to cling. What she clung to was "society," and a position in the world which a secret whisper told her she had never had and a voice more audible reminded her she was in danger of losing. To keep it, to recover it, to reconsecrate it, was the ambition of her heart; this was one of the many reasons why Providence had judged her worthy of having so wonderful a child. Verena was born not only to lead their common sex out of bondage, but to remodel a visiting-list which bulged and contracted in the wrong places, like a country-made garment. As the daughter of Abraham Greenstreet, Mrs. Tarrant had passed her youth in the first Abolitionist circles, and she was aware how much such a prospect was clouded by her union with a young man who had begun life as an itinerant vendor of lead pencils (he had called at Mr. Greenstreet's door in the exercise of this function), had afterwards been for a while a member of the celebrated Cayuga community, where there were no wives, or no husbands, or something of that sort (Mrs. Tarrant could never remember), and had still later (though before the development of the healing faculty) achieved distinction in the spiritualistic world. (He was an extraordinarily favored medium, only he had had to stop for reasons of which Mrs. Tarrant possessed her version.) Even in a society much occupied with the effacement of prejudice there had been certain dim presumptions against this versatile being, who naturally had not wanted arts to ingratiate himself with Miss Greenstreet, her eyes, like his own, being fixed exclusively on the future. The young couple (he was considerably her elder) had gazed on the future together until they found that the past had completely forsaken them and that the present offered but a slender foothold. Mrs. Tarrant, in other words, incurred the displeasure of her family, who gave her husband to understand that, much as they desired to remove the shackles from the slave, there were kinds of behavior which struck them as too unfettered. These had prevailed, to their thinking, at Cayuga, and they naturally felt it was no use for him to say that his residence there had been (for him—the community still existed) but a momentary episode, inasmuch as there was little more to be urged for the spiritual picnics and vegetarian camp meetings in which the discountenanced pair now sought consolation.

Such were the narrow views of people hitherto supposed capable of opening their hearts to all salutary novelties, but now put to a genuine test, as Mrs. Tarrant felt. Her husband's tastes rubbed off on her soft, moist moral surface, and the couple lived in an atmosphere of novelty, in which, occasionally, the accommodating wife encountered the fresh sensation of being in want of her dinner. Her father died, leaving, after all, very little money; he had spent his modest fortune upon the blacks. Selah Tarrant and his companion had strange adventures; she found herself completely enrolled in the great irregular army of nostrum-mongers, domiciled in humanitary Bohemia. It absorbed her like a social swamp; she sank into it a little more every day, without measuring the inches of her descent. Now she stood there up to her chin; it may probably be said of her that she had touched bottom. When she went to Miss Birdseye's it seemed to her that she re-entered society. The door that admitted her was not the door that admitted some of the others (she should never forget the tipped-up nose of Mrs. Farrinder), and the superior portal remained ajar, disclosing possible vistas. She had lived with long-haired men and short-haired women, she had contributed a flexible faith and an irremediable want of funds to a dozen social experiments, she had partaken of the comfort of a hundred religions, had followed innumerable dietary reforms, chiefly of the negative

order, and had gone of an evening to a *séance* or a lecture
as regularly as she had eaten her supper. Her husband always had tickets for lectures; in moments of irritation at the
want of a certain sequence in their career, she had remarked
to him that it was the only thing he did have. The memory
of all the winter nights they had tramped through the slush
(the tickets, alas! were not car-tickets) to hear Mrs. Ada
T. P. Foat discourse on the "Summer-land," came back to
her with bitterness. Selah was quite enthusiastic at one time
about Mrs. Foat, and it was his wife's belief that he had
been "associated" with her (that was Selah's expression in
referring to such episodes) at Cayuga. The poor woman,
matrimonially, had a great deal to put up with; it took, at
moments, all her belief in his genius to sustain her. She
knew that he was very magnetic (that, in fact, was his genius), and she felt that it was his magnetism that held her to
him. He had carried her through things where she really
didn't know what to think; there were moments when she
suspected that she had lost the strong moral sense for which
the Greenstreets were always so celebrated.

Of course a woman who had had the bad taste to marry
Selah Tarrant would not have been likely under any circumstances to possess a very straight judgment; but there is no
doubt that this poor lady had grown dreadfully limp. She
had blinked and compromised and shuffled; she asked herself whether, after all, it was any more than natural that she
should have wanted to help her husband, in those exciting
days of his mediumship, when the table, sometimes,
wouldn't rise from the ground, the sofa wouldn't float
through the air, and the soft hand of a lost loved one was
not so alert as it might have been to visit the circle. Mrs.
Tarrant's hand was soft enough for the most supernatural
effect, and she consoled her conscience on such occasions
by reflecting that she ministered to a belief in immortality.
She was glad, somehow, for Verena's sake, that they had
emerged from the phase of spirit-intercourse; her ambition
for her daughter took another form than desiring that she,

too, should minister to a belief in immortality. Yet among Mrs. Tarrant's multifarious memories these reminiscences of the darkened room, the waiting circle, the little taps on table and wall, the little touches on cheek and foot, the music in the air, the rain of flowers, the sense of something mysteriously flitting, were most tenderly cherished. She hated her husband for having magnetized her so that she consented to certain things, and even did them, the thought of which today would suddenly make her face burn; hated him for the manner in which, somehow, as she felt, he had lowered her social tone; yet at the same time she admired him for an impudence so consummate that it had ended (in the face of mortifications, exposures, failures, all the misery of a hand-to-mouth existence) by imposing itself on her as a kind of infallibility. She knew he was an awful humbug, and yet her knowledge had this imperfection, that he had never confessed it—a fact that was really grand when one thought of his opportunities for doing so. He had never allowed that he wasn't straight; the pair had so often been in the position of the two augurs behind the altar, and yet he had never given her a glance that the whole circle mightn't have observed. Even in the privacy of domestic intercourse he had phrases, excuses, explanations, ways of putting things, which, as she felt, were too sublime for just herself; they were pitched, as Selah's nature was pitched, altogether in the key of public life.

So it had come to pass, in her distended and demoralized conscience, that with all the things she despised in her life and all the things she rather liked, between being worn out with her husband's inability to earn a living and a kind of terror of his consistency (he had a theory that they lived delightfully), it happened, I say, that the only very definite criticism she made of him today was that he didn't know how to speak. That was where the shoe pinched—that was where Selah was slim. He couldn't hold the attention of an audience, he was not acceptable as a lecturer. He had plenty of thoughts, but it seemed as if he couldn't fit them into each other. Public speaking had been a Greenstreet tradition, and if Mrs. Tarrant had been asked whether in her younger years she had ever supposed she should marry a mesmeric healer, she would have replied: "Well, I never thought I should marry a gentleman who would be silent on the platform!" This was her most general humiliation; it included and exceeded every other, and it was a poor consolation that Selah possessed as a substitute—his career as a healer, to speak of none other, was there to prove it—the eloquence of the hand. The Greenstreets had never set much store on manual activity; they believed in the influence of the lips. It may be imagined, therefore, with what exultation, as time went on, Mrs. Tarrant found herself the mother of an inspired maiden, a young lady from whose lips eloquence flowed in streams. The Greenstreet tradition would not perish, and the dry places of her life would, perhaps, be plentifully watered. It must be added that, of late, this sandy surface had been irrigated, in moderation, from another source. Since Selah had addicted himself to the mesmeric mystery, their home had been a little more what the home of a Greenstreet should be. He had "considerable many" patients, he got about two dollars a sitting, and he had effected some most gratifying cures. A lady in Cambridge had been so much indebted to him that she had recently persuaded them to take a house near her, in order that Doctor Tarrant might drop in at any time. He availed himself of this convenience—they had taken so many houses that another, more or less, didn't matter—and Mrs. Tarrant began to feel as if they really had "struck" something.

Even to Verena, as we know, she was confused and confusing; the girl had not yet had an opportunity to ascertain the principles on which her mother's limpness was liable suddenly to become rigid. This phenomenon occurred when the vapors of social ambition mounted to her brain, when she extended an arm from which a crumpled dressing gown fluttered back to seize the passing occasion. Then she surprised her daughter by a volubility of exhortation as to the duty of making acquaintances, and by the apparent wealth of her knowledge of the mysteries of good society. She had, in particular, a way of explaining confidentially—and in her desire to be graphic she often made up the oddest faces—the interpretation that you must sometimes give to the manners of the best people, and the delicate dignity with which you should meet them, which made Verena wonder what secret sources of information she possessed. Verena took life, as yet, very simply; she was not conscious of so many differences of social complexion. She knew that some people were rich and others poor, and that her father's house had never been visited by such abundance as might make one ask one's self whether it were right, in a world so full of the disinherited, to roll in luxury. But except when her mother made her slightly dizzy by a resentment of some slight that she herself had never perceived, or a flutter over some opportunity that appeared already to have passed (while Mrs. Tarrant was looking for something to "put on"), Verena had no vivid sense that she was not as good as any one else, for no authority appealing really to her imagination had fixed the place of mesmeric healers in the scale of fashion. It was impossible to know in advance how Mrs. Tarrant would take things. Sometimes she was abjectly indifferent; at others she thought that every one who looked at her wished to insult her. At moments she was full of suspicion of the ladies (they were mainly ladies) whom Selah mesmerized; then again she appeared to have given up everything but her slippers and the evening paper (from this publication she derived inscrutable solace), so that if Mrs. Foat in person had returned from the summer-land (to which she had some time since taken her flight), she would not have disturbed Mrs. Tarrant's almost cynical equanimity.

It was, however, in her social subtleties that she was most beyond her daughter; it was when she discovered extraordinary though latent longings on the part of people they met to make their acquaintance, that the girl became conscious of how much she herself had still to learn. All her desire was to learn, and it must be added that she regarded her mother, in perfect good faith, as a wonderful teacher. She was perplexed sometimes by her worldliness; that, somehow, was not a part of the higher life which every one in such a house as theirs must wish above all things to lead; and it was not involved in the reign of justice, which they were all trying to bring about, that such a strict account should be kept of every little snub. Her father seemed to Verena to move more consecutively on the high plane; though his indifference to old-fashioned standards, his perpetual invocation of the brighter day, had not yet led her to ask herself whether, after all, men are more disinterested than women. Was it interest that prompted her mother to respond so warmly to Miss Chancellor, to say to Verena, with an air of knowingness, that the thing to do was to go in and see her *immediately?* No italics can represent the earnestness of Mrs. Tarrant's emphasis. Why hadn't she said, as she had done in former cases, that if people wanted to see them they could come out to their home; that she was not so low down in the world as not to know there was such a ceremony as leaving cards? When Mrs. Tarrant began on the question of ceremonies she was apt to go far; but she had waived it in this case; it suited her more to hold that Miss Chancellor had been very gracious, that she was a most desirable friend, that she had been more affected than any one by Verena's beautiful outpouring; that she would open to her the best salons in Boston; that when she said "Come soon" she meant the very next day, that this was the way to take it, anyhow (one must know when to go forward gracefully); and that in short she, Mrs. Tarrant, knew what she was talking about.

Verena accepted all this, for she was young enough to enjoy any journey in a horsecar, and she was ever-curious about the world; she only wondered a little how her mother knew so much about Miss Chancellor just from looking at her once. What Verena had mainly observed in the young lady who came up to her that way the night before was that she was rather dolefully dressed, that she looked as if she had been crying (Verena recognized that look quickly, she had seen it so much), and that she was in a hurry to get away. However, if she was as remarkable as her mother said, one would very soon see it; and meanwhile there was nothing in the girl's feeling about herself, in her sense of her importance, to make it a painful effort for her to run the risk of a mistake. She had no particular feeling about herself; she only cared, as yet, for outside things. Even the development of her "gift" had not made her think herself too precious for mere experiments; she had neither a particle of diffidence nor a particle of vanity. Though it would have seemed to you eminently natural that a daughter of Selah Tarrant and his wife should be an inspirational speaker, yet, as you knew Verena better, you would have wondered immensely how she came to issue from such a pair. Her ideas of enjoyment were very simple; she enjoyed putting on her new hat, with its redundancy of feather, and twenty cents appeared to her a very large sum.

II

"I was certain you would come—I have felt it all day—something told me!" It was with these words that Olive Chancellor greeted her young visitor, coming to her quickly from the window, where she might have been waiting for her arrival. Some weeks later she explained to Verena how definite this prevision had been, how it had filled her all day with a nervous agitation so violent as to be painful. She told her that such forebodings were a peculiarity of her organization, that she didn't know what to make of them, that she had to accept them; and she mentioned, as another example, the sudden dread that had come to her the evening before in the carriage, after proposing to Mr. Ransom to go with her to Miss Birdseye's. This had been as strange as it had been instinctive, and the strangeness, of course, was what must have struck Mr. Ransom; for the idea that he might come had been hers, and yet she suddenly veered round. She couldn't help it; her heart had begun to throb with the conviction that if he crossed that threshold some harm would come of it for her. She hadn't prevented him, and now she didn't care, for now, as she intimated, she had the interest of Verena, and that made her indifferent to every danger, to every ordinary pleasure. By this time Verena had learned how peculiarly her friend was constituted, how nervous and serious she was, how personal, how exclusive, what a force of will she had, what a concentration of purpose. Olive had taken her up, in the literal sense of the phrase, like a bird of the air, had spread an extraordinary pair of wings, and carried her through the dizzying void of space. Verena liked it, for the most part; liked to shoot upward without an effort of her own and look down upon all creation, upon all history, from such a height. From this first interview she felt that she was seized, and she gave herself up, only shutting her eyes a little, as we do whenever a person in whom we have perfect confidence proposes, with our assent, to subject us to some sensation.

"I want to know you," Olive said, on this occasion; "I felt that I must last night, as soon as I heard you speak. You seem to me very wonderful. I don't know what to make of you. I think we ought to be friends; so I just asked you to come to me straight off, without preliminaries, and I believed you would come. It is so *right* that you have come, and it proves how right I was." These remarks fell from Miss Chancellor's lips one by one, as she caught her breath, with the tremor that was always in her voice, even when she was the least excited, while she made Verena sit down near her on the sofa, and looked at her all over in a manner that caused the girl to rejoice at having put on the jacket with the gilt buttons. It was this glance that was the beginning; it was with this quick survey, omitting nothing, that Olive took possession of her. "You are very remarkable; I wonder if you know how remarkable!" she went on, murmuring the words as if she were losing herself, becoming inadvertent in admiration.

Verena sat there smiling, without a blush, but with a pure, bright look which, for her, would always make protests unnecessary. "Oh, it isn't me, you know; it's something outside!" She tossed this off lightly, as if she were in the habit of saying it, and Olive wondered whether it were a sincere disclaimer or only a phrase of the lips. The question was not a criticism, for she might have been satisfied that the girl was a mass of fluent catchwords and yet scarcely have liked her the less. It was just as she was that she liked her; she was so strange, so different from the girls one usually met, seemed to belong to some queer gypsy-land or transcendental Bohemia. With her bright, vulgar clothes, her salient appearance, she might have been a ropedancer or a fortuneteller; and this had the immense merit, for Olive, that it appeared to make her belong to the "people," threw her into the social dusk of that mysterious democracy which Miss Chancellor held that the fortunate classes know so little about, and with which (in a future possibly very near) they will have to count. Moreover, the girl had moved her as she had never been moved, and the power to do that, from whatever source it came, was a force that one must admire. Her emotion was still acute, however much she might speak to her visitor as if everything that had happened seemed to her natural; and what kept it, above all, from subsiding was her sense that she found here what she had been looking for so long—a friend of her own sex with whom she might have a union of soul. It took a double consent to make a friendship, but it was not possible that this intensely sympathetic girl would refuse. Olive had the penetration to discover in a moment that she was a creature of unlimited generosity. I know not what may have been the reality of Miss Chancellor's other premonitions, but there is no doubt that in this respect she took Verena's measure on the spot. This was what she wanted; after that the rest didn't matter; Miss Tarrant might wear gilt buttons from head to foot, her soul could not be vulgar.

"Mother told me I had better come right in," said Verena, looking now about the room, very glad to find herself in so pleasant a place, and noticing a great many things that she should like to see in detail.

"Your mother saw that I meant what I said; it isn't everybody that does me the honor to perceive that. She saw that I was shaken from head to foot. I could only say three words —I couldn't have spoken more! What a power—what a power, Miss Tarrant!"

"Yes, I suppose it is a power. If it wasn't a power, it couldn't do much with me!"

"You are so simple—so much like a child," Olive Chancellor said. That was the truth, and she wanted to say it because, quickly, without forms or circumlocutions, it made them familiar. She wished to arrive at this; her impatience was such that before the girl had been five minutes in the room she jumped to her point—inquired of her, interrupting herself, interrupting everything: "Will you be my friend, my friend of friends, beyond every one, everything, forever and forever?" Her face was full of eagerness and tenderness.

Verena gave a laugh of clear amusement, without a shade of embarrassment or confusion. "Perhaps you like me too much."

"Of course I like you too much! When I like, I like too much. But of course it's another thing, your liking me," Olive Chancellor added. "We must wait—we must wait. When I care for anything, I can be patient." She put out her hand to Verena, and the movement was at once so appealing and so confident that the girl instinctively placed her own in it. So, hand in hand, for some moments, these two young women sat looking at each other. "There is so much I want to ask you," said Olive.

"Well, I can't say much except when father has worked on me," Verena answered, with an ingenuousness beside which humility would have seemed pretentious.

"I don't care anything about your father," Olive Chancellor rejoined very gravely, with a great air of security.

"He is very good," Verena said simply. "And he's wonderfully magnetic."

"It isn't your father, and it isn't your mother; I don't think of them, and it's not them I want. It's only you—just as you are."

Verena dropped her eyes over the front of her dress. "Just as she was" seemed to her indeed very well.

"Do you want me to give up——?" she demanded, smiling.

Olive Chancellor drew in her breath for an instant, like a creature in pain; then, with her quavering voice, touched with a vibration of anguish, she said: "Oh, how can I ask you to give up? *I* will give up—I will give up everything!"

Filled with the impression of her hostess's agreeable interior, and of what her mother had told her about Miss Chancellor's wealth, her position in Boston society, Verena, in her fresh, diverted scrutiny of the surrounding objects, wondered what could be the need of this scheme of renunciation. Oh no, indeed, she hoped she wouldn't give up— at least not before she, Verena, had had a chance to see. She felt, however, that for the present there would be no answer for her save in the mere pressure of Miss Chancellor's eager nature, that intensity of emotion which made her suddenly exclaim, as if in a nervous ecstasy of anticipation, "But we must wait! Why do we talk of this? We must wait! All will be right," she added more calmly, with great sweetness.

Verena wondered afterward why she had not been more afraid of her—why, indeed, she had not turned and saved herself by darting out of the room. But it was not in this young woman's nature to be either timid or cautious; she had as yet to make acquaintance with the sentiment of fear. She knew too little of the world to have learned to mistrust sudden enthusiasms, and if she had had a suspicion it would have been (in accordance with common worldly knowledge) the wrong one—the suspicion that such a whimsical liking would burn itself out. She could not have that one, for there was a light in Miss Chancellor's magnified face which seemed to say that a sentiment, with her, might consume its object, might consume Miss Chancellor, but would never consume itself. Verena, as yet, had no sense of being scorched; she was only agreeably warmed. She also had dreamed of a friendship, though it was not what she had dreamed of most, and it came over her that this was the one which fortune might have been keeping. She never held back.

"Do you live here all alone?" she asked of Olive.

"I shouldn't if you would come and live with me!"

Even this really passionate rejoinder failed to make Verena shrink; she thought it so possible that in the wealthy class people made each other such easy proposals. It was a part of the romance, the luxury, of wealth; it belonged to the world of invitations, in which she had had so little share. But it seemed almost a mockery when she thought of the little house in Cambridge, where the boards were loose in the steps of the porch.

"I must stay with my father and mother," she said. "And then I have my work, you know. That's the way I must live now."

"Your work?" Olive repeated, not quite understanding.

"My gift," said Verena, smiling.

"Oh yes, you must use it. That's what I mean; you must move the world with it; it's divine."

It was so much what she meant that she had lain awake all night thinking of it, and the substance of her thought was that if she could only rescue the girl from the danger of

83

vulgar exploitation, could only constitute herself her protectress and devotee, the two, between them, might achieve the great result. Verena's genius was a mystery, and it might remain a mystery; it was impossible to see how this charming, blooming, simple creature, all youth and grace and innocence, got her extraordinary powers of reflection. When her gift was not in exercise she appeared anything but reflective, and as she sat there now, for instance, you would never have dreamed that she had had a vivid revelation. Olive had to content herself, provisionally, with saying that her precious faculty had come to her just as her beauty and distinction (to Olive she was full of that quality) had come; it had dropped straight from heaven, without filtering through her parents, whom Miss Chancellor decidedly did not fancy. Even among reformers she discriminated; she thought all wise people wanted great changes, but the votaries of change were not necessarily wise. She remained silent a little, after her last remark, and then she repeated again, as if it were the solution of everything, as if it represented with absolute certainty some immense happiness in the future—"We must wait, we must wait!" Verena was perfectly willing to wait, though she did not exactly know what they were to wait for, and the aspiring frankness of her assent shone out of her face, and seemed to pacify their mutual gaze. Olive asked her innumerable questions; she wanted to enter into her life. It was one of those talks which people remember afterwards, in which every word has been given and taken, and in which they see the signs of a beginning that was to be justified. The more Olive learnt of her visitor's life the more she wanted to enter into it, the more it took her out of herself. Such strange lives are led in America, she always knew that; but this was queerer than anything she had dreamed of, and the queerest part was that the girl herself didn't appear to think it queer. She had been nursed in darkened rooms, and suckled in the midst of manifestations; she had begun to "attend lectures," as she said, when she was quite an infant, because her mother had no one to leave her with at home. She had sat on the knees of somnambulists, and had been passed from hand to hand by trance-speakers; she was familiar with every kind of "cure," and had grown up among lady-editors of newspapers advocating new religions, and people who disapproved of the marriage-tie. Verena talked of the marriage-tie as she would have talked of the last novel—as if she had heard it as frequently discussed; and at certain times, listening to the answers she made to her questions, Olive Chancellor closed her eyes in the manner of a person waiting till giddiness passed. Her young friend's revelations actually gave her a vertigo; they made her perceive everything from which she should have rescued her. Verena was perfectly uncontaminated, and she would never be touched by evil; but though Olive had no views about the marriage-tie except that she should hate it for herself—that particular reform she did not propose to consider—she didn't like the "atmosphere" of circles in which such institutions were called into question. She had no wish now to enter into an examination of that particular one; nevertheless, to make sure, she would just ask Verena whether she disapproved of it.

"Well, I must say," said Miss Tarrant, "I prefer free unions."

Olive held her breath an instant; such an idea was so disagreeable to her. Then, for all answer, she murmured, irresolutely, "I wish you would let me help you!" Yet it seemed, at the same time, that Verena needed little help, for it was more and more clear that her eloquence, when she stood up that way before a roomful of people, was literally inspiration. She answered all her friend's questions with a good-nature which evidently took no pains to make things plausible, an effort to oblige, not to please; but, after all, she could give very little account of herself. This was very visible when Olive asked her where she had got her "intense realization" of the suffering of women; for her address at Miss Birdseye's showed that she, too (like Olive herself), had had that vision in the watches of the night. Verena thought a moment, as if to understand what her companion referred to, and then she inquired, always smiling, where Joan of Arc had got her idea of the suffering of France. This was so prettily said that Olive could scarcely keep from kissing her; she looked at the moment as if, like Joan, she might have had visits from the saints. Olive, of course, remembered afterwards that it had not literally answered the question; and she also reflected on something that made an answer seem more difficult—the fact that the girl had grown up among lady-doctors, lady-mediums, lady-editors, lady-preachers, lady-healers, women who, having rescued themselves from a passive existence, could illustrate only partially the misery of the sex at large. It was true that they might have illustrated it by their talk, by all they had "been through" and all they could tell a younger sister; but Olive was sure that Verena's prophetic impulse had not been stirred by the chatter of women (Miss Chancellor knew that sound as well as any one); it had proceeded rather out of their silence. She said to her visitor that whether or not the angels came down to her in glittering armor, she struck her as the only person she had yet encountered who had exactly the same tenderness, the same pity, for women that she herself had. Miss Birdseye had something of it, but Miss Birdseye wanted passion, wanted keenness, was capable of the weakest concessions. Mrs. Farrinder was not weak, of course, and she brought a great intellect to the matter; but she was not personal enough—she was too abstract. Verena was not abstract; she seemed to have lived in imagination through all the ages. Verena said she *did* think she had a certain amount of imagination; she supposed she couldn't be so effective on the platform if she hadn't a rich fancy. Then Olive said to her, taking her hand again, that she wanted her to assure her of this—that it was the only thing in all the world she cared for, the redemption of women, the thing she hoped under Providence to give her life to. Verena flushed a little at this appeal, and the deeper glow of her eyes was the first sign of exaltation she had offered. "Oh yes—I want to give my life!" she exclaimed, with a vibrating voice; and then she added gravely, "I want to do something great!"

"You will, you will, we both will!" Olive Chancellor cried, in rapture. But after a little she went on: "I wonder if you know what it means, young and lovely as you are—giving your life!"

Verena looked down for a moment in meditation.

"Well," she replied, "I guess I have thought more than I appear."

"Do you understand German? Do you know 'Faust'?" said Olive. " 'Entsagen sollst du, sollst entsagen!' "

"I don't know German; I should like so to study it; I want to know everything."

"We will work at it together—we will study everything," Olive almost panted; and while she spoke the peaceful picture hung before her of still winter evenings under the lamp, with falling snow outside, and tea on a little table, and successful renderings, with a chosen companion, of Goethe, almost the only foreign author she cared about; for she hated the writing of the French, in spite of the importance they have given to women. Such a vision as this was the highest indulgence she could offer herself; she had it only at considerable intervals. It seemed as if Verena caught a glimpse of it too, for her face kindled still more, and she said she should like that ever so much. At the same time she asked the meaning of the German words.

" 'Thou shalt renounce, refrain, abstain!' That's the way Bayard Taylor has translated them," Olive answered.

"Oh, well, I guess I can abstain!" Verena exclaimed, with a laugh. And she got up rather quickly, as if by taking leave she might give a proof of what she meant. Olive put out her hands to hold her, and at this moment one of the *portières* of the room was pushed aside, while a gentleman was ushered in by Miss Chancellor's little parlormaid.

12

Verena recognized him; she had seen him the night before at Miss Birdseye's, and she said to her hostess, "Now I must go—you have got another caller!" It was Verena's belief that in the fashionable world (like Mrs. Farrinder, she thought Miss Chancellor belonged to it—thought that, in standing there, she herself was in it)—in the highest social walks it was the custom of a prior guest to depart when another friend arrived. She had been told at people's doors that she could not be received because the lady of the house had a visitor, and she had retired on these occasions with a feeling of awe much more than a sense of injury. They had not been the portals of fashion, but in this respect, she deemed, they had emulated such bulwarks. Olive Chancellor offered Basil Ransom a greeting which she believed to be consummately ladylike, and which the young man, narrating the scene several months later to Mrs. Luna, whose susceptibilities he did not feel himself obliged to consider (she considered his so little), described by saying that she glared at him. Olive had thought it very possible he would come that day if he was to leave Boston; though she was perfectly mindful that she had given him no encouragement at the moment they separated. If he should not come she should be annoyed, and if he should come she should be furious; she was also sufficiently mindful of that. But she had a foreboding that, of the two grievances, fortune would confer upon her only the less; the only one she had as yet was that he had responded to her letter—a complaint rather wanting in richness. If he came, at any rate, he would be likely to come shortly before dinner, at the same hour as yesterday. He had now anticipated this period considerably, and it seemed to Miss Chancellor that he had taken a base advantage of her, stolen a march upon her privacy. She was startled, disconcerted, but as I have said, she was rigorously ladylike. She was determined not again to be fantastic, as she had been about his coming to Miss Birdseye's. The strange dread associating itself with that was something which, she devoutly trusted, she had felt once for all. She didn't know what he could do to her; he hadn't prevented, on the spot though he was, one of the happiest things that had befallen her for so long—this quick, confident visit of Verena Tarrant. It was only just at the last that he had come in, and Verena must go now; Olive's detaining hand immediately relaxed itself.

It is to be feared there was no disguise of Ransom's satisfaction at finding himself once more face to face with the charming creature with whom he had exchanged that final speechless smile the evening before. He was more glad to see her than if she had been an old friend, for it seemed to him that she had suddenly become a new one. "The delightful girl," he said to himself; "she smiles at me as if she liked me!" He could not know that this was fatuous, that she smiled so at every one; the first time she saw people she treated them as if she recognized them. Moreover, she did not seat herself again in his honor; she let it be seen that she was still going. The three stood there together in the middle of the long, characteristic room, and, for the first time in her life, Olive Chancellor chose not to introduce two persons who met under her roof. She hated Europe, but she could be European if it were necessary. Neither of her companions had an idea that in leaving them simply planted face to face (the terror of the American heart) she had so high a warrant; and presently Basil Ransom felt that he didn't care whether he were introduced or not, for the greatness of an evil didn't matter if the remedy were equally great.

"Miss Tarrant won't be surprised if I recognize her—if I take the liberty to speak to her. She is a public character; she must pay the penalty of her distinction." These words he boldly addressed to the girl, with his most gallant Southern manner, saying to himself meanwhile that she was prettier still by daylight.

"Oh, a great many gentlemen have spoken to me," Verena said. "There were quite a number at Topeka—" And her phrase lost itself in her look at Olive, as if she were wondering what was the matter with her.

"Now, I am afraid you are going the very moment I appear," Ransom went on. "Do you know that's very cruel to me? I know what your ideas are—you expressed them last night in such beautiful language; of course you convinced me. I am ashamed of being a man; but I am, and I can't help it, and I'll do penance any way you may prescribe. *Must* she go, Miss Olive?" he asked of his cousin. "Do you flee before the individual male?" And he turned again to Verena.

This young lady gave a laugh that resembled speech in liquid fusion. "Oh no; I like the individual!"

As an incarnation of a "movement," Ransom thought her more and more singular, and he wondered how she came to be closeted so soon with his kinswoman, to whom, only a few hours before, she had been a complete stranger. These, however, were doubtless the normal proceedings of women. He begged her to sit down again; he was sure Miss Chancellor would be sorry to part with her. Verena, looking at her friend, not for permission, but for sympathy, dropped again into a chair, and Ransom waited to see Miss Chancellor do the same. She gratified him after a moment, because she could not refuse without appearing to put a hurt upon Verena; but it went hard with her, and she was altogether discomposed. She had never seen any one so free in her own drawing room as this loud Southerner, to whom she

90

had so rashly offered a footing; he extended invitations to her guests under her nose. That Verena should do as he asked her was a signal sign of the absence of that "home-culture" (it was so that Miss Chancellor expressed the missing quality) which she never supposed the girl possessed: fortunately, as it would be supplied to her in abundance in Charles Street. (Olive of course held that home-culture was perfectly compatible with the widest emancipation.) It was with a perfectly good conscience that Verena complied with Basil Ransom's request; but it took her quick sensibility only a moment to discover that her friend was not pleased. She scarcely knew what had ruffled her, but at the same instant there passed before her the vision of the anxieties (of this sudden, unexplained sort, for instance, and much worse) which intimate relations with Miss Chancellor might entail.

"Now, I want you to tell me this," Basil Ransom said, leaning forward towards Verena, with his hands on his knees, and completely oblivious to his hostess. "Do you really believe all that pretty moonshine you talked last night? I could have listened to you for another hour; but I never heard such monstrous sentiments. I must protest—I must, as a calumniated, misrepresented man. Confess you meant it as a kind of *reductio ad absurdum*—a satire on Mrs. Farrinder?" He spoke in a tone of the freest pleasantry, with his familiar, friendly Southern cadence.

Verena looked at him with eyes that grew large. "Why, you don't mean to say you don't believe in our cause?"

"Oh, it won't do—it won't do!" Ransom went on, laughing. "You are on the wrong tack altogether. Do you really take the ground that your sex has been without influence? Influence? Why, you have led us all by the nose to where we are now! Wherever we are, it's all you. You are at the bottom of everything."

"Oh yes, and we want to be at the top," said Verena.

"Ah, the bottom is a better place, depend on it, when from there you move the whole mass! Besides, you are on the top as well; you are everywhere, you are everything. I am of the opinion of that historical character—wasn't he some king?—who thought there was a lady behind everything. Whatever it was, he held, you have only to look for her; she is the explanation. Well, I always look for her, and I always find her; of course, I am always delighted to do so; but it proves she is the universal cause. Now, you don't mean to deny that power, the power of setting men in motion. You are at the bottom of all the wars."

"Well, I am like Mrs. Farrinder; I like opposition," Verena exclaimed, with a happy smile.

"That proves, as I say, how in spite of your expressions of horror you delight in the shock of battle. What do you say to Helen of Troy and the fearful carnage she excited? It is well known that the Empress of France was at the bottom of the last war in that country. And as for our four fearful years of slaughter, of course you won't deny that there the ladies were the great motive power. The Abolitionists brought it on, and were not the Abolitionists principally females? Who was that celebrity that was mentioned last night?—Eliza P. Moseley. I regard Eliza as the cause of the biggest war of which history preserves the record."

Basil Ransom enjoyed his humor the more because Verena appeared to enjoy it; and the look with which she replied to him, at the end of this little tirade, "Why, sir, you ought to take the platform too; we might go round together as poison and antidote!"—this made him feel that he had convinced her, for the moment, quite as much as it was important he should. In Verena's face, however, it lasted but an instant—an instant after she had glanced at Olive Chancellor, who, with her eyes fixed intently on the ground (a look she was to learn to know so well), had a strange expression. The girl slowly got up; she felt that she must go. She guessed Miss Chancellor didn't like this handsome joker (it was so that Basil Ransom struck her); and it was impressed upon her ("in time," as she thought) that her new friend would be more serious even than she about the woman-question, serious as she had hitherto believed herself to be.

"I should like so much to have the pleasure of seeing you again," Ransom continued. "I think I should be able to interpret history for you by a new light."

"Well, I should be very happy to see you in my home." These words had barely fallen from Verena's lips (her mother told her they were, in general, the proper thing to say when people expressed such a desire as that; she must not let it be assumed that she would come first to them)— she had hardly uttered this hospitable speech when she felt the hand of her hostess upon her arm and became aware that a passionate appeal sat in Olive's eyes.

"You will just catch the Charles Street car," that young woman murmured, with muffled sweetness.

Verena did not understand further than to see that she ought already to have departed; and the simplest response was to kiss Miss Chancellor, an act which she briefly performed. Basil Ransom understood still less, and it was a melancholy commentary on his contention that men are not inferior, that this meeting could not come, however rapidly, to a close without his plunging into a blunder which necessarily aggravated those he had already made. He had been invited by the little prophetess, and yet he had not been invited; but he did not take that up, because he must absolutely leave Boston on the morrow, and, besides, Miss Chancellor appeared to have something to say to it. But he put out his hand to Verena and said, "Good-by, Miss Tarrant; are we not to have the pleasure of hearing you in New York? I am afraid we are sadly sunk."

"Certainly, I should like to raise my voice in the biggest city," the girl replied.

"Well, try to come on. I won't refute you. It would be a very stupid world, after all, if we always knew what women were going to say."

Verena was conscious of the approach of the Charles Street car, as well as of the fact that Miss Chancellor was in pain; but she lingered long enough to remark that she could see he had the old-fashioned idea—he regarded woman as the toy of man.

"Don't say the toy—say the joy!" Ransom exclaimed. "There is one statement I will venture to advance; I am quite as fond of you as you are of each other!"

"Much he knows about that!" said Verena, with a side-long smile at Olive Chancellor.

For Olive, it made her more beautiful than ever; still, there was no trace of this mere personal elation in the splendid sententiousness with which, turning to Mr. Ransom, she remarked: "What women may be, or may not be, to each other, I won't attempt just now to say; but what *the truth* may be to a human soul, I think perhaps even a woman may faintly suspect!"

"The truth? My dear cousin, your truth is a most vain thing!"

"Gracious me!" cried Verena Tarrant; and the gay vibration of her voice as she uttered this simple ejaculation was the last that Ransom heard of her. Miss Chancellor swept her out of the room, leaving the young man to extract a relish from the ineffable irony with which she uttered the words "even a woman." It was to be supposed, on general grounds, that she would reappear, but there was nothing in the glance she gave him, as she turned her back, that was an earnest of this. He stood there a moment, wondering; then his wonder spent itself on the page of a book which, according to his habit at such times, he had mechanically taken up, and in which he speedily became interested. He read it for five minutes in an uncomfortable-looking attitude, and quite forgot that he had been forsaken. He was recalled to this fact by the entrance of Mrs. Luna, arrayed as if for the street, and putting on her gloves again—she seemed always to be putting on her gloves. She wanted to know what in the world he was doing there alone—whether her sister had not been notified.

"Oh yes," said Ransom, "she has just been with me, but she has gone downstairs with Miss Tarrant."

"And who in the world is Miss Tarrant?"

Ransom was surprised that Mrs. Luna should not know of the intimacy of the two young ladies, in spite of the brevity of their acquaintance, being already so great. But, apparently, Miss Olive had not mentioned her new friend. "Well, she is an inspirational speaker—the most charming creature in the world!"

Mrs. Luna paused in her manipulations, gave an amazed, amused stare, then caused the room to ring with her laughter. "You don't mean to say you are converted—already?"

"Converted to Miss Tarrant, decidedly."

"You are not to belong to any Miss Tarrant; you are to belong to me," Mrs. Luna said, having thought over her Southern kinsman during the twenty-four hours, and made up her mind that he would be a good man for a lone woman to know. Then she added: "Did you come here to meet her —the inspirational speaker?"

"No; I came to bid your sister good-by."

"Are you really going? I haven't made you promise half the things I want yet. But we will settle that in New York. How do you get on with Olive Chancellor?" Mrs. Luna continued, making her points, as she always did, with eagerness, though her roundness and her dimples had hitherto prevented her from being accused of that vice. It was her practice to speak of her sister by her whole name, and you would have supposed, from her usual manner of alluding to her, that Olive was much the older, instead of having been born ten years later than Adeline. She had as many ways as possible of marking the gulf that divided them; but she bridged it over lightly now by saying to Basil Ransom: "Isn't she a dear old thing?"

This bridge, he saw, would not bear his weight, and her question seemed to him to have more audacity than sense. Why should she be so insincere? She might know that a man couldn't recognize Miss Chancellor in such a description as that. She was not old—she was sharply young; and it was inconceivable to him, though he had just seen the little prophetess kiss her, that she should ever become any one's "dear." Least of all was she a "thing"; she was intensely, fearfully, a person. He hesitated a moment, and then he replied: "She's a very remarkable woman."

"Take care—don't be reckless!" cried Mrs. Luna. "Do you think she is very dreadful?"

"Don't say anything against my cousin," Basil answered; and at that moment Miss Chancellor re-entered the room. She murmured some request that he would excuse her absence, but her sister interrupted her with an inquiry about Miss Tarrant.

"Mr. Ransom thinks her wonderfully charming. Why didn't you show her to me? Do you want to keep her all to yourself?"

Olive rested her eyes for some moments upon Mrs. Luna, without speaking. Then she said: "Your veil is not put on straight, Adeline."

"I look like a monster—that, evidently, is what you mean!" Adeline exclaimed, going to the mirror to rearrange the peccant tissue.

Miss Chancellor did not again ask Ransom to be seated; she appeared to take it for granted that he would leave her now. But instead of this he returned to the subject of Verena; he asked her whether she supposed the girl would come out in public—would go about like Mrs. Farrinder?

"Come out in public!" Olive repeated; "in public? Why, you don't imagine that pure voice is to be hushed?"

"Oh, hushed, no! it's too sweet for that. But not raised to a scream; not forced and cracked and ruined. She oughtn't to become like the others. She ought to remain apart."

"Apart—*apart?*" said Miss Chancellor; "when we shall all be looking to her, gathering about her, praying for her!"

There was an exceeding scorn in her voice. "If *I* can help her, she shall be an immense power for good."

"An immense power for quackery, my dear Miss Olive!" This broke from Basil Ransom's lips in spite of a vow he had just taken not to say anything that should "aggravate" his hostess, who was in a state of tension it was not difficult to detect. But he had lowered his tone to friendly pleading, and the offensive word was mitigated by his smile.

She moved away from him, backwards, as if he had given her a push. "Ah, well, now you are reckless," Mrs. Luna remarked, drawing out her ribbons before the mirror.

"I don't think you would interfere if you knew how little you understand us," Miss Chancellor said to Ransom.

"Whom do you mean by 'us'—your whole delightful sex? I don't understand *you*, Miss Olive."

"Come away with me, and I'll explain her as we go," Mrs. Luna went on, having finished her toilet.

Ransom offered his hand in farewell to his hostess; but Olive found it impossible to do anything but ignore the gesture. She could not have let him touch her. "Well, then, if you must exhibit her to the multitude, bring her on to New York," he said, with the same attempt at a light treatment.

"You'll have *me* in New York—you don't want any one else!" Mrs. Luna ejaculated, coquettishly. "I have made up my mind to winter there now."

Olive Chancellor looked from one to the other of her two relatives, one near and the other distant, but each so little in sympathy with her, and it came over her that there might be a kind of protection for her in binding them together, entangling them with each other. She had never had an idea of that kind in her life before, and that this sudden subtlety should have gleamed upon her as a momentary talisman gives the measure of her present nervousness.

"If I could take her to New York, I would take her farther," she remarked, hoping she was enigmatical.

91

"You talk about 'taking her,' as if you were a lecture-agent. Are you going into that business?" Mrs. Luna asked.

Ransom could not help noticing that Miss Chancellor would not shake hands with him, and he felt, on the whole, rather injured. He paused a moment before leaving the room—standing there with his hand on the knob of the door. "Look here, Miss Oilve, what did you write to me to come and see you for?" He made this inquiry with a countenance not destitute of gaiety, but his eyes showed something of that yellow light—just momentarily lurid—of which mention has been made. Mrs. Luna was on her way downstairs, and her companions remained face to face.

"Ask my sister—I think she will tell you," said Olive, turning away from him and going to the window. She remained there, looking out; she heard the door of the house close, and saw the two cross the street together. As they passed out of sight her fingers played, softly, a little air upon the pane; it seemed to her that she had had an inspiration.

Basil Ransom, meanwhile, put the question to Mrs. Luna. "If she was not going to like me, why in the world did she write to me?"

"Because she wanted you to know me—she thought *I* would like you!" And apparently she had not been wrong; for Mrs. Luna, when they reached Beacon Street, would not hear of his leaving her to go her way alone, would not in the least admit his plea that he had only an hour or two more in Boston (he was to travel, economically, by the boat) and must devote the time to his business. She appealed to his Southern chivalry, and not in vain; practically, at least, he admitted the rights of women.

13

Mrs. Tarrant was delighted, as may be imagined, with her daughter's account of Miss Chancellor's interior, and the reception the girl had found there; and Verena, for the next month, took her way very often to Charles Street. "Just you be as nice to her as you know how," Mrs. Tarrant had said to her; and she reflected with some complacency that her daughter did know—she knew how to do everything of that sort. It was not that Verena had been taught; that branch of the education of young ladies which is known as "manners and deportment" had not figured, as a definite head, in Miss Tarrant's curriculum. She had been told, indeed, that she must not lie nor steal; but she had been told very little else about behavior; her only great advantage, in short, had been the parental example. But her mother liked to think that she was quick and graceful, and she questioned her exhaustively as to the progress of this interesting episode; she didn't see why, as she said, it shouldn't be a permanent "stand-by" for Verena. In Mrs. Tarrant's meditations upon the girl's future she had never thought of a fine marriage as a reward of effort; she would have deemed herself very immoral if she had endeavored to capture for her child a rich husband. She had not, in fact, a very vivid sense of the existence of such agents of fate; all the rich men she had seen already had wives, and the unmarried men, who were generally very young, were distinguished from each other not so much by the figure of their income,

99

which came little into question, as by the degree of their interest in regenerating ideas. She supposed Verena would marry someone, some day, and she hoped the personage would be connected with public life—which meant, for Mrs. Tarrant, that his name would be visible, in the lamplight, on a colored poster, in the doorway of Tremont Temple. But she was not eager about this vision, for the implications of matrimony were for the most part wanting in brightness—consisted of a tired woman holding a baby over a furnace-register that emitted lukewarm air. A real lovely friendship with a young woman who had, as Mrs. Tarrant expressed it, "prop'ty," would occupy agreeably such an interval as might occur before Verena should meet her sterner fate; it would be a great thing for her to have a place to run into when she wanted a change, and there was no knowing but what it might end in her having two homes. For the idea of the home, like most American women of her quality, Mrs. Tarrant had an extreme reverence; and it was her candid faith that in all the vicissitudes of the past twenty years she had preserved the spirit of this institution. If it should exist in duplicate for Verena, the girl would be favored indeed.

All this was as nothing, however, compared with the fact that Miss Chancellor seemed to think her young friend's gift *was* inspirational, or at any rate, as Selah had so often said, quite unique. She couldn't make out very exactly, by Verena, what she thought; but if the way Miss Chancellor had taken hold of her didn't show that she believed she could rouse the people, Mrs. Tarrant didn't know what it showed. It was a satisfaction to her that Verena evidently responded freely; she didn't think anything of what she spent in car-tickets, and indeed she had told her that Miss Chancellor wanted to stuff her pockets with them. At first she went in because her mother liked to have her; but now, evidently, she went because she was so much drawn. She expressed the highest admiration of her new friend; she said it took her a little while to see into her, but now that she did, well, she was perfectly splendid. When Verena wanted to admire she went ahead of everyone, and it was delightful to see how she was stimulated by the young lady in Charles Street. They thought everything of each other—that was very plain; you could scarcely tell which thought most. Each thought the other so noble, and Mrs. Tarrant had a faith that between them they *would* rouse the people. What Verena wanted was someone who would know how to handle her (her father hadn't handled anything except the healing, up to this time, with real success), and perhaps Miss Chancellor would take hold better than some that made more of a profession.

"It's beautiful, the way she draws you out," Verena had said to her mother; "there's something so searching that the first time I visited her it quite realized my idea of the Day of Judgment. But she seems to show all that's in herself at the same time, and then you see how lovely it is. She's just as pure as she can live; you see if she is not, when you know her. She's so noble herself that she makes you feel as if you wouldn't want to be less so. She doesn't care for anything but the elevation of our sex; if she can work a little toward that, it's all she asks. I can tell you, she kindles me; she does, mother, really. She doesn't care a speck what she wears—only to have an elegant parlor. Well, she *has* got that; it's a regular dreamlike place to sit. She's going to have a tree in, next week; she says she wants to see me sitting under a tree. I believe it's some oriental idea; it has lately been introduced in Paris. She doesn't like French ideas as a general thing; but she says this has more nature than most. She has got so many of her own that I shouldn't think she would require to borrow any. I'd sit in a forest to hear her bring some of them out," Verena went on, with characteristic raciness. "She just quivers when she describes what our sex has been through. It's so interesting to me to hear what I have always felt. If she wasn't afraid of facing the public, she would go far ahead of me. But she doesn't want to speak herself; she only wants to call me out. Mother, if she doesn't attract attention to me there isn't any attention

101

to be attracted. She says I have got the gift of expression—it doesn't matter where it comes from. She says it's a great advantage to a movement to be personified in a bright young figure. Well, of course I'm young, and I feel bright enough when once I get started. She says my serenity while exposed to the gaze of hundreds is in itself a qualification; in fact, she seems to think my serenity is quite God-given. She hasn't got much of it herself; she's the most emotional woman I have met, up to now. She wants to know how I can speak the way I do unless I feel; and of course I tell her I do feel, so far as I realize. She seems to be realizing all the time; I never saw any one that took so little rest. She says I ought to do something great, and she makes me feel as if I should. She says I ought to have a wide influence, if I can obtain the ear of the public; and I say to her that if I do it will be all her influence."

Selah Tarrant looked at all this from a higher standpoint than his wife; at least such an altitude on his part was to be inferred from his increased solemnity. He committed himself to no precipitate elation at the idea of his daughter's being taken up by a patroness of movements who happened to have money; he looked at his child only from the point of view of the service she might render to humanity. To keep her ideal pointing in the right direction, to guide and animate her moral life—this was a duty more imperative for a parent so closely identified with revelations and panaceas than seeing that she formed profitable worldly connections. He was "off," moreover, so much of the time that he could keep little account of her comings and goings, and he had an air of being but vaguely aware of whom Miss Chancellor, the object now of his wife's perpetual reference, might be. Verena's initial appearance in Boston, as he called her performance at Miss Birdseye's, had been a great success; and this reflection added, as I say, to his habitually sacerdotal expression. He looked like the priest of a religion that was passing through the stage of miracles; he carried his responsibility in the general elongation of his person, of his gestures (his hands were now always in the air, as if he were being photographed in postures), of his words and sentences, as well as in his smile, as noiseless as a patent hinge, and in the folds of his eternal waterproof. He was incapable of giving an offhand answer or opinion on the simplest occasion, and his tone of high deliberation increased in proportion as the subject was trivial or domestic. If his wife asked him at dinner if the potatoes were good, he replied that they were strikingly fine (he used to speak of the newspaper as "fine"—he applied this term to objects the most dissimilar), and embarked on a parallel worthy of Plutarch, in which he compared them with other specimens of the same vegetable. He produced, or would have liked to produce, the impression of looking above and beyond everything, of not caring for the immediate, of reckoning only with the long run. In reality he had one all-absorbing solicitude—the desire to get paragraphs put into the newspapers, paragraphs of which he had hitherto been the subject, but of which he was now to divide the glory with his daughter. The newspapers were his world, the richest expression, in his eyes, of human life; and, for him, if a diviner day was to come upon earth, it would be brought about by copious advertisement in the daily prints. He looked with longing for the moment when Verena should be advertised among the "personals," and to his mind the supremely happy people were those (and there were a good many of them) of whom there was some journalistic mention every day in the year. Nothing less than this would really have satisfied Selah Tarrant; his ideal of bliss was to be as regularly and indispensably a component part of the newspaper as the title and date, or the list of fires, or the column of Western jokes. The vision of that publicity haunted his dreams, and he would gladly have sacrificed to it the innermost sanctities of home. Human existence to him, indeed, was a huge publicity, in which the only fault was that it was sometimes not sufficiently effective. There had been a Spiritualist paper of old which he used to pervade; but he

103

could not persuade himself that through this medium his personality had attracted general attention; and, moreover, the sheet, as he said, was played out anyway. Success was not success so long as his daughter's *physique,* the rumor of her engagement, were not included in the "Jottings," with the certainty of being extensively copied.

The account of her exploits in the West had not made their way to the seaboard with the promptitude that he had looked for; the reason of this being, he supposed, that the few addresses she had made had not been lectures, announced in advance, to which tickets had been sold, but incidents, of abrupt occurrence, of certain multitudinous meetings, where there had been other performers better known to fame. They had brought in no money; they had been delivered only for the good of the cause. If it could only be known that she spoke for nothing, that might deepen the reverberation; the only trouble was that her speaking for nothing was not the way to remind him that he had a remunerative daughter. It was not the way to stand out so very much either, Selah Tarrant felt; for there were plenty of others that knew how to make as little money as she would. To speak—that was the one thing that most people were willing to do for nothing; it was not a line in which it was easy to appear conspicuously disinterested. Disinterestedness, too, was incompatible with receipts; and receipts were what Selah Tarrant was, in his own parlance, after. He wished to bring about the day when they would flow in freely; the reader perhaps sees the gesture with which, in his colloquies with himself, he accompanied this mental image.

It seemed to him at present that the fruitful time was not far off; it had been brought appreciably nearer by that fortunate evening at Miss Birdseye's. If Mrs. Farrinder could be induced to write an "open letter" about Verena, that would do more than anything else. Selah was not remarkable for delicacy of perception, but he knew the world he lived in well enough to be aware that Mrs. Farrinder was liable to rear up, as they used to say down in Pennsylvania, where he lived before he began to peddle lead pencils. She wouldn't always take things as you might expect, and if it didn't meet her views to pay a public tribute to Verena, there wasn't any way known to Tarrant's ingenious mind of getting round her. If it was a question of a favor from Mrs. Farrinder, you just had to wait for it, as you would for a rise in the thermometer. He had told Miss Birdseye what he would like, and she seemed to think, from the way their celebrated friend had been affected, that the idea might take her some day of just letting the public know all she had felt. She was off somewhere now (since that evening), but Miss Birdseye had an idea that when she was back in Roxbury she would send for Verena and give her a few points. Meanwhile, at any rate, Selah was sure he had a card; he felt there was money in the air. It might already be said there were receipts from Charles Street; that rich, peculiar young woman seemed to want to lavish herself. He pretended, as I have intimated, not to notice this; but he never saw so much as when he had his eyes fixed on the cornice. He had no doubt that if he should make up his mind to take a hall some night, she would tell him where the bill might be sent. That was what he was thinking of now, whether he had better take a hall right away, so that Verena might leap at a bound into renown, or wait till she had made a few more appearances in private, so that curiosity might be worked up.

These meditations accompanied him in his multifarious wanderings through the streets and the suburbs of the New England capital. As I have also mentioned, he was absent for hours—long periods during which Mrs. Tarrant, sustaining nature with a hard-boiled egg and a doughnut, wondered how in the world he stayed his stomach. He never wanted anything but a piece of pie when he came in; the only thing about which he was particular was that it should be served up hot. She had a private conviction that he partook, at the houses of his lady patients, of little lunches;

she applied this term to any episodical repast, at any hour of the twenty-four. It is but fair to add that once, when she betrayed her suspicion, Selah remarked that the only refreshment *he* ever wanted was the sense that he was doing some good. This effort with him had many forms; it involved, among other things, a perpetual perambulation of the streets, a haunting of horsecars, railway-stations, shops that were "selling off." But the places that knew him best were the offices of the newspapers and the vestibules of the hotels—the big marble-paved chambers of informal reunion which offer to the streets, through high glass plates, the sight of the American citizen suspended by his heels. Here, amid the piled-up luggage, the convenient spittoons, the elbowing loungers, the disconsolate "guests," the truculent Irish porters, the rows of shaggy-backed men in strange hats, writing letters at a table inlaid with advertisements, Selah Tarrant made innumerable contemplative stations. He could not have told you, at any particular moment, what he was doing; he only had a general sense that such places were national nerve-centers, and that the more one looked in, the more one was "on the spot." The *penetralia* of the daily press were, however, still more fascinating, and the fact that they were less accessible, that here he found barriers in his path, only added to the zest of forcing an entrance. He abounded in pretexts; he even sometimes brought contributions; he was persistent and penetrating, he was known as the irrepressible Tarrant. He hung about, sat too long, took up the time of busy people, edged into the printing-rooms when he had been eliminated from the office, talked with the compositors till they set up his remarks by mistake, and to the newsboys when the compositors had turned their backs. He was always trying to find out what was "going in"; he would have liked to go in himself, bodily, and, failing in this, he hoped to get advertisements inserted gratis. The wish of his soul was that he might be interviewed; that made him hover at the editorial elbow. Once he thought he had been, and the headings, five or six deep, danced for days before his eyes; but the report never appeared. He expected his revenge for this the day after Verena should have burst forth; he saw the attitude in which he should receive the emissaries who would come after his daughter.

14

"We ought to have someone to meet her," Mrs. Tarrant said; "I presume she wouldn't care to come out just to see us." "She," between the mother and the daughter, at this period, could refer only to Olive Chancellor, who was discussed in the little house at Cambridge at all hours and from every possible point of view. It was never Verena now who began, for she had grown rather weary of the topic; she had her own ways of thinking of it, which were not her mother's, and if she lent herself to this lady's extensive considerations it was because that was the best way of keeping her thoughts to herself.

Mrs. Tarrant had an idea that she (Mrs. Tarrant) liked to study people, and that she was now engaged in an analysis of Miss Chancellor. It carried her far, and she came out at unexpected times with her results. It was still her purpose to interpret the world to the ingenuous mind of her daughter, and she translated Miss Chancellor with a confidence which made little account of the fact that she had seen her but once, while Verena had this advantage nearly every day. Verena felt that by this time she knew Olive very well, and her mother's most complicated versions of motive and temperament (Mrs. Tarrant, with the most imperfect idea of the meaning of the term, was always talking about people's temperament), rendered small justice to the phenomena it was now her privilege to observe in Charles Street. Olive was much more remarkable than Mrs. Tarrant suspected, remarkable as Mrs. Tarrant believed her to be. She had opened Verena's eyes to extraordinary pictures, made the girl believe that she had a heavenly mission, given her, as we have seen, quite a new measure of the interest of life. These were larger consequences than the possibility of meeting the leaders of society at Olive's house. She had met no one, as yet, but Mrs. Luna; her new friend seemed to wish to keep her quite for herself. This was the only reproach that Mrs. Tarrant directed to the new friend as yet; she was disappointed that Verena had not obtained more insight into the world of fashion. It was one of the prime articles of her faith that the world of fashion was wicked and hollow, and, moreover, Verena told her that Miss Chancellor loathed and despised it. She could not have informed you wherein it would profit her daughter (for the way those ladies shrank from any new gospel was notorious); nevertheless she was vexed that Verena shouldn't come back to her with a little more of the fragrance of Beacon Street. The girl herself would have been the most interested person in the world if she had not been the most resigned; she took all that was given her and was grateful, and missed nothing that was withheld; she was the most extraordinary mixture of eagerness and docility. Mrs. Tarrant theorized about temperaments and she loved her daughter; but she was only vaguely aware of the fact that she had at her side the sweetest flower of character (as one might say) that had ever bloomed on earth. She was proud of Verena's brightness, and of her special talent; but the commonness of her own surface was a non-conductor of the girl's quality. Therefore she thought that it would add to her success in life to know a few high-flyers, if only to put them to shame; as if anything could add to Verena's success, as if it were not supreme success simply to have been made as she was made.

Mrs. Tarrant had gone into town to call upon Miss Chancellor; she carried out this resolve, on which she had bestowed infinite consideration, independently of Verena. She had decided that she had a pretext; her dignity required one, for she felt that at present the antique pride of the Greenstreets was terribly at the mercy of her curiosity. She wished to see Miss Chancellor again, and to see her among her charming appurtenances, which Verena had described to her with great minuteness. The pretext that she would have valued most was wanting—that of Olive's having come out to Cambridge to pay the visit that had been solicited from the first; so she had to take the next best—she had to say to herself that it was her duty to see what she should think of a place where her daughter spent so much time. To Miss Chancellor she would appear to have come to thank her for her hospitality; she knew, in advance, just the air she should take (or she fancied she knew it—Mrs. Tarrant's airs were not always what she supposed), just the *nuance* (she had also an impression she knew a little French) of her tone. Olive, after the lapse of weeks, still showed no symptoms of presenting herself, and Mrs. Tarrant rebuked Verena with some sternness for not having made her feel that this attention was due to the mother of her friend. Verena could scarcely say to her she guessed Miss Chancellor didn't think much of that personage, true as it was that the girl had discerned this angular fact, which she attributed to Olive's extraordinary comprehensiveness of view. Verena herself did not suppose that her mother occupied a very important place in the universe; and Miss Chancellor never looked at anything smaller than that. Nor was she free to report (she was certainly now less frank at home, and, moreover, the suspicion was only just becoming distinct to her) that Olive would like to detach her from her parents altogether, and was therefore not interested in appearing to cultivate relations with them. Mrs. Tarrant, I may mention, had a further motive: she was consumed with the desire to behold Mrs. Luna. This circumstance may operate as a proof that the aridity of her life was great, and if it should have that effect I shall not be able to gainsay it. She had seen all the people who went to lectures, but there were hours when she desired, for a change, to see some who didn't go; and Mrs. Luna, from Verena's description of her, summed up the characteristics of this eccentric class.

Verena had given great attention to Olive's brilliant sister; she had told her friend everything now—everything but one little secret, namely, that if she could have chosen at the beginning she would have liked to resemble Mrs. Luna. This lady fascinated her, carried off her imagination to strange lands; she should enjoy so much a long evening with her alone, when she might ask her ten thousand questions. But she never saw her alone, never saw her at all but in glimpses. Adeline flitted in and out, dressed for dinners and concerts, always saying something worldly to the young woman from Cambridge, and something to Olive that had a freedom which she herself would probably never arrive at (a failure of foresight on Verena's part). But Miss Chancellor never detained her, never gave Verena a chance to see her, never appeared to imagine that she could have the least interest in such a person; only took up the subject again after Adeline had left them—the subject, of course, which was always the same, the subject of what they should do together for their suffering sex. It was not that Verena was not interested in that—gracious, no; it opened up before her, in those wonderful colloquies with Olive, in the most inspiring way; but her fancy would make a dart to right or left when other game crossed their path, and her companion led her, intellectually, a dance in which her feet—that is, her head—failed her at times for weariness. Mrs. Tarrant found Miss Chancellor at home, but she was not gratified by even the most transient glimpse of Mrs. Luna; a fact which, in her heart, Verena regarded as fortunate, inasmuch as (she said to herself) if her mother, returning from Charles Street, began to explain Miss Chancellor to her with fresh energy, and as if she (Verena) had never seen her, and up to this time they had had nothing to say about her, to what developments (of the same sort) would not an encounter with Adeline have given rise?

When Verena at last said to her friend that she thought she ought to come out to Cambridge—she didn't understand why she didn't—Olive expressed her reasons very frankly, admitted that she was jealous, that she didn't wish to think of the girl's belonging to any one but herself. Mr. and Mrs. Tarrant would have authority, opposed claims, and she didn't wish to see them, to remember that they existed. This was true, so far as it went; but Olive could not tell Verena everything—could not tell her that she hated that dreadful pair at Cambridge. As we know, she had forbidden herself this emotion as regards individuals; and she flattered herself that she considered the Tarrants as a type, a deplorable one, a class that, with the public at large, discredited the cause of the new truths. She had talked them over with Miss Birdseye (Olive was always looking after her now and giving her things—the good lady appeared at this period in wonderful caps and shawls—for she felt she couldn't thank her enough), and even Doctor Prance's fellow-lodger, whose animosity to flourishing evils lived in the happiest (though the most illicit) union with the mania for finding excuses, even Miss Birdseye was obliged to confess that if you came to examine his record, poor Selah didn't amount to so very much. How little he amounted to Olive perceived after she had made Verena talk, as the girl did immensely about her father and mother—quite unconscious, meanwhile, of the conclusions she suggested to Miss Chancellor. Tarrant was a moralist without moral sense—that was very clear to Olive as she listened to the history of his daughter's childhood and youth, which Verena related with an extraordinary artless vividness. This narrative, tremendously fascinating to Miss Chancellor, made her feel in all sorts of ways—prompted her to ask herself whether the girl was also destitute of the perception of right and wrong. No, she was only supremely innocent; she didn't understand, she didn't interpret nor see the *portée* of what she described; she had no idea whatever of judging her parents. Olive had wished to "realize" the conditions in which her wonderful young friend (she thought her more wonderful every day) had developed, and to this end, as I have related, she prompted her to infinite discourse. But now she was satisfied, the realization was complete, and what she would have liked to impose on the girl was an effectual rupture with her past. That past she by no means absolutely deplored, for it had the merit of having initiated Verena (and her patroness, through her agency) into the miseries and mysteries of the People. It was her theory that Verena (in spite of the blood of the Greenstreets, and, after all, who were they?) was a flower of the great Democracy, and that it was impossible to have had an origin less distinguished than Tarrant himself. His birth, in some unheard-of place in Pennsylvania, was quite inexpressibly low, and Olive would have been much disappointed if it had been wanting in this defect. She liked to think that Verena, in her childhood, had known almost the extremity of poverty, and there was a kind of ferocity in the joy with which she reflected that there had been moments when this delicate creature came near (if the pinch had only lasted a little longer) to literally going without food. These things added to her value for Olive; they made that young lady feel that their common undertaking would, in consequence, be so much more serious. It is always supposed that revolutionists have been goaded, and the goading would have been rather deficient here were it not for such happy accidents in Verena's past. When she conveyed from her mother a summons to Cambridge for a particular occasion, Olive perceived that the great effort must now be made. Great efforts were nothing new to her—it was a great effort to live at all —but this one appeared to her exceptionally cruel. She determined, however, to make it, promising herself that her first visit to Mrs. Tarrant should also be her last. Her only consolation was that she expected to suffer intensely; for the prospect of suffering was always, spiritually speaking, so much cash in her pocket. It was arranged that Olive should come to tea (the repast that Selah designated as his supper), when Mrs. Tarrant, as we have seen, desired to do her honor by inviting another guest. This guest, after much deliberation between that lady and Verena, was selected, and the first person Olive saw on entering the little parlor in Cambridge was a young man with hair prematurely, or, as one felt that one should say, precociously white, whom she had a vague impression she had encountered before, and who was introduced to her as Mr. Matthias Pardon.

She suffered less than she had hoped—she was so taken up with the consideration of Verena's interior. It was as bad as she could have desired; desired in order to feel that (to take her out of such a *milieu* as that) she should have a right to draw her altogether to herself. Olive wished more and more to extract some definite pledge from her; she could hardly say what it had best be as yet; she only felt that it must be something that would have an absolute sanctity for Verena and would bind them together for life. On this occasion it seemed to shape itself in her mind; she began to see what it ought to be, though she also saw that she would perhaps have to wait awhile. Mrs. Tarrant, too, in her own house, became now a complete figure; there was no manner of doubt left as to her being vulgar. Olive Chancellor despised vulgarity, had a scent for it which she followed up in her own family, so that often, with a rising flush, she detected the taint even in Adeline. There were times, indeed, when every one seemed to have it, every one but Miss Birdseye (who had nothing to do with it—she was an antique) and the poorest, humblest people. The toilers and spinners, the very obscure, these were the only persons who were safe from it. Miss Chancellor would have been much happier if the movements she was interested in could have been carried on only by the people she liked, and if revolutions, somehow, didn't always have to begin with one's self—with internal convulsions, sacrifices, executions. A common end, unfortunately, however fine as regards a special result, does not make community impersonal.

Mrs. Tarrant, with her soft corpulence, looked to her guest very bleached and tumid; her complexion had a kind of withered glaze; her hair, very scanty, was drawn off her forehead *à la Chinoise;* she had no eyebrows, and her eyes seemed to stare, like those of a figure of wax. When she talked and wished to insist, and she was always insisting, she puckered and distorted her face, with an effort to express the inexpressible, which turned out, after all, to be nothing. She had a kind of doleful elegance, tried to be confidential, lowered her voice and looked as if she wished to establish a secret understanding, in order to ask her visitor if she would venture on an apple-fritter. She wore a flowing mantle, which resembled her husband's waterproof —a garment which, when she turned to her daughter or talked about her, might have passed for the robe of a sort of priestess of maternity. She endeavored to keep the conversation in a channel which would enable her to ask sudden incoherent questions of Olive, mainly as to whether she knew the principal ladies (the expression was Mrs. Tarrant's), not only in Boston, but in the other cities which, in her nomadic course, she herself had visited. Olive knew some of them, and of some of them had never heard; but she was irritated, and pretended a universal ignorance (she was conscious that she had never told so many fibs), by which her hostess was much disconcerted, although her questions had apparently been questions pure and simple, leading nowhither and without bearings on any new truth.

15

Tarrant, however, kept an eye in that direction; he was solemnly civil to Miss Chancellor, handed her the dishes at table over and over again, and ventured to intimate that the apple fritters were very fine; but, save for this, alluded to nothing more trivial than the regeneration of humanity and the strong hope he felt that Miss Birdseye would again have one of her delightful gatherings. With regard to this latter point he explained that it was not in order that he might again present his daughter to the company, but simply because on such occasions there was a valuable interchange of hopeful thought, a contact of mind with mind. If Verena had anything suggestive to contribute to the social problem, the opportunity would come—that was part of their faith. They couldn't reach out for it and try and push their way; if they were wanted, their hour would strike; if they were not, they would just keep still and let others press forward who seemed to be called. If they were called, they would know it; and if they weren't, they could just hold on to each other as they had always done. Tarrant was very fond of alternatives, and he mentioned several others; it was never his fault if his listeners failed to think him impartial. They hadn't much, as Miss Chancellor could see; she could tell by their manner of life that they hadn't raked in the dollars; but they had faith that, whether one raised one's voice or simply worked on in silence, the principal difficulties would straighten themselves out; and they had also a considerable experience of great questions. Tarrant spoke as if, as a family, they were prepared to take charge of them on moderate terms. He always said "ma'am" in speaking to Olive, to whom, moreover, the air had never been so filled with the sound of her own name. It was always in her ear, save when Mrs. Tarrant and Verena conversed in prolonged and ingenuous asides; this was still for her benefit, but the pronoun sufficed them. She had wished to judge Doctor Tarrant (not that she believed he had come honestly by his title), to make up her mind. She had done these things now, and she expressed to herself the kind of man she believed him to be in reflecting that if she should offer him ten thousand dollars to renounce all claim to Verena, keeping—he and his wife—clear of her for the rest of time, he would probably say, with his fearful smile, "Make it twenty, money down, and I'll do it." Some image of this transaction, as one of the possibilities of the future, outlined itself for Olive among the moral incisions of that evening. It seemed implied in the very place, the bald bareness of Tarrant's temporary lair, a wooden cottage, with a rough front yard, a little naked piazza, which seemed rather to expose than to protect, facing upon an unpaved road, in which the footway was overlaid with a strip of planks. These planks were embedded in ice or in liquid thaw, according to the momentary mood of the weather, and the advancing pedestrian traversed them in the attitude, and with a good deal of the suspense, of a ropedancer. There was nothing in the house to speak of; nothing, to Olive's sense, but a smell of kerosene; though she had a consciousness of sitting down somewhere—the object creaked and rocked beneath her—and of the table at tea being covered with a cloth stamped in bright colors.

As regards the pecuniary transaction with Selah, it was strange how she should have seen it through the conviction that Verena would never give up her parents. Olive was sure that she would never turn her back upon them, would always share with them. She would have despised her had she thought her capable of another course; yet it baffled her to understand why, when parents were so trashy, this natural law should not be suspended. Such a question brought her back, however, to her perpetual enigma, the mystery she had already turned over in her mind for hours together —the wonder of such people being Verena's progenitors at all. She had explained it, as we explain all exceptional things, by making the part, as the French say, of the miraculous. She had come to consider the girl as a wonder of wonders, to hold that no human origin, however congruous it might superficially appear, would sufficiently account for her; that her springing up between Selah and his wife was an exquisite whim of the creative force; and that in such a case a few shades more or less of the inexplicable didn't matter. It was notorious that great beauties, great geniuses, great characters, take their own times and places for coming into the world, leaving the gaping spectators to make them "fit in," and holding from far-off ancestors, or even, perhaps, straight from the divine generosity, much more than from their ugly or stupid progenitors. They were incalculable phenomena, anyway, as Selah would have said. Verena, for Olive, was the very type and model of the "gifted being"; her qualities had not been bought and paid for; they were like some brilliant birthday-present, left at the door by an unknown messenger, to be delightful forever as an inexhaustible legacy, and amusing forever from the obscurity of its source. They were superabundantly crude as yet— happily for Olive, who promised herself, as we know, to train and polish them—but they were as genuine as fruit and flowers, as the glow of the fire or the plash of water. For her scrutinizing friend Verena had the disposition of the artist, the spirit to which all charming forms come easily and naturally. It required an effort at first to imagine an artist so untaught, so mistaught, so poor in experience; but then it required an effort also to imagine people like the old Tarrants, or a life so full as her life had been of ugly things. Only an exquisite creature could have resisted such associations, only a girl who had some natural light, some divine spark of taste. There were people like that, fresh from the hand of Omnipotence; they were far from common, but their existence was as incontestable as it was beneficent.

Tarrant's talk about his daughter, her prospects, her enthusiasm, was terribly painful to Olive; it brought back to her what she had suffered already from the idea that he laid his hands upon her to make her speak. That he should be mixed up in any way with this exercise of her genius was a great injury to the cause, and Olive had already determined that in future Verena should dispense with his cooperation. The girl had virtually confessed that she lent herself to it only because it gave him pleasure, and that anything else would do as well, anything that would make her quiet a little before she began to "give out." Olive took upon herself to believe that *she* could make her quiet, though, certainly, she had never had that effect upon any one; she would mount the platform with Verena if necessary, and lay her hands upon her head. Why in the world had a perverse fate decreed that Tarrant should take an interest in the affairs of Woman—as if she wanted *his* aid to arrive at her goal; a charlatan of the poor, lean, shabby sort, without the humor, brilliancy, prestige, which sometimes throw a drapery over shallowness? Mr. Pardon evidently took an interest as well, and there was something in his appearance that seemed to say that his sympathy would not be dangerous. He was much at his ease, plainly, beneath the roof of the Tarrants, and Olive reflected that though Verena had told her much about him, she had not given her the idea that he was as intimate as that. What she had mainly said was that he sometimes took her to the theatre. Olive could enter, to a certain extent, into that; she herself had had a phase (some time after her father's death—her mother's had preceded his—when she bought the little house in Charles Street and began to live alone), during which she accompanied gentlemen to respectable places of amusement. She was accordingly not shocked at the idea of such adventures on Verena's part; than which, indeed, judging from her own experience, nothing could well have been less adventurous. Her recollections of these expeditions were as of something solemn and edifying—of the earnest interest in her welfare exhibited by her companion (there were few occasions on which the young Bostonian appeared to more advantage), of the comfort of other friends sitting near, who were sure to know whom she was with, of serious discussion between the acts in regard to the behavior of the characters in the piece, and of the speech at the end with which, as the young man quitted her at her door, she rewarded his civility—"I must thank you for a very pleasant evening." She always felt that she made that too prim; her lips stiffened themselves as she spoke. But the whole affair had always a primness; this was discernible even to Olive's very limited sense of humor. It was not so religious as going to evening-service at King's Chapel; but it was the next thing to it. Of course all girls didn't do it; there were families that viewed such a custom with disfavor. But this was where the girls were of the romping sort; there had to be some things they were known not to do. As a general thing, moreover, the practice was confined to the decorous; it was a sign of culture and quiet tastes. All this made it innocent for Verena, whose life had exposed her to much worse dangers; but the thing referred itself in Olive's mind to a danger which cast a perpetual shadow there—the possibility of the girl's embarking with some ingenuous youth on an expedition that would last much longer than an evening. She was haunted, in a word, with the fear that Verena would marry, a fate to which she was altogether unprepared to surrender her; and this made her look with suspicion upon all male acquaintance.

Mr. Pardon was not the only one she knew; she had an example of the rest in the persons of two young Harvard law students, who presented themselves after tea on this same occasion. As they sat there Olive wondered whether Verena had kept something from her, whether she were, after all (like so many other girls in Cambridge), a college-"belle," an object of frequentation to undergraduates. It was natural that at the seat of a big university there should be girls like that, with students dangling after them, but she didn't want Verena to be one of them. There were some that received the Seniors and Juniors; others that were accessible to Sophomores and Freshmen. Certain young ladies distinguished the professional students; there was a group, even, that was on the best terms with the young men who were studying for the Unitarian ministry in that queer little barrack at the end of Divinity Avenue. The advent of the new visitors made Mrs. Tarrant bustle immensely; but after she had caused every one to change places two or three times with every one else the company subsided into a circle which was occasionally broken by wandering movements on the part of her husband, who, in the absence of anything to say on any subject whatever, placed himself at different points in listening attitudes, shaking his head slowly up and down, and gazing at the carpet with an air of supernatural attention. Mrs. Tarrant asked the young men from the Law School about their studies, and whether they meant to follow them up seriously; said she thought some of the laws were very unjust, and she hoped they meant to try and improve them. She had suffered by the laws herself, at the time her father died; she hadn't got half the prop'ty she should have got if they had been different. She thought they should be for public matters, not for people's private affairs; the idea always seemed to her to keep you down if you *were* down, and to hedge you in with difficulties. Sometimes she thought it was a wonder how she had developed in the face of so many; but it was a proof that freedom was everywhere, if you only knew how to look for it.

The two young men were in the best humor; they greeted these sallies with a merriment of which, though it was courteous in form, Olive was by no means unable to define the spirit. They talked naturally more with Verena than with her mother; and while they were so engaged Mrs. Tarrant explained to her who they were, and how one of them, the smaller, who was not quite so spruce, had brought the other, his particular friend, to introduce him. This friend, Mr. Burrage, was from New York; he was very fashionable, he went out a great deal in Boston ("I have no doubt you know some of the places," said Mrs. Tarrant); his "fam'ly" was very rich.

"Well, he knows plenty of that sort," Mrs. Tarrant went on, "but he felt unsatisfied; he didn't know any one like *us*. He told Mr. Gracie (that's the little one) that he felt as if he *must;* it seemed as if he couldn't hold out. So we told Mr. Gracie, of course, to bring him right round. Well, I hope he'll get something from us, I'm sure. He has been reported to be engaged to Miss Winkworth; I have no doubt you know who I mean. But Mr. Gracie says he hasn't looked at her more than twice. That's the way rumors fly round in that set, I presume. Well, I am glad we are not in it, wherever we are! Mr. Gracie is very different; he is intensely plain, but I believe he is very learned. You don't think him plain? Oh, you don't know? Well, I suppose you don't care, you must see so many. But I must say, when a young man looks like that, I call him painfully plain. I heard Doctor Tarrant make the remark the last time he was here. I don't say but what the plainest are the best. Well, I had no idea we were going to have a party when I asked you. I wonder whether Verena hadn't better hand the cake; we generally find the students enjoy it so much."

This office was ultimately delegated to Selah, who, after a considerable absence, reappeared with a dish of dainties, which he presented successively to each member of the company. Olive saw Verena lavish her smiles on Mr. Gracie and Mr. Burrage; the liveliest relation had established itself, and the latter gentleman in especial abounded in appreciative laughter. It might have been fancied, just from looking at the group, that Verena's vocation was to smile and talk with young men who bent toward her; might have been fancied, that is, by a person less sure of the contrary than Olive, who had reason to know that a "gifted being" is sent into the world for a very different purpose, and that making the time pass pleasantly for conceited young men is the last duty you are bound to think of if you happen to have a talent for embodying a cause. Olive tried to be glad that her friend had the richness of nature that makes a woman gracious without latent purposes; she reflected that Verena was not in the smallest degree a flirt, that she was only enchantingly and universally genial, that nature had given her a beautiful smile, which fell impartially on every one, man and woman, alike. Olive may have been right, but it shall be confided to the reader that in reality she never knew, by any sense of her own, whether Verena were a flirt or not. This young lady could not possibly have told her (even if she herself knew, which she didn't), and Olive, destitute for the quality, had no means of taking the measure in another of the subtle feminine desire to please. She could see the difference between Mr. Gracie and Mr. Burrage; her being bored by Mrs. Tarrant's attempting to point it out is perhaps a proof of that. It was a curious incident of her zeal for the regeneration of her sex that manly things were, perhaps on the whole, what she understood best. Mr. Burrage was rather a handsome youth, with a laughing, clever face, a certain sumptuosity of apparel, an air of belonging to the "fast set"—a precocious, good-natured man of the world, curious of new sensations and containing, perhaps, the making of a *dilettante*. Being, doubtless, a little ambitious, and liking to flatter himself that he appreciated worth in lowly forms, he had associated himself with the ruder but at the same time acuter personality of a genuine son of New England, who had a harder head than his own and a humor in reality more cynical, and who, having earlier knowledge of the Tarrants, had undertaken to show him something indigenous and curious, possibly even fascinating. Mr. Gracie was short, with a big head; he wore eyeglasses, looked unkempt, almost rustic, and said good things with his ugly lips. Verena had replies for a good many of them, and a pretty color came into her face as she talked. Olive could see that she produced herself quite as well as one of these gentlemen had foretold the other that she would. Miss Chancellor knew what had passed between them as well as if she had heard it; Mr. Gracie had promised that he would lead her on, that she should justify his description and prove the raciest of her class. They would laugh about her as they went away, lighting their cigars, and for many days afterwards their discourse would be enlivened with quotations from the "women's rights girl."

It was amazing how many ways men had of being antipathetic; these two were very different from Basil Ransom, and different from each other, and yet the manner of each conveyed an insult to one's womanhood. The worst of the case was that Verena would be sure not to perceive this outrage—not to dislike them in consequence. There were so many things that she hadn't yet learned to dislike, in spite of her friend's earnest efforts to teach her. She had the idea vividly (that was the marvel) of the cruelty of man, of his immemorial injustice; but it remained abstract, platonic; she didn't detest him in consequence. What was the use of her having that sharp, inspired vision of the history of the sex (it was, as she had said herself, exactly like Joan of Arc's absolutely supernatural apprehension of the state of France), if she wasn't going to carry it out, if she was going to behave as the ordinary pusillanimous, conventional young lady? It was all very well for her to have said that first day that she would renounce: did she look, at such a moment as this, like a young woman who had renounced? Suppose this glittering, laughing Burrage youth, with his chains and rings and shining shoes, should fall in love with her and try to bribe her, with his great possessions, to practice renunciations of another kind—to give up her holy work and to go with him to New York, there to live as his wife, partly bullied, partly pampered, in the accustomed Burrage manner? There was as little comfort for Olive as there had been on the whole alarm in the recollection of that offhand speech of Verena's about her preference for "free unions." This had been mere maiden flippancy; she had not known the meaning of what she said. Though she had grown up among people who took for granted all sorts of queer laxities, she had kept the consummate innocence of the American girl, that innocence which was the greatest of all, for it had survived the abolition of walls and locks; and of the various remarks that had dropped from Verena expressing this quality that startling observation certainly expressed it most. It implied, at any rate, that unions of some kind or other had her approval, and did not exclude the dangers that might arise from encounters with young men in search of sensations.

16

Mr. Pardon, as Olive observed, was a little out of this combination; but he was not a person to allow himself to droop. He came and seated himself by Miss Chancellor and broached a literary subject; he asked her if she were following any of the current "serials" in the magazines. On her telling him that she never followed anything of that sort, he undertook a defense of the serial system, which she presently reminded him that she had not attacked. He was not discouraged by this retort, but glided gracefully off to the question of Mount Desert; conversation on some subject or other being evidently a necessity of his nature. He talked very quickly and softly, with words, and even sentences, imperfectly formed; there was a certain amiable flatness in his tone, and he abounded in exclamations—"Goodness gracious!" and "Mercy on us!"—not much in use among the sex whose profanity is apt to be coarse. He had small, fair features, remarkably neat, and pretty eyes, and a mustache that he caressed, and an air of juvenility much at variance with his grizzled locks, and the free familiar reference in which he was apt to indulge to his career as a journalist. His friends knew that in spite of his delicacy and his prattle he was what they called a live man; his appearance was perfectly reconcilable with a large degree of literary enterprise. It should be explained that for the most part they attached to this idea the same meaning as Selah Tarrant—a state of intimacy with the newspapers, the cultivation of the great arts of publicity. For this ingenuous son of his age all distinction between the person and the artist had ceased to exist; the writer was personal, the person food for newsboys, and everything and everyone were everyone's business. All things, with him, referred themselves to print, and print meant simply infinite reporting, a promptitude of announcement, abusive when necessary, or even when not, about his fellow-citizens. He poured contumely on their private life, on their personal appearance, with the best conscience in the world. His faith, again, was the faith of Selah Tarrant—that being in the newspapers is a condition of bliss, and that it would be fastidious to question the terms of the privilege. He was an *enfant de la balle,* as the French say; he had begun his career, at the age of fourteen, by going the rounds of the hotels, to cull flowers from the big, greasy registers which lie on the marble counters; and he might flatter himself that he had contributed in his measure, and on behalf of a vigilant public opinion, the pride of a democratic State, to the great end of preventing the American citizen from attempting clandestine journeys. Since then he had ascended other steps of the same ladder; he was the most brilliant young interviewer on the Boston press. He was particularly successful in drawing out the ladies; he had condensed into shorthand many of

125

the most celebrated women of his time—some of these daughters of fame were very voluminous—and he was supposed to have a remarkably insinuating way of waiting upon *prime donne* and actresses the morning after their arrival, or sometimes the very evening, while their luggage was being brought up. He was only twenty-eight years old, and, with his hoary head, was a thoroughly modern young man; he had no idea of not taking advantage of all the modern conveniences. He regarded the mission of mankind upon earth as a perpetual evolution of telegrams; everything to him was very much the same, he had no sense of proportion or quality; but the newest thing was what came nearest exciting in his mind the sentiment of respect. He was an object of extreme admiration to Selah Tarrant, who believed that he had mastered all the secrets of success, and who, when Mrs. Tarrant remarked (as she had done more than once) that it looked as if Mr. Pardon was really coming after Verena, declared that if he was, he was one of the few young men he should want to see in that connection, one of the few he should be willing to allow to handle her. It was Tarrant's conviction that if Matthias Pardon should seek Verena in marriage, it would be with a view to producing her in public; and the advantage for the girl of having a husband who was at the same time reporter, interviewer, manager, agent, who had the command of the principal "dailies," would write her up and work her, as it were, scientifically—the attraction of all this was too obvious to be insisted on. Matthias had a mean opinion of Tarrant, thought him quite second-rate, a votary of played-out causes. It was his impression that he himself was in love with Verena, but his passion was not a jealous one, and included a remarkable disposition to share the object of his affection with the American people.

He talked some time to Olive about Mount Desert, told her that in his letters he had described the company at the different hotels. He remarked, however, that a correspondent suffered a good deal today from the competition of the "lady-writers"; the sort of article they produced was sometimes more acceptable to the papers. He supposed she would be glad to hear that—he knew she was so interested in woman's having a free field. They certainly made lovely correspondents; they picked up something bright before you could turn round; there wasn't much you could keep away from them; you had to be lively if you wanted to get there first. Of course, they were naturally more chatty, and that was the style of literature that seemed to take most today; only they didn't write much but what ladies would want to read. Of course, he knew there were millions of lady-readers, but he intimated that *he* didn't address himself exclusively to the gynecaeum; he tried to put in something that would interest all parties. If you read a lady's letter you knew pretty well in advance what you would find. Now, what he tried for was that you shouldn't have the least idea; he always tried to have something that would make you jump. Mr. Pardon was not conceited more, at least, than is proper when youth and success go hand in hand, and it was natural he should not know in what spirit Miss Chancellor listened to him. Being aware that she was a woman of culture his desire was simply to supply her with the pabulum that she would expect. She thought him very inferior; she had heard he was intensely bright, but there was probably some mistake; there couldn't be any danger for Verena from a mind that took merely a gossip's view of great tendencies. Besides, he wasn't half educated, and it was her belief, or at least her hope, that an educative process was now going on for Verena (under her own direction), which would enable her to make such a discovery for herself. Olive had a standing quarrel with the levity, the good-nature, of the judgments of the day; many of them seemed to her weak to imbecility, losing sight of all measures and standards, lavishing superlatives, delighted to be fooled. The age seemed to her relaxed and demoralized, and I believe she looked to the influx of the great feminine element to make it feel and speak more sharply.

"Well, it's a privilege to hear you two talk together," Mrs.

Tarrant said to her; "it's what I call real conversation. It isn't often we have anything so fresh; it makes me feel as if I wanted to join in. I scarcely know whom to listen to most; Verena seems to be having such a time with those gentlemen. First I catch one thing and then another; it seems as if I couldn't take it all in. Perhaps I ought to pay more attention to Mr. Burrage; I don't want him to think we are not so cordial as they are in New York."

She decided to draw nearer to the trio on the other side of the room, for she had perceived (as she devoutly hoped Miss Chancellor had not), that Verena was endeavoring to persuade either of her companions to go and talk to her dear friend, and that these unscrupulous young men, after a glance over their shoulder, appeared to plead for remission, to intimate that this was not what they had come round for. Selah wandered out of the room again with his collection of cakes, and Mr. Pardon began to talk to Olive about Verena, to say that he felt as if he couldn't say all he did feel with regard to the interest she had shown in her. Olive could not imagine why he was called upon to say or to feel anything, and she gave him short answers; while the poor young man, unconscious of his doom, remarked that he hoped she wasn't going to exercise any influence that would prevent Miss Tarrant from taking the rank that belonged to her. He thought there was too much hanging back; he wanted to see her in a front seat; he wanted to see her name in the biggest kind of bills and her portrait in the windows of the stores. She had genius, there was no doubt of that, and she would take a new line altogether. She had charm, and there was a great demand for that nowadays in connection with new ideas. There were so many that seemed to have fallen dead for want of it. She ought to be carried straight ahead; she ought to walk right up to the top. There was a want of bold action; he didn't see what they were waiting for. He didn't suppose they were waiting till she was fifty years old; there were old ones enough in the field. He knew that Miss Chancellor appreciated the advantage of her girlhood, because Miss Verena had told him so. Her father was dreadfully slack, and the winter was ebbing away. Mr. Pardon went so far as to say that if Dr. Tarrant didn't see his way to do something, he should feel as if he should want to take hold himself. He expressed a hope at the same time that Olive had not any views that would lead her to bring her influence to bear to make Miss Verena hold back; also that she wouldn't consider that he pressed in too much. He knew that was a charge that people brought against newspaper-men—that they were rather apt to cross the line. He only worried because he thought those who were no doubt nearer to Miss Verena than he could hope to be were not sufficiently alive. He knew that she had appeared in two or three parlors since that evening at Miss Birdseye's, and he had heard of the delightful occasion at Miss Chancellor's own house, where so many of the first families had been invited to meet her. (This was an allusion to a small luncheon-party that Olive had given, when Verena discoursed to a dozen matrons and spinsters, selected by her hostess with infinite consideration and many spiritual scruples; a report of the affair, presumably from the hand of the young Matthias, who naturally had not been present, appeared with extraordinary promptness in an evening-paper.) That was very well so far as it went, but he wanted something on another scale, something so big that people would have to go round if they wanted to get past. Then lowering his voice a little, he mentioned what it was: a lecture in the Music Hall, at fifty cents a ticket, without her father, right there on her own basis. He lowered his voice still more and revealed to Miss Chancellor his innermost thought, having first assured himself that Selah was still absent and that Mrs. Tarrant was inquiring of Mr. Burrage whether he visited much on the new land. The truth was, Miss Verena wanted to "shed" her father altogether; she didn't want him pawing round her that way before she began; it didn't add in the least to the attraction. Mr. Pardon expressed the conviction that Miss Chancellor agreed with him in this, and it required a great effort of mind on Olive's part, so small was her desire to act in concert with Mr. Pardon, to admit to herself that she did. She asked him, with a certain lofty coldness—he didn't make her shy, now, a bit—whether he took a great interest in the improvement of the position of women. The question appeared to strike the young man as abrupt and irrelevant, to come down on him from a height with which he was not accustomed to hold intercourse. He was used to quick operations, however, and he had only a moment of bright blankness before replying:

"Oh, there is nothing I wouldn't do for the ladies; just give me a chance and you'll see."

Olive was silent a moment. "What I mean is—is your sympathy a sympathy with our sex, or a particular interest in Miss Tarrant?"

"Well, sympathy is just sympathy—that's all I can say. It takes in Miss Verena and it takes in all others—except the lady-correspondents," the young man added, with a jocosity which, as he perceived even at the moment, was lost on Verena's friend. He was not more successful when he went on: "It takes in even you, Miss Chancellor!"

Olive rose to her feet, hesitating; she wanted to go away, and yet she couldn't bear to leave Verena to be exploited, as she felt that she would be after her departure, that indeed she had already been, by those offensive young men. She had a strange sense, too, that her friend had neglected her for the last half-hour, had not been occupied with her, had placed a barrier between them—a barrier of broad male backs, of laughter that verged upon coarseness, of glancing smiles directed across the room, directed to Olive, which seemed rather to disconnect her with what was going forward on that side than to invite her to take part in it. If Verena recognized that Miss Chancellor was not in report, as her father said, when jocose young men ruled the scene, the discovery implied no great penetration; but the poor girl might have reflected further that to see it taken for granted that she was unadapted for such company could scarcely be more agreeable to Olive than to be dragged into it. This young lady's worst apprehensions were now justified by Mrs. Tarrant's crying to her that she must not go, as Mr. Burrage and Mr. Gracie were trying to persuade Verena to give them a little specimen of inspirational speaking, and she was sure her daughter would comply in a moment if Miss Chancellor would just tell her to compose herself. They had got to own up to it, Miss Chancellor could do more with her than anyone else; but Mr. Gracie and Mr. Burrage had excited her so that she was afraid it would be rather an unsuccessful effort. The whole group had got up, and Verena came to Olive with her hands outstretched and no signs of a bad conscience in her bright face.

"I know you like me to speak so much—I'll try to say something if you want me to. But I'm afraid there are not enough people; I can't do much with a small audience."

"I wish we had brought some of our friends—they would have been delighted to come if we had given them a chance," said Mr. Burrage. "There is an immense desire throughout the University to hear you, and there is no such sympathetic audience as an audience of Harvard men. Gracie and I are only two, but Gracie is a host in himself, and I am sure he will say as much of me." The young man spoke these words freely and lightly, smiling at Verena, and even a little at Olive, with the air of one to whom a mastery of clever "chaff" was commonly attributed.

"Mr. Burrage listens even better than he talks," his companion declared. "We have the habit of attention at lectures, you know. To be lectured by you would be an advantage indeed. We are sunk in ignorance and prejudice."

"Ah, my prejudices," Burrage went on; "if you could see them—I assure you they are something monstrous!"

"Give them a regular ducking and make them gasp," Matthias Pardon cried. "If you want an opportunity to act on Harvard College, now's your chance. These gentlemen will carry the news; it will be the narrow end of the wedge."

"I can't tell what you like," Verena said, still looking into Olive's eyes.

"I'm sure Miss Chancellor likes everything here," Mrs. Tarrant remarked, with a noble confidence.

Selah had reappeared by this time; his lofty, contemplative person was framed by the doorway. "Want to try a little inspiration?" he inquired, looking round on the circle with an encouraging inflection.

"I'll do it alone, if you prefer," Verena said, soothingly to her friend. "It might be a good chance to try without father."

"You don't mean to say you ain't going to be supported?" Mrs. Tarrant exclaimed, with dismay.

"Ah, I beseech you, give us the whole program—don't omit any leading feature!" Mr. Burrage was heard to plead.

"My only interest is to draw her out," said Selah, defending his integrity. "I will drop right out if I don't seem to vitalize. I have no desire to draw attention to my own poor gifts." This declaration appeared to be addressed to Miss Chancellor.

"Well, there will be more inspiration if you don't touch her," Matthias Pardon said to him. "It will seem to come right down from—well, wherever it does come from."

"Yes, we don't pretend to say that," Mrs. Tarrant murmured.

This little discussion had brought the blood to Olive's face; she felt that every one present was looking at her—Verena most of all—and that here was a chance to take a more complete possession of the girl. Such chances were agitating; moreover, she didn't like, on any occasion, to be so prominent. But everything that had been said was benighted and vulgar; the place seemed thick with the very atmosphere out of which she wished to lift Verena. They were treating her as a show, as a social resource, and the two young men from the College were laughing at her shamelessly. She was not meant for that, and Olive would save her. Verena was so simple, she couldn't see herself; she was the only pure spirit in the odious group.

"I want you to address audiences that are worth addressing—to convince people who are serious and sincere." Olive herself, as she spoke, heard the great shake in her voice. "Your mission is not to exhibit yourself as a pastime for individuals, but to touch the heart of communities, of nations."

"Dear madam, I'm sure Miss Tarrant will touch my heart!" Mr. Burrage objected, gallantly.

"Well, I don't know but she judges you young men fairly," said Mrs. Tarrant, with a sigh.

Verena, diverted a moment from her communion with her friend, considered Mr. Burrage with a smile. "I don't believe you have got any heart, and I shouldn't care much if you had!"

"You have no idea how much the way you say that increases my desire to hear you speak."

"Do as you please, my dear," said Olive, almost inaudibly. "My carriage must be there—I must leave you, in any case."

"I can see you don't want it," said Verena, wondering. "You would stay if you liked it, wouldn't you?"

"I don't know what I should do. Come out with me!" Olive spoke almost with fierceness.

"Well, you'll send them away no better than they came," said Matthias Pardon.

"I guess you had better come round some other night," Selah suggested pacifically, but with a significance which fell upon Olive's ear.

Mr. Gracie seemed inclined to make the sturdiest protest. "Look here, Miss Tarrant; do you want to save Harvard College, or do you not?" he demanded, with a humorous frown.

"I didn't know *you* were Harvard College!" Verena returned as humorously.

"I am afraid you are rather disappointed in your evening if you expected to obtain some insight into our ideas," said Mrs. Tarrant, with an air of impotent sympathy, to Mr. Gracie.

"Well, good night, Miss Chancellor," she went on; "I hope you've got a warm wrap. I suppose you'll think we go a good deal by what you say in this house. Well, most people don't object to that. There's a little hole right there in the porch; it seems as if Doctor Tarrant couldn't remember to go for the man to fix it. I am afraid you'll think we're too much taken up with all these new hopes. Well, we *have* enjoyed seeing you in our home; it quite raises my appetite for social intercourse. Did you come out on wheels? I can't stand a sleigh myself; it makes me sick."

This was her hostess's response to Miss Chancellor's very summary farewell, uttered as the three ladies proceeded together to the door of the house. Olive had got herself out of the little parlor with a sort of blind, defiant dash; she had taken no perceptible leave of the rest of the company. When she was calm she had very good manners, but when she was agitated she was guilty of lapses, every one of which came back to her, magnified, in the watches of the night. Sometimes they excited remorse, and sometimes triumph; in the latter case she felt that she could not have been so justly vindictive in cold blood. Tarrant wished to guide her down the steps, out of the little yard, to her carriage; he reminded her that they had had ashes sprinkled on the planks on purpose. But she begged him to let her alone, she almost pushed him back; she drew Verena out into the dark freshness, closing the door of the house behind her. There was a splendid sky, all blue-black and silver—a sparkling wintry vault, where the stars were like a myriad points of ice. The air was silent and sharp, and the vague snow looked cruel. Olive knew now very definitely what the promise was that she wanted Verena to make; but it was too cold, she could keep her there bareheaded but an instant. Mrs. Tarrant, meanwhile, in the parlor, remarked that it seemed as if she couldn't trust Verena with her own parents; and Selah intimated that, with a proper invitation, his daughter would be very happy to address Harvard College at large. Mr. Burrage and Mr. Gracie said they would invite her on the spot, in the name of the University; and Matthias Pardon reflected (and asserted) with glee that this would be the newest thing yet. But he added that they would have a high time with Miss Chancellor first, and this was evidently the conviction of the company.

"I can see you are angry at something," Verena said to Olive, as the two stood there in the starlight. "I hope it isn't me. What have I done?"

"I am not angry—I am anxious. I am so afraid I shall lose you. Verena, don't fail me—don't fail me!" Olive spoke low, with a kind of passion.

"Fail you? How can I fail?"

"You can't, of course you can't. Your star is above you. But don't listen to *them*."

"To whom do you mean, Olive? To my parents?"

"Oh no, not your parents," Miss Chancellor replied, with some sharpness. She paused a moment, and then she said: "I don't care for your parents. I have told you that before; but now that I have seen them—as they wished, as you wished, and I didn't—I don't care for them; I must repeat it, Verena. I should be dishonest if I let you think I did."

"Why, Olive Chancellor!" Verena murmured, as if she were trying, in spite of the sadness produced by this declaration, to do justice to her friend's impartiality.

"Yes, I am hard; perhaps I am cruel; but we must be hard if we wish to triumph. Don't listen to young men when they try to mock and muddle you. They don't care for you; they don't care for *us*. They care only for their pleasure, for what they believe to be the right of the stronger. The stronger? I am not so sure!"

"Some of them care so much—are supposed to care too much—for us," Verena said, with a smile that looked dim in the darkness.

135

"Yes, if we will give up everything. I have asked you before—are you prepared to give up?"

"Do you mean, to give *you* up?"

"No, all our wretched sisters—all our hopes and purposes—all that we think sacred and worth living for!"

"Oh, they don't want that, Olive." Verena's smile became more distinct, and she added: "They don't want so much as that!"

"Well, then, go in and speak for them—and sing for them—and dance for them!"

"Olive, you are cruel!"

"Yes, I am. But promise me one thing, and I shall be—oh, so tender!"

"What a strange place for promises," said Verena, with a shiver, looking about her into the night.

"Yes, I am dreadful; I know it. But promise." And Olive drew the girl nearer to her, flinging over her with one hand the fold of a cloak that hung ample upon her own meager person, and holding her there with the other, while she looked at her, suppliant but half hesitating. "Promise!" she repeated.

"Is it something terrible?"

"Never to listen to one of them, never to be bribed——"

At this moment the house door was opened again, and the light of the hall projected itself across the little piazza. Matthias Pardon stood in the aperture, and Tarrant and his wife, with the two other visitors, appeared to have come forward as well, to see what detained Verena.

"You seem to have started a kind of lecture out here," Mr. Pardon said. "You ladies had better look out, or you'll freeze together!"

Verena was reminded by her mother that she would catch her death, but she had already heard sharply, low as they were spoken, five last words from Olive, who now abruptly released her and passed swiftly over the path from the porch to her waiting carriage. Tarrant creaked along, in pursuit, to assist Miss Chancellor; the others drew Verena into the house. "Promise me not to marry!"—that was what echoed in her startled mind, and repeated itself there when Mr. Burrage returned to the charge, asking her if she wouldn't at least appoint some evening when they might listen to her. She knew that Olive's injunction ought not to have surprised her; she had already felt it in the air; she would have said at any time, if she had been asked, that she didn't suppose Miss Chancellor would want her to marry. But the idea, uttered as her friend had uttered it, had a new solemnity, and the effect of that quick, violent colloquy was to make her nervous and impatient, as if she had had a sudden glimpse of futurity. That was rather awful, even if it represented the fate one would like.

When the two young men from the College pressed their petition, she asked, with a laugh that surprised them, whether they wished to "mock and muddle" her. They went away, assenting to Mrs. Tarrant's last remark: "I am afraid you'll feel that you don't quite understand us yet." Matthias Pardon remained; her father and mother, expressing their perfect confidence that he would excuse them, went to bed and left him sitting there. He stayed a good while longer, nearly an hour, and said things that made Verena think that *he,* perhaps, would like to marry her. But while she listened to him, more abstractedly than her custom was, she remarked to herself that there could be no difficulty in promising Olive so far as he was concerned. He was very pleasant, and he knew an immense deal about everything, or, rather, about everyone, and he would take her right into the midst of life. But she didn't wish to marry him, all the same, and after he had gone she reflected that, once she came to think of it, she didn't want to marry anyone. So it would be easy, after all, to make Olive that promise, and it would give her so much pleasure!

17

The next time Verena saw Olive, she said to her that she was ready to make the promise she had asked the other night; but, to her great surprise, this young woman answered her by a question intended to check such rashness. Miss Chancellor raised a warning finger; she had an air of dissuasion almost as solemn as her former pressure; her passionate impatience appeared to have given way to other considerations, to be replaced by the resignation that comes with deeper reflection. It was tinged in this case, indeed, by such bitterness as might be permitted to a young lady who cultivated the brightness of a great faith.

"Don't you want any promise at present?" Verena asked. "Why, Olive, how you change!"

"My dear child, you are so young—so strangely young. I am a thousand years old; I have lived through generations —through centuries. I know what I know by experience; you know it by imagination. That is consistent with your being the fresh, bright creature that you are. I am constantly forgetting the difference between us—that you are a mere child as yet, though a child destined for great things. I forgot it the other night, but I have remembered it since. You must pass through a certain phase, and it would be very wrong in me to pretend to suppress it. That is all clear to me now; I see it was my jealousy that spoke—my restless, hungry jealousy. I have far too much of that; I oughtn't to give anyone the right to say that it's a woman's quality. I don't want your signature; I only want your confidence— only what springs from that. I hope with all my soul that you won't marry; but if you don't it must not be because you have promised me. You know what I think—that there is something noble done when one makes a sacrifice for a great good. Priests—when they were real priests—never married, and what you and I dream of doing demands of us a kind of priesthood. It seems to me very poor, when friendship and faith and charity and the most interesting occupation in the world—when such a combination as this doesn't seem, by itself, enough to live for. No man that I have ever seen cares a straw in his heart for what we are trying to accomplish. They hate it; they scorn it; they will try to stamp it out whenever they can. Oh yes, I know there are men who pretend to care for it; but they are not really men, and I wouldn't be sure even of them! Any man that one would look at—with him, as a matter of course, it is war upon us to the knife. I don't mean to say there are not some male beings who are willing to patronize us a little; to pat us on the back and recommend a few moderate concessions; to say that there *are* two or three little points in which society has not been quite just to us. But any man who pretends to accept our program *in toto,* as you and I understand it, of his own free will, before he is forced to—such a person simply schemes to betray us. There are gentlemen in plenty who would be glad to stop your mouth by kissing you! If you become dangerous some day to their selfishness, to their vested interests, to their immorality—as I pray heaven every day, my dear friend, that you may!—it will be a grand thing for one of them if he can persuade you that he loves you. Then you will see what he will do with you, and how far his love will take him! It would be a sad day for you and for me and for all of us, if you were to believe something of that kind. You see I am very calm now; I have thought it all out."

Verena had listened with earnest eyes. "Why, Olive, you

are quite a speaker yourself!" she exclaimed. "You would far surpass me if you would let yourself go."

Miss Chancellor shook her head with a melancholy that was not devoid of sweetness. "I can speak to *you;* but that is no proof. The very stones of the street—all the dumb things of nature—might find a voice to talk to you. I have no facility; I am awkward and embarrassed and dry." When this young lady, after a struggle with the winds and waves of emotion, emerged into the quiet stream of a certain high reasonableness, she presented her most graceful aspect; she had a tone of softness and sympathy, a gentle dignity, a serenity of wisdom, which sealed the appreciation of those who knew her well enough to like her, and which always impressed Verena as something almost august. Such moods, however, were not often revealed to the public at large; they belonged to Miss Chancellor's very private life. One of them had possession of her at present, and she went on to explain the inconsequence which had puzzled her friend with the same quiet clearness, the detachment from error, of a woman whose self-scrutiny has been as sharp as her deflection.

"Don't think me capricious if I say I would rather trust you without a pledge. I owe you, I owe every one, an apology for my rudeness and fierceness at your mother's. It came over me—just seeing those young men—how exposed you are; and the idea made me (for the moment) frantic. I see your danger still, but I see other things too, and I have recovered my balance. You must be safe, Verena—you must be saved; but your safety must not come from your having tied your hands. It must come from the growth of your perception; from your seeing things, of yourself, sincerely and with conviction, in the light in which I see them; from your feeling that for your work your freedom is essential, and that there is no freedom for you and me save in religiously *not* doing what you will often be asked to do—and I never!" Miss Chancellor brought out these last words with a proud jerk which was not without its pathos. "Don't promise, don't promise!" she went on. "I would far rather you didn't. But don't fail me—don't fail me, or I shall die!"

Her manner of repairing her inconsistency was altogether feminine: she wished to extract a certainty at the same time that she wished to deprecate a pledge, and she would have been delighted to put Verena into the enjoyment of that freedom which was so important for her by preventing her exercising it in a particular direction. The girl was now completely under her influence; she had latent curiosities and distractions—left to herself, she was not always thinking of the unhappiness of women; but the touch of Olive's tone worked a spell, and she found something to which at least a portion of her nature turned with eagerness in her companion's wider knowledge, her elevation of view. Miss Chancellor was historic and philosophic; or, at any rate, she appeared so to Verena, who felt that through such an association one might at last intellectually command all life. And there was a simpler impulse; Verena wished to please her if only because she had such a dread of displeasing her. Olive's displeasures, disappointments, disapprovals were tragic, truly memorable; she grew white under them, not shedding many tears, as a general thing, like inferior women (she cried when she was angry, not when she was hurt), but limping and panting, morally, as if she had received a wound that she would carry for life. On the other hand, her commendations, her satisfactions were as soft as a west wind; and she had this sign, the rarest of all, of generosity, that she liked obligations of gratitude when they were not laid upon her by men. Then, indeed, she scarcely recognized them. She considered men in general as so much in the debt of the opposite sex that any individual woman had an unlimited credit with them; she could not possibly overdraw the general feminine account. The unexpected temperance of her speech on this subject of Verena's accessibility to matrimonial error seemed to the girl to have an antique beauty, a wisdom purged of worldly elements; it reminded her of qualities that she believed to have been proper to Electra or Antigone. This made her wish the more to do something that would gratify Olive; and in spite of her friend's dissuasion she declared that she should like to promise. "I will promise, at any rate, not to marry any of those gentlemen that were at the house," she said. "Those seemed to be the ones you were principally afraid of."

"You will promise not to marry anyone you don't like," said Olive. "That would be a great comfort!"

"But I do like Mr. Burrage and Mr. Gracie."

"And Mr. Matthias Pardon? What a name!"

"Well, he knows how to make himself agreeable. He can tell you everything you want to know."

"You mean everything you don't! Well, if you like everyone, I haven't the least objection. It would only be preferences that I should find alarming. I am not the least afraid of your marrying a repulsive man; your danger would come from an attractive one."

"I'm glad to hear you admit that some *are* attractive!" Verena exclaimed, with the light laugh which her reverence for Miss Chancellor had not yet quenched. "It sometimes seems as if there weren't any you could like!"

"I can imagine a man I should like very much," Olive replied, after a moment. "But I don't like those I see. They seem to me poor creatures." And, indeed, her uppermost feeling in regard to them was a kind of cold scorn; she thought most of them palterers and bullies. The end of the colloquy was that Verena, having assented, with her usual docility, to her companion's optimistic contention that it was a "phase," this taste for evening calls from collegians and newspapermen, and would consequently pass away with the growth of her mind, remarked that the injustice of men might be an accident or might be a part of their nature, but at any rate she should have to change a good deal before she should want to marry.

About the middle of December, Miss Chancellor received a visit from Matthias Pardon, who had come to ask her what she meant to do about Verena. She had never invited him to call upon her, and the appearance of a gentleman whose desire to see her was so irrepressible as to dispense with such a preliminary was not in her career an accident frequent enough to have taught her equanimity. She thought Mr. Pardon's visit a liberty; but, if she expected to convey this idea to him by withholding any suggestion that he should sit down, she was greatly mistaken, inasmuch as he cut the ground from under her feet by himself offering her a chair. His manner represented hospitality enough for both of them, and she was obliged to listen, on the edge of her sofa (she could at least seat herself where she liked), to his extraordinary inquiry. Of course she was not obliged to answer it, and indeed she scarcely understood it. He explained that it was prompted by the intense interest he felt in Miss Verena; but that scarcely made it more comprehensible, such a sentiment (on his part) being such a curious mixture. He had a sort of enamel of good humor which showed that his indelicacy was his profession; and he asked for revelations of the *vie intime* of his victims with the bland confidence of a fashionable physician inquiring about symptoms. He wanted to know what Miss Chancellor meant to do, because if she didn't mean to do anything, he had an idea—which he wouldn't conceal from her—of going into the enterprise himself. "You see, what I should like to know is this: do you consider that she belongs to you, or that she belongs to the people? If she belongs to you, why don't you bring her out?"

He had no purpose and no consciousness of being impertinent; he only wished to talk over the matter sociably with Miss Chancellor. He knew, of course, that there was a presumption she would not be sociable, but no presumption had yet deterred him from presenting a surface which he believed to be polished till it shone; there was always a larger one in favor of his power to penetrate and of the majesty of the "great dailies." Indeed, he took so many things for granted that Olive remained dumb while she regarded them; and he availed himself of what he considered as a fortunate opening to be really very frank. He reminded her that he had known Miss Verena a good deal longer than she; he had traveled out to Cambridge the other winter (when he could get an off-night), with the thermometer at ten below zero. He had always thought her attractive, but it wasn't till this season that his eyes had been fully opened. Her talent had matured, and now he had no hesitation in calling her brilliant. Miss Chancellor could imagine whether, as an old friend, he could watch such a beautiful unfolding with indifference. She would fascinate the people, just as she had fascinated her (Miss Chancellor), and, he might be permitted to add, himself. The fact was, she was a great card, and some one ought to play it. There never had been a more attractive female speaker before the American public; she would walk right past Mrs. Farrinder, and Mrs. Farrinder knew it. There was room for both, no doubt, they had such a different style; anyhow, what he wanted to show was that there was room for Miss Verena. She didn't want any more tuning-up, she wanted to break right out. Moreover, he felt that any gentleman who should lead her to success would win her esteem; he might even attract her more powerfully—who could tell? If Miss Chancellor wanted to attach her permanently, she ought to push her right forward. He gathered from what Miss Verena had told him that she wanted to make her study up the subject a while longer—follow some kind of course. Well, now, he could assure her that there was no preparation so good as just seeing a couple of thousand people down there before you who have paid their money to have you tell them something. Miss Verena was a natural genius, and he hoped very much she wasn't going to take the nature out of her. She could study up as she went along; she had got the great thing that you couldn't learn, a kind of divine afflatus, as the ancients used to say, and she had better just begin on that. He wouldn't deny what was the matter with *him;* he was quite under the spell, and his admiration made him want to see her where she belonged. He shouldn't care so much how she got there, but it would certainly add to his pleasure if he could show her up to her place. Therefore, would Miss Chancellor just tell him this: How long did she expect to hold her back; how long did she expect a humble admirer to wait? Of course he hadn't come there to cross-question her; there was one thing he trusted he always kept clear of; when he was indiscreet he wanted to know it. He had come with a proposal of his own, and he hoped it would seem a sufficient warrant for his visit. Would Miss Chancellor be willing to divide a—the—well, he might call it the responsibilities? Couldn't they run Miss Verena together? In this case, every one would be satisfied. She could travel round with her as her companion, and he would see that the American people walked up. If Miss Chancellor would just let her go a little, he would look after the rest. He wanted no odds; he only wanted her for about an hour and a half three or four evenings a week.

Olive had time, in the course of this appeal, to make her faculties converge, to ask herself what she could say to this prodigious young man that would make him feel as how base a thing she held his proposal that they should constitute themselves into a company for drawing profit from Verena. Unfortunately, the most sarcastic inquiry that could occur to her as a response was also the most obvious one, so that he hesitated but a moment with his rejoinder after she had asked him how many thousands of dollars he expected to make.

"For Miss Verena? It depends upon the time. She'd run for ten years, at least. I can't figure it up till all the States have been heard from," he said, smiling.

"I don't mean for Miss Tarrant, I mean for you," Olive returned, with the impression that she was looking him straight in the eye.

"Oh, as many as you'll leave me!" Matthias Pardon answered, with a laugh that contained all, and more than all, the jocularity of the American press. "To speak seriously," he added, "I don't want to make money out of it."

145

"What do you want to make, then?"

"Well, I want to make history! I want to help the ladies."

"The ladies?" Olive murmured. "What do you know about ladies?" she was on the point of adding, when his promptness checked her.

"All over the world. I want to work for their emancipation. I regard it as the great modern question."

Miss Chancellor got up now; this was rather too strong. Whether, eventually, she was successful in what she attempted, the reader of her history will judge; but at this moment she had not that promise of success which resides in a willingness to make use of every aid that offers. Such is the penalty of being of a fastidious, exclusive, uncompromising nature; of seeing things not simply and sharply, but in perverse relations, in interwisted strands. It seemed to our young lady that nothing could be less attractive than to owe her emancipation to such a one as Matthias Pardon; and it is curious that those qualities which he had in common with Verena, and which in her seemed to Olive romantic and touching—her having sprung from the "people," had an acquaintance with poverty, a hand-to-mouth development, and an experience of the seamy side of life—availed in no degree to conciliate Miss Chancellor. I suppose it was because he was a man. She told him that she was much obliged to him for his offer, but that he evidently didn't understand Verena and herself. No, not even Miss Tarrant, in spite of his long acquaintance with her. They had no desire to be notorious; they only wanted to be useful. They had no wish to make money; there would always be plenty of money for Miss Tarrant. Certainly, she should come before the public, and the world would acclaim her and hang upon her words; but crude, precipitate action was what both of them least desired. The change in the dreadful position of women was not a question for today simply, or for tomorrow, but for many years to come; and there would be a great deal to think of, to map out. One thing they were determined upon—that men shouldn't

146

taunt them with being superficial. When Verena should appear it would be armed at all points, like Joan of Arc (this analogy had lodged itself in Olive's imagination); she should have facts and figures; she should meet men on their own ground. "What we mean to do, we mean to do well," Miss Chancellor said to her visitor, with considerable sternness; leaving him to make such an application to himself as his fancy might suggest.

This announcement had little comfort for him; he felt baffled and disheartened—indeed, quite sick. Was it not sickening to hear her talk of this dreary process of preparation?—as if any one cared about that, and would know whether Verena were prepared or not! Had Miss Chancellor no faith in her girlhood? didn't she know what a card that would be? This was the last inquiry Olive allowed him the opportunity of making. She remarked to him that they might talk for ever without coming to an agreement—their points of view were so far apart. Besides, it was a woman's question; what they wanted was for women, and it should be by women. It had happened to the young Matthias more than once to be shown the way to the door, but the path of retreat had never yet seemed to him so unpleasant. He was naturally amiable, but it had not hitherto befallen him to be made to feel that he was not—and could not be—a factor in contemporary history: here was a rapacious woman who proposed to keep that favorable setting for herself. He let her know that she was right-down selfish, and that if she chose to sacrifice a beautiful nature to her antediluvian theories and love of power, a vigilant daily press—whose business it was to expose wrongdoing—would demand an account from her. She replied that, if the newspapers chose to insult her, that was their own affair; one outrage the more to the sex in her person was of little account. And after he had left her she seemed to see the glow of dawning success; the battle had begun, and something of the ecstasy of the martyr.

18

Verena told her, a week after this, that Mr. Pardon wanted so much she should say she would marry him; and she added, with evident pleasure at being able to give her so agreeable a piece of news, that she had declined to say anything of the sort. She thought that now, at least, Olive must believe in her; for the proposal was more attractive than Miss Chancellor seemed able to understand. "He does place things in a very seductive light," Verena said; "he says that if I become his wife I shall be carried straight along by a force of excitement of which at present I have no idea. I shall wake up famous, if I marry him; I have only got to give out my feelings, and he will take care of the rest. He says every hour of my youth is precious to me, and that we should have a lovely time traveling round the country. I think you ought to allow that all that is rather dazzling—for I am not naturally concentrated, like you!"

"He promises you success. What do you call success?" Olive inquired, looking at her friend with a kind of salutary coldness—a suspension of sympathy—with which Verena was now familiar (though she liked it no better than at first), and which made approbation more gracious when approbation came.

Verena reflected a moment, and then answered, smiling, but with confidence: "Producing a pressure that shall be irresistible. Causing certain laws to be repealed by Congress and by the State legislatures, and others to be enacted."

She repeated the words as if they had been part of a catechism committed to memory, while Olive saw that this mechanical tone was in the nature of a joke that she could not deny herself; they had had that definition so often before, and Miss Chancellor had had occasion so often to remind her what success *really* was. Of course it was easy to prove to her now that Mr. Pardon's glittering bait was a very different thing; was a mere trap and lure, a bribe to vanity and impatience, a device for making her give herself away—let alone fill his pockets while she did so. Olive was conscious enough of the girl's want of continuity; she had seen before how she could be passionately serious at times, and then perversely, even if innocently, trivial—as just now, when she seemed to wish to convert one of their most sacred formulas into a pleasantry. She had already quite recognized, however, that it was not of importance that Verena should be just like herself; she was all of one piece, and Verena was of many pieces, which had, where they fitted together, little capricious chinks, through which mocking inner lights seemed sometimes to gleam. It was a part of Verena's being unlike her that she should feel Mr. Pardon's promise of eternal excitement to be a brilliant thing, should indeed consider Mr. Pardon with any tolerance at all. But Olive tried afresh to allow for such aberrations, as a phase of youth and suburban culture; the more so that, even when she tried most, Verena reproached her—so far as Verena's incurable softness could reproach—with not allowing enough. Olive didn't appear to understand that, while Matthias Pardon drew that picture and tried to hold her hand (this image was unfortunate), she had given one long, fixed, wistful look, through the door he opened, at the bright tumult of the world, and then had turned away, solely for her friend's sake, to an austerer probation and a purer effort; solely for her friend's, that is, and that of the whole enslaved sisterhood. The fact remained, at any rate, that Verena had made a sacrifice; and this thought, after a while, gave Olive a greater sense of security. It seemed almost to seal the future; for Olive knew that the young interviewer would not easily be shaken off, and yet she was sure that Verena would never yield to him.

It was true that at present Mr. Burrage came a great deal to the little house at Cambridge; Verena told her about that, told her so much that it was almost as good as if she had told her all. He came without Mr. Gracie now; he could find his way alone, and he seemed to wish that there should be no one else. He had made himself so pleasant to her mother that she almost always went out of the room; that was the highest proof Mrs. Tarrant could give of her appreciation of a "gentleman-caller." They knew everything about him by this time; that his father was dead, his mother very fashionable and prominent, and he himself in possession of a handsome patrimony. They thought ever so much of him in New York. He collected beautiful things, pictures and antiques and objects that he sent for to Europe on purpose, many of which were arranged in his rooms at Cambridge. He had intaglios and Spanish altar-cloths and drawings by the old masters. He was different from most others; he seemed to want so much to enjoy life, and to think you easily could if you would only let yourself go. Of course—judging by what *he* had—he appeared to think you required a great many things to keep you up. And then Verena told Olive—she could see it was after a little delay —that he wanted her to come round to his place and see his treasures. He wanted to show them to her, he was so sure she would admire them. Verena was sure also, but she wouldn't go alone, and she wanted Olive to go with her. They would have tea, and there would be other ladies, and Olive would tell her what she thought of a life that was so crowded with beauty. Miss Chancellor made her reflections on all this, and the first of them was that it was happy for her that she had determined for the present to accept these accidents, for otherwise might she not now have had a deeper alarm? She wished to heaven that conceited young men with time on their hands would leave Verena alone; but evidently they wouldn't, and her best safety was in seeing as many as should turn up. If the type should become frequent, she would very soon judge it. If Olive had not been so grim, she would have had a smile to spare for the frankness with which the girl herself adopted this theory. She was eager to explain that Mr. Burrage didn't seem at all to want what poor Mr. Pardon had wanted; he made her talk about her views far more than that gentleman, but gave no sign of offering himself either as a husband or as a lecture-agent. The furthest he had gone as yet was to tell her that he liked her for the same reason that he liked old enamels and old embroideries; and when she said that she didn't see how she resembled such things, he had replied that it was because she was so peculiar and so delicate. She might be peculiar, but she had protested against the idea that she was delicate; it was the last thing that she wanted to be thought; and Olive could see from this how far she was from falling in with everything he said. When Miss Chancellor asked if she respected Mr. Burrage (and how solemn Olive could make that word she by this time knew), she answered, with her sweet, vain laugh, but apparently with perfect good faith, that it didn't matter whether she did or not, for what was the whole thing but simply a phase—the very one they had talked about? The sooner she got through it the better, was it not?—and she seemed to think that her transit would be materially quickened by a visit to Mr. Burrage's rooms. As I say, Verena was pleased to regard the phase as quite inevitable, and she had said more than once to Olive that if their struggle was to be with men, the more they knew about them the better. Miss Chancellor asked her why her mother should not go with her to see the curiosities, since she mentioned that their possessor had not neglected to invite Mrs. Tarrant; and Verena said that this, of course, would be very simple—only her mother wouldn't be able to tell her so well as Olive whether she ought to respect Mr. Burrage. This decision as to whether Mr. Burrage should be respected assumed in the life of these two remarkable young women, pitched in so high a moral key, the proportions of a momentous event. Olive shrank at first from facing it—not, indeed, the decision—for we know that her own mind had long since been made up in regard to the quantity of esteem due to almost any member of the other sex—but the incident itself, which, if Mr. Burrage should exasperate her further, might expose her to the danger of appearing to Verena to be unfair to him. It was her belief that he was playing a deeper game than the young Matthias, and she was very willing to watch him; but she thought it prudent not to attempt to cut short the phase (she adopted that classification) prematurely—an imputation she should incur if, without more delay, she were to "shut down," as Verena said, on the young connoisseur.

It was settled, therefore, that Mrs. Tarrant should, with her daughter, accept Mr. Burrage's invitation; and in a few days these ladies paid a visit to his apartments. Verena subsequently, of course, had much to say about it, but she dilated even more upon her mother's impressions than upon her own. Mrs. Tarrant had carried away a supply which would last her all winter; there had been some New York ladies present who were "on" at that moment, and with whom her intercourse was rich in emotions. She had told them all that she should be happy to see them in her home, but they had not yet picked their way along the little planks of the front yard. Mr. Burrage, at all events, had been quite lovely, and had talked about his collections, which were wonderful, in the most interesting manner. Verena inclined to think he was to be respected. He admitted that he was not really studying law at all; he had only come to Cambridge for the form; but she didn't see why it wasn't enough when you made yourself as pleasant as that. She went so far as to ask Olive whether taste and art were not something, and her friend could see that she was certainly very much involved in the phase. Miss Chancellor, of course, had her answer ready. Taste and art were good when they enlarged the mind, not when they narrowed it. Verena assented to this, and said it remained to be seen what effect they had had upon Mr. Burrage—a remark which led Olive to fear that at such a rate much would remain, especially when Verena told her, later, that another visit to the young man's rooms was projected, and that this time she must come, he having expressed the greatest desire for the honor, and her own wish being greater still that they should look at some of his beautiful things together.

A day or two after this, Mr. Henry Burrage left a card at Miss Chancellor's door, with a note in which he expressed the hope that she would take tea with him on a certain day on which he expected the company of his mother. Olive responded to this invitation, in conjunction with Verena; but in doing so she was in the position, singular for her, of not quite understanding what she was about. It seemed to her strange that Verena should urge her to take such a step when she was free to go without her, and it proved two things: first, that she was much interested in Mr. Henry Burrage, and second, that her nature was extraordinarily beautiful. Could anything, in effect, be less underhand than such an indifference to what she supposed to be the best opportunities for carrying on a flirtation? Verena wanted to know the truth, and it was clear that by this time she believed Olive Chancellor to have it, for the most part, in her keeping. Her insistence, therefore, proved, above all, that she cared more for her friend's opinion of Henry Burrage than for her own—a reminder, certainly, of the responsibility that Olive had incurred in undertaking to form this generous young mind, and of the exalted place that she now occupied in it. Such revelations ought to have been satisfactory; if they failed to be completely so, it was only on account of the elder girl's regret that the subject as to which her judgment was wanted should be a young man destitute of the worst vices. Henry Burrage had contributed to throw Miss Chancellor into a "state," as these young ladies called it, the night she met him at Mrs. Tarrant's; but it had none the less been conveyed to Olive by the voices of the air that he was a gentleman and a good fellow.

This was painfully obvious when the visit to his rooms took place; he was so good-humored, so amusing, so friendly and considerate, so attentive to Miss Chancellor, he did the honors of his bachelor-nest with so easy a grace, that Olive, part of the time, sat dumbly shaking her conscience, like a watch that wouldn't go, to make it tell her some better reason why she shouldn't like him. She saw that there would be no difficulty in disliking his mother; but that, unfortunately, would not serve her purpose nearly so well. Mrs. Burrage had come to spend a few days near her son; she was staying at an hotel in Boston. It presented itself to Olive that after this entertainment it would be an act of courtesy to call upon her; but here, at least, was the comfort that she could cover herself with the general absolution extended to the Boston temperament and leave her alone. It was slightly provoking, indeed, that Mrs. Burrage should have so much the air of a New Yorker who didn't particularly notice whether a Bostonian called or not; but there is ever an imperfection, I suppose, in even the sweetest revenge. She was a woman of society, large and voluminous, fair (in complexion) and regularly ugly, looking as if she ought to be slow and rather heavy, but disappointing this expectation by a quick, amused utterance, a short, bright, summary laugh, with which she appeared to dispose of the joke (whatever it was) forever, and an air of recognizing on the instant everything she saw and heard. She was evidently accustomed to talk, and even to listen, if not kept waiting too long for details and parentheses; she was not continuous, but frequent, as it were, and you could see that she hated explanations, though it was not to be supposed that she had anything to fear from them. Her favors were general, not particular; she was civil enough to everyone, but not in any case endearing, and perfectly genial without being confiding, as people were in Boston when (in moments of exaltation) they wished to mark that they were not suspicious. There was something in her whole manner which seemed to say to Olive that she belonged to a larger world than hers; and our young lady was vexed at not hearing that she had lived for a good many years in Europe, as this would have made it easy to classify her as one of the corrupt. She learned, almost with a sense of injury, that neither the mother nor the son had been longer beyond the seas than she herself; and if they were to be judged as triflers they must be dealt with individually. Was it an aid to such a judgment to see that Mrs. Burrage was very much pleased with Boston, with Harvard College, with her son's interior, with her cup of tea (it was old Sèvres), which was not half so bad as she had expected, with the company he had asked to meet her (there were three or four gentlemen, one of whom was Mr. Gracie), and, last, not least, with Verena Tarrant, whom she addressed as a celebrity, kindly, cleverly, but without maternal tenderness or anything to mark the difference in their age? She spoke to her as if they were equals in that respect, as if Verena's genius and fame would make up the disparity, and the girl had no need of encouragement and patronage. She made no direct allusion, however, to her particular views, and asked her no question about her "gift"—an omission which Verena thought strange, and, with the most speculative candor, spoke of to Olive afterwards. Mrs. Burrage seemed to imply that every one present had some distinction and some talent, that they were all good company together. There was nothing in her manner to indicate that she was afraid of Verena on her son's account; she didn't resemble a person who would like him to marry the daughter of a mesmeric healer, and yet she appeared to think it charming that he should have such a young woman there to give gusto to her hour at Cambridge. Poor Olive was, in the nature of things, entangled in contradictions; she had a horror of the idea of Verena's marrying Mr. Burrage, and yet she was angry when his mother demeaned herself as if the little girl with red hair, whose freshness she enjoyed, could not be a serious danger. She saw all this through the blur of her shyness, the conscious, anxious silence to which she was so much of the time condemned. It may therefore be imagined how sharp her vision would have been could she only have taken the situation more simply; for she was intelligent enough not to have needed to be morbid, even for purposes of self-defense.

I must add, however, that there was a moment when she came near being happy—or, at any rate, reflected that it was a pity she could not be so. Mrs. Burrage asked her son to play "some little thing," and he sat down to his piano and revealed a talent that might well have gratified that lady's pride. Olive was extremely susceptible to music, and it was impossible to her not to be soothed and beguiled by the young man's charming art. One "little thing" succeeded another; his selections were all very happy. His guests sat scattered in the red firelight, listening, silent, in comfortable attitudes; there was a faint fragrance from the burning logs, which mingled with the perfume of Schubert and Mendelssohn; the covered lamps made a glow here and there, and the cabinets and brackets produced brown shadows, out of which some precious object gleamed—some ivory carving or cinque-cento cup. It was given to Olive, under these circumstances, for half an hour, to surrender herself, to enjoy the music, to admit that Mr. Burrage played with exquisite taste, to feel as if the situation were a kind of truce. Her nerves were calmed, her problems—for the time—subsided. Civilization, under such an influence, in such a setting, appeared to have done its work; harmony ruled the scene; human life ceased to be a battle. She went so far as to ask herself why one should have a quarrel with it; the relations of men and women, in that picturesque grouping, had not the air of being internecine. In short, she had an interval of unexpected rest, during which she kept her eyes mainly on Verena, who sat near Mrs. Burrage, letting herself go, evidently, more completely than Olive. To her, too, music was a delight, and her listening face turned itself to different parts of the room, unconsciously, while her eyes vaguely rested on the *bibelots* that emerged into the fire-light. At moments Mrs. Burrage bent her countenance upon her and smiled, at random, kindly; and then Verena smiled back, while her expression seemed to say that, oh yes, she was giving up everything, all principles, all projects. Even before it was time to go, Olive felt that they were both (Verena and she) quite demoralized, and she only summoned energy to take her companion away when she heard Mrs. Burrage propose to her to come and spend a fortnight in New York. Then Olive exclaimed to herself, "Is it a plot? Why in the world can't they let her alone?" and prepared to throw a fold of her mantle, as she had done before, over her young friend. Verena answered, somewhat impetuously, that she should be delighted to visit Mrs. Burrage; then checked her impetuosity, after a glance from Olive, by adding that perhaps this lady wouldn't ask her if she knew what strong ground she took on the emancipation of women. Mrs. Burrage looked at her son and laughed; she said she was perfectly aware of Verena's views, and that it was impossible to be more in sympathy with them than she herself. She took the greatest interest in the emancipation of women; she thought there was so much to be done. These were the only remarks that passed in reference to the great subject; and nothing more was said to Verena, either by Henry Burrage or by his friend Gracie, about her addressing the Harvard students. Verena had told her father that Olive had put her veto upon that, and Tarrant had said to the young men that it seemed as if Miss Chancellor was going to put the thing through in her own way. We know that he thought this way very circuitous; but Miss Chancellor made him feel that she was in earnest, and that idea frightened the resistance out of him—it had such terrible associations. The people he had ever seen who were most in earnest were a committee of gentlemen who had investigated the phenomena of the "materialization" of spirits, some ten years before, and had bent the fierce light of the scientific method upon him. To Olive it appeared that Mr. Burrage and Mr. Gracie had ceased to be jocular; but that did not make them any less cynical. Henry Burrage said to Verena, as she was going, that he hoped she would think seriously of his mother's invitation; and she replied that she didn't know whether she should have much time in the future to give to people who already approved of her views: she expected to have her hands full with the others, who didn't.

"Does your scheme of work exclude all distraction, all recreation, then?" the young man inquired; and his look expressed real suspense.

Verena referred the matter, as usual, with her air of bright, ungrudging deference, to her companion. "Does it, should you say—our scheme of work?"

"I am afraid the distraction we have had this afternoon must last us for a long time," Olive said, without harshness, but with considerable majesty.

"Well, now, *is* he to be respected?" Verena demanded, as the two young women took their way through the early darkness, pacing quietly side by side, in their winter robes, like women consecrated to some holy office.

Olive turned it over a moment. "Yes, very much—as a pianist!"

Verena went into town with her in the horsecar—she was staying in Charles Street for a few days—and that evening she startled Olive by breaking out into a reflection very similar to the whimsical falterings of which she herself had been conscious while they sat in Mr. Burrage's pretty rooms, but against which she had now violently reacted.

"It would be very nice to do that always—just to take men as they are, and not to have to think about their badness. It would be very nice not to have so many questions, but to think they were all comfortably answered, so that one could sit there on an old Spanish leather chair, with the curtains drawn and keeping out the cold, the darkness, all the big, terrible, cruel world—sit there and listen for ever to Schubert and Mendelssohn. *They* didn't care anything about female suffrage! And I didn't feel the want of a vote today at all, did you?" Verena inquired, ending, as she always ended in these few speculations, with an appeal to Olive.

This young lady thought it necessary to give her a very firm answer. "I always feel it—everywhere—night and day. I feel it *here*"; and Olive laid her hand solemnly on her heart. "I feel it as a deep, unforgettable wrong; I feel it as one feels a stain that is on one's honor."

Verena gave a clear laugh, and after that a soft sigh, and then said, "Do you know, Olive, I sometimes wonder whether, if it wasn't for you, I should feel it so very much!"

"My own friend," Olive replied, "you have never yet said anything to me which expressed so clearly the closeness and sanctity of our union."

"You do keep me up," Verena went on. "You are my conscience."

"I should like to be able to say that you are my form—my envelope. But you are too beautiful for that!" So Olive returned her friend's compliment; and later she said that, of course, it would be far easier to give up everything and draw the curtains to and pass one's life in an artificial atmosphere, with rose-colored lamps. It would be far easier to abandon the struggle, to leave all the unhappy women of the world to their immemorial misery, to lay down one's burden, close one's eyes to the whole dark picture, and, in short, simply expire. To this Verena objected that it would not be easy for her to expire at all; that such an idea was darker than anything the world contained; that she had not done with life yet, and that she didn't mean to allow her responsibilities to crush her. And then the two young women concluded, as they had concluded before, by finding themselves completely, inspiringly in agreement, full of the purpose to live indeed, and with high success; to become great, in order not to be obscure, and powerful, in order not to be useless. Olive had often declared before that her conception of life was as something sublime or as nothing at all. The world was full of evil, but she was glad to have been born before it had been swept away, while it was still there to face, to give one a task and a reward. When the great reforms should be consummated, when the day of justice should have dawned, would not life perhaps be rather poor and pale? She had never pretended to deny that the hope of fame, of the very highest distinction, was one of her strongest incitements; and she held that the most effective way of protesting against the state of bondage of women was for an individual member of the sex to become illustrious. A person who might have overheard some of the talk of this possibly infatuated pair would have been touched by their extreme familiarity with the idea of earthly glory. Verena had not invented it, but she had taken it eagerly from her friend, and she returned it with interest. To Olive it appeared that just this partnership of their two minds—each of them, by itself, lacking an important group of facets—made an organic whole which, for the work in hand, could not fail to be brilliantly effective. Verena was often far more irresponsive than she liked to see her; but the happy thing in her composition was that, after a short contact with the divine idea—Olive was always trying to flash it at her, like a jewel in an uncovered case—she kindled, flamed up, took the words from her friend's less persuasive lips, resolved herself into a magical voice, became again the pure young sibyl. Then Olive perceived how fatally, without Verena's tender notes, her crusade would lack sweetness, what the Catholics call unction; and, on the other hand, how weak Verena would be on the statistical and logical side if she herself should not bring up the rear. Together, in short, they would be complete, they would have everything, and together they would triumph.

19

This idea of their triumph, a triumph as yet ultimate and remote, but preceded by the solemn vista of an effort so religious as never to be wanting in ecstasy, became tremendously familiar to the two friends, but especially to Olive, during the winter of 187-, a season which ushered in the most momentous period of Miss Chancellor's life. About Christmas a step was taken which advanced her affairs immensely, and put them, to her apprehension, on a regular footing. This consisted in Verena's coming in to Charles Street to stay with her, in pursuance of an arrangement on Olive's part with Selah Tarrant and his wife that she should remain for many months. The coast was now perfectly clear. Mrs. Farrinder had started on her annual grand tour; she was rousing the people, from Maine to Texas; Matthias Pardon (it was to be supposed) had received, temporarily at least, his quietus; and Mrs. Luna was established in New York, where she had taken a house for a year, and whence she wrote to her sister that she was going to engage Basil Ransom (with whom she was in communication for this purpose) to do her law business. Olive wondered what law business Adeline could have, and hoped she would get into a pickle with her landlord or her milliner, so that repeated interviews with Mr. Ransom might become necessary. Mrs. Luna let her know very soon that these interviews had begun; the young Mississippian had come to dine with her; he hadn't got started much, by what she could make out, and she was even afraid that he didn't dine every day. But he wore a tall hat now, like a Northern gentleman, and Adeline intimated that she found him really attractive. He had been very nice to Newton, told him all about the war (quite the Southern version, of course, but Mrs. Luna didn't care anything about American politics, and she wanted her son to know all sides), and Newton did nothing but talk about him, calling him "Rannie," and imitating his pronunciation of certain words. Adeline subsequently wrote that she had made up her mind to put her affairs into his hands (Olive sighed, not unmagnanimously, as she thought of her sister's "affairs"), and later still she mentioned that she was thinking strongly of taking him to be Newton's tutor. She wished this interesting child to be privately educated, and it would be more agreeable to have in that relation a person who was already, as it were, a member of the family. Mrs. Luna wrote as if he were prepared to give up his profession to take charge of her son, and Olive was pretty sure that this was only a part of her grandeur, of the habit she had contracted, especially since living in Europe, of speaking as if in every case she required special arrangements.

In spite of the difference in their age, Olive had long since judged her, and made up her mind that Adeline lacked every quality that a person needed to be interesting in her eyes. She was rich (or sufficiently so), she was conventional and timid, very fond of attentions from men (with whom indeed she was reputed bold, but Olive scorned such boldness as that), given up to a merely personal, egotistical, instinctive life, and as unconscious of the tendencies of the age, the revenges of the future, the new truths and the great social questions, as if she had been a mere bundle of dress-trimmings, which she very nearly was. It was perfectly observable that she had no conscience, and it irritated Olive deeply to see how much trouble a woman was spared when she was constructed on that system. Adeline's "affairs," as I have intimated, her social relations, her views of Newton's education, her practice and her theory (for she had plenty of that, such as it was, heaven save the mark!), her spasmodic disposition to marry again, and her still sillier retreats in the presence of danger (for she had not even the courage of her frivolity), these things had been a subject of tragic consideration to Olive ever since the return of the elder sister to America. The tragedy was not in any particular harm that Mrs. Luna could do her (for she did her good, rather, that is, she did her honor, by laughing at her), but in the spectacle itself, the drama, guided by the hand of fate, of which the small, ignoble scenes unrolled themselves so logically. The *dénouement* would of course be in keeping, and would consist simply of the spiritual death of Mrs. Luna, who would end by understanding no common speech of Olive's at all, and would sink into mere worldly plumpness, into the last complacency, the supreme imbecility, of petty, genteel conservatism. As for Newton, he would be more utterly odious, if possible, as he grew up, than he was already; in fact, he would not grow up at all, but only grow down, if his mother should continue her infatuated system with him. He was insufferably forward and selfish; under the pretext of keeping him, at any cost, refined, Adeline had coddled and caressed him, having him always in her petticoats, remitting his lessons when he pretended he had an earache, drawing him into the conversation, letting him answer her back, with an impertinence beyond his years, when she administered the smallest check. The place for him, in Olive's eyes, was one of the public schools, where the children of the people would teach him his small importance, teach it, if necessary, by the aid of an occasional drubbing; and the two ladies had a grand discussion on this point before Mrs. Luna left Boston—a scene which ended in Adeline's clutching the irrepressible Newton to her bosom (he came in at the moment), and demanding of him a vow that he would live and die in the principles of his mother. Mrs. Luna declared that if she must be trampled upon—and very likely it was her fate!—she would rather be trampled upon by men than by women, and that if Olive and her friends should get possession of the government they would be worse despots than those who were celebrated in history. Newton took an infant oath that he would never be a destructive, impious radical, and Olive felt that after this she needn't trouble herself any more about her sister, whom she simply committed to her fate. That fate might very properly be to marry an enemy of her country, a man who, no doubt, desired to treat women with the lash and manacles, as he and his people had formerly treated the wretched colored race. If she was so fond of the fine old institutions of the past, he would supply them to her in abundance; and if she wanted so much to be a conservative, she could try first how she liked being a conservative's wife. If Olive troubled herself little about Adeline, she troubled herself more about Basil Ransom; she said to herself that since he hated women who respected themselves (and each other), destiny would use him rightly in hanging a person like Adeline round his neck. That would be the way poetic justice ought to work, for him—and the law that our prejudices, when they act themselves out, punish us in doing so. Olive considered all this, as it was her effort to consider everything, from a very high point of view, and ended by feeling sure it was not for the sake of any nervous personal security that she desired to see her two relations in New York get mixed up together. If such an event as their marriage would gratify her sense of fitness, it would be simply as an illustration of certain laws. Olive, thanks to the philosophic cast of her mind, was exceedingly fond of illustrations of laws.

I hardly know, however, what illumination it was that sprang from her consciousness (now a source of considerable comfort), that Mrs. Farrinder was carrying the war into distant territories, and would return to Boston only in time to preside at a grand Female Convention, already advertised to take place in Boston in the month of June. It was agreeable to her that this imperial woman should be away; it made the field more free, the air more light; it suggested an exemption from official criticism. I have not taken space to mention certain episodes of the more recent intercourse of these ladies, and must content myself with tracing them, lightly, in their consequences. These may be summed up in the remark, which will doubtless startle no one by its freshness, that two imperial women are scarcely more likely to hit it off together, as the phrase is, than two imperial men. Since that party at Miss Birdseye's, so important in its results for Olive, she had had occasion to approach Mrs. Farrinder more nearly, and those overtures brought forth the knowledge that the great leader of the feminine revolution was the one person (in that part of the world) more concentrated, more determined, than herself. Miss Chancellor's aspirations, of late, had been immensely quickened; she had begun to believe in herself to a livelier tune than she had ever listened to before; and she now perceived that when spirit meets spirit there must either be mutual absorption or a sharp concussion. It had long been familiar to her that she should have to count with the obstinacy of the world at large, but she now discovered that she should have to count also with certain elements in the feminine camp. This complicated the problem, and such a complication, naturally, could not make Mrs. Farrinder appear more easy to assimilate. If Olive's was a high nature and so was hers, the fault was in neither; it was only an admonition that they were not needed as landmarks in the same part of the field. If such perceptions are delicate as between men, the reader need not be reminded of the exquisite form they may assume in natures more refined. So it was that Olive passed, in three months, from the stage of veneration to that of competition; and the process had been accelerated by the introduction of Verena into the fold. Mrs. Farrinder had behaved in the strangest way about Verena. First she had been struck with her, and then she hadn't; first she had seemed to want to take her in, then she had shied at her unmistakably—intimating to Olive that there were enough of that kind already. Of "that kind" indeed!—the phrase reverberated in Miss Chancellor's resentful soul. Was it possible she didn't know the kind Verena was of, and with what vulgar aspirants to notoriety did she confound her? It had been Olive's original desire to obtain Mrs. Farrinder's stamp for her *protégée,* she wished her to hold a commission from the commander-in-chief. With this view the two young women had made more than one pilgrimage to Roxbury, and on one of these occasions the sibylline mood (in its most charming form) had descended upon Verena. She had fallen into it, naturally and gracefully, in the course of talk, and poured out a stream of eloquence even more touching than her regular discourse at Miss Birdseye's. Mrs. Farrinder had taken it rather drily, and certainly it didn't resemble her own style of oratory, remarkable and cogent as this was. There had been considerable question of her writing a letter to the New York *Tribune,* the effect of which should be to launch Miss Tarrant into renown; but this beneficent epistle never appeared, and now Olive saw that there was no favor to come from the prophetess of Roxbury. There had been primnesses, pruderies, small reserves, which ended by staying her pen. If Olive didn't say at once that she was jealous of Verena's more attractive manner, it was only because such a declaration was destined to produce more effect a little later. What she did say was that evidently Mrs. Farrinder wanted to keep the movement in her own hands—viewed with suspicion certain romantic, aesthetic elements which Olive and Verena seemed to be trying to introduce into it. They insisted so much, for instance, on the historic unhappiness of women; but Mrs. Farrinder didn't appear to care anything for that, or indeed to know much about history at all. She seemed to begin just today, and she demanded their rights for them whether they were unhappy or not. The upshot of this was that Olive threw herself on Verena's neck with a movement which was half indignation, half rapture; she exclaimed that they would have to fight the battle without human help, but, after all, ⌐ better so. If they were all in all to each other, what ⌐uld they want? They would be isolated, but they would be free; and this view of the situation brought with it a feeling that they had almost already begun to be a force. It was not, indeed, that Olive's resentment faded quite away; for not only had she the sense, doubtless very presumptuous, that Mrs. Farrinder was the only person thereabouts of a stature to judge her (a sufficient cause of antagonism in itself, for if we like to be praised by our betters we prefer that censure should come from the other sort), but the kind of opinion she had unexpectedly betrayed, after implying such esteem in the earlier phase of their intercourse, made Olive's cheeks occasionally flush. She prayed heaven that *she* might never become so personal, so narrow. She was frivolous, worldly, an amateur, a trifler, a frequenter of Beacon Street; her taking up Verena Tarrant was only a kind of elderly, ridiculous doll-dressing: this was the light in which Miss Chancellor had reason to believe that it now suited Mrs. Farrinder to regard her! It was fortunate, perhaps, that the misrepresentation was so gross; yet, none the less, tears of wrath rose more than once to Olive's eyes when she reflected that this particular wrong had been put upon her. Frivolous, worldly, Beacon Street! She appealed to Verena to share in her pledge that the world should know in due time how much of that sort of thing there was about her. As I have already hinted, Verena at such moments quite rose to the occasion; she had private pangs at committing herself to give the cold shoulder to Beacon Street forever; but she was now so completely in Olive's hands that there was no sacrifice to which she would not have consented in order to prove that her benefactress was not frivolous.

The matter of her coming to stay for so long in Charles Street was arranged during a visit that Selah Tarrant paid there at Miss Chancellor's request. This interview, which had some curious features, would be worth describing, but I am forbidden to do more than mention the most striking of these. Olive wished to have an understanding with him; wished the situation to be clear, so that, disagreeable as it would be to her to receive him, she sent him a summons for a certain hour—an hour at which she had planned that Verena should be out of the house. She withheld this incident from the girl's knowledge, reflecting with some solemnity that it was the first deception (for Olive her silence was a deception) that she had yet practiced on her friend, and wondering whether she should have to practice others in the future. She then and there made up her mind that she would not shrink from others should they be necessary. She notified Tarrant that she should keep Verena a long time, and Tarrant remarked that it was certainly very pleasant to see her so happily located. But he also intimated that he should like to know what Miss Chancellor laid out to do with her; and the tone of this suggestion made Olive feel how right she had been to forsee that their interview would have the stamp of business. It assumed that complexion very definitely when she crossed over to her desk and wrote Mr. Tarrant a check for a very considerable amount. "Leave us alone—entirely alone—for a year, and then I will write you another": it was with these words she handed him the little strip of paper that meant so much, feeling, as she did so, that surely Mrs. Farrinder herself could not be less amateurish than that. Selah looked at the check, at Miss Chancellor, at the check again, at the ceiling, at the floor, at the clock, and once more at his hostess; then the document disappeared beneath the folds of his waterproof, and she saw that he was putting it into some queer place on his queer person. "Well, if I didn't believe you were going to help her to develop," he remarked; and he stopped, while his hands continued to fumble, out of sight, and he treated Olive to his large joyless smile. She assured him that he need have no fear on that score; Verena's development was the thing in the world in which she took most interest; she should have every opportunity for a free expansion. "Yes, that's the great thing," Selah said; "it's more important than attracting a crowd. That's all we shall ask of you; let her act out her nature. Don't all the trouble of humanity come from our being pressed back? Don't shut

down the cover, Miss Chancellor; just let her overflow!"
And again Tarrant illuminated his inquiry, his metaphor, by
the strange and silent lateral movement of his jaws. He
added, presently, that he supposed he should have to fix it
with Mis' Tarrant; but Olive made no answer to that; she
only looked at him with a face in which she intended to
express that there was nothing that need detain him longer.
She knew it had been fixed with Mrs. Tarrant; she had been
over all that with Verena, who had told her that her mother
was willing to sacrifice her for her highest good. She had
reason to know (not through Verena, of course), that Mrs.
Tarrant had embraced, tenderly, the idea of a pecuniary
compensation, and there was no fear of her making a scene
when Tarrant should come back with a check in his pocket.
"Well, I trust she *may* develop, richly, and that you may
accomplish what you desire; it seems as if we had only a
little way to go further," that worthy observed, as he
erected himself for departure.

"It's not a little way; it's a very long way," Olive replied,
rather sternly.

Tarrant was on the threshold; he lingered a little, embarrassed by her grimness, for he himself had always inclined to rose-colored views of progress, of the march of
truth. He had never met any one so much in earnest as
this definite, literal young woman, who had taken such an
unhoped-for fancy to his daughter; whose longing for the
new day had such perversities of pessimism, and who, in
the midst of something that appeared to be terribly searching in her honesty, was willing to corrupt him, as a father,
with the most extravagant orders on her bank. He hardly
knew in what language to speak to her; it seemed as if
there was nothing soothing enough, when a lady adopted
that tone about a movement which was thought by some of
the brightest to be so promising. "Oh, well, I guess there's
some kind of mysterious law . . ." he murmured, almost
timidly; and so he passed from Miss Chancellor's sight.

20

She hoped she should not soon see him again, and there
appeared to be no reason she should, if their intercourse
was to be conducted by means of checks. The understanding with Verena was, of course, complete; she had promised
to stay with her friend as long as her friend should require
it. She had said at first that she couldn't give up her mother,
but she had been made to feel that there was no question
of giving up. She should be as free as air, to go and come;
she could spend hours and days with her mother, whenever
Mrs. Tarrant required her attention; all that Olive asked
of her was that, for the time, she should regard Charles
Street as her home. There was no struggle about this, for
the simple reason that by the time the question came to
the front Verena was completely under the charm. The idea
of Olive's charm will perhaps make the reader smile; but
I use the word not in its derived, but in its literal sense.
The fine web of authority, of dependence, that her strenuous companion had woven about her, was now as dense as
a suit of golden mail; and Verena was thoroughly interested
in their great undertaking; she saw it in the light of an active,
enthusiastic faith. The benefit that her father desired for
her was now assured; she expanded, developed, on the most
liberal scale. Olive saw the difference, and you may imagine
how she rejoiced in it; she had never known a greater
pleasure. Verena's former attitude had been girlish submission, grateful, curious sympathy. She had given herself,

in her young, amused surprise, because Olive's stronger will and the incisive proceedings with which she pointed her purpose drew her on. Besides, she was held by hospitality, the vision of new social horizons, the sense of novelty, and the love of change. But now the girl was disinterestedly attached to the precious things they were to do together; she cared about them for themselves, believed in them ardently, had them constantly in mind. Her share in the union of the two young women was no longer passive, purely appreciative; it was passionate, too, and it put forth a beautiful energy. If Olive desired to get Verena into training, she could flatter herself that the process had already begun, and that her colleague enjoyed it almost as much as she. Therefore she could say to herself, without the imputation of heartlessness, that when she left her mother it was for a noble, a sacred use. In point of fact, she left her very little, and she spent hours in jingling, aching, jostled journeys between Charles Street and the stale suburban cottage. Mrs. Tarrant sighed and grimaced, wrapped herself more than ever in her mantle, said she didn't know as she was fit to struggle alone, and that, half the time, if Verena was away, she wouldn't have the nerve to answer the doorbell; she was incapable, of course, of neglecting such an opportunity to posture as one who paid with her heart's blood for leading the van of human progress. But Verena had an inner sense (she judged her mother now, a little, for the first time), that she would be sorry to be taken at her word, and that she felt safe enough in trusting to her daughter's generosity. She could not divest herself of the faith—even now that Mrs. Luna was gone, leaving no trace, and the gray walls of a sedentary winter were apparently closing about the two young women—she could not renounce the theory that a residence in Charles Street must at least produce some contact with the brilliant classes. She was vexed at her daughter's resignation to not going to parties and to Miss Chancellor's not giving them; but it was nothing new for her to have to practice patience, and she could feel, at least, that it was just as handy for Mr. Burrage to call on the child in town, where he spent half his time, sleeping constantly at Parker's.

It was a fact that this fortunate youth called very often, and Verena saw him with Olive's full concurrence whenever she was at home. It had now been quite agreed between them that no artificial limits should be set to the famous phase; and Olive had, while it lasted, a sense of real heroism in steeling herself against uneasiness. It seemed to her, moreover, only justice that she should make some concession; if Verena made a great sacrifice of filial duty in coming to live with her (this, of course, should be permanent—she would buy off the Tarrants from year to year), she must not incur the imputation (the world would judge her, in that case, ferociously) of keeping her from forming common social ties. The friendship of a young man and a young woman was, according to the pure code of New England, a common social tie; and as the weeks elapsed Miss Chancellor saw no reason to repent of her temerity. Verena was not falling in love; she felt that she should know it, should guess it on the spot. Verena was fond of human intercourse; she was essentially a sociable creature; she liked to shine and smile and talk and listen; and so far as Henry Burrage was concerned he introduced an element of easy and convenient relaxation into a life now a good deal stiffened (Olive was perfectly willing to own it) by great civic purposes. But the girl was being saved, without interference, by the simple operation of her interest in those very designs. From this time there was no need of putting pressure on her; her own springs were working; the fire with which she glowed came from within. Sacredly, brightly single she would remain; her only espousals would be at the altar of a great cause. Olive always absented herself when Mr. Burrage was announced; and when Verena afterwards attempted to give some account of his conversation she checked her, said she would rather know nothing about it—all with a very solemn mildness; this made her feel very superior, truly noble. She knew by this time (I scarcely can tell how, since Verena could give her no report), exactly what sort of a youth Mr. Burrage was: he was weakly pretentious, softly original, cultivated eccentricity, patronized progress, liked to have mysteries, sudden appointments to keep, anonymous persons to visit, the air of leading a double life, of being devoted to a girl whom people didn't know, or at least didn't meet. Of course he liked to make an impression on Verena; but what he mainly liked was to play her off upon the other girls, the daughters of fashion, with whom he danced at Papanti's. Such were the images that proceeded from Olive's rich moral consciousness. "Well, he *is* greatly interested in our movement": so much Verena once managed to announce; but the words rather irritated Miss Chancellor, who, as we know, did not care to allow for accidental exceptions in the great masculine conspiracy.

In the month of March Verena told her that Mr. Burrage was offering matrimony—offering it with much insistence, begging that she would at least wait and think of it before giving him a final answer. Verena was evidently very glad to be able to say to Olive that she had assured him she couldn't think of it, and that if he expected this he had better not come any more. He continued to come, and it was therefore to be supposed that he had ceased to count on such a concession; it was now Olive's opinion that he really didn't desire it. She had a theory that he proposed to almost any girl who was not likely to accept him—did it because he was making a collection of such episodes—a mental album of declarations, blushes, hesitations, refusals that just missed imposing themselves as acceptances, quite as he collected enamels and Cremona violins. He would be very sorry indeed to ally himself to the house of Tarrant; but such a fear didn't prevent him from holding it becoming in a man of taste to give that encouragement to low-born girls who were pretty, for one looked out for the special cases in which, for reasons (even the lowest might have reasons), they wouldn't "rise." "I told you I wouldn't marry him, and I won't," Verena said, delightedly, to her friend; her tone suggested that a certain credit belonged to her for the way she carried out her assurance. "I never thought you would, if you didn't want to," Olive replied to this; and Verena could have no rejoinder but the good-humor that sat in her eyes, unable as she was to say that she had wanted to. They had a little discussion, however, when she intimated that she pitied him for his discomfiture, Olive's contention being that, selfish, conceited, pampered and insincere, he might properly be left now to digest his affront. Miss Chancellor felt none of the remorse now that she would have felt six months before at standing in the way of such a chance for Verena, and she would have been very angry if any one had asked her if she were not afraid of taking too much upon herself. She would have said, moreover, that she stood in no one's way, and that even if she were not there Verena would never think seriously of a frivolous little man who fiddled while Rome was burning. This did not prevent Olive from making up her mind that they had better go to Europe in the spring; a year's residence in that quarter of the globe would be highly agreeable to Verena, and might even contribute to the evolution of her genius. It cost Miss Chancellor an effort to admit that any virtue still lingered in the elder world, and that it could have any important lesson for two such good Americans as her friend and herself; but it suited her just then to make this assumption, which was not altogether sincere. It was recommended by the idea that it would get her companion out of the way—out of the way of officious fellow-citizens—till she should be absolutely firm on her feet, and would also give greater intensity to their own long conversation. On that continent of strangers they would cleave more closely still to each other. This, of course, would be to fly before the inevitable "phase," much more than to face it; but Olive decided that if they should reach unscathed the term of their delay (the first of July) she should have faced it as much as either justice or generosity demanded. I may as well say at once that she traversed most of this period without further serious alarms and with a great many little thrills of bliss and hope.

Nothing happened to dissipate the good omens with which her partnership with Verena Tarrant was at present surrounded. They threw themselves into study; they had innumerable big books from the Athenaeum, and consumed the midnight oil. Henry Burrage, after Verena had shaken her head at him so sweetly and sadly, returned to New York, giving no sign; they only heard that he had taken refuge under the ruffled maternal wing. (Olive, at least, took for granted the wing was ruffled; she could fancy how Mrs. Burrage would be affected by the knowledge that her son had been refused by the daughter of a mesmeric healer. She would be almost as angry as if she had learnt that he had been accepted.) Matthias Pardon had not yet taken his revenge in the newspapers; he was perhaps nursing his thunderbolts; at any rate, now that the operatic season had begun, he was much occupied in interviewing the principal singers, one of whom he described in one of the leading journals (Olive, at least, was sure it was only he who could write like that), as " a dear little woman with baby dimples and kittenish movements." The Tarrants were apparently given up to a measure of sensual ease with which they had not hitherto been familiar, thanks to the increase of income that they drew from their eccentric protectress. Mrs. Tarrant now enjoyed the ministrations of a "girl"; it was partly her pride (at any rate, she chose to give it this turn), that her house had for many years been conducted without the element—so debasing on both sides—of servile, mercenary labor. She wrote to Olive (she was perpetually writing to her now, but Olive never answered), that she was conscious of having fallen to a lower plane, but she admitted that it was a prop to her wasted spirit to have some one to converse with when Selah was off. Verena, of course, perceived the difference, which was inadequately explained by the theory of a sudden increase of her father's practice (nothing of her father's had ever increased like that), and ended by guessing the cause of it—a discovery which did not in the least disturb her equanimity. She accepted the idea that her parents should receive a pecuniary tribute from the extraordinary friend whom she had encountered on the threshold of womanhood, just as she herself accepted that friend's irresistible hospitality. She had no worldly pride, no traditions of independence, no ideas of what was done and what was not done; but there was only one thing that equalled this perfectly gentle and natural insensibility to favors— namely, the inveteracy of her habit of not asking them. Olive had had an apprehension that she would flush a little at learning the terms on which they should now be able to pursue their career together; but Verena never changed color; it was either not new or not disagreeable to her that the authors of her being should be bought off, silenced by money, treated as the troublesome of the lower orders are treated when they are not locked up; so that her friend had a perception, after this, that it would probably be impossible in any way ever to offend her. She was too rancorless, too detached from conventional standards, too free from private self-reference. It was too much to say of her that she forgave injuries, since she was not conscious of them; there was in forgiveness a certain arrogance of which she was incapable, and her bright mildness glided over the many traps that life sets for our consistency. Olive had always held that pride was necessary to character, but there was no peculiarity of Verena's that could make her spirit seem less pure. The added luxuries in the little house at Cambridge, which even with their help was still such a penal settlement, made her feel afresh that before she came to the rescue the daughter of that house had traversed a desert of sordid misery. She had cooked and washed and swept and stitched; she had worked harder than any of Miss Chancellor's servants. These things had left no trace upon her person or her mind; everything fresh and fair renewed itself in her with extraordinary facility, everything ugly and tiresome evaporated as soon as it touched her; but Olive deemed that, being what she was, she had a right to immense compensations. In the future she should have exceeding luxury and ease, and Miss Chancellor had no difficulty in persuading herself that persons doing the high intellectual and moral work to which the two young ladies in Charles Street were now committed owed it to themselves, owed it to the groaning sisterhood, to cultivate the best material conditions. She herself was nothing of a sybarite, and she had proved, visiting the alleys and slums of Boston in the service of the Associated Charities, that there was no foulness of disease or misery she feared to look in the face; but her house had always been thoroughly well regulated, she was passionately clean, and she was an excellent woman of business. Now, however, she elevated daintiness to a religion; her interior shone with superfluous friction, with punctuality, with winter roses. Among these soft influences Verena herself bloomed like the flower that attains such perfection in Boston. Olive had always rated high the native refinement of her countrywomen, their latent "adaptability," their talent for accommodating themselves at a glance to changed conditions; but the way her companion rose with the level of the civilization that surrounded her, the way she assimilated all delicacies and absorbed all traditions, left this friendly theory halting behind. The winter days were still, indoors, in Charles Street, and the winter nights secure from interruption. Our two young women had plenty of duties, but Olive had never favored the custom of running in and out. Much conference on social and reformatory topics went forward under her roof, and she received her colleagues—she belonged to twenty associations and committees—only at preappointed hours, which she expected them to observe rigidly. Verena's share in these proceedings was not active; she hovered over them, smiling, listening, dropping occasionally a fanciful though never an idle word, like some gently animated image placed there for good omen. It was understood that her part was before the scenes, not behind; that she was not a prompter, but (potentially, at least) a "popular favorite," and that the work over which Miss Chancellor presided so efficiently was a general preparation of the platform on which, later, her companion would execute the most striking steps.

The western windows of Olive's drawing room, looking over the water, took in the red sunsets of winter; the long, low bridge that crawled, on its staggering posts, across the Charles; the casual patches of ice and snow; the desolate suburban horizons, peeled and made bald by the rigor of the season; the general hard, cold void of the prospect; the extrusion, at Charlestown, at Cambridge, of a few chimneys and steeples, straight, sordid tubes of factories and engine-shops, or spare, heavenward finger of the New England meeting house. There was something inexorable in the poverty of the scene, shameful in the meanness of its details, which gave a collective impression of boards and tin and frozen earth, sheds and rotting piles, railwaylines striding flat across a thoroughfare of puddles, and tracks of the humbler, the universal horsecar, traversing obliquely this path of danger; loose fences, vacant lots, mounds of refuse, yards bestrewn with iron pipes, telegraph poles, and bare wooden backs of places. Verena thought such a view lovely, and she was by no means without excuse when, as the afternoon closed, the ugly picture was tinted with a clear, cold rosiness. The air, in its windless chill, seemed to tinkle like a crystal, the faintest gradations of tone were perceptible in the sky, the west became deep and delicate, everything grew doubly distinct before taking on the dimness of evening. There were pink flushes on snow, "tender" reflections in patches of stiffened marsh, sounds of car-bells, no longer vulgar, but almost silvery, on the long bridge, lonely outlines of distant dusky undulations against the fading glow. These agreeable effects used to light up that end of the drawing room, and Olive often sat at the window with her companion before it was time for the lamp. They admired the sunsets, they rejoiced in the ruddy spots projected upon the parlor wall, they followed the darkening perspective in fanciful excursions. They watched the stellar points come out at last in a colder heaven, and then, shuddering a little, arm in arm, they turned away, with a sense that the winter night was even more cruel than the tyranny of men—turned back to drawn curtains and a brighter fire and a glittering tea-tray and more and more talk about the long martyrdom of women, a subject as to which Olive was inexhaustible and really most interesting. There were some nights of deep snowfall, when Charles Street was white and muffled and the doorbell foredoomed to silence, which seemed little islands of lamplight, of enlarged and intensified vision. They read a great deal of history together, and read it ever with the same thought—that of finding confirmation in it for this idea that their sex had suffered inexpressibly, and that at any moment in the course of human affairs the state of the world would have been so much less horrible (history seemed to them in every way horrible), if women had been able to press down the scale. Verena was full of suggestions which stimulated discussions; it was she, oftenest, who kept in view the fact that a good many women in the past had been intrusted with power and had not always used it amiably, who brought up the wicked queens, the profligate mistresses of kings. These ladies were easily disposed of between the two, and the public crimes of Bloody Mary, the private misdemeanors of Faustina, wife of the pure Marcus Aurelius, were very satisfactorily classified. If the influence of women in the past accounted for every act of virtue that men had happened to achieve, it only made the matter balance properly that the influence of men should explain the casual irregularities of the other sex. Olive could see how few books had passed through Verena's hands, and how little the home of the Tarrants had been a house of reading; but the girl now traversed the fields of literature with her characteristic lightness of step. Everything she turned to or took up became an illustration of the facility, the "giftedness," which Olive, who had so little of it, never ceased to wonder at and prize. Nothing frightened her; she always smiled at it, she could do anything she tried. As she knew how to do other things, she knew how to study; she read quickly and remembered infallibly; could repeat, days afterward, passages that she appeared only to have glanced at. Olive, of course, was more and more happy to think that their cause should have the services of an organization so rare.

All this doubtless sounds rather dry, and I hasten to add that our friends were not always shut up in Miss Chancellor's strenuous parlor. In spite of Olive's desire to keep her precious inmate to herself and to bend her attention upon their common studies, in spite of her constantly reminding Verena that this winter was to be purely educative and that the platitudes of the satisfied and unregenerate would have little to teach her, in spite, in short, of the severe and constant duality of our young women, it must not be supposed that their life had not many personal confluents and tributaries. Individual and original as Miss Chancellor was universally acknowledged to be, she was yet a typical Bostonian, and as a typical Bostonian she could not fail to belong in some degree to a "set." It had been said of her that she was in it but not of it; but she was of it enough to go occasionally into other houses and to receive their occupants in her own. It was her belief that she filled her teapot with the spoon of hospitality, and made a good many select spirits feel that they were welcome under her roof at convenient hours. She had a preference for what she called *real* people, and there were several whose reality she had tested by arts known to herself. This little society was rather suburban and miscellaneous; it was prolific in ladies who trotted about, early and late, with books from the Athenæum nursed behind their muff, or little nosegays of exquisite flowers that they were carrying as presents to each other. Verena, who, when Olive was not with her, indulged in a good deal of desultory contemplation at the window, saw them pass the house in Charles Street, always apparently straining a little, as if they might be too late for something. At almost any time, for she envied their preoccupation, she would have taken the chance with them. Very often, when she described them to her mother, Mrs. Tarrant didn't know who they were; they were even days (she had so many discouragements) when it seemed as if she didn't want to know. So long as they were not someone else, it seemed to be no use that they were themselves; whoever they were, they were sure to have that defect. Even after all her mother's disquisitions Verena had but vague ideas as to whom she would have liked them to be; and it was only when the girl talked of the concerts, to all of which Olive subscribed and conducted her inseparable friend, that Mrs. Tarrant appeared to feel in any degree that her daughter was living up to the standard formed for her in their Cambridge home. As all the world knows, the opportunities in Boston for hearing good music are numerous and excellent, and it had long been Miss Chancellor's practice to cultivate the best. She went in, as the phrase is, for the superior programs, and that high, dim, dignified Music Hall, which has echoed in its time to so much eloquence and so much melody, and of which the very proportions and color seem to teach respect and attention, shed the protection of its illuminated cornice, this winter, upon no faces more intelligently upturned than those of the young women for whom Bach and Beethoven only repeated, in a myriad form, the idea that was always with them. Symphonies and fugues only stimulated their convictions, excited their revolutionary passion, led their imagination further in the direction in which it was always pressing. It lifted them to immeasurable heights; and as they sat looking at the great florid, somber organ, overhanging the bronze statue of Beethoven, they felt that this was the only temple in which the votaries of their creed could worship.

And yet their music was not their greatest joy, for they had two others which they cultivated at least as zealously. One of these was simply the society of old Miss Birdseye.

of whom Olive saw more this winter than she had ever seen before. It had become apparent that her long and beautiful career was drawing to a close, her earnest, unremitting work was over, her old-fashioned weapons were broken and dull. Olive would have liked to hang them up as venerable relics of a patient fight, and this was what she seemed to do when she made the poor lady relate her battles—never glorious and brilliant, but obscure and wastefully heroic—call back the figures of her companions in arms, exhibit her medals and scars. Miss Birdseye knew that her uses were ended; she might pretend still to go about the business of unpopular causes, might fumble for papers in her immemorial satchel and think she had important appointments, might sign petitions, attend conventions, say to Doctor Prance that if she would only make her sleep she should live to see a great many improvements yet; she ached and was weary, growing almost as glad to look back (a great anomaly for Miss Birdseye) as to look forward. She let herself be coddled now by her friends of the new generation; there were days when she seemed to want nothing better than to sit by Olive's fire and ramble on about the old struggles, with a vague, comfortable sense—no physical rapture of Miss Birdseye's could be very acute—of immunity from wet feet, from the draughts that prevail at thin meetings, of independence of streetcars that would probably arrive overflowing; and also a pleased perception, not that she was an example to these fresh lives which began with more advantages than hers, but that she was in some degree an encouragement, as she helped them to measure the way the new truths had advanced—being able to tell them of such a different state of things when she was a young lady, the daughter of a very talented teacher (indeed her mother had been a teacher too), down in Connecticut. She had always had for Olive a kind of aroma of martyrdom, and her battered, unremunerated, unpensioned old age brought angry tears, springing from depths of outraged theory, into Miss Chancellor's eyes. For Verena, too, she was a picturesque humanitary figure. Verena had been in the habit of meeting martyrs from her childhood up, but she had seen none with so many reminiscences as Miss Birdseye, or who had been so nearly scorched by penal fires. She had had escapes, in the early days of abolitionism, which it was a marvel she could tell with so little implication that she had shown courage. She had roamed through certain parts of the South, carrying the Bible to the slave; and more than one of her companions, in the course of these expeditions, had been tarred and feathered. She herself, at one season, had spent a month in a Georgian jail. She had preached temperance in Irish circles where the doctrine was received with missiles; she had interfered between wives and husbands mad with drink; she had taken filthy children, picked up in the street, to her own poor rooms, and had removed their pestilent rags and washed their sore bodies with slippery little hands. In her own person she appeared to Olive and Verena a representative of suffering humanity; the pity they felt for her was part of their pity for all who were weakest and most hardly used; and it struck Miss Chancellor (more especially) that this frumpy little missionary was the last link in a tradition, and that when she should be called away the heroic age of New England life—the age of plain living and high thinking, of pure ideals and earnest effort, of moral passion and noble experiment—would effectually be closed. It was the perennial freshness of Miss Birdseye's faith that had had such a contagion for these modern maidens, the unquenched flame of her transcendentalism, the simplicity of her vision, the way in which, in spite of mistakes, deceptions, the changing fashions of reform, which make the remedies of a previous generation look as ridiculous as their bonnets, the only thing that was still actual for her was the elevation of the species by the reading of Emerson and the frequentation of Tremont Temple. Olive had been active enough, for years, in the city-missions; she too had scoured dirty children, and, in squalid lodging-houses, had gone into rooms where the domestic situation was strained and the noises made the neighbors turn pale. But she reflected that after such exertions she had the refreshment of a pretty house, a drawing room full of flowers, a crackling hearth, where she threw in pine-cones and made them snap, an imported tea-service, a Chickering piano, and the *Deutsche Rundschau;* whereas Miss Birdseye had only a bare, vulgar room, with a hideous flowered carpet (it looked like a dentist's), a cold furnace, the evening-paper, and Doctor Prance. Olive and Verena were present at another of her gatherings before the winter ended; it resembled the occasion that we described at the beginning of this history, with the difference that Mrs. Farrinder was not there to oppress the company with her greatness, and that Verena made a speech without the co-operation of her father. This young lady had delivered herself with even finer effect than before, and Olive could see how much she had gained, in confidence and range of allusion, since the educative process in Charles Street began. Her *motif* was now a kind of unprepared tribute to Miss Birdseye, the fruit of the occasion and of the unanimous tenderness of the younger members of the circle, which made her a willing mouthpiece. She pictured her laborious career, her early associates (Eliza P. Moseley was not neglected as Verena passed), her difficulties and dangers and triumphs, her humanizing effect upon so many, her serene and honored old age—expressed, in short, as one of the ladies said, just the very way they all felt about her. Verena's face brightened and grew triumphant as she spoke, but she brought tears into the eyes of most of the others. It was Olive's opinion that nothing could be more graceful and touching, and she saw that the impression made was now deeper than on the former evening. Miss Birdseye went about with her eighty years of innocence, her undiscriminating spectacles, asking her friends if it wasn't perfectly splendid; she took none of it to herself, she regarded it only as a brilliant expression of Verena's gift. Olive thought, afterwards, that if a collection could only be taken up on the spot, the good lady would be made easy for the rest of her days; then she remembered that most of her guests were as impecunious as herself.

I have intimated that our young friends had a source of fortifying emotion which was distinct from the hours they spent with Beethoven and Bach, or in hearing Miss Birdseye describe Concord as it used to be. This consisted in the wonderful insight they had obtained into the history of feminine anguish. They perused that chapter perpetually and zealously, and they derived from it the purest part of their mission. Olive had pored over it so long, so earnestly, that she was now in complete possession of the subject; it was the one thing in life which she felt she had really mastered. She was able to exhibit it to Verena with the greatest authority and accuracy, to lead her up and down, in and out, through all the darkest and most tortuous passages. We know that she was without belief in her own eloquence, but she was very eloquent when she reminded Verena how the exquisite weakness of women had never been their defense, but had only exposed them to sufferings more acute than masculine grossness can conceive. Their odious partner had trampled upon them from the beginning of time, and their tenderness, their abnegation, had been his opportunity. All the bullied wives, the stricken mothers, the dishonored, deserted maidens who have lived on the earth and longed to leave it, passed and repassed before her eyes, and the interminable dim procession seemed to stretch out a myriad hands to her. She sat with them at their trembling vigils, listened for the tread, the voice, at which they grew pale and sick, walked with them by the dark waters that offered to wash away misery and shame, took with them, even, when the vision grew intense, the last shuddering leap. She had analyzed to an extraordinary fineness their susceptibility, their softness; she knew (or she thought she knew) all the possible tortures of anxiety, of suspense and dread; and she had made up her mind that it was women, in the end, who had paid for everything. In the last resort the whole burden of the human lot came upon them; it pressed upon them far more than on the others, the intolerable load of fate. It was they who sat cramped and chained to receive it; it was they who had done all the waiting and taken all the wounds. The sacrifices, the blood, the tears, the terrors were theirs. Their organism was in itself a challenge to suffering, and men had practiced upon it with an impudence that knew no bounds. As they were the weakest most had been wrung from them, and as they were the most generous they had been most deceived. Olive Chancellor would have rested her case, had it been necessary, on those general facts; and her simple and comprehensive contention was that the peculiar wretchedness which had been the very essence of the feminine lot was a monstrous artificial imposition, crying aloud for redress. She was willing to admit that women, too, could be bad; that there were many about the world who were false, immoral, vile. But their errors were as nothing to their sufferings; they had expiated, in advance, an eternity, if need be, of misconduct. Olive poured forth these views to her listening and responsive friend; she presented them again and again, and there was no light in which they did not seem to palpitate with truth. Verena was immensely wrought upon; a subtle fire passed into her; she was not so hungry for revenge as Olive, but at the last, before they went to Europe (I shall take no place to describe the manner in which she threw herself into that project), she quite agreed with her companion that after so many ages of wrong (it would also be after the European journey) men must take *their* turn, men must pay!

Book Second

21

Basil Ransom lived in New York, rather far to the eastward, and in the upper reaches of the town; he occupied two small shabby rooms in a somewhat decayed mansion which stood next to the corner of the Second Avenue. The corner itself was formed by a considerable grocer's shop, the near neighborhood of which was fatal to any pretensions Ransom and his fellow-lodgers might have had in regard to gentility of situation. The house had a red, rusty face, and faded green shutters, of which the slats were limp and at variance with each other. In one of the lower windows was suspended a fly-blown card, with the words "Table Board" affixed in letters cut (not very neatly) out of colored paper, of graduated tints, and surrounded with a small band of stamped gilt. The two sides of the shop were protected by an immense penthouse shed, which projected over a greasy pavement and was supported by wooden posts fixed in the curbstone. Beneath it, on the dislocated flags, barrels and baskets were freely and picturesquely grouped; an open cellarway yawned beneath the feet of those who might pause to gaze too fondly on the savory wares displayed in the window; a strong odor of smoked fish, combined with a fragrance of molasses, hung about the spot; the pavement, toward the gutters, was fringed with dirty panniers, heaped with potatoes, carrots, and onions; and a smart, bright wagon, with the horse detached from the shafts, drawn up on the edge of the abominable road (it contained holes and ruts a foot deep, and immemorial accumulations of stagnant mud), imparted an idle, rural, pastoral air to a scene otherwise perhaps expressive of a rank civilization. The establishment was of the kind known to New Yorkers as a Dutch grocery; and red-faced, yellow-haired, bare-armed vendors might have been observed to lounge in the doorway. I mention it not on account of any particular influence it may have had on the life or the thought of Basil Ransom, but for old acquaintance sake and that of local color; besides which, a figure is nothing without a setting, and our young man came and went every day, with rather an indifferent, unperceiving step, it is true, among the objects I have briefly designated. One of his rooms was directly above the street-door of the house; such a dormitory, when it is so exiguous, is called in the nomenclature of New York a "hall bedroom." The sitting room, beside it, was slightly larger, and they both commanded a row of tenements no less degenerate than Ransom's own habitation—houses built forty years before, and already sere and superannuated. These were also painted red, and the bricks were accentuated by a white line; they were garnished, on the first floor, with balconies covered with small tin roofs, striped in different colors, and with an elaborate iron lattice-work, which gave them a repressive, cagelike appearance, and caused them slightly to resemble the little boxes for peeping unseen into the street, which are a feature of oriental towns. Such posts of observation commanded a view of the grocery on the corner, of the relaxed and disjointed roadway, enlivened at the curbstone with an occasional ash-barrel or with gas-lamps drooping from the perpendicular, and westward, at the end of the truncated vista, of the fantastic skeleton of the Elevated Railway, overhanging the transverse longitudinal street, which it darkened and smothered with the immeasurable spinal column and myriad clutching paws of an antediluvian monster. If the opportunity were not denied me here, I should like to give some account of Basil Ransom's interior, of certain curious persons of both sexes, for the most part not favorites of fortune, who had found an obscure asylum there; some picture of the crumpled little *table d'hôte,* at two dollars and a half a week, where everything felt sticky, which went forward in the low-ceiled basement, under the conduct of a couple of shuffling negresses, who mingled in the conversation and indulged in low, mysterious chuckles when it took a facetious turn. But we need, in strictness, concern ourselves with it no further than to gather the implication that the young Mississippian, even a year and a half after that momentous visit of his to Boston, had not made his profession very lucrative.

He had been diligent, he had been ambitious, but he had not yet been successful. During the few weeks preceding the moment at which we meet him again, he had even begun to lose faith altogether in his earthly destiny. It became much of a question with him whether success in any form was written there; whether for a hungry young Mississippian, without means, without friends, wanting, too, in the highest energy, the wisdom of the serpent, personal arts and national prestige, the game of life was to be won in New York. He had been on the point of giving it up and returning to the home of his ancestors, where, as he heard from his mother, there was still just a sufficient supply of hot corn-cake to support existence. He had never believed much in his luck, but during the last year it had been guilty of aberrations surprising even to a constant, an imperturbable, victim of fate. Not only had he not extended his connection, but he had lost most of the little business which was an object of complacency to him a twelvemonth before. He had had none but small jobs, and he had made a mess of more than one of them. Such accidents had not had a happy effect upon his reputation; he had been able to perceive that this fair flower may be nipped when it is so tender a bud as scarcely to be palpable. He had formed a partnership with a person who seemed likely to repair some of his deficiencies—a young man from Rhode Island, acquainted, according to his own expression, with the inside track. But this gentleman himself, as it turned out, would have been better for a good deal of remodeling, and Ransom's principal deficiency, which was, after all, that of cash, was not less apparent to him after his colleague, prior to a sudden and unexplained departure for Europe, had drawn the slender accumulations of the firm out of the bank. Ransom sat for hours in his office, waiting for clients who either did not come, or, if they did come, did not seem to find him encouraging, as they usually left him with the remark that they would think what they would do. They thought to little purpose, and seldom reappeared, so that at last he began to wonder whether there were not a prejudice against his Southern complexion. Perhaps they didn't like the way he spoke. If they could show him a better way, he was willing to adopt it; but the manner of New York could not be acquired by precept, and example, somehow, was not in this case contagious. He wondered whether he were stupid and unskilled, and he was finally obliged to confess to himself that he was unpractical.

This confession was in itself a proof of the fact, for nothing could be less fruitful than such a speculation, terminating in such a way. He was perfectly aware that he cared a great deal for the theory, and so his visitors must have thought when they found him, with one of his long legs twisted round the other, reading a volume of De Tocqueville.

That was the kind of reading he liked; he had thought a great deal about social and economical questions, forms of government and the happiness of peoples. The convictions he had arrived at were not such as mix gracefully with the time-honored verities a young lawyer looking out for business is in the habit of taking for granted; but he had to reflect that these doctrines would probably not contribute any more to his prosperity in Mississippi than in New York. Indeed, he scarcely could think of the country where they would be a particular advantage to him. It came home to him that his opinions were stiff, whereas in comparison his effort was lax; and he accordingly began to wonder whether he might not make a living by his opinions. He had always had a desire for public life; to cause one's ideas to be embodied in national conduct appeared to him the highest form of human enjoyment. But there was little enough that was public in his solitary studies, and he asked himself what was the use of his having an office at all, and why he might not as well carry on his profession at the Astor Library, where, in his spare hours and on chance holidays, he did an immense deal of suggestive reading. He took copious notes and memoranda, and these things sometimes shaped themselves in a way that might possibly commend them to the editors of periodicals. Readers perhaps would come, if clients didn't; so he produced, with a great deal of labor, half a dozen articles, from which, when they were finished, it seemed to him that he had omitted all the points he wished most to make, and addressed them to the powers that preside over weekly and monthly publications. They were all declined with thanks, and he would have been forced to believe that the accent of his linguid clime brought him luck as little under the pen as on the lips, had not another explanation been suggested by one of the more explicit of his oracles, in relation to a paper on the rights of minorities. This gentleman pointed out that his doctrines were about three hundred years behind the age; doubtless some magazine of the sixteenth century would have been very happy

193

to print them. This threw light on his own suspicion that he was attached to causes that could only, in the nature of things, be unpopular. The disagreeable editor was right about his being out of date, only he had got the time wrong. He had come centuries too soon; he was not too old, but too new. Such an impression, however, would not have prevented him from going into politics, if there had been any other way to represent constituencies than by being elected. People might be found eccentric enough to vote for him in Mississippi, but meanwhile where should he find the twenty-dollar greenbacks which it was his ambition to transmit from time to time to his female relations, confined so constantly to a farinaceous diet? It came over him with some force that his opinions would not yield interest, and the evaporation of this pleasing hypothesis made him feel like a man in an open boat, at sea, who should just have parted with his last rag of canvas.

I shall not attempt a complete description of Ransom's ill-starred views, being convinced that the reader will guess them as he goes, for they had a frolicsome, ingenious way of peeping out of the young man's conversation. I shall do them sufficient justice in saying that he was by natural disposition a good deal of a stoic, and that, as the result of a considerable intellectual experience, he was, in social and political matters, a reactionary. I suppose he was very conceited, for he was much addicted to judging his age. He thought it talkative, querulous, hysterical, maudlin, full of false ideas, of unhealthy germs, of extravagant, dissipated habits, for which a great reckoning was in store. He was an immense admirer of the late Thomas Carlyle, and was very suspicious of the encroachments of modern democracy. I know not exactly how these queer heresies had planted themselves, but he had a longish pedigree (it had flowered at one time with English royalists and cavaliers), and he seemed at moments to be inhabited by some transmitted spirit of a robust but narrow ancestor, some broad-faced wig-wearer or sword-bearer, with a more primitive conception of manhood than our modern temperament appears to require, and a program of human felicity much less varied. He liked his pedigree, he revered his forefathers, and he rather pitied those who might come after him. In saying so, however, I betray him a little, for he never mentioned such feelings as these. Though he thought the age too talkative, as I have hinted, he liked to talk as well as anyone; but he could hold his tongue, if that were more expressive, and he usually did so when his perplexities were greatest. He had been sitting for several evenings in a beer-cellar, smoking his pipe with a profundity of reticence. This attitude was so unbroken that it marked a crisis—the complete, the acute consciousness of his personal situation. It was the cheapest way he knew of spending an evening. At this particular establishment the *Schoppen* were very tall and the beer was very good; and as the host and most of the guests were German, and their colloquial tongue was unknown to him, he was not drawn into any undue expenditure of speech. He watched his smoke and he thought, thought so hard that at last he appeared to himself to have exhausted the thinkable. When this moment of combined relief and dismay arrived (on the last of the evenings that we are concerned with), he took his way down Third Avenue and reached his humble dwelling. Till within a short time there had been a resource for him at such an hour and in such a mood; a little variety-actress, who lived in the house, and with whom he had established the most cordial relations, was often having her supper (she took it somewhere, every night, after the theater), in the dim, close dining room, and he used to drop in and talk to her. But she had lately married, to his great amusement, and her husband had taken her on a wedding-tour, which was to be at the same time professional. On this occasion he mounted, with rather a heavy tread, to his rooms, where (on the rickety writing-table in the parlor) he found a note from Mrs. Luna. I need not reproduce it *in extenso;* a pale reflection of it will serve. She reproached him with neglecting her, wanted to know what had become of him, whether he had grown too fashionable for a person who cared only for serious society. She accused him of having changed, and inquired as to the reason of his coldness. Was it too much to ask whether he could tell her at least in what manner she had offended him? She used to think they were so much in sympathy—he expressed her own ideas about everything so vividly. She liked intellectual companionship, and she had none now. She hoped very much he would come and see her—as he used to do six months before—the following evening; and however much she might have sinned or he might have altered, she was at least always his affectionate cousin Adeline.

"What the deuce does she want of me now?" It was with this somewhat ungracious exclamation that he tossed away his cousin Adeline's missive. The gesture might have indicated that he meant to take no notice of her; nevertheless, after a day had elapsed, he presented himself before her. He knew what she wanted of old—that is, a year ago; she had wanted him to look after her property and to be tutor to her son. He had lent himself, good-naturedly, to this desire—he was touched by so much confidence—but the experiment had speedily collapsed. Mrs. Luna's affairs were in the hands of trustees, who had complete care of them, and Ransom instantly perceived that his function would be simply to meddle in things that didn't concern him. The levity with which she had exposed him to the derision of the lawful guardians of her fortune opened his eyes to some of the dangers of cousinship; nevertheless he said to himself that he might turn an honest penny by giving an hour to two every day to the education of her little boy. But this, too, proved a brief illusion. Ransom had to find his time in the afternoon; he left his business at five o'clock and remained with his young kinsman till the hour of dinner. At the end of a few weeks he thought himself lucky in retiring without broken shins. That Newton's little nature was remarkable had often been insisted on by his mother;

but it was remarkable, Ransom saw, for the absence of any of the qualities which attach a teacher to a pupil. He was in truth an insufferable child, entertaining for the Latin language a personal, physical hostility, which expressed itself in convulsions of rage. During these paroxysms he kicked furiously at every one and everything—at poor "Rannie," at his mother, at Messrs. Andrews and Stoddard, at the illustrious men of Rome, at the universe in general, to which, as he lay on his back on the carpet, he presented a pair of singularly active little heels. Mrs. Luna had a way of being present at his lessons, and when they passed, as sooner or later they were sure to, into the stage I have described, she interceded for her overwrought darling, reminded Ransom that these were the signs of an exquisite sensibility, begged that the child might be allowed to rest a little, and spent the remainder of the time in conversation with the preceptor. It came to seem to him, very soon, that he was not earning his fee; besides which, it was disagreeable to him to have pecuniary relations with a lady who had not the art of concealing from him that she liked to place him under obligations. He resigned his tutorship, and drew a long breath, having a vague feeling that he had escaped a danger. He could not have told you exactly what it was, and he had a certain sentimental, provincial respect for women which even prevented him from attempting to give a name to it in his own thoughts. He was addicted with the ladies to the old forms of address and of gallantry; he held that they were delicate, agreeable creatures, whom Providence had placed under the protection of the bearded sex; and it was not merely a humorous idea with him that whatever might be the defects of Southern gentlemen, they were at any rate remarkable for their chivalry. He was a man who still, in a slangy age, could pronounce that word with a perfectly serious face.

This boldness did not prevent him from thinking that women were essentially inferior to men, and infinitely tiresome when they declined to accept the lot which men had made for them. He had the most definite notions about their place in nature, in society, and was perfectly easy in his mind as to whether it excluded them from any proper homage. The chivalrous man paid that tax with alacrity. He admitted their rights; these consisted in a standing claim to the generosity and tenderness of the stronger race. The exercise of such feelings was full of advantage for both sexes, and they flowed most freely, of course, when women were gracious and grateful. It may be said that he had a higher conception of politeness than most of the persons who desired the advent of female law-makers. When I have added that he hated to see women eager and argumentative, and thought that their softness and docility were the inspiration, the opportunity (the highest) of man, I shall have sketched a state of mind which will doubtless strike many readers as painfully crude. It had prevented Basil Ransom, at any rate, from putting the dots on his *i*'s, as the French say, in this gradual discovery that Mrs. Luna was making love to him. The process went on a long time before he became aware of it. He had perceived very soon that she was a tremendously familiar little woman—that she took, more rapidly than he had ever known, a high degree of intimacy for granted. But as she had seemed to him neither very fresh nor very beautiful, so he could not easily have represented to himself why she should take it into her head to marry (it would never have occurred to him to doubt that she wanted marriage), an obscure and penniless Mississippian, with womenkind of his own to provide for. He could not guess that he answered to a certain secret ideal of Mrs. Luna's, who loved the landed gentry even when landless, who adored a Southerner under any circumstances, who thought her kinsman a fine, manly, melancholy, disinterested type, and who was sure that her views of public matters, the questions of the age, the vulgar character of modern life, would meet with a perfect response in his mind. She could see by the way he talked that he was a conservative, and this was the motto inscribed upon her own silken banner. She took this unpopular line both by temperament and by reaction from her sister's "extreme" views, the sight of the dreadful people that they brought about her. In reality, Olive was distinguished and discriminating, and Adeline was the dupe of confusions in which the worse was apt to be mistaken for the better. She talked to Ransom about the inferiority of republics, the distressing persons she had met abroad in the legations of the United States, the bad manners of servants and shopkeepers in that country, the hope she entertained that "the good old families" would make a stand; but he never suspected that she cultivated these topics (her treatment of them struck him as highly comical), for the purpose of leading him to the altar, of beguiling the way. Least of all could he suppose that she would be indifferent to his want of income—a point in which he failed to do her justice; for, thinking the fact that he had remained poor a proof of delicacy in that shopkeeping age, it gave her much pleasure to reflect that, as Newton's little property was settled on him (with safeguards which showed how long-headed poor Mr. Luna had been, and large-hearted, too, since to what he left *her* no disagreeable conditions, such as eternal mourning, for instance, were attached)— that as Newton, I say, enjoyed the pecuniary independence which befitted his character, her own income was ample even for two, and she might give herself the luxury of taking a husband who should owe her something. Basil Ransom did not divine all this, but he divined that it was not for nothing that Mrs. Luna wrote him little notes every other day, that she proposed to drive him in the Park at unnatural hours, and that when he said he had his business to attend to, she replied: "Oh, a plague on your business! I am sick of that word—one hears of nothing else in America. There are ways of getting on without business, if you would only take them!" He seldom answered her notes, and he disliked extremely the way in which, in spite of her love of form and order, she attempted to clamber in at the window of one's house when one had locked the door; so that he began to interspace his visits considerably, and at last made them very rare. When I reflect on his habits of almost superstitious politeness to women, it comes over me that some very strong motive must have operated to make him give his friendly—his only too friendly—cousin the cold shoulder. Nevertheless, when he received her reproachful letter (after it had had time to work a little), he said to himself that he had perhaps been unjust and even brutal, and as he was easily touched by remorse of this kind, he took up the broken thread.

22

As he sat with Mrs. Luna, in her little back drawing room, under the lamp, he felt rather more tolerant than before of the pressure she could not help putting upon him. Several months had elapsed, and he was no nearer to the sort of success he had hoped for. It stole over him gently that there was another sort, pretty visibly open to him, not so elevated nor so manly, it is true, but on which he should after all, perhaps, be able to reconcile it with his honor to fall back. Mrs. Luna had had an inspiration; for once in her life she had held her tongue. She had not made him a scene, there had been no question of an explanation; she had received him as if he had been there the day before, with the addition of a spice of mysterious melancholy. She might have made up her mind that she had lost him as what she had hoped, but that it was better than desolation to try and keep him as a friend. It was as if she wished him to see now how she tried. She was subdued and consolatory, she waited upon him, moved away a screen that intercepted the fire, remarked that he looked very tired, and rang for some tea. She made no inquiry about his affairs, never asked if he had been busy and prosperous; and this reticence struck him as unexpectedly delicate and discreet; it was as if she had guessed, by a subtle feminine faculty, that his professional career was nothing to boast of. There was a simplicity in him which permitted him to wonder whether she had not improved. The lamplight was soft, the fire crackled pleasantly, everything that surrounded him betrayed a woman's taste and touch; the place was decorated and cushioned in perfection, delightfully private and personal, the picture of a well-appointed home. Mrs. Luna had complained of the difficulties of installing one's self in America, but Ransom remembered that he had received an impression similar to this in her sister's house in Boston, and reflected that these ladies had, as a family-trait, the art of making themselves comfortable. It was better for a winter's evening than the German beer-cellar (Mrs. Luna's tea was excellent), and his hostess herself appeared tonight almost as amiable as the variety-actress. At the end of an hour he felt, I will not say almost marriageable, but almost married. Images of leisure played before him, leisure in which he saw himself covering foolscap paper with his views on several subjects, and with favorable illustrations of Southern eloquence. It became tolerably vivid to him that if editors wouldn't print one's lucubrations, it would be a comfort to feel that one was able to publish them at one's own expense.

He had a moment of almost complete illusion. Mrs. Luna had taken up her bit of crochet; she was sitting opposite to him, on the other side of the fire. Her white hands moved with little jerks as she took her stitches, and her rings flashed and twinkled in the light of the hearth. Her head fell a little to one side, exhibiting the plumpness of her chin and neck, and her dropped eyes (it gave her a little modest air), rested quietly on her work. A silence of a few moments had fallen upon their talk, and Adeline—who decidedly *had* improved —appeared also to feel the charm of it, not to wish to break it. Basil Ransom was conscious of all this, and at the same time he was vaguely engaged in a speculation. If it gave one time, if it gave one leisure, was not that in itself a high motive? Thorough study of the question he cared for most— was not the chance for *that* an infinitely desirable good? He seemed to see himself, to feel himself, in that very chair, in the evenings of the future, reading some indispensable book in the still lamplight—Mrs. Luna knew where to get such pretty mellowing shades. Should he not be able to act in that way upon the public opinion of his time, to check certain tendencies, to point out certain dangers, to indulge in much salutary criticism? Was it not one's duty to put one's self in the best conditions for such action? And as the silence continued he almost fell to musing on his duty, almost persuaded himself that the moral law commanded him to marry Mrs. Luna. She looked up presently from her work, their eyes met, and she smiled. He might have believed she had guessed what he was thinking of. This idea startled him, alarmed him a little, so that when Mrs. Luna said, with her sociable manner, "There is nothing I like so much, of a winter's night, as a cozy *tête-à-tête* by the fire. It's quite like Darby and Joan; what a pity the kettle has ceased singing!" —when she uttered these insinuating words he gave himself a little imperceptible shake, which was, however, enough to break the spell, and made no response more direct than to ask her, in a moment, in a tone of cold, mild curiosity, whether she had lately heard from her sister, and how long Miss Chancellor intended to remain in Europe.

"Well, you *have* been living in your hole!" Mrs. Luna exclaimed. "Olive came home six weeks ago. How long did you expect her to endure it?"

"I am sure I don't know; I have never been there," Ransom replied.

"Yes, that's what I like you for," Mrs. Luna remarked

202

sweetly. "If a man is nice without it, it's such a pleasant change."

The young man started, then gave a natural laugh. "Lord, how few reasons there must be!"

"Oh, I mention that one because I can tell it. I shouldn't care to tell the others."

"I am glad you have some to fall back upon, the day I should go," Ransom went on. "I thought you thought so much of Europe."

"So I do; but it isn't everything," said Mrs. Luna, philosophically. "You had better go there with me," she added, with a certain inconsequence.

"One would go to the end of the world with so irresistible a lady!" Ransom exclaimed, falling into the tone which Mrs. Luna always found so unsatisfactory. It was a part of his Southern gallantry—his accent always came out strongly when he said anything of that sort—and it committed him to nothing in particular. She had had occasion to wish, more than once, that he wouldn't be so beastly polite, as she used to hear people say in England. She answered that she didn't care about ends, she cared about beginnings; but he didn't take up the declaration; he returned to the subject of Olive, wanted to know what she had done over there, whether she had worked them up much.

"Oh, of course, she fascinated every one," said Mrs. Luna. "With her grace and beauty, her general style, how could she help that?"

"But did she bring them round, did she swell the host that is prepared to march under her banner?"

"I suppose she saw plenty of the strong-minded, plenty of vicious old maids, and fanatics, and frumps. But I haven't the least idea what she accomplished—what they call 'wonders,' I suppose."

"Didn't you see her when she returned?" Basil Ransom asked.

"How could I see her? I can see pretty far, but I can't see

all the way to Boston." And then, in explaining that it was at this port that her sister had disembarked, Mrs. Luna further inquired whether he could imagine Olive doing anything in a first-rate way, as long as there were inferior ones. "Of course she likes bad ships—Boston steamers—just as she likes common people, and red-haired hoydens, and preposterous doctrines."

Ransom was silent a moment. "Do you mean the—a—rather striking young lady whom I met in Boston a year ago last October? What was her name?—Miss Tarrant? Does Miss Chancellor like her as much as ever?"

"Mercy! don't you know she took her to Europe? It was to form *her* mind she went. Didn't I tell you that last summer? You used to come to see me then."

"Oh yes, I remember," Ransom said, rather musingly. "And did she bring her back?"

"Gracious, you don't suppose she would leave her! Olive thinks she's born to regenerate the world."

"I remember you telling me that, too. It comes back to me. Well, is her mind formed?"

"As I haven't seen it, I cannot tell you."

"Aren't you going on there to see——"

"To see whether Miss Tarrant's mind is formed?" Mrs. Luna broke in. "I will go if you would like me to. I remember your being immensely excited about her that time you met her. Don't you recollect that?"

Ransom hesitated an instant. "I can't say I do. It is too long ago."

"Yes, I have no doubt that's the way you change, about women! Poor Miss Tarrant, if she thinks she made an impression on you!"

"She won't think about such things as that, if her mind has been formed by your sister," Ransom said. "It does come back to me now, what you told me about the growth of their intimacy. And do they mean to go on living together forever?"

"I suppose so—unless some one should take it into his head to marry Verena."

"Verena—is that her name?" Ransom asked.

Mrs. Luna looked at him with a suspended needle. "Well! have you forgotten that too? You told me yourself you thought it so pretty, that time in Boston, when you walked me up the hill." Ransom declared that he remembered that walk, but didn't remember everything he had said to her; and she suggested, very satirically, that perhaps he would like to marry Verena himself—he seemed so interested in her. Ransom shook his head sadly, and said he was afraid he was not in a position to marry; whereupon Mrs. Luna asked him what he meant—did he mean (after a moment's hesitation) that he was too poor?

"Never in the world—I am very rich; I make an enormous income!" the young man exclaimed; so that, remarking his tone, and the slight flush of annoyance that rose to his face, Mrs. Luna was quick enough to judge that she had overstepped the mark. She remembered (she ought to have remembered before), that he had never taken her in the least into his confidence about his affairs. That was not the Southern way, and he was at least as proud as he was poor. In this surmise she was just; Basil Ransom would have despised himself if he had been capable of confessing to a woman that he couldn't make a living. Such questions were none of their business (their business was simply to be provided for, practice the domestic virtues, and be charmingly grateful), and there was, to his sense, something almost indecent in talking about them. Mrs. Luna felt doubly sorry for him as she perceived that he denied himself the luxury of sympathy (that is, of hers), and the vague but comprehensive sigh that passed her lips as she took up her crochet again was unusually expressive of helplessness. She said that of course she knew how great his talents were—he could do anything he wanted; and Basil Ransom wondered for a moment whether, if she were to ask him point-blank to marry

205

her, it would be consistent with the high courtesy of a Southern gentleman to refuse. After she should be his wife he might of course confess to her that he was too poor to marry, for in that relation even a Southern gentleman of the highest tone must sometimes unbend. But he didn't in the least long for this arrangement, and was conscious that the most pertinent sequel to her conjecture would be for him to take up his hat and walk away.

Within five minutes, however, he had come to desire to do this almost as little as to marry Mrs. Luna. He wanted to hear more about the girl who lived with Olive Chancellor. Something had revived in him—an old curiosity, an image half effaced—when he learned that she had come back to America. He had taken a wrong impression from what Mrs. Luna said, nearly a year before, about her sister's visit to Europe; he had supposed it was to be a long absence, that Miss Chancellor wanted perhaps to get the little prophetess away from her parents, possibly even away from some amorous entanglement. Then, no doubt, they wanted to study up the woman-question with the facilities that Europe would offer; he didn't know much about Europe, but he had an idea that it was a great place for facilities. His knowledge of Miss Chancellor's departure, accompanied by her young companion, had checked at the time, on Ransom's part, a certain habit of idle but none the less entertaining retrospect. His life, on the whole, had not been rich in episode, and that little chapter of his visit to his queer, clever, capricious cousin, with his evening at Miss Birdseye's, and his glimpse, repeated on the morrow, of the strange, beautiful, ridiculous, red-haired young *improvisatrice,* unrolled itself in his memory like a page of interesting fiction. The page seemed to fade, however, when he heard that the two girls had gone, for an indefinite time, to unknown lands; this carried them out of his range, spoiled the perspective, diminished their actuality; so that for several months past, with his increase of anxiety about his own affairs, and the low pitch of his spirits, he had not thought at all about Verena

Tarrant. The fact that she was once more in Boston, with a certain contiguity that it seemed to imply between Boston and New York, presented itself now as important and agreeable. He was conscious that this was rather an anomaly, and his consciousness made him, had already made him, dissimulate slightly. He did not pick up his hat to go; he sat in his chair taking his chance of the tax which Mrs. Luna might lay upon his urbanity. He remembered that he had not made, as yet, any very eager inquiry about Newton, who at this late hour had succumbed to the only influence that tames the untamable and was sleeping the sleep of childhood, if not of innocence. Ransom repaired his neglect in a manner which elicited the most copious response from his hostess. The boy had had a good many tutors since Ransom gave him up, and it could not be said that his education languished. Mrs. Luna spoke with pride of the manner in which he went through them; if he did not master his lessons, he mastered his teachers, and she had the happy conviction that she gave him every advantage. Ransom's delay was diplomatic, but at the end of ten minutes he returned to the young ladies in Boston; he asked why, with their aggressive program, one hadn't begun to feel their onset, why the echoes of Miss Tarrant's eloquence hadn't reached his ears. Hadn't she come out yet in public? was she not coming to stir them up in New York? He hoped she hadn't broken down.

"She didn't seem to break down last summer, at the Female Convention," Mrs. Luna replied. "Have you forgotten that too? Didn't I tell you of the sensation she produced there, and of what I heard from Boston about it? Do you mean to say I didn't give you that 'Transcript,' with the report of her great speech? It was just before they sailed for Europe; she went off with flying colors, in a blaze of fireworks." Ransom protested that he had not heard this affair mentioned till that moment, and then, when they compared dates, they found it had taken place just after his last visit to Mrs. Luna. This, of course, gave her a chance to say that he had treated her even worse than she supposed; it had been her impression, at any rate, that they had talked together about Verena's sudden bound into fame. Apparently she confounded him with someone else, that was very possible; he was not to suppose that he occupied such a distinct place in her mind, especially when she might die twenty deaths before he came near her. Ransom demurred to the implication that Miss Tarrant was famous; if she were famous, wouldn't she be in the New York papers? He hadn't seen her there, and he had no recollection of having encountered any mention at the time (last June, was it?) of her exploits at the Female Convention. A local reputation doubtless she had, but that had been the case a year and a half before, and what was expected of her then was to become a first-class national glory. He was willing to believe that she had created some excitement in Boston, but he shouldn't attach much importance to that till one began to see her photograph in the stores. Of course, one must give her time, but he had supposed Miss Chancellor was going to put her through faster.

If he had taken a contradictious tone on purpose to draw Mrs. Luna out, he could not have elicited more of the information he desired. It was perfectly true that he had seen no reference to Verena's performances in the preceding June; there were periods when the newspapers seemed to him so idiotic that for weeks he never looked at one. He learned from Mrs. Luna that it was not Olive who had sent her the "Transcript" and in letters had added some private account of the doings at the convention to the testimony of that amiable sheet; she had been indebted for this service to a "gentleman-friend," who wrote her everything that happened in Boston, and what every one had every day for dinner. Not that it was necessary for her happiness to know; but the gentleman she spoke of didn't know what to invent to please her. A Bostonian couldn't imagine that one didn't want to know, and that was their idea of ingratiating themselves, or, at any rate, it was his, poor man. Olive would never have gone into particulars about Verena; she regarded her sister as quite too much one of the profane, and knew Adeline couldn't understand why, when she took to herself a bosom-friend, she should have been at such pains to select her in just the most dreadful class in the community. Verena was a perfect little adventuress, and quite third-rate into the bargain; but, of course, she was a pretty girl enough, if one cared for hair of the color of cochineal. As for her people, they were too absolutely awful; it was exactly as if she, Mrs. Luna, had struck up an intimacy with the daughter of her chiropodist. It took Olive to invent such monstrosities, and to think she was doing something great for humanity when she did so; though, in spite of her wanting to turn everything over, and put the lowest highest, she could be just as contemptuous and invidious, when it came to really mixing, as if she were some grand old duchess. She must do her the justice to say that she hated the Tarrants, the father and mother; but, all the same, she let Verena run to and fro between Charles Street and the horrible hole they lived in, and Adeline knew from that gentleman who wrote so copiously that the girl now and then spent a week at a time at Cambridge. Her mother, who had been ill for some weeks, wanted her to sleep there. Mrs. Luna knew further, by her correspondent, that Verena had—or had had the winter before—a great deal of attention from gentlemen. She didn't know how she worked that into the idea that the female sex was sufficient to itself; but she had grounds for saying that this was one reason why Olive had taken her abroad. She was afraid Verena would give in to some man, and she wanted to make a break. Of course, any such giving in would be very awkward for a young woman who shrieked out on platforms that old maids were the highest type. Adeline guessed Olive had perfect control of her now, unless indeed she used the expeditions to Cambridge as a cover for meeting gentlemen. She was an artful little minx, and cared as much for the rights of women as she did for the Panama Canal; the only right of a woman she wanted was to climb up on top of something, where the men could look at her. She would stay with Olive as long as it served her purpose, because Olive, with her great respectability, could push her, and counteract the effect of her low relations, to say nothing of paying all her expenses and taking her the tour of Europe. "But, mark my words," said Mrs. Luna, "she will give Olive the greatest cut she has ever had in her life. She will run off with some lion-tamer; she will marry a circus-man!" And Mrs. Luna added that it would serve Olive Chancellor right. But she would take it hard; look out for tantrums then!

Basil Ransom's emotions were peculiar while his hostess delivered herself, in a manner at once casual and emphatic, of these rather insidious remarks. He took them all in, for they represented to him certain very interesting facts; but he perceived at the same time that Mrs. Luna didn't know what she was talking about. He had seen Verena Tarrant only twice in his life, but it was no use telling him that she was an adventuress—though, certainly, it *was* very likely she would end by giving Miss Chancellor a cut. He chuckled, with a certain grimness, as this image passed before him; it was not unpleasing, the idea that he should be avenged (for it would avenge him to know it), upon the wanton young woman who had invited him to come and see her in order simply to slap his face. But he had an odd sense of having lost something in not knowing of the other girl's appearance at the Women's Convention—a vague feeling that he had been cheated and trifled with. The complaint was idle, inasmuch as it was not probable he could have gone to Boston to listen to her; but it represented to him that he had not shared, even dimly and remotely, in an event which concerned her very closely. Why should he share, and what was more natural than that the things which concerned her closely should not concern him at all? This question came to him only as he walked home that evening; for the moment it remained quite in abeyance: therefore he was free to feel also that his imagination had been rather starved by his ignorance of the fact that she was near him again (comparatively), that she was in the dimness of the horizon (no longer beyond the curve of the globe), and yet he had not perceived it. This sense of personal loss, as I have called it, made him feel, further, that he had something to make up, to recover. He could scarcely have told you how he would go about it; but the idea, formless though it was, led him in a direction very different from the one he had been following a quarter of an hour before. As he watched it dance before him he fell into another silence, in the midst of which Mrs. Luna gave him another mystic smile. The effect of it was to make him rise to his feet; the whole landscape of his mind had suddenly been illuminated. Decidedly, it was *not* his duty to marry Mrs. Luna, in order to have means to pursue his studies; he jerked himself back, as if he had been on the point of it.

"You don't mean to say you are going already? I haven't said half I wanted to!" she exclaimed.

He glanced at the clock, saw it was not yet late, took a turn about the room, then sat down again in a different place, while she followed him with her eyes, wondering what was the matter with him. Ransom took good care not to ask her what it was she had still to say, and perhaps it was to prevent her telling him that he now began to talk, freely, quickly, in quite a new tone. He stayed half an hour longer, and made himself very agreeable. It seemed to Mrs. Luna now that he had every distinction (she had known he had most), that he was really a charming man. He abounded in conversation, till at last he took up his hat in earnest; he talked about the state of the South, its social peculiarities, the ruin wrought by the war, the dilapidated gentry, the queer types of superannuated fire-eaters, ragged and unreconciled, all the pathos and all the comedy of it, making her laugh at one moment, almost cry at another, and say to herself throughout that when he took it into his head there was no one who could make a lady's evening pass so pleasantly. It was only afterwards that she asked herself why he had not taken it into his head till the last, so quickly. She delighted in the dilapidated gentry; her taste was completely different from her sister's, who took an interest only in the lower class, as it struggled to rise; what Adeline cared for was the fallen aristocracy (it seemed to be falling everywhere very much; was not Basil Ransom an example of it? was he not like a French *gentilhomme de province* after the Revolution? or an old monarchical *émigré* from the Languedoc?), the despoiled patriciate, I say, whose attitude was noble and touching, and toward whom one might exercise a charity as discreet as their pride was sensitive. In all Mrs. Luna's visions of herself, her discretion was the leading feature. "Are you going to let ten years elapse again before you come?" she asked, as Basil Ransom bade her good night. "You must let me know, because between this and your next visit I shall have time to go to Europe and come back. I shall take care to arrive the day before."

Instead of answering this sally, Ransom said, "Are you not going one of these days to Boston? Are you not going to pay your sister another visit?"

Mrs. Luna stared. "What good will that do *you*? Excuse my stupidity," she added; "of course, it gets me away. Thank you very much!"

"I don't want you to go away; but I want to hear more about Miss Olive."

"Why in the world? You know you loathe her!" Here, before Ransom could reply, Mrs. Luna again overtook herself. "I verily believe that by Miss Olive you mean Miss Verena!" Her eyes charged him a moment with this perverse intention; then she exclaimed, "Basil Ransom, *are* you in love with that creature?"

He gave a perfectly natural laugh, not pleading guilty, in order to practice on Mrs. Luna, but expressing the simple state of the case. "How should I be? I have seen her but twice in my life."

"If you had seen her more, I shouldn't be afraid! Fancy your wanting to pack me off to Boston!" his hostess went on.

"I am in no hurry to stay with Olive again; besides, that girl takes up the whole house. You had better go there yourself."

"I should like nothing better," said Ransom.

"Perhaps you would like me to ask Verena to spend a month with me—it might be a way of attracting you to the house," Adeline went on, in the tone of exuberant provocation.

Ransom was on the point of replying that it would be a better way than any other, but he checked himself in time; he had never yet, even in joke, made so crude, so rude a speech to a lady. You only knew when he was joking with women by his superadded civility. "I beg you to believe there is nothing I would do for any woman in the world that I wouldn't do for you," he said, bending, for the last time, over Mrs. Luna's plump hand.

"I shall remember that and keep you up to it!" she cried after him, as he went. But even with this rather lively exchange of vows he felt that he had got off rather easily. He walked slowly up Fifth Avenue, into which, out of Adeline's cross-street, he had turned, by the light of a fine winter moon; and at every corner he stopped a minute, lingered in meditation, while he exhaled a soft, vague sigh. This was an unconscious, involuntary expression of relief, such as a man might utter who had seen himself on the point of being run over and yet felt that he was whole. He didn't trouble himself much to ask what had saved him; whatever it was it had produced a reaction, so that he felt rather ashamed of having found his look-out of late so blank. By the time he reached his lodgings, his ambition, his resolution, had rekindled; he had remembered that he formerly supposed he was a man of ability, that nothing particular had occurred to make him doubt it (the evidence was only negative, not positive), and that at any rate he was young enough to have another try. He whistled that night as he went to bed.

23

Three weeks afterward he stood in front of Olive Chancellor's house, looking up and down the street and hesitating. He had told Mrs. Luna that he should like nothing better than to make another journey to Boston; and it was not simply because he liked it that he had come. I was on the point of saying that a happy chance had favored him, but it occurs to me that one is under no obligation to call chances by flattering epithets when they have been waited for so long. At any rate, the darkest hour is before the dawn; and a few days after that melancholy evening I have described, which Ransom spent in his German beer-cellar, before a single glass, soon emptied, staring at his future with an unremunerated eye, he found that the world appeared to have need of him yet. The "party," as he would have said (I cannot pretend that his speech was too heroic for that), for whom he had transacted business in Boston so many months before, and who had expressed at the time but a limited appreciation of his services (there had been between the lawyer and his client a divergence of judgment), observing, apparently, that they proved more fruitful than he expected, had reopened the affair and presently requested Ransom to transport himself again to the sister city. His errand demanded more time than before, and for three days he gave it his constant attention. On the fourth he found he was still detained; he should have to wait till the evening—some important papers were to be prepared. He determined to treat the interval as a holiday, and he wondered what one could do in Boston to give one's morning a festive complexion. The weather was brilliant enough to minister to any illusion, and he strolled along the streets, taking it in. In front of the Music Hall and of Tremont Temple he stopped, looking at the posters in the doorway; for was it not possible that Miss Chancellor's little friend might be just then addressing her fellow-citizens? Her name was absent, however, and this resource seemed to mock him. He knew no one in the place but Olive Chancellor, so there was no question of a visit to pay. He was perfectly resolved that he would never go near *her* again; she was doubtless a very superior being, but she had been too rough with him to tempt him further. Politeness, even a largely interpreted "chivalry," required nothing more than he had already done; he had quitted her, the other year, without telling her that she was a vixen, and that reticence was chivalrous enough. There was also Verena Tarrant, of course; he saw no reason to dissemble when he spoke of her to himself, and he allowed himself the entertainment of feeling that he should like very much to see her again. Very likely she wouldn't seem to him the same; the impression she had made upon him was due to some accident of mood or circumstance; and, at any rate, any charm she might have exhibited then had probably been obliterated by the coarsening effect of publicity and the tonic influence of his kinswoman. It will be observed that in this reasoning of Basil Ransom's the impression was freely recognized, and recognized as a phenomenon still present. The attraction might have vanished, as he said to himself, but the mental picture of it was yet vivid. The greater the pity that he couldn't call upon Verena (he called her by her name in his thoughts, it was so pretty), without calling upon Olive, and that Olive was so disagreeable as to place that effort beyond his strength. There was another consideration, with Ransom, which eminently belonged to the man; he believed that Miss Chancellor had conceived, in the course of those few hours, and in a manner that formed so absurd a sequel to her having gone out of her way to make his acquaintance, such a dislike to him that it would be odious to her to see him again within her doors; and he would have felt indelicate in taking warrant from her original invitation (before she had seen him), to inflict on her a presence which he had no reason to suppose the lapse of time had made less offensive. She had given him no sign of pardon or penitence in any of the little ways that are familiar to women—by sending him a message through her sister, or even a book, a photograph, a Christmas card, or a newspaper, by the post. He felt, in a word, not at liberty to ring at her door; he didn't know what kind of a fit the sight of his long Mississippian person would give her, and it was characteristic of him that he should wish so to spare the sensibilities of a young lady whom he had not found tender; being ever as willing to let women off easily in the particular case as he was fixed in the belief that the sex in general requires watching.

Nevertheless, he found himself, at the end of half an hour, standing on the only spot in Charles Street which had any significance for him. It had occurred to him that if he couldn't call upon Verena without calling upon Olive, he should be exempt from that condition if he called upon Mrs. Tarrant. It was not her mother, truly, who had asked him, it was the girl herself; and he was conscious, as a candid young American, that a mother is always less accessible, more guarded by social prejudice, than a daughter. But he was at a pass in which it was permissible to strain a point, and he took his way in the direction in which he knew that Cambridge lay, remembering that Miss Tarrant's invitation had reference to that quarter and that Mrs. Luna had given him further evidence. Had she not said that Verena often went back there for visits of several days—that her mother had been ill and she gave her much care? There was nothing inconceivable in her being engaged at that hour (it was getting to be one o'clock), in one of those expeditions—nothing impossible in the chance that he might find her in Cambridge. The chance, at any rate, was worth taking;

Cambridge, moreover, was worth seeing, and it was as good a way as another of keeping his holiday. It occurred to him, indeed, that Cambridge was a big place, and that he had no particular address. This reflection overtook him just as he reached Olive's house, which, oddly enough, he was obliged to pass on his way to the mysterious suburb. That is partly why he paused there; he asked himself for a moment why he shouldn't ring the bell and obtain his needed information from the servant, who would be sure to be able to give it to him. He had just dismissed this method, as of questionable taste, when he heard the door of the house open, within the deep embrasure in which, in Charles Street, the main portals are set, and which are partly occupied by a flight of steps protected at the bottom by a second door, whose upper half, in either wing, consists of a sheet of glass. It was a minute before he could see who had come out, and in that minute he had time to turn away and then to turn back again, and to wonder which of the two inmates would appear to him, or whether he should behold neither or both.

The person who had issued from the house descended the steps very slowly, as if on purpose to give him time to escape; and when at last the glass doors were divided they disclosed a little old lady. Ransom was disappointed; such an apparition was so scantily to his purpose. But the next minute his spirits rose again, for he was sure that he had seen the little old lady before. She stopped on the sidewalk and looked vaguely about her, in the manner of a person waiting for an omnibus or a streetcar; she had a dingy, loosely-habited air, as if she had worn her clothes for many years and yet was even now imperfectly acquainted with them; a large, benignant face, caged in by the glass of her spectacles, which seemed to cover it almost equally everywhere, and a fat, rusty satchel, which hung low at her side, as if it wearied her to carry it. This gave Ransom time to recognize her; he knew in Boston no such figure as that save Miss Birdseye. Her party, her person, the exalted account Miss Chancellor gave of her, had kept a very distinct place in his mind; and while she stood there in dim circumspection she came back to him as a friend of yesterday. His necessity gave a point to the reminiscences she evoked; it took him only a moment to reflect that she would be able to tell him where Verena Tarrant was at that particular time, and where, if need be, her parents lived. Her eyes rested on him, and as she saw that he was looking at her she didn't go through the ceremony (she had broken so completely with all conventions), of removing them; he evidently represented nothing to her but a sentient fellow citizen in the enjoyment of his rights, which included that of staring. Miss Birdseye's modesty had never pretended that it was not to be publicly challenged; there were so many bright new motives and ideas in the world that there might even be reasons for looking at her. When Ransom approached her and, raising his hat with a smile, said, "Shall I stop this car for you, Miss Birdseye?" she only looked at him more vaguely, in her complete failure to seize the idea that this might be simply Fame. She had trudged about the streets of Boston for fifty years, and at no period had she received that amount of attention from dark-eyed young men. She glanced, in an unprejudiced way, at the big party-colored human van which now jingled toward them from out of the Cambridge road. "Well, I should like to get into it, if it will take me home," she answered. "Is this a South End car?"

The vehicle had been stopped by the conductor, on his perceiving Miss Birdseye; he evidently recognized her as a frequent passenger. He went, however, through none of the forms of reassurance beyond remarking, "You want to get right in here—quick," but stood with his hand raised, in a threatening way, to the cord of his signal-bell.

"You must allow me the honor of taking you home, madam; I will tell you who I am," Basil Ransom said, in obedience to a rapid reflection. He helped her into the car, the conductor pressed a fraternal hand upon her back, and in a moment the young man was seated beside her, and the jingling had recommenced. At that hour of the day the car was almost empty, and they had it virtually to themselves.

"Well, I know you are someone; I don't think you belong round here," Miss Birdseye declared, as they proceeded.

"I was once at your house—on a very interesting occasion. Do you remember a party you gave, a year ago last October, to which Miss Chancellor came, and another young lady, who made a wonderful speech?"

"Oh yes! when Verena Tarrant moved us all so! There were a good many there; I don't remember all."

"I was one of them," Basil Ransom said; "I came with Miss Chancellor, who is a kind of relation of mine, and you were very good to me."

"What did I do?" asked Miss Birdseye, candidly. Then, before he could answer her, she recognized him. "I remember you now, and Olive bringing you! You're a Southern gentleman—she told me about you afterwards. You don't approve of our great struggle—you want us to be kept down." The old lady spoke with perfect mildness, as if she had long ago done with passion and resentment. Then she added, "Well, I presume we can't have the sympathy of all."

"Doesn't it look as if you had my sympathy, when I get into a car on purpose to see you home—one of the principal agitators?" Ransom inquired, laughing.

"Did you get in on purpose?"

"Quite on purpose. I am not so bad as Miss Chancellor thinks me."

"Oh, I presume you have your ideas," said Miss Birdseye. "Of course, Southerners have peculiar views. I suppose they retain more than one might think. I hope you won't ride too far—I know my way round Boston."

"Don't object to me, or think me officious," Ransom replied. "I want to ask you something."

Miss Birdseye looked at him again. "Oh yes, I place you now; you conversed some with Doctor Prance."

"To my great edification!" Ransom exclaimed. "And I hope Doctor Prance is well."

"She looks after every one's health but her own," said

Miss Birdseye, smiling. "When I tell her that, she says she hasn't got any to look after. She says she's the only woman in Boston that hasn't got a doctor. She was determined she wouldn't be a patient, and it seemed as if the only way not to be one was to be a doctor. She is trying to make me sleep; that's her principal occupation."

"Is it possible you don't sleep yet?" Ransom asked, almost tenderly.

"Well, just a little. But by the time I get to sleep I have to get up. I can't sleep when I want to live."

"You ought to come down South," the young man suggested. "In that languid air you would doze deliciously!"

"Well, I don't want to be languid," said Miss Birdseye. "Besides, I have been down South, in the old times, and I can't say they let me sleep very much; they were always round after me!"

"Do you mean on account of the negroes?"

"Yes, I couldn't think of anything else then. I carried them the Bible."

Ransom was silent a moment; then he said, in a tone which evidently was carefully considerate, "I should like to hear all about that!"

"Well, fortunately, we are not required now; we are required for something else." And Miss Birdseye looked at him with a wandering, tentative humor, as if he would know what she meant.

"You mean for the other slaves!" he exclaimed, with a laugh. "You can carry them all the Bibles you want."

"I want to carry them the Statute-book; that must be our Bible now."

Ransom found himself liking Miss Birdseye very much, and it was quite without hypocrisy or a tinge too much of the local quality in his speech that he said: "Wherever you go, madam, it will matter little what you carry. You will always carry your goodness."

For a minute she made no response. Then she murmured: "That's the way Olive Chancellor told me you talked."

"I am afraid she has told you little good of me."

"Well, I am sure she thinks she is right."

"Thinks it?" said Ransom. "Why, she knows it, with supreme certainty! By the way, I hope she is well."

Miss Birdseye stared again. "Haven't you seen her? Are you not visiting?"

"Oh no, I am not visiting! I was literally passing her house when I met you."

"Perhaps you live here now," said Miss Birdseye. And when he had corrected this impression, she added, in a tone which showed with what positive confidence he had now inspired her, "Hadn't you better drop in?"

"It would give Miss Chancellor no pleasure," Basil Ransom rejoined. "She regards me as an enemy in the camp."

"Well, she is very brave."

"Precisely. And I am very timid."

"Didn't you fight once?"

"Yes; but it was in such a good cause!"

Ransom meant this allusion to the great Secession and, by comparison, to the attitude of the resisting male (laudable even as that might be), to be decently jocular; but Miss Birdseye took it very seriously, and sat there for a good while as speechless as if she meant to convey that she had been going on too long now to be able to discuss the propriety of the late rebellion. The young man felt that he had silenced her, and he was very sorry; for, with all deference to the distinterested Southern attitude toward the unprotected female, what he had got into the car with her for was precisely to make her talk. He had wished for general, as well as for particular, news of Verena Tarrant; it was a topic on which he had proposed to draw Miss Birdseye out. He preferred not to broach it himself, and he waited awhile for another opening. At last, when he was on the point of exposing himself by a direct inquiry (he reflected that the exposure would in any case not be long averted), she anticipated him by saying, in a manner which showed that her thoughts had continued in the same train, "I wonder very much that Miss Tarrant didn't affect you that evening!"

"Ah, but she did!" Ransom said, with alacrity. "I thought her very charming!"

"Didn't you think her very reasonable?"

"God forbid, madam! I consider women have no business to be reasonable."

His companion turned upon him, slowly and mildly, and each of her glasses, in her aspect of reproach, had the glitter of an enormous tear. "Do you regard us, then, simply as lovely baubles?"

The effect of this question, as coming from Miss Birdseye, and referring in some degree to her own venerable identity, was such as to move him to irresistible laughter. But he controlled himself quickly enough to say, with genuine expression, "I regard you as the dearest thing in life, the only thing which makes it worth living!"

"Worth living for—you! But for us?" suggested Miss Birdseye.

"It's worth any woman's while to be admired as I admire you. Miss Tarrant, of whom we were speaking, affected me, as you say, in this way—that I think more highly still, if possible, of the sex which produced such a delightful young lady."

"Well, we think everything of her here," said Miss Birdseye. "It seems as if it were a real gift."

"Does she speak often—is there any chance of my hearing her now?"

"She raises her voice a good deal in the places round—like Framingham and Billerica. It seems as if she were gathering strength, just to break over Boston like a wave. In fact she did break, last summer. She is a growing power since her great success at the convention."

"Ah! her success at the convention was very great?" Ransom inquired, putting discretion into his voice.

Miss Birdseye hesitated a moment, in order to measure her response by the bounds of righteousness. "Well," she said, with the tenderness of a long retrospect, "I have seen nothing like it since I last listened to Eliza P. Moseley."

"What a pity she isn't speaking somewhere tonight!" Ransom exclaimed.

"Oh, tonight she's out in Cambridge. Olive Chancellor mentioned that."

"Is she making a speech there?"

"No; she's visiting her home."

"I thought her home was in Charles Street?"

"Well, no; that's her residence—her principal one—since she became so united to your cousin. Isn't Miss Chancellor your cousin?"

"We don't insist on the relationship," said Ransom, smiling. "Are they very much united, the two young ladies?"

"You would say so if you were to see Miss Chancellor when Verena rises to eloquence. It's as if the chords were strung across her own heart; she seems to vibrate, to echo with every word. It's a very close and very beautiful tie, and we think everything of it here. They will work together for a great good!"

"I hope so," Ransom remarked. "But in spite of it Miss Tarrant spends a part of her time with her father and mother."

"Yes, she seems to have something for everyone. If you were to see her at home, you would think she was all the daughter. She leads a lovely life!" said Miss Birdseye.

"See her at home? That's exactly what I want!" Ransom rejoined, feeling that if he was to come to this he needn't have had scruples at first. "I haven't forgotten that she invited me, when I met her."

"Oh, of course she attracts many visitors," said Miss Birdseye, limiting her encouragement to this statement.

"Yes; she must be used to admirers. And where, in Cambridge, do her family live?"

"Oh, it's on one of those little streets that don't seem to

have very much of a name. But they do call it—they do call it——" she meditated, audibly.

This process was interrupted by an abrupt allocution from the conductor. "I guess you change here for *your* place. You want one of them blue cars."

The good lady returned to a sense of the situation, and Ransom helped her out of the vehicle, with the aid, as before, of a certain amount of propulsion from the conductor. Her road branched off to the right, and she had to wait on the corner of a street, there being as yet no blue car within hail. The corner was quiet and the day favorable to patience—a day of relaxed rigor and intense brilliancy. It was as if the touch of the air itself were gloved, and the street-coloring had the richness of a superficial thaw. Ransom, of course, waited with his philanthropic companion, though she now protested more vigorously against the idea that a gentleman from the South should pretend to teach an old abolitionist the mysteries of Boston. He promised to leave her when he should have consigned her to the blue car; and meanwhile they stood in the sun, with their backs against an apothecary's window, and she tried again, at his suggestion, to remember the name of Doctor Tarrant's street. "I guess if you ask for Doctor Tarrant, anyone can tell you," she said; and then suddenly the address came to her —the residence of the mesmeric healer was in Monadnoc Place.

"But you'll have to ask for that, so it comes to the same," she went on. After this she added, with a friendliness more personal, "Ain't you going to see your cousin too?"

"Not if I can help it!"

Miss Birdseye gave a little ineffectual sigh. "Well, I suppose every one must act out their ideal. That's what Olive Chancellor does. She's a very noble character."

"Oh yes, a glorious nature."

"You know their opinions are just the same—hers and Verena's," Miss Birdseye placidly continued. "So why should you make a distinction?"

"My dear madam," said Ransom, "does a woman consist of nothing but her opinions? I like Miss Tarrant's lovely face better, to begin with."

"Well, she *is* pretty-looking." And Miss Birdseye gave another sigh, as if she had had a theory submitted to her—that one about a lady's opinions—which, with all that was unfamiliar and peculiar lying behind it, she was really too old to look into much. It might have been the first time she really felt her age. "There's a blue car," she said, in a tone of mild relief.

"It will be some moments before it gets here. Moreover, I don't believe that at bottom they *are* Miss Tarrant's opinions," Ransom added.

"You mustn't think she hasn't a strong hold of them," his companion exclaimed, more briskly. "If you think she is not sincere, you are very much mistaken. Those views are just her life."

"Well, *she* may bring me round to them," said Ransom, smiling.

Miss Birdseye had been watching her blue car, the advance of which was temporarily obstructed. At this, she transferred her eyes to him, gazing at him solemnly out of the pervasive window of her spectacles. "Well, I shouldn't wonder if she did! Yes, that will be a good thing. I don't see how you can help being a good deal shaken by her. She has acted on so many."

"I see; no doubt she will act on me." Then it occurred to Ransom to add: "By the way, Miss Birdseye, perhaps you will be so kind as not to mention this meeting of ours to my cousin, in case of your seeing her again. I have a perfectly good conscience in not calling upon her, but I shouldn't like her to think that I announced my slighting intention all over the town. I don't want to offend her, and she had better not know that I have been in Boston. If you don't tell her, no one else will."

"Do you wish me to conceal——?" murmured Miss Birdseye, panting a little.

"No, I don't want you to conceal anything. I only want you to let this incident pass—to say nothing."

"Well, I never did anything of that kind."

"Of what kind?" Ransom was half vexed, half touched by her inability to enter into his point of view, and her resistance made him hold to his idea the more. "It is very simple, what I ask of you. You are under no obligation to tell Miss Chancellor everything that happens to you, are you?"

His request seemed still something of a shock to the poor old lady's candor. "Well, I see her very often, and we talk a great deal. And then—won't Verena tell her?"

"I have thought of that—but I hope not."

"She tells her most everything. Their union is so close."

"She won't want her to be wounded," Ransom said, ingeniously.

"Well, you *are* considerate." And Miss Birdseye continued to gaze at him. "It's a pity you can't sympathize."

"As I tell you, perhaps Miss Tarrant will bring me round. You have before you a possible convert," Ransom went on, without, I fear, putting up the least little prayer to heaven that his dishonesty might be forgiven.

"I should be very happy to think that—after I have told you her address in this secret way." A smile of infinite mildness glimmered in Miss Birdseye's face, and she added: "Well, I guess that will be your fate. She *has* affected so many. I would keep very quiet if I thought that. Yes, she will bring you round."

"I will let you know as soon as she does," Basil Ransom said. "Here is your car at last."

"Well, I believe in the victory of the truth. I won't say anything." And she suffered the young man to lead her to the car, which had now stopped at their corner.

"I hope very much I shall see you again," he remarked, as they went.

"Well, I am always round the streets, in Boston." And while, lifting and pushing, he was helping again to insert her into the oblong receptacle, she turned a little and repeated,

226

"She *will* affect you! If that's to be your secret, I will keep it," Ransom heard her subjoin. He raised his hat and waved her a farewell, but she didn't see him; she was squeezing further into the car and making the discovery that this time it was full and there was no seat for her. Surely, however, he said to himself, every man in the place would offer his own to such an innocent old dear.

24

A little more than an hour after this he stood in the parlor of Doctor Tarrant's suburban residence, in Monadnoc Place. He had induced a juvenile maid-servant, by an appeal somewhat impassioned, to let the ladies know that he was there; and she had returned, after a long absence, to say that Miss Tarrant would come down to him in a little while. He possessed himself, according to his wont, of the nearest book (it lay on the table, with an old magazine and a little japanned tray containing Tarrant's professional cards —his denomination as a mesmeric healer), and spent ten minutes in turning it over. It was a biography of Mrs. Ada T. P. Foat, the celebrated trance-lecturer, and was embellished by a portrait representing the lady with a surprised expression and innumerable ringlets. Ransom said to himself, after reading a few pages, that much ridicule had been cast upon Southern literature; but if that was a fair specimen of Northern!—and he threw it back upon the table with a gesture almost as contemptuous as if he had not known perfectly, after so long a residence in the North, that it was not, while he wondered whether this was the sort of thing Miss Tarrant had been brought up on. There was no other book to be seen, and he remembered to have read the magazine; so there was finally nothing for him, as the occupants of the house failed still to appear, but to stare before him, into the bright, bare, common little room, which was so hot that he wished to open a window, and of which an ugly, undraped cross-light seemed to have taken upon itself to reveal the poverty. Ransom, as I have mentioned, had not a high standard of comfort, and noticed little, usually, how people's houses were furnished—it was only when they were very pretty that he observed; but what he saw while he waited at Doctor Tarrant's made him say to himself that it was no wonder Verena liked better to live with Olive Chancellor. He even began to wonder whether it were for the sake of that superior softness she had cultivated Miss Chancellor's favor, and whether Mrs. Luna had been right about her being mercenary and insincere. So many minutes elapsed before she appeared that he had time to remember he really knew nothing to the contrary, as well as to consider the oddity (so great when one did consider it), of his coming out to Cambridge to see her, when he had only a few hours in Boston to spare, a year and a half after she had given him her very casual invitation. She had not refused to receive him, at any rate; she was free to, if it didn't please her. And not only this, but she was apparently making herself fine in his honor, inasmuch as he heard a rapid footstep move to and fro above his head, and even, through the slightness which in Monadnoc Place did service for an upper floor, the sound of drawers and presses opened and closed. Some one was "flying round," as they said in Mississippi. At last the stairs creaked under a light tread, and the next moment a brilliant person came into the room.

His reminiscence of her had been very pretty; but now that she had developed and matured, the little prophetess was prettier still. Her splendid hair seemed to shine; her cheek and chin had a curve which struck him by its fineness; her eyes and lips were full of smiles and greetings. She had

228

appeared to him before as a creature of brightness, but now she lighted up the place, she irradiated, she made everything that surrounded her of no consequence; dropping upon the shabby sofa with an effect as charming as if she had been a nymph sinking on a leopard-skin, and with the native sweetness of her voice forcing him to listen till she spoke again. It was not long before he perceived that this added luster was simply success; she was young and tender still, but the sound of a great applauding audience had been in her ears; it formed an element in which she felt buoyant and floated. Still, however, her glance was as pure as it was direct, and that fantastic fairness hung about her which had made an impression on him of old, and which reminded him of unworldly places—he didn't know where—convent-cloisters or vales of Arcady. At that other time she had been party-colored and bedizened, and she had always an air of costume, only now her costume was richer and more chastened. It was her line, her condition, part of her expression. If at Miss Birdseye's, and afterwards in Charles Street, she might have been a ropedancer, today she made a "scene" of the mean little room in Monadnoc Place, such a scene as a prima donna makes of daubed canvas and dusty boards. She addressed Basil Ransom as if she had seen him the other week and his merits were fresh to her, though she let him, while she sat smiling at him, explain in his own rather ceremonious way why it was he had presumed to call upon her on so slight an acquaintance—on an invitation which she herself had had more than time to forget. His explanation, as a finished and satisfactory thing, quite broke down; there was no more impressive reason than that he had simply wished to see her. He became aware that this motive loomed large, and that her listening smile, innocent as it was, in the Arcadian manner, of mockery, seemed to accuse him of not having the courage of his inclination. He had alluded especially to their meeting at Miss Chancellor's; there it was that she had told him she should be glad to see him in her home.

"Oh yes, I remember perfectly, and I remember quite as well seeing you at Miss Birdseye's the night before. I made a speech—don't you remember? That was delightful."

"It was delightful indeed," said Basil Ransom.

"I don't mean my speech; I mean the whole thing. It was then I made Miss Chancellor's acquaintance. I don't know whether you know how we work together. She has done so much for me."

"Do you still make speeches?" Ransom asked, conscious, as soon as he had uttered it, that the question was below the mark.

"Still? Why, I should hope so; it's all I'm good for! It's my life—or it's going to be. And it's Miss Chancellor's too. We are determined to do something."

"And does she make speeches too?"

"Well, she makes mine—or the best part of them. She tells me what to say—the real things, the strong things. It's Miss Chancellor as much as me!" said the singular girl, with a generous complacency which was yet half ludicrous.

"I should like to hear you again," Basil Ransom rejoined.

"Well, you must come some night. You will have plenty of chances. We are going on from triumph to triumph."

Her brightness, her self-possession, her air of being a public character, her mixture of the girlish and the comprehensive, startled and confounded her visitor, who felt that if he had come to gratify his curiosity he should be in danger of going away still more curious than satiated. She added in her gay, friendly, trustful tone—the tone of facile intercourse, the tone in which happy, flower-crowned maidens may have talked to sunburnt young men in the golden age —"I am very familiar with your name; Miss Chancellor has told me all about you."

"All about me?" Ransom raised his black eyebrows. "How could she do that? She doesn't know anything about me!"

"Well, she told me you are a great enemy to our movement. Isn't that true? I think you expressed some unfavorable idea that day I met you at her house."

"If you regard me as an enemy, it's very kind of you to receive me."

"Oh, a great many gentlemen call," Verena said, calmly and brightly. "Some call simply to inquire. Some call because they have heard of me, or been present on some occasion when I have moved them. Everyone is so interested."

"And you have been in Europe," Ransom remarked, in a moment.

"Oh yes, we went over to see if they were in advance. We had a magnificent time—we saw all the leaders."

"The leaders?" Ransom repeated.

"Of the emancipation of our sex. There are gentlemen there, as well as ladies. Olive had splendid introductions in all countries, and we conversed with all the earnest people. We heard much that was suggestive. And as for Europe!" —and the young lady paused, smiling at him and ending in a happy sigh, as if there were more to say on the subject than she could attempt on such short notice.

"I suppose it's very attractive," said Ransom, encouragingly.

"It's just a dream!"

"And did you find that they were in advance?"

"Well, Miss Chancellor thought they were. She was surprised at some things we observed, and concluded that perhaps she hadn't done the Europeans justice—she has got such an open mind, it's as wide as the sea!—while I incline to the opinion that on the whole *we* make the better show. The state of the movement there reflects their general culture, and their general culture is higher than ours (I mean taking the term in its broadest sense). On the other hand, the *special* condition—moral, social, personal—of our sex seems to me to be superior in this country; I mean regarded in relation—in proportion as it were—to the social phase at large. I must add that we did see some noble specimens over

there. In England we met some lovely women, highly cultivated, and of immense organizing power. In France we saw
some wonderful, contagious types; we passed a delightful
evening with the celebrated Marie Verneuil; she was released from prison, you know, only a few weeks before. Our
total impression was that it is only a question of time—the
future is ours. But everywhere we heard one cry—'How
long, O Lord, how long?' "

Basil Ransom listened to this considerable statement with
a feeling which, as the current of Miss Tarrant's facile utterance flowed on, took the form of an hilarity charmed into
stillness by the fear of losing something. There was indeed a
sweet comicality in seeing this pretty girl sit there and, in
answer to a casual, civil inquiry, drop into oratory as a natural thing. Had she forgotten where she was, and did she
take him for a full house? She had the same turns and cadences, almost the same gestures, as if she had been on the
platform; and the great queerness of it was that, with such a
manner, she should escape being odious. She was not odious,
she was delightful; she was not dogmatic, she was genial. No
wonder she was a success, if she speechified as a bird sings!
Ransom could see, too, from her easy lapse, how the lecture-
tone was the thing in the world with which, by education, by
association, she was most familiar. He didn't know what to
make of her; she was an astounding young phenomenon.
The other time came back to him afresh, and how she had
stood up at Miss Birdseye's; it occurred to him that an element, here, had been wanting. Several moments after she
had ceased speaking he became conscious that the expression of his face presented a perceptible analogy to a broad
grin. He changed his posture, saying the first thing that
came into his head. "I presume you do without your father
now."

"Without my father?"

"To set you going, as he did that time I heard you."

"Oh, I see; you thought I had begun a lecture!" And she
laughed, in perfect good humor. "They tell me I speak as I

talk, so I suppose I talk as I speak. But you mustn't put me on what I saw and heard in Europe. That's to be the title of an address I am now preparing, by the way. Yes, I don't depend on father any more," she went on, while Ransom's sense of having said too sarcastic a thing was deepened by her perfect indifference to it. "He finds his patients draw off about enough, anyway. But I owe him everything; if it hadn't been for him, no one would ever have known I had a gift—not even myself. He started me so, once for all, that I now go alone."

"You go beautifully," said Ransom, wanting to say something agreeable, and even respectfully tender, to her, but troubled by the fact that there was nothing he could say that didn't sound rather like chaff. There was no resentment in her, however, for in a moment she said to him, as quickly as it occurred to her, in the manner of a person repairing an accidental omission, "It was very good of you to come so far."

This was a sort of speech it was never safe to make to Ransom; there was no telling what retribution it might entail. "Do you suppose any journey is too great, too wearisome, when it's a question of so great a pleasure?" On this occasion it was not worse than that.

"Well, people *have* come from other cities," Verena answered, not with pretended humility, but with pretended pride. "Do you know Cambridge?"

"This is the first time I have ever been here."

"Well, I suppose you have heard of the university; it's so celebrated."

"Yes—even in Mississippi. I suppose it's very fine."

"I presume it is," said Verena; "but you can't expect me to speak with much admiration of an institution of which the doors are closed to our sex."

"Do you then advocate a system of education in common?"

"I advocate equal rights, equal opportunities, equal privileges. So does Miss Chancellor," Verena added, with just a perceptible air of feeling that her declaration needed support.

"Oh, I thought what she wanted was simply a different inequality—simply to turn out the men altogether," Ransom said.

"Well, she thinks we have great arrears to make up. I do tell her, sometimes, that what she desires is not only justice but vengeance. I think she admits that," Verena continued, with a certain solemnity. The subject, however, held her but an instant, and before Ransom had time to make any comment, she went on, in a different tone: "You don't mean to say you live in Mississippi *now*? Miss Chancellor told me when you were in Boston before, that you had located in New York." She persevered in this reference to himself, for when he had assented to her remark about New York, she asked him whether he had quite given up the South.

"Given it up—the poor, dear, desolate old South? Heaven forbid!" Basil Ransom exclaimed.

She looked at him for a moment with an added softness. "I presume it is natural you should love your home. But I am afraid you think I don't love mine much; I have been here—for so long—so little. Miss Chancellor *has* absorbed me—there is no doubt about that. But it's a pity I wasn't with her today." Ransom made no answer to this; he was incapable of telling Miss Tarrant that if she had been he would not have called upon her. It was not, indeed, that he was not incapable of hypocrisy, for when she had asked him if he had seen his cousin the night before, and he had replied that he hadn't seen her at all, and she had exclaimed with a candor which the next minute made her blush, "Ah, you don't mean to say you haven't forgiven her!"—after this he put on a look of innocence sufficient to carry off the inquiry, "Forgiven her for what?"

Verena colored at the sound of her own words. "Well, I could see how much she felt, that time at her house."

"What did she feel?" Basil Ransom asked, with the natural provokingness of a man.

I know not whether Verena was provoked, but she answered with more spirit than sequence: "Well, you know you *did* pour contempt on us, ever so much; I could see how it worked Olive up. Are you not going to see her at all?"

"Well, I shall think about that; I am here only for three or four days," said Ransom, smiling as men smile when they are perfectly unsatisfactory.

It is very possible that Verena was provoked, inaccessible as she was, in a general way, to irritation; for she rejoined in a moment, with a little deliberate air: "Well, perhaps it's as well you shouldn't go, if you haven't changed at all."

"I haven't changed at all," said the young man, smiling still, with his elbows on the arms of his chair, his shoulders pushed up a little, and his thin brown hands interlocked in front of him.

"Well, I have had visitors who were quite opposed!" Verena announced, as if such news could not possibly alarm her. Then she added, "How then did you know I was out here?"

"Miss Birdseye told me."

"Oh, I am so glad you went to see *her!*" the girl cried, speaking again with the impetuosity of a moment before.

"I didn't go to see her. I met her in the street, just as she was leaving Miss Chancellor's door. I spoke to her, and accompanied her some distance. I passed that way because I knew it was the direct way to Cambridge—from the Common—and I was coming out to see you anyway—on the chance."

"On the chance?" Verena repeated.

"Yes; Mrs. Luna, in New York, told me you were sometimes here, and I wanted, at any rate, to make the attempt to find you."

It may be communicated to the reader that it was very agreeable to Verena to learn that her visitor had made this arduous pilgrimage (for she knew well enough how people in Boston regarded a winter journey to the academic suburb) with only half the prospect of a reward; but her pleasure was mixed with other feelings, or at least with the consciousness that the whole situation was rather less simple than the elements of her life had been hitherto. There was the germ of disorder in this invidious distinction which Mr. Ransom had suddenly made between Olive Chancellor, who was related to him by blood, and herself, who had never been related to him in any way whatever. She knew Olive by this time well enough to wish not to reveal it to her, and yet it would be something quite new for her to undertake to conceal such an incident as her having spent an hour with Mr. Ransom during a flying visit he had made to Boston. She had spent hours with other gentlemen, whom Olive didn't see; but that was different, because her friend knew about her doing it and didn't care, in regard to the persons —didn't care, that is, as she would care in this case. It was vivid to Verena's mind that now Olive *would* care. She had talked about Mr. Burrage, and Mr. Pardon, and even about some gentlemen in Europe, and she had not (after the first few days, a year and a half before) talked about Mr. Ransom.

Nevertheless there were reasons, clear to Verena's view, for wishing either that he would go and see Olive or would keep away from *her;* and the responsibility of treating the fact that he had not so kept away as a secret seemed the greater, perhaps, in the light of this other fact, that so far as simply seeing Mr. Ransom went—why, she quite liked it. She had remembered him perfectly after their two former meetings, superficial as their contact then had been; she had thought of him at moments and wondered whether she should like him if she were to know him better. Now, at the end of twenty minutes, she did know him better, and found that he had rather a curious, but still a pleasant way. There he was, at any rate, and she didn't wish his call to be spoiled by any uncomfortable implication of consequences. So she glanced off, at the touch of Mrs. Luna's name; it seemed to afford relief. "Oh yes, Mrs. Luna—isn't she fascinating?"

Ransom hesitated a little. "Well, no, I don't think she is."

"You ought to like her—she hates our movement!" And Verena asked, further, numerous questions about the brilliant Adeline; whether he saw her often, whether she went out much, whether she was admired in New York, whether he thought her very handsome. He answered to the best of his ability, but soon made the reflection that he had not come out to Monadnoc Place to talk about Mrs. Luna; in consequence of which, to change the subject (as well as to acquit himself of a social duty), he began to speak of Verena's parents, to express regret that Mrs. Tarrant had been sick, and fear that he was not to have the pleasure of seeing her. "She is a great deal better," Verena said; "but she's lying down; she lies down a great deal when she has got nothing else to do. Mother's very peculiar," she added in a moment; "she lies down when she feels well and happy, and when she's sick she walks about—she roams all round the house. If you hear her on the stairs a good deal, you can be pretty sure she's very bad. She'll be very much interested to hear about you after you have left."

Ransom glanced at his watch. "I hope I am not staying too long—that I am not taking you away from her."

"Oh no; she likes visitors, even when she can't see them. If it didn't take her so long to rise, she would have been down here by this time. I suppose you think she has missed me, since I have been so absorbed. Well, so she has, but she knows it's for my good. She would make any sacrifice for affection."

The fancy suddenly struck Ransom of asking, in response to this, "And you? would you make any?"

Verena gave him a bright natural stare. "Any sacrifice for affection?" She thought a moment, and then she said: "I don't think I have a right to say, because I have never been asked. I don't remember ever to have had to make a sacrifice—not an important one."

"Lord! you must have had a happy life!"

"I have been very fortunate, I know that. I don't know what to do when I think how some women—how most women—suffer. But I must not speak of that," she went on, with her smile coming back to her. "If you oppose our movement, you won't want to hear of the suffering of women!"

"The suffering of women is the suffering of all humanity," Ransom returned. "Do you think any movement is going to stop that—or all the lectures from now to doomsday? We are born to suffer—and to bear it, like decent people."

"Oh, I adore heroism!" Verena interposed.

"And as for women," Ransom went on, "they have one source of happiness that is closed to us—the consciousness that their presence here below lifts half the load of *our* suffering."

Verena thought this very graceful, but she was not sure it was not rather sophistical; she would have liked to have Olive's judgment upon it. As that was not possible for the present, she abandoned the question (since learning that Mr. Ransom had passed over Olive, to come to her, she had become rather fidgety), and inquired of the young man, irrelevantly, whether he knew any one else in Cambridge.

"Not a creature; as I tell you, I have never been here before. Your image alone attracted me; this charming interview will be henceforth my only association with the place."

"It's a pity you couldn't have a few more," said Verena, musingly.

"A few more interviews? I should be unspeakably delighted!"

"A few more associations. Did you see the colleges as you came?"

"I had a glimpse of a large enclosure, with some big buildings. Perhaps I can look at them better as I go back to Boston."

"Oh yes, you ought to see them—they have improved so much of late. The inner life, of course, is the greatest interest, but there is some fine architecture, if you are not familiar with Europe." She paused a moment, looking at him with an eye that seemed to brighten, and continued quickly,

238

like a person who had collected herself for a little jump, "If you would like to walk round a little, I shall be very glad to show you."

"To walk round—with you to show me?" Ransom repeated. "My dear Miss Tarrant, it would be the greatest privilege—the greatest happiness—of my life. What a delightful idea—what an ideal guide!"

Verena got up; she would go and put on her hat; he must wait a little. Her offer had a frankness and friendliness which gave him a new sensation, and he could not know that as soon as she had made it (though she had hesitated too, with a moment of intense reflection), she seemed to herself strangely reckless. An impulse pushed her; she obeyed it with her eyes open. She felt as a girl feels when she commits her first conscious indiscretion. She had done many things before which many people would have called indiscreet, but that quality had not even faintly belonged to them in her own mind; she had done them in perfect good faith and with a remarkable absence of palpitation. This superficially ingenuous proposal to walk around the colleges with Mr. Ransom had really another color; it deepened the ambiguity of her position, by reason of a prevision which I shall presently mention. If Olive was not to know that she had seen him, this extension of their interview would double her secret. And yet, while she saw it grow—this monstrous little mystery—she couldn't feel sorry that she was going out with Olive's cousin. As I have already said, she had become nervous. She went to put on her hat, but at the door of the room she stopped, turned round, and presented herself to her visitor with a small spot in either cheek, which had appeared there within the instant. "I have suggested this, because it seems to me I ought to do something for you—in return," she said. "It's nothing, simply sitting there with me. And we haven't got anything else. This is our only hospitality. And the day seems so splendid."

The modesty, the sweetness, of this little explanation, with a kind of intimated desire, constituting almost an appeal, for rightness, which seemed to pervade it, left a fragrance in the air after she had vanished. Ransom walked up and down the room, with his hands in his pockets, under the influence of it, without taking up even once the book about Mrs. Foat. He occupied the time in asking himself by what perversity of fate or of inclination such a charming creature was ranting upon platforms and living in Olive Chancellor's pocket, or how a ranter and sycophant could possibly be so engaging. And she was so disturbingly beautiful, too. This last fact was not less evident when she came down arranged for their walk. They left the house, and as they proceeded he remembered that he had asked himself earlier how he could do honor to such a combination of leisure and ethereal mildness as he had waked up to that morning—a mildness that seemed the very breath of his own latitude. This question was answered now; to do exactly what he was doing at that moment was an observance sufficiently festive.

25

They passed through two or three small, short streets, which, with their little wooden houses, with still more wooden dooryards, looked as if they had been constructed by the nearest carpenter and his boy—a sightless, soundless, interspaced, embryonic region—and entered a long avenue which, fringed on either side with fresh villas, offering themselves trustfully to the public, had the distinction of a wide pavement of neat red brick. The new paint on the square detached houses shone afar off in the transparent air: they had, on top, little cupolas and belvederes, in front a pillared piazza, made bare by the indoor life of winter, on either side a bow-window or two, and everywhere an embellishment of scallops, brackets, cornices, wooden flourishes. They stood, for the most part, on small eminences, lifted above the impertinence of hedge or paling, well up before the world, with all the good conscience which in many cases came, as Ransom saw (and he had noticed the same ornament when he traversed with Olive the quarter of Boston inhabited by Miss Birdseye), from a silvered number, affixed to the glass above the door, in figures huge enough to be read by the people who, in the periodic horsecars, traveled along the middle of the avenue. It was to these glittering badges that many of the houses on either side owed their principal identity. One of the horsecars now advanced in the straight, spacious distance; it was almost the only object that animated the prospect, which, in its large cleanness, its implication of strict business habits on the part of all the people who were not there, Ransom thought very impressive. As he went on with Verena he asked her about the Women's Convention, the year before; whether it had accomplished much work and she had enjoyed it.

"What do you care about the work it accomplished?" said the girl. "You don't take any interest in that."

"You mistake my attitude. I don't like it, but I greatly fear it."

In answer to this Verena gave a free laugh. "I don't believe you fear much!"

"The bravest men have been afraid of women. Won't you even tell me whether you enjoyed it? I am told you made an immense sensation there—that you leaped into fame."

Verena never waved off an allusion to her ability, her eloquence; she took it seriously, without any flutter or protest, and had no more manner about it than if it concerned the goddess Minerva. "I believe I attracted considerable attention; of course, that's what Olive wants—it paves the way for future work. I have no doubt I reached many that wouldn't have been reached otherwise. They think that's my great use—to take hold of the outsiders, as it were; of those who are prejudiced or thoughtless, or who don't care about anything unless it's amusing. I wake up the attention."

"That's the class to which I belong," Ransom said. "Am I not an outsider? I wonder whether you would have reached me—or waked up my attention!"

Verena was silent awhile, as they walked; he heard the light click of her boots on the smooth bricks. Then—"I think I *have* waked it up a little," she replied, looking straight before her.

"Most assuredly! You have made me wish tremendously to contradict you."

"Well, that's a good sign."

"I suppose it was very exciting—your convention," Ransom went on, in a moment; "the sort of thing you would miss very much if you were to return to the ancient fold."

"The ancient fold, you say very well, where women were slaughtered like sheep! Oh, last June, for a week, we just quivered! There were delegates from every State and every city; we lived in a crowd of people and of ideas; the heat was intense, the weather magnificent, and great thoughts and brilliant sayings flew round like darting fireflies. Olive had six celebrated, high-minded women staying in her house— two in a room; and in the summer evenings we sat in the open windows, in her parlor, looking out on the bay, with the lights gleaming in the water, and talked over the doings of the morning, the speeches, the incidents, the fresh contributions to the cause. We had some tremendously earnest discussions, which it would have been a benefit to you to hear, or any man who doesn't think that we can rise to the highest point. Then we had some refreshment—we consumed quantities of ice cream!" said Verena, in whom the note of gaiety alternated with that of earnestness, almost of exaltation, in a manner which seemed to Basil Ransom absolutely and fascinatingly original. "Those were great nights!" she added, between a laugh and a sigh.

Her description of the convention put the scene before him vividly; he seemed to see the crowded, overheated hall, which he was sure was filled with carpetbaggers, to hear flushed women, with loosened bonnet-strings, forcing thin voices into ineffectual shrillness. It made him angry, and all the more angry, that he hadn't a reason, to think of the charming creature at his side being mixed up with such elements, pushed and elbowed by them, conjoined with them in emulation, in unsightly strainings and clappings and shoutings, in wordy, windy iteration of inanities. Worst of all was the idea that she should have expressed such a congregation to itself so acceptably, have been acclaimed and applauded by hoarse throats, have been lifted up, to all the vulgar multitude, as the queen of the occasion. He made the reflection, afterwards, that he was singularly ill-grounded in his wrath, inasmuch as it was none of his business what use Miss Tarrant chose to make of her energies, and, in addition to this, nothing else was to have been expected of her. But that reflection was absent now, and in its absence he saw only the fact that his companion had been odiously perverted. "Well, Miss Tarrant," he said, with a deeper seriousness than showed in his voice, "I am forced to the painful conclusion that you are simply ruined."

"Ruined? Ruined yourself!"

"Oh, I know the kind of women that Miss Chancellor had at her house, and what a group you must have made when you looked out at the Back Bay! It depresses me very much to think of it."

"We made a lovely, interesting group, and, if we had had a spare minute we would have been photographed," Verena said.

This led him to ask her if she had ever subjected herself to the process; and she answered that a photographer had been after her as soon as she got back from Europe, and that she had sat for him, and that there were certain shops in Boston where her portrait could be obtained. She gave him this information very simply, without pretense of vagueness of knowledge, spoke of the matter rather respectfully, indeed, as if it might be of some importance; and when he said that he should go and buy one of the little pictures as soon as he returned to town, contented herself with replying, "Well, be sure you pick out a good one!" He had not been altogether without a hope that she would offer to give him one, with her name written beneath, which was a mode of acquisition he would greatly have preferred; but this, evidently, had not occurred to her, and now, as they went further, her thought was following a different train. That was proved by her remarking, at the end of a silence, inconsequently, "Well, it showed I have a great use!" As he stared, wondering what she meant, she explained that she referred to the brilliancy of her success at the convention. "It proved I have a great use," she repeated, "and that is all I care for!"

"The use of a truly amiable woman is to make some honest man happy," Ransom said, with a sententiousness of which he was perfectly aware.

It was so marked that it caused her to stop short in the middle of the broad walk, while she looked at him with shining eyes. "See here, Mr. Ransom, do you know what strikes me?" she exclaimed. "The interest you take in me isn't really controversial—a bit. It's quite personal!" She was the most extraordinary girl; she could speak such words as those without the smallest look of added consciousness coming into her face, without the least supposable intention of coquetry, or any visible purpose of challenging the young man to say more.

"My interest in you—my interest in you," he began. Then hesitating, he broke off suddenly. "It is certain your discovery doesn't make it any less!"

"Well, that's better," she went on; "for we needn't dispute."

He laughed at the way she arranged it, and they presently reached the irregular group of heterogeneous buildings —chapels, dormitories, libraries, halls—which, scattered among slender trees, over a space reserved by means of a low rustic fence, rather than inclosed (for Harvard knows nothing either of the jealousy or the dignity of high walls and guarded gateways), constitutes the great university of Massachusetts. The yard, or college-precinct, is traversed by a number of straight little paths, over which, at certain hours of the day, a thousand undergraduates, with books under their arm and youth in their step, flit from one school to another. Verena Tarrant knew her way round, as she said to her companion; it was not the first time she had taken an admiring visitor to see the local monuments. Basil Ransom, walking with her from point to point, admired them all, and thought several of them exceedingly quaint and venerable. The rectangular structures of old red brick especially gratified his eye; the afternoon sun was yellow on their homely faces; their windows showed a peep of flower-pots and bright-colored curtains; they wore an expression of scholastic quietude, and exhaled for the young Missis-sippian a tradition, an antiquity. "This is the place where I ought to have been," he said to his charming guide. "I should have had a good time if I had been able to study here."

"Yes; I presume you feel yourself drawn to any place where ancient prejudices are garnered up," she answered, not without archness. "I know by the stand you take about our cause that you share the superstitions of the old book-men. You ought to have been at one of those really mediæval universities that we saw on the other side, at Oxford, or Göttingen, or Padua. You would have been in perfect sym-pathy with their spirit."

"Well, I don't know much about those old haunts," Ran-som rejoined. "I reckon this is good enough for me. And then it would have had the advantage that your residence isn't far, you know."

"Oh, I guess we shouldn't have seen you much at my residence! As you live in New York, you come, but here you wouldn't; that is always the way." With this light philosophy Verena beguiled the transit to the library, into which she introduced her companion with the air of a person familiar with the sanctified spot. This edifice, a diminished copy of the chapel of King's College, at the greater Cambridge, is a rich and impressive institution; and as he stood there, in the bright, heated stillness, which seemed suffused with the odor of old print and old bindings, and looked up 'into the high, light vaults that hung over quiet book-laden galleries, alcoves and tables, and glazed cases where rarer treasures gleamed more vaguely, over busts of benefactors and portraits of worthies, bowed heads of working students and the gentle creak of passing messengers—as he took possession, in a comprehensive glance, of the wealth and wisdom of the place, he felt more than ever the soreness of an opportunity missed; but he abstained from expressing it (it was too deep for that), and in a moment Verena had introduced him to a young lady, a friend of hers, who, as she explained, was working on the catalogue, and whom she had asked for on entering the library, at a desk where another young lady was occupied. Miss Catching, the first-mentioned young lady, presented herself with promptness, offered Verena a low-toned but appreciative greeting, and, after a little, undertook to explain to Ransom the mysteries of the catalogue, which consisted of a myriad little cards, disposed alphabetically in immense chests of drawers. Ransom was deeply interested, and as, with Verena, he followed Miss Catching about (she was so good as to show them the establishment in all its ramifications), he considered with attention the young lady's fair ringlets and refined, anxious expression, saying to himself that this was in the highest degree a New England type. Verena found an opportunity to mention to him that she was wrapped up in the cause, and there was a moment during which he was afraid that his companion would expose him to her as one of its traducers; but there was that in Miss Catching's manner (and in the influence of the lofty halls), which deprecated loud pleasantry, and seemed to say, moreover, that if she were treated to such a revelation she should not know under what letter to range it.

"Now there is one place where perhaps it would be indelicate to take a Mississippian," Verena said, after this episode. "I mean the great place that towers above the others—that big building with the beautiful pinnacles, which you see from every point." But Basil Ransom had heard of the great Memorial Hall; he knew what memories it enshrined, and the worst that he should have to suffer there; and the ornate, overtopping structure, which was the finest piece of architecture he had ever seen, had moreover solicited his enlarged curiosity for the last half-hour. He thought there was rather too much brick about it, but it was buttressed, cloistered, turreted, dedicated, superscribed, as he had never seen anything; though it didn't look old, it looked significant; it covered a large area, and it sprang majestic into the winter air. It was detached from the rest of the collegiate group, and stood in a grassy triangle of its own. As he approached it with Verena, she suddenly stopped, to decline responsibility. "Now mind, if you don't like what's inside, it isn't my fault."

He looked at her an instant, smiling. "Is there anything against Mississippi?"

"Well, no, I don't think she is mentioned. But there is great praise of our young men in the war."

"It says they were brave, I suppose."

"Yes, it says so in Latin."

"Well, so they were—I know something about that," Basil Ransom said. "I must be brave enough to face them—it isn't the first time." And they went up the low steps and passed into the tall doors. The Memorial Hall of Harvard consists of three main divisions: one of them a theatre, for academic ceremonies; another a vast refectory, covered with a timbered roof, hung about with portraits and lighted by stained windows, like the halls of the colleges of Oxford; and the third, the most interesting, a chamber high, dim, and severe, consecrated to the sons of the university who fell in the long Civil War. Ransom and his companion wandered from one part of the building to another, and stayed their steps at several impressive points; but they lingered longest in the presence of the white, ranged tablets, each of which, in its proud, sad clearness, is inscribed with the name of a student-soldier. The effect of the place is singularly noble and solemn, and it is impossible to feel it without a lifting of the heart. If stands there for duty and honor, it speaks of sacrifice and example, seems a kind of temple to youth, manhood, generosity. Most of them were young, all were in their prime, and all of them had fallen; this simple idea hovers before the visitor and makes him read with tenderness each name and place—names often without other history, and forgotten Southern battles. For Ransom these things were not a challenge nor a taunt; they touched him with respect, with the sentiment of beauty. He was capable of being a generous foeman, and he forgot, now, the whole question of sides and parties; the simple emotion of the old fighting-time came back to him, and the monument around him seemed an embodiment of that memory; it arched over friends as well as enemies, the victims of defeat as well as the sons of triumph.

"It is very beautiful—but I think it is very dreadful!" This remark, from Verena, called him back to the present. "It's a real sin to put up such a building, just to glorify a lot of bloodshed. If it wasn't so majestic, I would have it pulled down."

"That is delightful feminine logic!" Ransom answered. "If, when women have the conduct of affairs, they fight as well as they reason, surely for them too we shall have to set up memorials."

Verena retorted that they would reason so well they would have no need to fight—they would usher in the reign of peace. "But this is very peaceful too," she added, looking about her; and she sat down on a low stone ledge, as if to enjoy the influence of the scene. Ransom left her alone for ten minutes; he wished to take another look at the inscribed tablets, and read again the names of the various engagements, at several of which he had been present. When he came back to her she greeted him abruptly, with a question which had no reference to the solemnity of the spot. "If Miss Birdseye knew you were coming out to see me, can't *she* easily tell Olive? Then won't Olive make her reflections about your neglect of herself?"

"I don't care for her reflections. At any rate, I asked Miss Birdseye, as a favor, not to mention to her that she had met me," Ransom added.

Verena was silent a moment. "Your logic is almost as good as a woman's. Do change your mind and go to see her now," she went on. "She will probably be at home by the time you get to Charles Street. If she was a little strange, a little stiff with you before (I know just how she must have been), all that will be different today."

"Why will it be different?"

"Oh, she will be easier, more genial, much softer."

"I don't believe it," said Ransom; and his skepticism seemed none the less complete because it was light and smiling.

"She is much happier now—she can afford not to mind you."

"Not to mind me? That's a nice inducement for a gentleman to go and see a lady!"

"Well, she will be more gracious, because she feels now that she is more successful."

"You mean because she has brought you out? Oh, I have no doubt that has cleared the air for her immensely, and you have improved her very much. But I have got a charming impression out here, and I have no wish to put another —which won't be charming, anyhow you arrange it—on top of it."

"Well, she will be sure to know you have been round here, at any rate," Verena rejoined.

"How will she know, unless you tell her?"

249

"I tell her everything," said the girl; and now as soon as she had spoken, she blushed. He stood before her, tracing a figure on the mosaic pavement with his cane, conscious that in a moment they had become more intimate. They were discussing their affairs, which had nothing to do with the heroic symbols that surrounded them; but their affairs had suddenly grown so serious that there was no want of decency in their lingering there for the purpose. The implication that his visit might remain as a secret between them made them both feel it differently. To ask her to keep it so would have been, as it seemed to Ransom, a liberty, and, moreover, he didn't care so much as that; but if she were to prefer to do so such a preference would only make him consider the more that his expedition had been a success.

"Oh, then, you can tell her this!" he said in a moment.

"If I shouldn't, it would be the first—" And Verena checked herself.

"You must arrange that with your conscience," Ransom went on, laughing.

They came out of the hall, passed down the steps, and emerged from the Delta, as that portion of the college precinct is called. The afternoon had begun to wane, but the air was filled with a pink brightness, and there was a cool, pure smell, a vague breath of spring.

"Well, if I don't tell Olive, then you must leave me here," said Verena, stopping in the path and putting out a hand of farewell.

"I don't understand. What has that to do with it? Besides I thought you said you *must* tell," Ransom added. In playing with the subject this way, in enjoying her visible hesitation, he was slightly conscious of a man's brutality—of being pushed by an impulse to test her good nature, which seemed to have no limit. It showed no sign of perturbation as she answered:

"Well, I want to be free—to do as I think best. And, if there is a chance of my keeping it back, there mustn't

250

be anything more—there must not, Mr. Ransom, really."

"Anything more? Why, what are you afraid there will be —if I should simply walk home with you?"

"I must go alone, I must hurry back to mother," she said, for all reply. And she again put out her hand, which he had not taken before.

Of course he took it now, and even held it a moment; he didn't like being dismissed, and was thinking of pretexts to linger. "Miss Birdseye said you would convert me, but you haven't yet," it came into his head to say.

"You can't tell yet; wait a little. My influence is peculiar; it sometimes comes out a long time afterwards!" This speech, on Verena's part, was evidently perfunctory, and the grandeur of her self-reference jocular; she was much more serious when she went on quickly, "Do you mean to say Miss Birdseye promised you that?"

"Oh yes. Talk about influence! you should have seen the influence I obtained over her."

"Well, what good will it do, if I'm going to tell Olive about your visit?"

"Well, you see, I think she hopes you won't. She believes you are going to convert me privately—so that I shall blaze forth, suddenly, out of the darkness of Mississippi, as a first-class proselyte: very effective and dramatic."

Verena struck Basil Ransom as constantly simple, but there were moments when her candor seemed to him preternatural. "If I thought that would be the effect, I might make an exception," she remarked, speaking as if such a result were, after all, possible.

"Oh, Miss Tarrant, you will convert me enough, anyway," said the young man.

"Enough? What do you mean by enough?"

"Enough to make me terribly unhappy."

She looked at him a moment, evidently not understanding; but she tossed him a retort at a venture, turned away, and took her course homeward. The retort was that if he should be unhappy it would serve him right—a form of

251

words that committed her to nothing. As he returned to Boston he saw how curious he should be to learn whether she had betrayed him, as it were, to Miss Chancellor. He might learn through Mrs. Luna; that would almost reconcile him to going to see her again. Olive would mention it in writing to her sister, and Adeline would repeat the complaint. Perhaps she herself would even make him a scene about it; that would be, for him, part of the unhappiness he had foretold to Verena Tarrant.

26

"Mrs. Henry Burrage, at home Wednesday evening, March 26th, at half-past nine o'clock." It was in consequence of having received a card with these words inscribed upon it that Basil Ransom presented himself, on the evening she had designated, at the house of a lady he had never heard of before. The account of the relation of effect to cause is not complete, however, unless I mention that the card bore, furthermore, in the left-hand lower corner, the words: "An Address from Miss Verena Tarrant." He had an idea (it came mainly from the look and even the odor of the engraved pasteboard), that Mrs. Burrage was a member of the fashionable world, and it was with considerable surprise that he found himself in such an element. He wondered what had induced a denizen of that fine air to send him an invitation; then he said to himself that, obviously, Verena Tarrant had simply requested that this should be done. Mrs. Henry Burrage, whoever she might be, had asked her if she shouldn't like some of her own friends to be present, and she had said, Oh yes, and mentioned him in the happy group. She had been able to give Mrs. Burrage his address, for had it not been contained in the short letter he despatched to Monadnoc Place soon after his return from Boston, in which he thanked Miss Tarrant afresh for the charming hour she had enabled him to spend at Cambridge? She had not answered his letter at the time, but Mrs. Burrage's card was a very good answer. Such a missive deserved a rejoinder, and it was by way of rejoinder that he entered the streetcar which, on the evening of March 26th, was to deposit him at a corner adjacent to Mrs. Burrage's dwelling. He almost never went to evening parties (he knew scarcely any one who gave them, though Mrs. Luna had broken him in a little), and he was sure this occasion was of festive intention, would have nothing in common with the nocturnal "exercises" at Miss Birdseye's; but he would have exposed himself to almost any social discomfort in order to see Verena Tarrant on the platform. The platform it evidently was to be—private if not public—since one was admitted by a ticket given away if not sold. He took his in his pocket, quite ready to present it at the door. It would take some time for me to explain the contradiction to the reader; but Basil Ransom's desire to be present at one of Verena's regular performances was not diminished by the fact that he detested her views and thought the whole business a poor perversity. He understood her now very well (since his visit to Cambridge); he saw she was honest and natural; she had queer, bad lecture-blood in her veins, and a comically false idea of the aptitude of little girls for conducting movements; but her enthusiasm was of the purest, her illusions had a fragrance, and so far as the mania for producing herself personally was concerned, it had been distilled into her by people who worked her for ends which to Basil Ransom could only appear insane. She was a touching, ingenuous victim, unconscious of the pernicious forces which were hurrying her to her ruin. With this idea of ruin there had already associated itself in the young man's mind, the idea —a good deal more dim and incomplete—of rescue; and it was the disposition to confirm himself in the view that her charm was her own, and her fallacies, her absurdity, a mere reflection of unlucky circumstance, that led him to make an effort to behold her in the position in which he could least bear to think of her. Such a glimpse was all that was wanted to prove to him that she was a person for whom he might open an unlimited credit of tender compassion. He expected to suffer—to suffer deliciously.

By the time he had crossed Mrs. Burrage's threshold there was no doubt whatever in his mind that he was in the fashionable world. It was embodied strikingly in the stout, elderly, ugly lady, dressed in a brilliant color, with a twinkle of jewels and a bosom much uncovered, who stood near the door of the first room, and with whom the people passing in before him were shaking hands. Ransom made her a Mississippian bow, and she said she was delighted to see him, while people behind him pressed him forward. He yielded to the impulse, and found himself in a great salon, amid lights and flowers, where the company was dense, and there were more twinkling, smiling ladies, with uncovered bosoms. It was certainly the fashionable world, for there was no one there whom he had ever seen before. The walls of the room were covered with pictures—the very ceiling was painted and framed. The people pushed each other a little, edged about, advanced and retreated, looking at each other with differing faces—sometimes blandly, unperceivingly, sometimes with a harshness of contemplation, a kind of cruelty, Ransom thought; sometimes with sudden nods and grimaces, inarticulate murmurs, followed by a quick reaction, a sort of gloom. He was now absolutely certain that he was in the best society. He was carried further and further forward, and saw that another room stretched beyond the one he had entered, in which there was a sort of little stage, covered with a red cloth, and an immense collection of chairs, arranged in rows. He became aware that people looked at him, as well as at each other, rather more, indeed, than at each other, and he wondered whether it were very visible in his appearance that his being there was a kind of exception. He didn't know how much his head looked over the heads of others, or that his brown complexion, fuliginous eye, and straight black hair, the leonine fall of which I mentioned in the first pages of this narrative, gave him that relief which, in the best society, has the great advantage of suggesting a topic. But there were other topics besides, as was proved by a fragment of conversation, between two ladies, which reached his ear while he stood rather wistfully wondering where Verena Tarrant might be.

"Are you a member?" one of the ladies said to the other. "I didn't know you had joined."

"Oh, I haven't; nothing would induce me."

"That's not fair; you have all the fun and none of the responsibility."

"Oh, the fun—the fun!" exclaimed the second lady.

"You needn't abuse us, or I will never invite you," said the first.

"Well, I thought it was meant to be improving; that's all I mean; very good for the mind. Now, this woman tonight; isn't she from Boston?"

"Yes, I believe they have brought her on, just for this."

"Well, you must be pretty desperate when you have got to go to Boston for your entertainment."

"Well, there's a similar society there, and I never heard of their sending to New York."

"Of course not, they think they have got everything. But doesn't it make your life a burden, thinking what you can possibly have?"

"Oh dear, no. I am going to have Professor Gougenheim —all about the Talmud. You must come."

"Well, I'll come," said the second lady; "but nothing would induce me to be a regular member."

Whatever the mystic circle might be, Ransom agreed with the second lady that regular membership must have terrors,

255

and he admired her independence in such an artificial world. A considerable part of the company had now directed itself to the further apartment—people had begun to occupy the chairs, to confront the empty platform. He reached the wide doors, and saw that the place was a spacious music-room, decorated in white and gold, with a polished floor and marble busts of composers, on brackets attached to the delicate panels. He forbore to enter, however, being shy about taking a seat, and seeing that the ladies were arranging themselves first. He turned back into the first room, to wait till the audience had massed itself, conscious that even if he were behind every one he should be able to make a long neck; and here, suddenly, in a corner, his eyes rested upon Olive Chancellor. She was seated a little apart, in an angle of the room, and she was looking straight at him; but as soon as she perceived that he saw her she dropped her eyes, giving no sign of recognition. Ransom hesitated a moment, but the next he went straight over to her. It had been in his mind that if Verena Tarrant was there, *she* would be there; an instinct told him that Miss Chancellor would not allow her dear friend to come to New York without her. It was very possible she meant to "cut" him—especially if she knew of his having cut her, the other week, in Boston; but it was his duty to take for granted she would speak to him, until the contrary should be definitely proved. Though he had seen her only twice he remembered well how acutely shy she was capable of being, and he thought it possible one of these spasms had seized her at the present time.

When he stood before her he found his conjecture perfectly just; she was white with the intensity of her self-consciousness; she was altogether in a very uncomfortable state. She made no response to his offer to shake hands with her, and he saw that she would never go through that ceremony again. She looked up at him when he spoke to her, and her lips moved; but her face was intensely grave and her eye had almost a feverish light. She had evidently got into her corner to be out of the way; he recognized in her the air of an interloper, as he had felt it in himself. The small sofa on which she had placed herself had the form to which the French give the name of *causeuse;* there was room on it for just another person, and Ransom asked her, with a cheerful accent, if he might sit down beside her. She turned toward him when he had done so, turned every-thing but her eyes, and opened and shut her fan while she waited for her fit of diffidence to pass away. Ransom himself did not wait; he took a jocular tone about their encounter, asking her if she had come to New York to rouse the people. She glanced round the room; the backs of Mrs. Burrage's guests, mainly, were presented to them, and their position was partly masked by a pyramid of flowers which rose from a pedestal close to Olive's end of the sofa and diffused a fragrance in the air.

"Do you call these the 'people'?" she asked.

"I haven't the least idea. I don't know who any of them are, not even who Mrs. Henry Burrage is. I simply received an invitation."

Miss Chancellor gave him no information on the point he had mentioned; she only said, in a moment: "Do you go wherever you are invited?"

"Why, I go if I think I may find you there," the young man replied, gallantly. "My card mentioned that Miss Tarrant would give an address, and I knew that wherever she is you are not far off. I have heard you are inseparable, from Mrs. Luna."

"Yes, we are inseparable. That is exactly why I am here."

"It's the fashionable world, then, you are going to stir up."

Olive remained for some time with her eyes fastened to the floor; then she flashed them up at her interlocutor. "It's a part of our life to go anywhere—to carry our work where it seems most needed. We have taught ourselves to stifle repulsion, distaste."

"Oh, I think this is very amusing," said Ransom. "It's

a beautiful house, and there are some very pretty faces. We haven't anything so brilliant in Mississippi."

To everything he said Olive offered at first a momentary silence, but the worst of her shyness was apparently leaving her.

"Are you successful in New York? do you like it?" she presently asked, uttering the inquiry in a tone of infinite melancholy, as if the eternal sense of duty forced it from her lips.

"Oh, successful! I am not successful as you and Miss Tarrant are; for (to my barbaric eyes) it is a great sign of prosperity to be the heroines of an occasion like this."

"Do I look like the heroine of an occasion?" asked Olive Chancellor, without an intention of humor, but with an effect that was almost comical.

"You would if you didn't hide yourself away. Are you not going into the other room to hear the speech? Everything is prepared."

"I am going when I am notified—when I am invited."

There was considerable majesty in her tone, and Ransom saw that something was wrong, that she felt neglected. To see that she was as ticklish with others as she had been with him made him feel forgiving, and there was in his manner a perfect disposition to forget their differences as he said, "Oh, there is plenty of time; the place isn't half full yet."

She made no direct rejoinder to this, but she asked him about his mother and sisters, what news he received from the South. "Have they any happiness?" she inquired, rather as if she warned him to take care not to pretend they had. He neglected her warning to the point of saying that there was one happiness they always had—that of having learned not to think about it too much, and to make the best of their circumstances. She listened to this with an air of great reserve, and apparently thought he had wished to give her a lesson; for she suddenly broke out, "You mean that you

258

have traced a certain line for them, and that that's all you know about it!"

Ransom stared at her, surprised; he felt, now, that she would always surprise him. "Ah, don't be rough with me," he said, in his soft Southern voice; "don't you remember how you knocked me about when I called on you in Boston?"

"You hold us in chains, and then, when we writhe in our agony, you say we don't behave prettily!" These words, which did not lessen Ransom's wonderment, were the young lady's answer to his deprecatory speech. She saw that he was honestly bewildered and that in a moment more he would laugh at her, as he had done a year and a half before (she remembered it as if it had been yesterday); and to stop that off, at any cost, she went on hurriedly— "If you listen to Miss Tarrant, you will know what I mean."

"Oh, Miss Tarrant—Miss Tarrant!" And Basil Ransom's laughter came.

She had not escaped that mockery, after all, and she looked at him sharply now, her embarrassment having quite cleared up. "What do you know about her? What observation have you had?"

Ransom met her eye, and for a moment they scrutinized each other. Did she know of his interview with Verena a month before, and was her reserve simply the wish to place on him the burden of declaring that he had been to Boston since they last met, and yet had not called in Charles Street? He thought there was suspicion in her face; but in regard to Verena she would always be suspicious. If he had done at that moment just what would gratify him he would have said to her that he knew a great deal about Miss Tarrant, having lately had a long walk and talk with her; but he checked himself, with the reflection that if Verena had not betrayed him it would be very wrong in him to betray her. The sweetness of the idea that she should have thought the episode of his visit to Monadnoc Place

259

worth placing under the rose, was quenched for the moment in his regret at not being able to let his disagreeable cousin know that he had passed *her* over. "Don't you remember my hearing her speak that night at Miss Birdseye's?" he said, presently. "And I met her the next day at your house, you know."

"She has developed greatly since then," Olive remarked drily; and Ransom felt sure that Verena had held her tongue.

At this moment a gentleman made his way through the clusters of Mrs. Burrage's guests and presented himself to Olive. "If you will do me the honor to take my arm I will find a good seat for you in the other room. It's getting to be time for Miss Tarrant to reveal herself. I have been taking her into the picture-room; there were some things she wanted to see. She is with my mother now," he added, as if Miss Chancellor's grave face constituted a sort of demand for an explanation of her friend's absence. "She said she was a little nervous; so I thought we would just move about."

"It's the first time I have ever heard of that!" said Olive Chancellor, preparing to surrender herself to the young man's guidance. He told her that he had reserved the best seat for her; it was evidently his desire to conciliate her, to treat her as a person of importance. Before leading her away, he shook hands with Ransom and remarked that he was very glad to see him; and Ransom saw that he must be the master of the house, though he could scarcely be the son of the stout lady in the doorway. He was a fresh, pleasant, handsome young man, with a bright friendly manner; he recommended Ransom to take a seat in the other room, without delay; if he had never heard Miss Tarrant he would have one of the greatest pleasures of his life.

"Oh, Mr. Ransom only comes to ventilate his prejudices," Miss Chancellor said, as she turned her back to her kinsman. He shrank from pushing into the front of the company, which was now rapidly filling the music-room, and contented himself with lingering in the doorway, where several gentlemen were stationed. The seats were all occupied; all, that is, save one, toward which he saw Miss Chancellor and her companion direct themselves, squeezing and edging past the people who were standing up against the walls. This was quite in front, close to the little platform; every one noticed Olive as she went, and Ransom heard a gentleman near him say to another—"I guess she's one of the same kind." He looked for Verena, but she was apparently keeping out of sight. Suddenly he felt himself smartly tapped on the back, and, turning round, perceived Mrs. Luna, who had been prodding him with her fan.

27

"You won't speak to me in my own house—that I have almost grown used to; but if you are going to pass me over in public I think you might give me warning first." This was only her archness, and he knew what to make of that now; she was dressed in yellow and looked very plump and gay. He wondered at the unerring instinct by which she had discovered his exposed quarter. The outer room was completely empty; she had come in at the further door and found the field free for her operations. He offered to find her a place where she could see and hear Miss Tarrant, to get her a chair to stand on, even, if she wished to look over the heads of the gentlemen in the doorway; a proposal which she greeted with the inquiry—"Do you suppose I came here for the sake of that chatterbox? haven't I told you what I think of her?"

"Well, you certainly did not come here for my sake," said Ransom, anticipating this insinuation; "for you couldn't possibly have known I was coming."

"I guessed it—a presentiment told me!" Mrs. Luna declared; and she looked up at him with searching, accusing eyes. "I know what you have come for," she cried in a moment. "You never mentioned to me that you knew Mrs. Burrage!"

"I don't—I never had heard of her till she asked me."

"Then why in the world *did* she ask you?"

Ransom had spoken a trifle rashly; it came over him, quickly, that there were reasons why he had better not have said that. But almost as quickly he covered up his mistake. "I suppose your sister was so good as to ask for a card for me."

"My sister? My grandmother! I know how Olive loves you. Mr. Ransom, you are very deep." She had drawn him well into the room, out of earshot of the group in the doorway, and he felt that if she should be able to compass her wish she would organize a little entertainment for herself, in the outer drawing room, in opposition to Miss Tarrant's address. "Please come and sit down here a moment; we shall be quite undisturbed. I have something very particular to say to you." She led the way to the little sofa in the corner, where he had been talking with Olive a few minutes before, and he accompanied her, with extreme reluctance, grudging the moments that he should be obliged to give to her. He had quite forgotten that he once had a vision of spending his life in her society, and he looked at his watch as he made the observation:

"I haven't the least idea of losing any of the sport in there, you know."

He felt, the next instant, that he oughtn't to have said that either; but he was irritated, disconcerted, and he couldn't help it. It was in the nature of a gallant Mississippian to do everything a lady asked him, and he had never, remarkable as it may appear, been in the position of finding such a request so incompatible with his own desires as now. It was a new predicament, for Mrs. Luna evidently meant to keep him if she could. She looked round the room, more and more pleased at their having it to themselves, and for the moment said nothing more about the singularity of his being there. On the contrary, she became freshly jocular, remarked that now they had got hold of him they wouldn't easily let him go, they would make him entertain them, induce him to gave a lecture—on the "Lights and Shadows of Southern Life," or the "Social Peculiarities of Mississippi" —before the Wednesday Club.

"And what in the world is the Wednesday Club? I suppose it's what those ladies were talking about," Ransom said.

"I don't know your ladies, but the Wednesday Club is this thing. I don't mean you and me here together, but all those deluded beings in the other room. It is New York trying to be like Boston. It is the culture, the good form, of the metropolis. You might not think it, but it is. It's the "quiet set"; they *are* quiet enough; you might hear a pin drop, in there. Is someone going to offer up a prayer? How happy Olive must be, to be taken so seriously! They form an association for meeting at each other's houses, every week, and having some performance, or some paper read, or some subject explained. The more dreary it is and the more fearful the subject, the more they think it is what it ought to be. They have an idea this is the way to make New York society intellectual. There's a sumptuary law— isn't that what you call it?—about suppers, and they restrict themselves to a kind of Spartan broth. When it's made by their French cooks it isn't bad. Mrs. Burrage is one of the principal members—one of the founders, I believe; and when her turn has come round, formerly—it comes only once in the winter for each—I am told she has usually had very good music. But that is thought rather a base evasion,

263

a begging of the question; the vulgar set can easily keep up with them on music. So Mrs. Burrage conceived the extraordinary idea"—and it was wonderful to hear how Mrs. Luna pronounced that adjective—"of sending on to Boston for that girl. It was her son, of course, who put it into her head; he has been at Cambridge for some years—that's where Verena lived, you know—and he was as thick with her as you please out there. Now that he is no longer there it suits him very well to have her here. She is coming on a visit to his mother when Olive goes. I asked them to stay with me, but Olive declined, majestically; she said they wished to be in some place where they would be free to receive "sympathizing friends." So they are staying at some extraordinary kind of New Jerusalem boarding house, in Tenth Street; Olive thinks it's her duty to go to such places. I was greatly surprised that she should let Verena be drawn into such a worldly crowd as this; but she told me they had made up their minds not to let *any* occasion slip, that they could sow the seed of truth in drawing rooms as well as in workshops, and that if a single person was brought round to their ideas they should have been justified in coming on. That's what they are doing in there—sowing the seed; but you shall not be the one that's brought round, I shall take care of that. Have you seen my delightful sister yet? The way she *does* arrange herself when she wants to protest against frills! She looks as if she thought it pretty barren ground round here, now she has come to see it. I don't think she thinks you can be saved in a French dress, anyhow. I must say I call it a *very* base evasion of Mrs. Burrage's, producing Verena Tarrant; it's worse than the meretricious music. Why didn't she honestly send for a *ballerina* from Niblo's—if she wanted a young woman capering about on a platform? They don't care a fig about poor Olive's ideas; it's only because Verena has strange hair, and shiny eyes, and gets herself up like a prestidigitator's assistant. I have never understood how Olive can reconcile herself to Verena's really low style of dress. I suppose it's only because her clothes are so fearfully made. You look as if you didn't believe me—but I assure you that the cut is revolutionary; and that's a salve to Olive's conscience."

Ransom was surprised to hear that he looked as if he didn't believe her, for he had found himself, after his first uneasiness, listening with considerable interest to her account of the circumstances under which Miss Tarrant was visiting New York. After a moment, as the result of some private reflection, he propounded this question: "Is the son of the lady of the house a handsome young man, very polite, in a white vest?"

"I don't know the color of his vest—but he has a kind of fawning manner. Verena judges from that that he is in love with her."

"Perhaps he is," said Ransom. "You say it was his idea to get her to come on."

"Oh, he likes to flirt; that is highly probable."

"Perhaps she has brought him round."

"Not to where she wants, I think. The property is very large; he will have it all one of these days."

"Do you mean she wishes to impose on him the yoke of matrimony?" Ransom asked, with Southern languor.

"I believe she thinks matrimony an exploded superstition; but there is here and there a case in which it is still the best thing; when the gentleman's name happens to be Burrage and the young lady's Tarrant. I don't admire 'Burrage' so much myself. But I think she would have captured this present scion if it hadn't been for Olive. Olive stands between them—she wants to keep her in the single sisterhood; to keep her, above all, for herself. Of course she won't listen to her marrying, and she has put a spoke in the wheel. She has brought her to New York; that may seem against what I say; but the girl pulls hard, she has to humor her, to give her her head sometimes, to throw something overboard, in short, to save the rest. You may say, as regards Mr. Burrage, that it's a queer taste in a gentleman; but there is no arguing about that. It's queer taste in a lady, too; for she is a lady, poor Olive. You can see that tonight. She is dressed like a book-agent, but she is more distinguished than anyone here. Verena, beside her, looks like a walking advertisement."

When Mrs. Luna paused, Basil Ransom became aware that, in the other room, Verena's address had begun; the sound of her clear, bright, ringing voice, an admirable voice for public uses, came to them from the distance. His eagerness to stand where he could hear her better, and see her into the bargain, made him start in his place, and this movement produced an outgush of mocking laughter on the part of his companion. But she didn't say—"Go, go, deluded man, I take pity on you!" she only remarked, with light impertinence, that he surely wouldn't be so wanting in gallantry as to leave a lady absolutely alone in a public place— it was so Mrs. Luna was pleased to qualify Mrs. Burrage's drawing room—in the face of her entreaty that he would remain with her. She had the better of poor Ransom, thanks to the superstitions of Mississippi. It was in his simple code a gross rudeness to withdraw from conversation with a lady at a party before another gentleman should have come to take one's place; it was to inflict on the lady a kind of outrage. The other gentlemen, at Mrs. Burrage's, were all too well occupied; there was not the smallest chance of one of them coming to his rescue. He couldn't leave Mrs. Luna, and yet he couldn't stay with her and lose the only thing he had come so much out of his way for. "Let me at least find you a place over there, in the doorway. You can stand upon a chair—you can lean on me."

"Thank you very much; I would much rather lean on this sofa. And I am much too tired to stand on chairs. Besides, I wouldn't for the world that either Verena or Olive should see me craning over the heads of the crowd—as if I attached the smallest importance to their perorations!"

"It isn't time for the peroration yet," Ransom said, with savage dryness; and he sat forward, with his elbow on his knees, his eyes on the ground, a flush in his sallow cheek.

"It's never time to say such things as those," Mrs. Luna remarked, arranging her laces.

"How do you know what she is saying?"

"I can tell by the way her voice goes up and down. It sounds so silly."

Ransom sat there five minutes longer—minutes which, he felt, the recording angel ought to write down to his credit —and asked himself how Mrs. Luna could be such a goose as not to see that she was making him hate her. But she was goose enough for anything. He tried to appear indifferent, and it occurred to him to doubt whether the Mississippi system could be right, after all. It certainly hadn't foreseen such a case as this. "It's as plain as day that Mr. Burrage intends to marry her—if he can," he said in a minute; that remark being better calculated than any other he could think of to dissimulate his real state of mind.

It drew no rejoinder from his companion, and after an instant he turned his head a little and glanced at her. The result of something that silently passed between them was to make her say, abruptly: "Mr. Ransom, my sister never sent you an invitation to this place. Didn't it come from Verena Tarrant?"

"I haven't the least idea."

"As you hadn't the least acquaintance with Mrs. Burrage, who else could it have come from?"

"If it came from Miss Tarrant, I ought at least to recognize her courtesy by listening to her."

"If you rise from this sofa I will tell Olive what I suspect. She will be perfectly capable of carrying Verena off to China—or anywhere out of your reach."

"And pray what is it you suspect?"

"That you two have been in correspondence."

"Tell her whatever you like, Mrs. Luna," said the young man, with the grimness of resignation.

"You are quite unable to deny it, I see."

"I never contradict a lady."

"We shall see if I can't make you tell a fib. Haven't you been seeing Miss Tarrant, too?"

"Where should I have seen her? I can't see all the way to Boston, as you said the other day."

"Haven't you been there—on secret visits?"

Ransom started just perceptibly; but to conceal it, the next instant, he stood up.

"They wouldn't be secret if I were to tell you."

Looking down at her he saw that her words were a happy hit, not the result of definite knowledge. But she appeared to him vain, egotistical, grasping, odious.

"Well, I shall give the alarm," she went on; "this is, I will if you leave me. Is that the way a Southern gentleman treats a lady? Do as I wish, and I will let you off!"

"You won't let me off from staying with you."

"Is it such a *corvée?* I never heard of such rudeness!" Mrs. Luna cried. "All the same, I am determined to keep you if I can!"

Ransom felt that she must be in the wrong, and yet superficially she seemed (and it was quite intolerable), to have right on her side. All this while Verena's golden voice, with her words indistinct, solicited, tantalized his ear. The question had evidently got on Mrs. Luna's nerves; she had reached that point of feminine embroilment when a woman is perverse for the sake of perversity, and even with a clear vision of bad consequences.

"You have lost your head," he relieved himself by saying, as he looked down at her.

"I wish you would go and get me some tea."

"You say that only to embarrass me." He had hardly spoken when a great sound of applause, the clapping of many hands, and the cry from fifty throats of "Brava, brava!" floated in and died away. All Ransom's pulses throbbed, he flung his scruples to the winds, and after remarking to Mrs. Luna—still with all due ceremony—that he feared he must resign himself to forfeiting her good opinion, turned his back upon her and strode away to the open door of the music-room. "Well, I have never been so insulted!" he heard her exclaim, with exceeding sharpness, as he left her; and, glancing back at her, as he took up his position, he saw her still seated on her sofa—alone in the lamp-lit desert—with her eyes making, across the empty space, little vindictive points. Well, she could come where he was, if she wanted him so much; he would support her on an ottoman, and make it easy for her to see. But Mrs. Luna was uncompromising; he became aware, after a minute, that she had withdrawn, majestically, from the place, and he did not see her again that evening.

28

He could command the music-room very well from where he stood, behind a thick outer fringe of intently listening men. Verena Tarrant was erect on her little platform, dressed in white, with flowers in her bosom. The red cloth beneath her feet looked rich in the light of lamps placed on high pedestals on either side of the stage; it gave her figure a setting of color which made it more pure and salient. She moved freely in her exposed isolation, yet with great sobriety of gesture; there was no table in front of her, and she had no notes in her hand, but stood there like an actress before the footlights, or a singer spinning vocal sounds to a silver thread. There was such a risk that a slim provincial girl, pretending to fascinate a couple of hundred *blasé* New Yorkers by simply giving them her ideas, would fail of her effect, that at the end of a few moments Basil Ransom became aware that he was watching her in very much the same excited way as if she had been performing, high above his head, on the trapeze. Yet, as one listened, it was impossible not to perceive that she was in perfect possession of her faculties, her subject, her audience; and he remembered the other time at Miss Birdseye's well enough to be able to measure the ground she had traveled since then. This exhibition was much more complete, her manner much more assured; she seemed to speak and survey the whole place from a much greater height. Her voice, too, had developed; he had forgotten how beautiful it could be when she raised it to its full capacity. Such a tone as that, so pure and rich, and yet so young, so natural, constituted in itself a talent; he didn't wonder that they had made a fuss about her at the Female Convention, if she filled their hideous hall with such a music. He had read, of old, of the *improvisatrice* of Italy, and this was a chastened, modern, American version of the type, a New England Corinna, with a mission instead of a lyre. The most graceful part of her was her earnestness, the way her delightful eyes, wandering over the "fashionable audience" (before which she was so perfectly unabashed), as if she wished to resolve it into a single sentient personality, seemed to say that the only thing in life she cared for was to put the truth into a form that would render conviction irresistible. She was as simple as she was charming, and there was not a glance or motion that did not seem part of the pure, still-burning passion that animated her. She had indeed—it was manifest—reduced the company to unanimity; their attention was anything but languid; they smiled back at her when she smiled; they were noiseless, motionless when she was solemn; and it was evident that the entertainment which Mrs. Burrage had had the happy thought of offering to her friends would be memorable in the annals of the Wednesday Club. It was agreeable to Basil Ransom to think that Verena noticed him in his corner; her eyes played over her listeners so freely that you couldn't say they rested in one place more than another; nevertheless, a single rapid ray, which, however, didn't in the least strike him as a deviation from her ridiculous, fantastic, delightful argument, let him know that he had been missed and now was particularly spoken to. This glance was a sufficient assurance that his invitation had come to him by the girl's request. He took for granted the matter of her speech was ridiculous; how could it help being, and what did it signify if it was? She was none the less charming for that, and the moonshine she had been plied with was none the less moonshine for her being charming. After he had stood there a quarter of an hour he became conscious that he should not be able to repeat a word she had said; he had not definitely heeded it, and yet he had not lost a vibration of her voice. He had discovered Olive Chancellor by this time; she was in the front row of chairs, at the end, on the left; her back was turned to him, but he could see half her sharp profile, bent down a little and absolutely motionless. Even across the wide interval her attitude expressed to him a kind of rapturous stillness, the concentration of triumph. There were several irrepressible effusions of applause, instantly self-checked, but Olive never looked up, at the loudest, and such a calmness as that could only be the result of passionate volition. Success was in the air, and she was tasting it; she tasted it, as she did everything, in a way of her own. Success for Verena was success for her, and Ransom was sure that the only thing wanting to her triumph was that he should have been placed in the line of her vision, so that she might enjoy his embarrassment and confusion, might say to him, in one of her dumb, cold flashes—*"Now* do you think our movement is not a force—*now* do you think that women are meant to be slaves?" Honestly, he was not conscious of any confusion; it subverted none of his heresies to perceive that Verena Tarrant had even more power to fix his attention than he had hitherto supposed. It was fixed in a way it had not been yet, however, by his at last understanding her speech, feeling it reach his inner sense through the impediment of mere dazzled vision. Certain phrases took on a meaning for him—an appeal she was making to those who still resisted the beneficent influence of the truth. They appeared to be mocking, cynical men, mainly; many of whom were such triflers and idlers, so heartless and brainless that it didn't matter much what they thought on any subject; if the old tyranny needed to be propped up by *them* it showed it was in a pretty bad way. But there were others whose prejudice was stronger and more cultivated, pretended to rest upon study and argument. To those she wished particularly to address herself; she wanted to waylay them, to say, "Look here, you're all wrong; you'll be so much happier when I have convinced you. Just give me five minutes," she should like to say; "just sit down here and let me ask a simple question. Do you think any state of society can come to good that is based upon an organized wrong?" That was the simple question that Verena desired to propound, and Basil smiled across the room at her with an amused tenderness as he gathered that she conceived it to be a poser. He didn't think it would frighten him much if she were to ask him that, and he would sit down with her for as many minutes as she liked.

He, of course, was one of the systematic scoffers, one of those to whom she said—"Do you know how you strike me? You strike me as men who are starving to death while they have a cupboard at home, all full of bread and meat and wine; or as blind, demented beings who let themselves be cast into a debtor's prison, while in their pocket they have the key of vaults and treasure-chests heaped up with gold and silver. The meat and wine, the gold and silver," Verena went on, "are simply the suppressed and wasted force, the precious sovereign remedy, of which society insanely deprives itself—the genius, the intelligence, the inspiration of women. It is dying, inch by inch, in the midst of old superstitions which it invokes in vain, and yet it has the elixir of life in its hands. Let it drink but a draught, and it will bloom once more; it will be refreshed, radiant; it will find its youth again. The heart, the heart is cold, and nothing but the touch of woman can warm it, make it act. We *are* the Heart of humanity, and let us have the courage to insist on it! The public life of the world will move in the same barren, mechanical, vicious circle—the circle of egotism, cruelty, ferocity, jealousy, greed, of blind striving to do things only for *some,* at the cost of others, instead of trying to do everything for all. All, all? Who dares to say 'all' when we are not there? We are an equal, a splendid, an inestimable part. Try us and you'll see—you will wonder how, without us, society has ever dragged itself even this distance—so wretchedly small compared with what it might have been—on its painful earthly pilgrimage. That is what I should like above all to pour into the ears of those who still hold out, who stiffen their necks and repeat hard, empty formulas, which are as dry as a broken gourd that has been flung away in the desert. I would take them by their selfishness, their indolence, their interest. I am not here to recriminate, nor to deepen the gulf that already yawns between the sexes, and I don't accept the doctrine that they are natural enemies, since my plea is for a union far more intimate—provided it be equal—than any that the sages and philosophers of former times have ever dreamed of. Therefore I shall not touch upon the subject of men's being most easily influenced by considerations of what is most agreeable and profitable for *them;* I shall simply assume that they *are* so influenced, and I shall say to them that our cause would long ago have been gained if their vision were not so dim, so veiled, even in matters in which their own interests are concerned. If they had the same quick sight as women, if they had the intelligence of the heart, the world would be very different now; and I assure you that half the bitterness of our lot is to see so clearly and not to be able to do! Good gentlemen all, if I could make you believe how much brighter and fairer and sweeter the garden of life would be for you, if you would only let us help

273

you to keep it in order! You would like so much better to walk there, and you would find grass and trees and flowers that would make you think you were in Eden. That is what I should like to press home to each of you, personally, individually—to give him the vision of the world as it hangs perpetually before me, redeemed, transfigured, by a new moral tone. There would be generosity, tenderness, sympathy, where there is now only brute force and sordid rivalry. But you really do strike me as stupid even about your own welfare! Some of you say that we have already all the influence we can possibly require, and talk as if we ought to be grateful that we are allowed even to breathe. Pray, who shall judge what we require if not we ourselves? We require simply freedom; we require the lid to be taken off the box in which we have been kept for centuries. You say it's a very comfortable, cozy, convenient box, with nice glass sides, so that we can see out, and that all that's wanted is to give another quiet turn to the key. That is very easily answered. Good gentlemen, you have never been in the box, and you haven't the least idea how it feels!"

The historian who has gathered these documents together does not deem it necessary to give a larger specimen of Verena's eloquence, especially as Basil Ransom, through whose ears we are listening to it, arrived, at this point, at a definite conclusion. He had taken her measure as a public speaker, judged her importance in the field of discussion, the cause of reform. Her speech, in itself, had about the value of a pretty essay, committed to memory and delivered by a bright girl at an "academy"; it was vague, thin, rambling, a tissue of generalities that glittered agreeably enough in Mrs. Burrage's veiled lamplight. From any serious point of view it was neither worth answering nor worth considering, and Basil Ransom made his reflections on the crazy character of the age in which such a performance as that was treated as an intellectual effort, a contribution to a question. He asked himself what either he or anyone else would think of it if Miss Chancellor—or even Mrs. Luna

—had been on the platform instead of the actual declaimer. Nevertheless, its importance was high, and consisted precisely, in part, of the fact that the voice was not the voice of Olive or of Adeline. Its importance was that Verena was unspeakably attractive, and this was all the greater for him in the light of the fact, which quietly dawned upon him as he stood there, that he was falling in love with her. It had tapped at his heart for recognition, and before he could hesitate or challenge, the door had sprung open and the mansion was illuminated. He gave no outward sign; he stood gazing as at a picture; but the room wavered before his eyes, even Verena's figure danced a little. This did not make the sequel of her discourse more clear to him; her meaning faded again into the agreeable vague, and he simply felt her presence, tasted her voice. Yet the act of reflection was not suspended; he found himself rejoicing that she was so weak in argument, so inevitably verbose. The idea that she was brilliant, that she counted as a factor only because the public mind was in a muddle, was not an humiliation but a delight to him; it was a proof that her apostleship was all nonsense, the most passing of fashions, the veriest of delusions, and that she was meant for something divinely different—for privacy, for him, for love. He took no measure of the duration of her talk; he only knew, when it was over and succeeded by a clapping of hands, an immense buzz of voices and shuffling of chairs, that it had been capitally bad, and that her personal success, wrapping it about with a glamour like the silver mist that surrounds a fountain, was such as to prevent its badness from being a cause of mortification to her lover. The company—such of it as did not immediately close together around Verena—filed away into the other rooms, bore him in its current into the neighborhood of a table spread for supper, where he looked for signs of the sumptuary law mentioned to him by Mrs. Luna. It appeared to be embodied mainly in the glitter of crystal and silver, and the fresh tints of mysterious viands and jellies, which looked desirable in the soft circle projected by lace-fringed lamps. He heard the popping of corks, he felt a pressure of elbows, a thickening of the crowd, perceived that he was glowered at, squeezed against the table, by contending gentlemen who observed that he usurped space, was neither feeding himself nor helping others to feed. He had lost sight of Verena; she had been borne away in clouds of compliment; but he found himself thinking—almost paternally—that she must be hungry after so much chatter, and he hoped some one was getting her something to eat. After a moment, just as he was edging away, for his own opportunity to sup much better than usual was not what was uppermost in his mind, this little vision was suddenly embodied—embodied by the appearance of Miss Tarrant, who faced him, in the press, attached to the arm of a young man now recognizable to him as the son of the house—the smiling, fragrant youth who an hour before had interrupted his colloquy with Olive. He was leading her to the table, while people made way for them, covering Verena with gratulations of word and look. Ransom could see that, according to a phrase which came back to him just then, oddly, out of some novel or poem he had read of old, she was the cynosure of every eye. She looked beautiful, and they were a beautiful couple. As soon as she saw him, she put out her left hand to him—the other was in Mr. Burrage's arm—and said: "Well, don't you think it's all true?"

"No, not a word of it!" Ransom answered, with a kind of joyous sincerity. "But it doesn't make any difference."

"Oh, it makes a great deal of difference to me!" Verena cried.

"I mean to me. I don't care in the least whether I agree with you," Ransom said, looking askance at young Mr. Burrage, who had detached himself and was getting something for Verena to eat.

"Ah, well, if you are so indifferent!"

"It's not because I'm indifferent!" His eyes came back to her own, the expression of which had changed before they quitted them. She began to complain to her companion, who brought her something very dainty on a plate, that Mr. Ransom was "standing out," that he was about the hardest subject she had encountered yet. Henry Burrage smiled upon Ransom in a way that was meant to show he remembered having already spoken to him, while the Mississippian said to himself that there was nothing on the face of it to make it strange there should be between these fair, successful young persons some such question of love or marriage as Mrs. Luna had tattled about. Mr. Burrage was successful, he could see that in the turn of an eye; not perhaps as having a commanding intellect or a very strong character, but as being rich, polite, handsome, happy, amiable, and as wearing a splendid camellia in his buttonhole. And that *he,* at any rate, thought Verena had succeeded was proved by the casual, civil tone, and the contented distraction of eye, with which he exclaimed, "You don't mean to say you were not moved by that! It's my opinion that Miss Tarrant will carry everything before her." He was so pleased himself, and so safe in his conviction, that it didn't matter to him what anyone else thought; which was, after all, just Basil Ransom's own state of mind.

'Oh! I didn't say I wasn't moved,' the Mississippian remarked.

"Moved the wrong way!" said Verena. "Never mind; you'll be left behind."

"If I am, you will come back to console me."

"Back? I shall never come back!" the girl replied, gaily.

"You'll be the very first!" Ransom went on, feeling himself now, and as if by a sudden clearing up of his spiritual atmosphere, no longer in the vein for making the concessions of chivalry, and yet conscious that his words were an expression of homage.

"Oh, I call that presumptuous!" Mr. Burrage exclaimed, turning away to get a glass of water for Verena, who had refused to accept champagne, mentioning that she had never drunk any in her life and that she associated a kind of iniquity with it. Olive had no wine in her house (not that Verena gave this explanation), but her father's old madeira and a little claret; of the former of which liquors Basil Ransom had highly approved the day he dined with her.

"Does he believe in all those lunacies?" he inquired, knowing perfectly what to think about the charge of presumption brought by Mr. Burrage.

"Why, he's crazy about our movement," Verena responded. "He's one of my most gratifying converts."

"And don't you despise him for it?"

"Despise him? Why, you seem to think I swing round pretty often!"

"Well, I have an idea that I shall see you swing round yet," Ransom remarked, in a tone in which it would have appeared to Henry Burrage, had he heard these words, that presumption was pushed to fatuity.

On Verena, however, they produced no impression that prevented her from saying simply, without the least rancor, "Well, if you expect to draw me back five hundred years, I hope you won't tell Miss Birdseye." And as Ransom did not seize immediately the reason of her allusion, she went on, "You know she is convinced it will be just the other way. I went to see her after you had been at Cambridge—almost immediately."

"Darling old lady—I hope she's well," the young man said.

"Well, she's tremendously interested."

"She's always interested in something, isn't she?"

"Well, this time it's in our relations, yours and mine," Verena replied, in a tone in which only Verena could say a thing like that. "You ought to see how she throws herself into them. She is sure it will all work round for your good.

"All what, Miss Tarrant?" Ransom asked.

"Well, what I told her. She is sure you are going to become one of our leaders, that you are very gifted for treating great questions and acting on masses of people, that you will become quite enthusiastic about our uprising, and that when you go up to the top as one of our champions it will all have been through me."

Ransom stood there, smiling at her; the dusky glow in his eyes expressed a softness representing no prevision of such laurels, but which testified none the less to Verena's influence. "And what you want is that I shouldn't undeceive her?"

"Well, I don't want you to be hypocritical—if you shouldn't take our side; but I do think that it would be sweet if the dear old thing could just cling to her illusion. She won't live so very long, probably; she told me the other day she was ready for her final rest; so it wouldn't interfere much with your freedom. She feels quite romantic about it —your being a Southerner and all, and not naturally in sympathy with Boston ideas, and your meeting her that way in the street and making yourself known to her. She won't believe but what I shall move you."

"Don't fear, Miss Tarrant, she shall be satisfied," Ransom said, with a laugh which he could see she but partially understood. He was prevented from making his meaning more clear by the return of Mr. Burrage, bringing not only Verena's glass of water but a smooth-faced, rosy, smiling old gentleman, who had a velvet waistcoat, and thin white hair, brushed effectively, and whom he introduced to Verena under a name which Ransom recognized as that of a rich and venerable citizen, conspicuous for his public spirit and his large almsgiving. Ransom had lived long enough in New York to know that a request from this ancient worthy to be made known to Miss Tarrant would mark her for the approval of the respectable, stamp her as a success of no vulgar sort; and as he turned away, a faint, inaudible sigh passed his lips, dictated by the sense that he himself belonged to a terribly small and obscure minority. He turned away because, as we know, he had been taught that a gentleman talking to a lady must always do that when a new gentleman is presented; though he observed, looking back, after a minute, that young Mr. Burrage evidently had no intention of abdicating in favor of the eminent philanthropist. He thought he had better go home; he didn't know what might happen at such a party as that, nor when the proceedings might be supposed to terminate; but after considering it a minute he dismissed the idea that there was a chance of Verena's speaking again. If he was a little vague about this, however, there was no doubt in his mind as to the obligation he was under to take leave first of Mrs. Burrage. He wished he knew where Verena was staying; he wanted to see her alone, not in a supper-room crowded with millionaires. As he looked about for the hostess it occurred to him that she would know, and that if he were able to quench a certain shyness sufficiently to ask her, she would tell him. Having satisfied himself presently that she was not in the supper-room, he made his way back to the parlors, where the company now was much diminished. He looked again into the music-room, tenanted only by half a dozen couples, who were cultivating privacy among the empty chairs, and here he perceived Mrs. Burrage sitting in conversation with Olive Chancellor (the latter, apparently, had not moved from her place), before the deserted scene of Verena's triumph. His search had been so little for Olive that at the sight of her he faltered a moment; then he pulled himself together, advancing with a consciousness of the Mississippi manner. He felt Olive's eyes receiving him; she looked at him as if it was just the hope that she shouldn't meet him again that had made her remain where she was. Mrs. Burrage got up, as he bade her good night, and Olive followed her example.

"So glad you were able to come. Wonderful creature, isn't she? She can do anything she wants."

These words from the elder lady Ransom received at first with a reserve which, as he trusted, suggested extreme respect; and it was a fact that his silence had a kind if Southern solemnity in it. Then he said, in a tone equally expressive of great deliberation:

"Yes, madam, I think I never was present at an exhibition, an entertainment of any kind, which held me more completely under the charm."

"Delighted you liked it. I didn't know what in the world to have, and this has proved an inspiration—for me as well as for Miss Tarrant. Miss Chancellor has been telling me how they have worked together; it's really quite beautiful. Miss Chancellor is Miss Tarrant's great friend and colleague. Miss Tarrant assures me that she couldn't do anything without her." After which explanation, turning to Olive, Mrs. Burrage murmured: "Let me introduce Mr.—— introduce Mr.——"

But she had forgotten poor Ransom's name, forgotten who had asked her for a card for him; and, perceiving it, he came to her rescue with the observation that he was a kind of cousin of Miss Olive's, if she didn't repudiate him, and that he knew what a tremendous partnership existed between the two young ladies. "When I applauded I was applauding the firm—that is, you too," he said, smiling, to his kinswoman.

"Your applause? I confess I don't understand it," Olive replied, with much promptitude.

"Well, to tell the truth, I didn't myself!"

"Oh yes, of course I know; that's why—that's why——" And this further speech of Mrs. Burrage's, in reference to the relationship between the young man and her companion, faded also into vagueness. She had been on the point of saying it was the reason why he was in her house; but she had bethought herself in time that this ought to pass as a matter of course. Basil Ransom could see she was a woman who could carry off an awkwardness like that, and he considered her with a sense of her importance. She had a brisk, familiar, slightly impatient way, and if she had not spoken so fast, and had more of the softness of the Southern matron, she would have reminded him of a certain type of woman he had seen of old, before the changes in his own part of the world—the clever, capable, hospitable proprietress, widowed or unmarried, of a big plantation carried on by herself. "If you are her cousin, do take Miss Chancellor to have some supper—instead of going away," she went on, with her infelicitous readiness.

At this Olive instantly seated herself again.

"I am much obliged to you; I never touch supper. I shall not leave this room—I like it."

"Then let me send you something—or let Mr.——, your cousin, remain with you."

Olive looked at Mrs. Burrage with a strange beseeching-ness, "I am very tired, I must rest. These occasions leave me exhausted."

"Ah yes, I can imagine that. Well, then, you shall be quite quiet—I shall come back to you." And with a smile of farewell for Basil Ransom, Mrs. Burrage moved away.

Basil lingered a moment, though he saw that Olive wished to get rid of him. "I won't disturb you further than to ask you a single question," he said. "Where are you staying? I want to come and see Miss Tarrant. I don't say I want to come and see you, because I have an idea that it would give you no pleasure." It had occurred to him that he might obtain their address from Mrs. Luna—he only knew vaguely it was Tenth Street; much as he had displeased her she couldn't refuse him that; but suddenly the greater simplicity and frankness of applying directly to Olive, even at the risk of appearing to brave her, recommended itself. He couldn't, of course, call upon Verena without her knowing it, and she might as well make her protest (since he proposed to pay no heed to it), sooner as later. He had seen nothing, personally, of their life together, but it had come over him that what Miss Chancellor most disliked in him (had she not, on the very threshold of their acquaintance, had a sort of mystical foreboding of it?) was the possibility that he would interfere. It was quite on the cards that he might; yet it was decent, all the same, to ask her rather than anyone else. It was better that his interference should be accompanied with all the forms of chivalry.

Olive took no notice of his remark as to how she herself

might be affected by his visit; but she asked in a moment why he should think it necessary to call on Miss Tarrant. "You know you are not in sympathy," she added, in a tone which contained a really touching element of entreaty that he would not even pretend to prove he was.

I know not whether Basil was touched, but he said, with every appearance of a conciliatory purpose—"I wish to thank her for all the interesting information she has given me this evening."

"If you think it generous to come and scoff at her, of course she has no defense; you will be glad to know that."

"Dear Miss Chancellor, if you are not a defense—a battery of many guns!" Ransom exclaimed.

"Well, she at least is not mine!" Olive returned, springing to her feet. She looked round her as if she were really pressed too hard, panting like a hunted creature.

"Your defense is your certain immunity from attack. Perhaps if you won't tell me where you are staying, you will kindly ask Miss Tarrant herself to do so. Would she send me a word on a card?"

"We are in West Tenth Street," Olive said; and she gave the number. "Of course you are free to come."

"Of course I am! Why shouldn't I be? But I am greatly obliged to you for the information. I will ask her to come out, so that you won't see us." And he turned away, with the sense that it was really insufferable, her attempt always to give him the air of being in the wrong. If that was the kind of spirit in which women were going to act when they had more power!

29

Mrs. Luna was early in the field the next day, and her sister wondered to what she owed the honor of a visit from her at eleven o'clock in the morning. She very soon saw, when Adeline asked her whether it had been she who procured for Basil Ransom an invitation to Mrs. Burrage's.

"Me—why in the world should it have been me?" Olive asked, feeling something of a pang at the implication that it had not been Adeline, as she supposed.

"I didn't know—but you took him up so."

"Why, Adeline Luna, when did I ever——?" Miss Chancellor exclaimed, staring and intensely grave.

"You don't mean to say you have forgotten how you brought him on to see you, a year and a half ago!"

"I didn't bring him on—I said if he happened to be there."

"Yes, I remember how it was: he did happen, and then you happened to hate him, and tried to get out of it."

Miss Chancellor saw, I say, why Adeline had come to her at the hour she knew she was always writing letters, after having given her all the attention that was necessary the day before; she had come simply to make herself disagreeable, as Olive knew, of old, the spirit sometimes moved her irresistibly to do. It seemed to her that Adeline had been disagreeable enough in not having beguiled Basil Ransom into a marriage, according to that memorable calculation of probabilities in which she indulged (with a license that she scarcely liked definitely to recall), when the pair made acquaintance under her eyes in Charles Street, and Mrs. Luna seemed to take to him as much as she herself did little. She would gladly have accepted him as a brother-in-law, for the harm such a relation could do one was limited and definite; whereas in his general capacity of being at large in her life the ability of the young Mississippian to injure her seemed somehow immense. "I wrote to him—that time —for a perfectly definite reason," she said. "I thought mother would have liked us to know him. But it was a mistake."

"How do you know it was a mistake? Mother would have liked him, I dare say."

"I mean my acting as I did; it was a theory of duty which I allowed to press me too much. I always do. Duty should be obvious; one shouldn't hunt round for it."

"Was it very obvious when it brought you on here?" asked Mrs. Luna, who was distinctly out of humor.

Olive looked for a moment at the toe of her shoe. "I had an idea that you would have married him by this time," she presently remarked.

"Marry him yourself, my dear! What put such an idea into your head?"

"You wrote to me at first so much about him. You told me he was tremendously attentive, and that you liked him."

"His state of mind is one thing and mine is another. How can I marry every man that hangs about me—that dogs my footsteps? I might as well become a Mormon at once!" Mrs. Luna delivered herself of this argument with a certain charitable air, as if her sister could not be expected to understand such a situation by her own light.

Olive waived the discussion, and simply said: "I took for granted *you* had got him the invitation."

"I, my dear? That would be quite at variance with my attitude of discouragement."

"Then she simply sent it herself."

"Whom do you mean by 'she'?"

"Mrs. Burrage, of course."

"I thought that you might mean Verena," said Mrs. Luna, casually.

"Verena—to him? Why in the world——?" And Olive gave the cold glare with which her sister was familiar.

"Why in the world not—since she knows him?"

"She had seen him twice in her life before last night, when she met him for the third time and spoke to him."

"Did she tell you that?"

"She tells me everything."

"Are you very sure?"

"Adeline Luna, what *do* you mean?" Miss Chancellor murmured.

"Are you very sure that last night was only the third time?" Mrs. Luna went on.

Olive threw back her head and swept her sister from her bonnet to her lowest flounce. "You have no right to hint at such a thing as that unless you know!"

"Oh, I know—I know, at any rate, more than you do!" And then Mrs. Luna, sitting with her sister, much withdrawn, in one of the windows of the big, hot, faded parlor of the boarding house in Tenth Street, where there was a rug before the chimney representing a Newfoundland dog saving a child from drowning, and a row of chromo-lithographs on the walls, imparted to her the impression she had received the evening before—the impression of Basil Ransom's keen curiosity about Verena Tarrant. Verena must have asked Mrs. Burrage to send him a card, and asked it without mentioning the fact to Olive—for wouldn't Olive certainly have remembered it? It was no use her saying that Mrs. Burrage might have sent it of her own movement, because she wasn't aware of his existence, and why should she be? Basil Ransom himself had told her he didn't know Mrs. Burrage. Mrs. Luna knew whom he knew and whom he didn't, or at least the sort of people, and they were not the sort that belonged to the Wednesday Club. That was one reason why she didn't care about him for any intimate relation—that he didn't seem to have any taste for making nice friends. Olive would know what *her* taste was in this respect, though it wasn't that young woman's own any more than his. It was positive that the suggestion about the card could only have come from Verena. At any rate Olive could easily ask, or if she was afraid of her telling a fib she could ask Mrs. Burrage. It was true Mrs. Burrage might have been put on her guard by Verena, and would perhaps invent some other account of the matter; therefore Olive had better just believe what *she* believed, that Verena had secured his presence at the party and had had private reasons for doing so. It is to be feared that Ransom's remark to Mrs. Luna the night before about her having lost her head was near to the mark; for if she had not been blinded by her rancor she would have guessed the horror with which she inspired her sister when she spoke in that offhand way of Verena's lying and Mrs. Burrage's lying. Did people lie like that in Mrs. Luna's set? It was Olive's plan of life not to lie, and attributing a similar disposition to people she liked, it was impossible for her to believe that Verena had had the intention of deceiving her. Mrs. Luna, in a calmer hour, might also have divined that Olive would make her private comments on the strange story of Basil Ransom's having made up to Verena out of pique at Adeline's rebuff; for this was the account of the matter that she now offered to Miss Chancellor. Olive did two things: she listened intently and eagerly, judging there was distinct danger in the air (which, however, she had not wanted Mrs. Luna to tell her, having perceived it for herself the night before); and she saw that poor Adeline was fabricating fearfully, that the "rebuff" was altogether an invention. Mr. Ransom was evidently preoccupied with Verena, but he had not needed Mrs. Luna's cruelty to make him so. So Olive maintained an attitude of great reserve; she did not take upon herself to announce that her own version was that Adeline, for reasons absolutely imperceptible to others, had tried to catch Basil Ransom, had failed in her attempt, and, furious at seeing Verena preferred to a person of her importance (Olive remembered the *spretæ injuria formæ*), now wished to do both him and the girl an ill turn. This would be accomplished if she could induce Olive to interfere. Miss Chancellor was conscious of an abundant readiness to interfere, but it was not because she cared for Adeline's mortification. I am not sure, even, that she did not think her *fiasco* but another illustration of her sister's general uselessness, and rather despise her for it; being perfectly able at once to hold that nothing is baser than the effort to entrap a man, and to think it very ignoble to have to renounce it because you can't. Olive kept these reflections to herself, but she went so far as to say to her sister that she didn't see where the "pique" came in. How could it hurt Adeline that he should turn his attention to Verena? What was Verena to her?

"Why, Olive Chancellor, how can you ask?" Mrs. Luna boldly responded. "Isn't Verena everything to you, and aren't you everything to me, and wouldn't an attempt—a successful one—to take Verena away from you knock you up fearfully, and shouldn't I suffer, as you know I suffer, by sympathy?"

I have said that it was Miss Chancellor's plan of life not to lie, but such a plan was compatible with a kind of consideration for the truth which led her to shrink from producing it on poor occasions. So she didn't say, "Dear me, Adeline, what humbug! you know you hate Verena and would be very glad if she were drowned!" She only said, "Well, I see; but it's very roundabout." What she did see was that Mrs. Luna was eager to help her to stop off Basil Ransom from "making head," as the phrase was; and the fact that her motive was spite, and not tenderness for the Bostonians, would not make her assistance less welcome if the danger were real. She herself had a nervous dread, but she had that about everything; still, Adeline had perhaps seen something, and what in the world did she mean by her reference to Verena's having had secret meetings? When pressed on this point, Mrs. Luna could only say that she didn't pretend to give definite information, and she wasn't a spy anyway, but that the night before he had positively flaunted in her face his admiration for the girl, his enthusiasm for her way of standing up there. Of course he hated her ideas, but he was quite conceited enough to think she would give them up. Perhaps it was all directed at *her*—as if she cared! It would depend a good deal on the girl herself; certainly, if there was any likelihood of Verena's being affected, she should advise Olive to look out. She knew best what to do; it was only Adeline's duty to give her the benefit of her own impression, whether she was thanked for it or not. She only wished to put her on her guard, and it was just like Olive to receive such information so coldly; she was the most disappointing woman she knew.

Miss Chancellor's coldness was not diminished by this rebuke; for it had come over her that, after all, she had never opened herself at that rate to Adeline, had never let her see the real intensity of her desire to keep the sort of danger there was now a question of away from Verena, had given her no warrant for regarding her as her friend's keeper; so that she was taken aback by the flatness if Mrs. Luna's assumption that she was ready to enter into a conspiracy to circumvent and frustrate the girl. Olive put on all her majesty to dispel this impression, and if she could not help being aware that she made Mrs. Luna still angrier, on the whole, than at first, she felt that she would much rather disappoint her than give herself away to her—especially as she was intensely eager to profit by her warning!

30

Mrs. Luna would have been still less satisfied with the manner in which Olive received her proffered assistance had she known how many confidences that reticent young woman might have made her in return. Olive's whole life now was a matter for whispered communications; she felt this herself, as she sought the privacy of her own apartment after her interview with her sister. She had for the moment time to think; Verena having gone out with Mr. Burrage, who had made an appointment the night before to call for her to drive at that early hour. They had other engagements in the afternoon—the principal of which was to meet a group of earnest people at the house of one of the great local promoters. Olive would whisk Verena off to these appointments directly after lunch; she flattered herself that she could arrange matters so that there would not be half an hour in the day during which Basil Ransom, complacently calling, would find the Bostonians in the house. She had had this well in mind when, at Mrs. Burrage's, she was driven to give him their address; and she had had it also in mind that she would ask Verena, as a special favor, to accompany her back to Boston on the next day but one, which was the morning of the morrow. There had been considerable talk of her staying a few days with Mrs. Burrage—staying on after her own departure; but Verena backed out of it spontaneously, seeing how the idea worried her friend. Olive had accepted the sacrifice, and their visit to New York was now cut down, in intention, to four days, one of which, the moment she perceived whither Basil Ransom was tending, Miss Chancellor promised herself also to suppress. She had not mentioned that to Verena yet; she hesitated a little, having a slightly bad conscience about the concessions she had already obtained from her friend. Verena made such concessions with a generosity which caused one's heart to ache for admiration, even while one asked for them; and never once had Olive known her to demand the smallest credit for any virtue she showed in this way, or to bargain for an instant about any effort she made to oblige. She had been delighted with the idea of spending a week under Mrs. Burrage's roof; she had said, too, that she believed her mother would die happy (not that there was the least prospect of Mrs. Tarrant's dying), if she could hear of her having such an experience as that; and yet, perceiving how solemn Olive looked about it, how she blanched and brooded at the prospect, she had offered to give it up, with a smile sweeter, if possible, than any that had ever sat in her eyes. Olive knew what that meant for her, knew what a power of enjoyment she still had, in spite of the tension of their common purpose, their vital work, which had now, as they equally felt, passed into the stage of realization, of fruition; and that is why her conscience rather pricked her for consenting to this further act of renunciation, especially as their position seemed really so secure, on the part of one who had already given herself away so sublimely.

Secure as their position might be, Olive called herself a blind idiot for having, in spite of all her first shrinkings, agreed to bring Verena to New York. Verena had jumped at the invitation, the very unexpectedness of which on Mrs. Burrage's part—it was such an odd idea to have come to a mere worldling—carried a kind of persuasion with it. Olive's immediate sentiment had been an instinctive general fear; but, later, she had dismissed that as unworthy; she had decided (and such a decision was nothing new), that where their mission was concerned they ought to face everything.

Such an opportunity would contribute too much to Verena's reputation and authority to justify a refusal at the bidding of apprehensions which were after all only vague. Olive's specific terrors and dangers had by this time very much blown over; Basil Ransom had given no sign of life for ages, and Henry Burrage had certainly got his quietus before they went to Europe. If it had occurred to his mother that she might convert Verena into the animating principle of a big soirée, she was at least acting in good faith, for it could be no more her wish today that he should marry Selah Tarrant's daughter than it was her wish a year before. And then they should do some good to the benighted, the most benighted, the fashionable benighted; they should perhaps make them furious—there was always some good in that. Lastly, Olive was conscious of a personal temptation in the matter; she was not insensible to the pleasure of appearing in a distinguished New York circle as a representative woman, an important Bostonian, the prompter, colleague, associate of one of the most original girls of the time. Basil Ransom was the person she had least expected to meet at Mrs. Burrage's; it had been her belief that they might easily spend four days in a city of more than a million of inhabitants without that disagreeable accident. But it had occurred; nothing was wanting to make it seem serious; and, setting her teeth, she shook herself, morally, hard, for having fallen into the trap of fate. Well, she would scramble out, with only a scare, probably. Henry Burrage was very attentive, but somehow she didn't fear him now; and it was only natural he should feel that he couldn't be polite enough, after they had consented to be exploited in that worldly way by his mother. The other danger was the worst; the palpitation of her strange dread, the night of Miss Birdseye's party, came back to her. Mr. Burrage seemed, indeed, a protection; she reflected, with relief, that it had been arranged that after taking Verena to drive in the Park and see the Museum of Art in the morning, they should in the evening dine with him at Delmonico's (he was to invite another gentleman), and go afterwards to the German opera. Olive had kept all this to herself, as I have said; revealing to her sister neither the vividness of her prevision that Basil Ransom would look blank when he came down to Tenth Street and learned they had flitted, nor the eagerness of her desire just to find herself once more in the Boston train. It had been only this prevision that sustained her when she gave Mr. Ransom their number.

Verena came to her room shortly before luncheon, to let her know she had returned; and while they sat there, waiting to stop their ears when the gong announcing the repast was beaten, at the foot of the stairs, by a negro in a white jacket, she narrated to her friend her adventures with Mr. Burrage—expatiated on the beauty of the park, the splendor and interest of the Museum, the wonder of the young man's acquaintance with everything it contained, the swiftness of his horses, the softness of his English cart, the pleasure of rolling at that pace over roads as firm as marble, the entertainment he promised them for the evening. Olive listened in serious silence; she saw Verena was quite carried away; of course she hadn't gone so far with her without knowing that phase.

"Did Mr. Burrage try to make love to you?" Miss Chancellor inquired at last, without a smile.

Verena had taken off her hat to arrange her feather, and as she placed it on her head again, her uplifted arms making a frame for her face, she said: "Yes, I suppose it was meant for love."

Olive waited for her to tell more, to tell how she had treated him, kept him in his place, made him feel that that question was over long ago; but as Verena gave her no farther information she did not insist, conscious as she always was that in such a relation as theirs there should be a great respect on either side for the liberty of each. She had never yet infringed on Verena's, and of course she wouldn't begin now. Moreover, with the request that she meant presently to make of her she felt that she must be discreet. She wondered whether Henry Burrage were really going to begin again; whether his mother had only been acting in his interest in getting them to come on. Certainly, the bright spot in such a prospect was that if she listened to him she couldn't listen to Basil Ransom; and he *had* told Olive herself last night, when he put them into their carriage, that he hoped to prove to her yet that he had come round to her gospel. But the old sickness stole upon her again, the faintness of discouragement, as she asked herself why in the name of pity Verena should listen to any one at all but Olive Chancellor. Again it came over her, when she saw the brightness, the happy look, the girl brought back, as it had done in the earlier months, that the great trouble was that weak spot of Verena's, that sole infirmity and subtle flaw, which she had expressed to her very soon after they began to live together, in saying (she remembered it through the ineffaceable impression made by her friend's avowal),"I'll tell you what is the matter with you—you don't dislike men as a class!" Verena had replied on this occasion, "Well, no, I don't dislike them when they are pleasant!" As if organized atrociousness could ever be pleasant! Olive disliked them most when they were least unpleasant. After a little, at present, she remarked, referring to Henry Burrage: "It is not right of him, not decent, after your making him feel how, while he was at Cambridge, he wearied you, tormented you."

"Oh, I didn't show anything," said Verena, gaily. "I am learning to dissimulate," she added in a moment. "I suppose you have to as you go along. I pretend not to notice."

At this moment the gong sounded for luncheon, and the two young women covered up their ears, face to face, Verena with her quick smile, Olive with her pale patience. When they could hear themselves speak, the latter said abruptly:

"How did Mrs. Burrage come to invite Mr. Ransom to her party? He told Adeline he had never seen her before."

"Oh, I asked her to send him an invitation—after she

had written to me, to thank me, when it was definitely settled we should come on. She asked me in her letter if there were any friends of mine in the city to whom I should like her to send cards, and I mentioned Mr. Ransom."

Verena spoke without a single instant's hesitation, and the only sign of embarrassment she gave was that she got up from her chair, passing in this manner a little out of Olive's scrutiny. It was easy for her not to falter, because she was glad of the chance. She wanted to be very simple in all her relations with her friend, and of course it was not simple so soon as she began to keep things back. She could at any rate keep back as little as possible, and she felt as if she were making up for a dereliction when she answered Olive's inquiry so promptly.

"You never told me of that," Miss Chancellor remarked, in a low tone.

"I didn't want to. I know you don't like him, and I thought it would give you pain. Yet I wanted him to be there—I wanted him to hear."

"What does it matter—why should you care about him?"

"Well, because he is so awfully opposed!"

"How do you know that, Verena?"

At this point Verena began to hesitate. It was not, after all, so easy to keep back only a little; it appeared rather as if one must either tell everything or hide everything. The former course had already presented itself to her as unduly harsh; it was because it seemed so that she had ended by keeping the incident of Basil Ransom's visit to Monadnoc Place buried in unspoken, in unspeakable, considerations, the only secret she had in the world—the only thing that was all her own. She was so glad to say what she could without betraying herself that it was only after she had spoken that she perceived there was a danger of Olive's pushing the inquiry to the point where, to defend herself as it were, she should be obliged to practice a positive deception; and she was conscious at the same time that the moment her secret was threatened it became dearer to her. She began to pray

295

silently that Olive might not push; for it would be odious, it would be impossible, to defend herself by a lie. Meanwhile, however, she had to answer, and the way she answered was by exclaiming, much more quickly than the reflections I note might have appeared to permit, "Well, if you can't tell from his appearance! He's the type of the reactionary."

Verena went to the toilet-glass to see that she had put on her hat properly, and Olive slowly got up, in the manner of a person not in the least eager for food. "Let him react as he likes—for heaven's sake don't mind him!" That was Miss Chancellor's rejoinder, and Verena felt that it didn't say all that was in her mind. She wished she would come down to luncheon, for she, at least, was honestly hungry. She even suspected Olive had an idea she was afraid to express, such distress it would bring with it. "Well, you know, Verena, this isnt our *real* life—it isn't our work," Olive went on.

"Well, no, it isn't, certainly," said Verena, not pretending at first that she did not know what Olive meant. In a moment, however, she added, "Do you refer to this social intercourse with Mr. Burrage?"

"Not to that only." Then Olive asked abruptly, looking at her, "How did you know his address?"

"His address?"

"Mr. Ransom's—to enable Mrs. Burrage to invite him?"

They stood for a moment interchanging a gaze. "It was in a letter I got from him."

At these words there came into Olive's face an expression which made her companion cross over to her directly and take her by the hand. But the tone was different from what Verena expected when she said, with cold surprise: "Oh, you are in correspondence!" It showed an immense effort of self-control.

"He wrote to me once—I never told you," Verena rejoined, smiling. She felt that her friend's strange, uneasy eyes searched very far; a little more and they would go to the very bottom. Well, they might go if they would; she didn't, after all, care so much about her secret as that. For

296

the moment, however, Verena did not learn what Olive had discovered, inasmuch as she only remarked presently that it was really time to go down. As they descended the staircase she put her arm into Miss Chancellor's and perceived that she was trembling.

Of course there were plenty of people in New York interested in the uprising, and Olive had made appointments, in advance, which filled the whole afternoon. Everybody wanted to meet them, and wanted everybody else to do so, and Verena saw they could easily have quite a vogue, if they only chose to stay and work that vein. Very likely, as Olive said, it wasn't their real life, and people didn't seem to have such a grip of the movement as they had in Boston; but there was something in the air that carried one along, and a sense of vastness and variety, of the infinite possibilities of a great city, which—Verena hardly knew whether she ought to confess it to herself—might in the end make up for the want of the Boston earnestness. Certainly, the people seemed very much alive, and there was no other place where so many cheering reports could flow in, owing to the number of electric feelers that stretched away everywhere. The principal center appeared to be Mrs. Croucher's, on Fifty-sixth Street, where there was an informal gathering of sympathizers who didn't seem as if they could forgive her when they learned that she had been speaking the night before in a circle in which none of them were acquainted. Certainly, they were very different from the group she had addressed at Mrs. Burrage's, and Verena heaved a thin, private sigh, expressive of some helplessness, as she thought what a big, complicated world it was, and how it evidently contained a little of everything. There was a general demand that she should repeat her address in a more congenial atmosphere; to which she replied that Olive made her engagements for her, and that as the address had been intended just to lead people on, perhaps she would think Mrs. Croucher's friends had reached a higher point. She was as cautious as this because she saw that Olive was now just straining to get out of the city; she didn't want to say anything that would tie them. When she felt her trembling that way before luncheon it made her quite sick to realize how much her friend was wrapped up in her—how terribly she would suffer from the least deviation. After they had started for their round of engagements the very first thing Verena spoke of in the carriage (Olive had taken one, in her liberal way, for the whole time), was the fact that her correspondence with Mr. Ransom, as her friend had called it, had consisted on his part of only one letter. It was a very short one, too; it had come to her a little more than a month before. Olive knew she got letters from gentlemen; she didn't see why she should attach such importance to this one. Miss Chancellor was leaning back in the carriage, very still, very grave, with her head against the cushioned surface, only turning her eyes towards the girl.

"You attach importance yourself; otherwise you would have told me."

"I knew you wouldn't like it—because you don't like *him*."

"I don't think of him," said Olive; "he's nothing to me." Then she added, suddenly, "Have you noticed that I am afraid to face what I don't like?"

Verena could not say that she had, and yet it was not just on Olive's part to speak as if she were an easy person to tell such a thing to: the way she lay there, white and weak, like a wounded creature, sufficiently proved the contrary. "You have such a fearful power of suffering," she replied in a moment.

To this at first Miss Chancellor made no rejoinder; but after a little she said, in the same attitude, "Yes, *you* could make me."

Verena took her hand and held it awhile. "I never will, till I have been through everything myself."

"*You* were not made to suffer—you were made to enjoy," Olive said, in very much the same tone in which she had told her that what was the matter with her was that she didn't dislike men as a class—a tone which implied that the contrary would have been much more natural and perhaps rather higher. Perhaps it would; but Verena was unable to rebut the charge; she felt this, as she looked out of the window of the carriage at the bright, amusing city, where the elements seemed so numerous, the animation so immense, the shops so brilliant, the women so strikingly dressed, and knew that these things quickened her curiosity, all her pulses.

"Well, I suppose I mustn't presume on it," she remarked, glancing back at Olive with her natural sweetness, her un-contradicting grace.

That young lady lifted her hand to her lips—held it there a moment; the movement seemed to say, "When you are so divinely docile, how can I help the dread of losing you?" This idea, however, was unspoken, and Olive Chancellor's uttered words, as the carriage rolled on, were different.

"Verena, I don't understand why he wrote to you."

"He wrote to me because he likes me. Perhaps you'll say you don't understand why he likes me," the girl continued, laughing. "He liked me the first time he saw me."

"Oh, that time!" Olive murmured.

"And still more the second."

"Did he tell you that in his letter?" Miss Chancellor inquired.

"Yes, my dear, he told me that. Only he expressed it more gracefully." Verena was very happy to say that; a written phrase of Basil Ransom's sufficiently justified her.

"It was my intuition—it was my foreboding!" Olive exclaimed, closing her eyes.

"I thought you said you didn't dislike him."

"It isn't dislike—it's simple dread. Is that all there is between you?"

"Why, Olive Chancellor, what do you think?" Verena asked, feeling now distinctly like a coward. Five minutes afterwards she said to Olive that if it would give her pleasure they would leave New York on the morrow, without taking a fourth day; and as soon as she had done so she felt better, especially when she saw how gratefully Olive looked at her for the concession, how eagerly she rose to the offer in saying, "Well, if you *do* feel that it isn't our own life—our very own!" It was with these words, and others besides, and with an unusually weak, indefinite kiss, as if she wished to protest that, after all, a single day didn't matter, and yet accepted the sacrifice and was a little ashamed of it—it was in this manner that the agreement as to an immediate retreat was sealed. Verena could not shut her eyes to the fact that for a month she had been less frank, and if she wished to do penance this abbreviation of their pleasure in New York, even if it made her almost completely miss Basil Ransom, was easier than to tell Olive just now that the letter was *not* all, that there had been a long visit, a talk, and a walk besides, which she had been covering up for ever so many weeks. And of what consequence, anyway, was the missing? Was it such a pleasure to converse with a gentleman who only wanted to let you know—and why he should want it so much Verena couldn't guess—that he thought you quite preposterous? Olive took her from place to place, and she ended by forgetting everything but the present hour, and the bigness and variety of New York, and the entertainment of rolling about in a carriage with silk cushions, and meeting new faces, new expressions of curiosity and sympathy, assurances that one was watched and followed. Mingled with this was a bright consciousness, sufficient for the moment, that one was moreover to dine at Delmonico's and go to the German opera. There was enough of the epicurean in Verena's composition to make it easy for her in certain conditions to live only for the hour.

31

When she returned with her companion to the establishment in Tenth Street she saw two notes lying on the table in the hall; one of which she perceived to be addressed to Miss Chancellor, the other to herself. The hand was different, but she recognized both. Olive was behind her on the steps, talking to the coachman about sending another carriage for them in half an hour (they had left themselves but just time to dress); so that she simply possessed herself of her own note and ascended to her room. As she did so she felt that all the while she had known it would be there, and was conscious of a kind of treachery, an unfriendly wilfulness, in not being more prepared for it. If she could roll about New York the whole afternoon and forget that there might be difficulties ahead, that didn't alter the fact that there *were* difficulties, and that they might even become considerable—might not be settled by her simply going back to Boston. Half an hour later, as she drove up the Fifth Avenue with Olive (there seemed to be so much crowded into that one day), smoothing her light gloves, wishing her fan were a little nicer, and proving by the answering, familiar brightness with which she looked out on the lamp-lighted streets that, whatever theory might be entertained as to the genesis of her talent and her personal nature, the blood of the lecture-going, night-walking Tarrants did distinctly flow in her veins; as the pair proceeded, I say, to the celebrated restaurant, at the door of which Mr. Burrage had promised to be in vigilant expectancy of their carriage, Verena found a sufficiently gay and natural tone of voice for remarking to her friend that Mr. Ransom had called upon her while they were out, and had left a note in which there were many compliments for Miss Chancellor.

"That's wholly your own affair, my dear," Olive replied, with a melancholy sigh, gazing down the vista of Fourteenth Street (which they happened just then to be traversing, with much agitation), toward the queer barrier of the elevated railway.

It was nothing new to Verena that if the great striving of Olive's life was for justice she yet sometimes failed to arrive at it in particular cases; and she reflected that it was rather late for her to say, like that, that Basil Ransom's letters were only his correspondent's business. Had not his kinswoman quite made the subject her own during their drive that afternoon? Verena determined now that her companion should hear all there was to be heard about the letter; asking herself whether, if she told her at present more than she cared to know, it wouldn't make up for her hitherto having told her less. "He brought it with him, written, in case I should be out. He wants to see me to-morrow—he says he has ever so much to say to me. He proposes an hour—says he hopes it won't be inconvenient for me to see him about eleven in the morning; thinks I may have no other engagement so early as that. Of course our return to Boston settles it," Verena added, with serenity.

Miss Chancellor said nothing for a moment; then she replied, "Yes, unless you invite him to come on with you in the train."

"Why, Olive, how bitter you are!" Verena exclaimed, in genuine surprise.

Olive could not justify her bitterness by saying that her companion had spoken as if she were disappointed, because Verena had not. So she simply remarked, "I don't see what he can have to say to you—that would be worth your hearing."

"Well, of course, it's the other side. He has got it on the brain!" said Verena, with a laugh which seemed to relegate the whole matter to the category of the unimportant.

"If we should stay, would you see him—at eleven o'clock?" Olive inquired.

"Why do you ask that—when I have given it up?"

"Do you consider it such a tremendous sacrifice?"

"No," said Verena good-naturedly; "but I confess I am curious."

"Curious—how do you mean?"

"Well, to hear the other side."

"Oh heaven!" Olive Chancellor murmured, turning her face upon her.

"You must remember I have never heard it." And Verena smiled into her friend's wan gaze.

"Do you want to hear all the infamy that is in the world?"

"No, it isn't that; but the more he should talk the better chance he would give me. I guess I can meet him."

"Life is too short. Leave him as he is."

"Well," Verena went on, "there are many I haven't cared to move at all, whom I might have been more interested in than in him. But to make him give in just at two or three points—that I should like better than anything I have done."

"You have no business to enter upon a contest that isn't equal; and it wouldn't be, with Mr. Ransom."

"The inequality would be that I have right on my side."

"What is that—for a man? For what was their brutality given them, but to make that up?"

"I don't think he's brutal; I should like to see," said Verena gaily.

Olive's eyes lingered a little on her own; then they turned away, vaguely, blindly, out of the carriage-window, and Verena made the reflection that she looked strangely little like a person who was going to dine at Delmonico's. How terribly she worried about everything, and how tragical was her nature; how anxious, suspicious, exposed to

303

subtle influences! In their long intimacy Verena had come to revere most of her friend's peculiarities; they were a proof of her depth and devotion, and were so bound up with what was noble in her that she was rarely provoked to criticize them separately. But at present, suddenly, Olive's earnestness began to appear as inharmonious with the scheme of the universe as if it had been a broken saw; and she was positively glad she had not told her about Basil Ransom's appearance in Monadnoc Place. If she worried so about what she knew, how much would she not have worried about the rest! Verena had by this time made up her mind that her acquaintance with Mr. Ransom was the most episodical, most superficial, most unimportant of all possible relations.

Olive Chancellor watched Henry Burrage very closely that evening; she had a special reason for doing so, and her entertainment, during the successive hours, was derived much less from the delicate little feast over which this insinuating proselyte presided, in the brilliant public room of the establishment, where French waiters flitted about on deep carpets and parties at neighboring tables excited curiosity and conjecture, or even from the magnificent music of "Lohengrin," than from a secret process of comparison and verification, which shall presently be explained to the reader. As some discredit has possibly been thrown upon her impartiality it is a pleasure to be able to say that on her return from the opera she took a step dictated by an earnest consideration of justice—of the promptness with which Verena had told her of the note left by Basil Ransom in the afternoon. She drew Verena into her room with her. The girl, on the way back to Tenth Street, had spoken only of Wagner's music, of the singers, the orchestra, the immensity of the house, her tremendous pleasure. Olive could see how fond she might become of New York, where that kind of pleasure was so much more in the air.

"Well, Mr. Burrage was certainly very kind to us—no one could have been more thoughtful," Olive said; and she

colored a little at the look with which Verena greeted this
tribute of appreciation from Miss Chancellor to a single
gentleman.

"I am so glad you were struck with that, because I do
think we have been a little rough to him." Verena's *we* was
angelic. "He was particularly attentive to you, my dear; he
has got over me. He looked at you so sweetly. Dearest
Olive, if you marry him——!" And Miss Tarrant, who was
in high spirits, embraced her companion, to check her own
silliness.

"He wants you to stay there, all the same. They haven't
given *that* up," Olive remarked, turning to a drawer, out of
which she took a letter.

"Did he tell you that, pray? He said nothing more about
it to me."

"When we came in this afternoon I found this note from
Mrs. Burrage. You had better read it." And she presented
the document, open, to Verena.

The purpose of it was to say that Mrs. Burrage could
really not reconcile herself to the loss of Verena's visit, on
which both she and her son had counted so much. She was
sure they would be able to make it as interesting to Miss
Tarrant as it would be to themselves. She, Mrs. Burrage,
moreover, felt as if she hadn't heard half she wanted about
Miss Tarrant's views, and there were so many more who
were present at the address, who had come to her that
afternoon (losing not a minute, as Miss Chancellor could
see), to ask how in the world they too could learn more—
how they could get at the fair speaker and question her
about certain details. She hoped so much, therefore, that
even if the young ladies should be unable to alter their
decision about the visit they might at least see their way
to staying over long enough to allow her to arrange an
informal meeting for some of these poor thirsty souls. Might
she not at least talk over the question with Miss Chancellor?
She gave her notice that she would attack her on the subject
of the visit too. Might she not see her on the morrow, and

might she ask of her the very great favor that the interview should be at Mrs. Burrage's own house? She had something very particular to say to her, as regards which perfect privacy was a great consideration, and Miss Chancellor would doubtless recognize that this would be best secured under Mrs. Burrage's roof. She would therefore send her carriage for Miss Chancellor at any hour that would be convenient to the latter. She really thought much good might come from their having a satisfactory talk.

Verena read this epistle with much deliberation; it seemed to her mysterious, and confirmed the idea she had received the night before—the idea that she had not got quite a correct impression of this clever, worldly, curious woman on the occasion of her visit to Cambridge, when they met her at her son's rooms. As she gave the letter back to Olive she said, "That's why he didn't seem to believe we are really leaving tomorrow. He knows she had written that, and he thinks it will keep us."

"Well, if I were to say it may—should you think me too miserably changeful?"

Verena stared, with all her candor, and it was so very queer that Olive should now wish to linger that the sense of it, for the moment, almost covered the sense of its being pleasant. But that came out after an instant, and she said, with great honesty, "You needn't drag me away for consistency's sake. It would be absurd for me to pretend that I don't like being here."

"I think perhaps I ought to see her." Olive was very thoughtful.

"How lovely it must be to have a secret with Mrs. Burrage!" Verena exclaimed.

"It won't be a secret from you."

"Dearest, you needn't tell me unless you want," Verena went on, thinking of her own unimparted knowledge.

"I thought it was our plan to divide everything. It was certainly mine."

"Ah, don't talk about plans!" Verena exclaimed, rather ruefully. "You see, if we *are* going to stay tomorrow, how foolish it was to have any. There is more in her letter than is expressed," she added, as Olive appeared to be studying in her face the reasons for and against making this concession to Mrs. Burrage, and that was rather embarrassing.

"I thought it over all the evening—so that if now you will consent we will stay."

"Darling—what a spirit you have got! All through all those dear little dishes—all through 'Lohengrin!' As I haven't thought it over at all, you must settle it. You know I am not difficult."

"And would you go and stay with Mrs. Burrage, after all, if she should say anything to me that seems to make it desirable?"

Verena broke into a laugh. "You know it's not our real life!"

Olive said nothing for a moment; then she replied: "Don't think *I* can forget that. If I suggest a deviation, it's only because it sometimes seems to me that perhaps, after all, almost anything is better than the form reality *may* take with us." This was slightly obscure, as well as very melancholy, and Verena was relieved when her companion remarked, in a moment, "You must think me strangely inconsequent"; for this gave her a chance to reply, soothingly:

"Why, you don't suppose I expect you to keep always screwed up! I will stay a week with Mrs. Burrage, or a fortnight, or a month, or anything you like," she pursued; "anything it may seem to you best to tell her after you have seen her."

"Do you leave it all to me? You don't give me much help," Olive said.

"Help to what?"

"Help to help *you*."

"I don't want any help; I am quite strong enough!"

Verena cried, gaily. The next moment she inquired, in an appeal half comical, half touching, "My dear colleague, why do you make me say such conceited things?"

"And if you do stay—just even tomorrow—shall you be —very much of the time—with Mr. Ransom?"

As Verena for the moment appeared ironically-minded, she might have found a fresh subject for hilarity in the tremulous, tentative tone in which Olive made this inquiry. But it had not that effect; it produced the first manifestation of impatience—the first, literally, and the first note of re-proach—that had occurred in the course of their remark-able intimacy. The color rose to Verena's cheek, and her eye for an instant looked moist.

"I don't know what you always think, Olive, nor why you don't seem able to trust me. You didn't, from the first, with gentlemen. Perhaps you were right then—I don't say; but surely it is very different now. I don't think I ought to be suspected so much. Why have you a manner as if I had to be watched, as if I wanted to run away with every man that speaks to me? I should think I had proved how little I care. I thought you had discovered by this time that I am serious; that I have dedicated my life; that there is something un-speakably dear to me. But you begin again, every time— you don't do me justice. I must take everything that comes. I mustn't be afraid. I thought we had agreed that we were to do our work in the midst of the world, facing everything, keeping straight on, always taking hold. And now that it all opens out so magnificently, and victory is really sitting on our banners, it is strange of you to doubt of me, to suppose I am not more wedded to all our old dreams than ever. I told you the first time I saw you that I could renounce, and knowing better today, perhaps, what that means, I am ready to say it again. That I can, that I will! Why, Olive Chancellor," Verena cried, panting, a moment, with her eloquence, and with the rush of a culminating idea, "haven't you discovered by this time that I *have* renounced?"

The habit of public speaking, the training, the practice,

in which she had been immersed, enabled Verena to unroll a coil of propositions dedicated even to a private interest with the most touching, most cumulative effect. Olive was completely aware of this, and she stilled herself, while the girl uttered one soft, pleading sentence after another, into the same rapt attention she was in the habit of sending up from the benches of an auditorium. She looked at Verena fixedly, felt that she was stirred to her depths, that she was exquisitely passionate and sincere, that she was a quivering, spotless, consecrated maiden, that she really had renounced, that they were both safe, and that her own injustice and indelicacy had been great. She came to her slowly, took her in her arms and held her long—giving her a silent kiss. From which Verena knew that she believed her.

32

The hour that Olive proposed to Mrs. Burrage, in a note sent early the next morning, for the interview to which she consented to lend herself, was the stroke of noon; this period of the day being chosen in consequence of a prevision of many subsequent calls upon her time. She remarked in her note that she did not wish any carriage to be sent for her, and she surged and swayed up the Fifth Avenue on one of the convulsive, clattering omnibuses which circulate in that thoroughfare. One of her reasons for mentioning twelve o'clock had been that she knew Basil Ransom was to call at Tenth Street at eleven, and (as she supposed he didn't intend to stay all day) this would give her time to see him come and go. It had been tacitly agreed between them, the night before, that Verena was quite firm enough in her faith to submit to his visit, and that such a course would be much more dignified than dodging it. This understanding passed from one to the other during that dumb embrace which I have described as taking place before they separated for the night. Shortly before noon, Olive, passing out of the house, looked into the big, sunny double parlor, where, in the morning, with all the husbands absent for the day and all the wives and spinsters launched upon the town, a young man desiring to hold a debate with a young lady might enjoy every advantage in the way of a clear field. Basil Ransom was still there; he and Verena, with the place to themselves, were standing in the recess of a window, their backs presented to the door. If he had got up, perhaps he was going, and Olive, softly closing the door again, waited a little in the hall, ready to pass into the back part of the house if she should hear him coming out. No sound, however, reached her ear; apparently he did mean to stay all day, and she should find him there on her return. She left the house, knowing they were looking at her from the window as she descended the steps, but feeling she could not bear to see Basil Ransom's face. As she walked, averting her own, toward the Fifth Avenue, on the sunny side, she was barely conscious of the loveliness of the day, the perfect weather, all suffused and tinted with spring, which sometimes descends upon New York when the winds of March have been stilled; she was given up only to the remembrance of that moment when she herself had stood at a window (the second time he came to see her in Boston), and watched Basil Ransom pass out with Adeline—with Adeline who had seemed capable then of getting such a hold on him but had proved as ineffectual in this respect as she was in every other. She recalled the vision she had allowed to dance before her as she saw the pair cross the street together, laughing and talking, and how it seemed to interpose itself against the fears which already then—so

strangely—haunted her. Now that she saw it so fruitless—
and that Verena, moreover, had turned out really so great—
she was rather ashamed of it; she felt associated, however
remotely, in the reasons which had made Mrs. Luna tell her
so many fibs the day before, and there could be nothing
elevating in that. As for the other reasons why her fidgety
sister had failed and Mr. Ransom had held his own course,
naturally Miss Chancellor didn't like to think of them.

If she had wondered what Mrs. Burrage wished so particularly to talk about, she waited some time for the clearing-
up of the mystery. During this interval she sat in a
remarkably pretty boudoir, where there were flowers and
faïences and little French pictures, and watched her hostess
revolve round the subject in circles the vagueness of which
she tried to dissimulate. Olive believed she was a person
who never could enjoy asking a favor, especially of a votary
of the new ideas; and that was evidently what was coming.
She had asked one already, but that had been handsomely
paid for; the note from Mrs. Burrage which Verena found
awaiting her in Tenth Street, on her arrival, contained the
largest check this young woman had ever received for an
address. The request that hung fire had reference to Verena
too, of course; and Olive needed no prompting to feel that
her friend's being a young person who took money could
not make Mrs. Burrage's present effort more agreeable. To
this taking of money (for when it came to Verena it was as if
it came to her as well), she herself was now completely
inured; money was a tremendous force, and when one
wanted to assault the wrong with every engine one was
happy not to lack the sinews of war. She liked her hostess
better this morning than she had liked her before; she had
more than ever the air of taking all sorts of sentiments and
views for granted between them; which could only be flattering to Olive so long as it was really Mrs. Burrage who
made each advance, while her visitor sat watchful and
motionless. She had a light, clever, familiar way of traversing an immense distance with a very few words, as when

she remarked, "Well then, it is settled that she will come, and will stay till she is tired."

Nothing of the kind had been settled, but Olive helped Mrs. Burrage (this time) more than she knew by saying, "Why do you want her to visit you, Mrs. Burrage? why do you want her socially? Are you not aware that your son, a year ago, desired to marry her?"

"My dear Miss Chancellor, that is just what I wish to talk to you about. I am aware of everything; I don't believe you ever met anyone who is aware of more things than I." And Olive had to believe this, as Mrs. Burrage held up, smiling, her intelligent, proud, good-natured, successful head. "I knew a year ago that my son was in love with your friend, I know that he has been so ever since, and that in consequence he would like to marry her today. I daresay you don't like the idea of her marrying at all; it would break up a friendship which is so full of interest" (Olive wondered for a moment whether she had been going to say "so full of profit"), "for you. This is why I hesitated; but since you are willing to talk about it, that is just what I want."

"I don't see what good it will do," Olive said.

"How can we tell till we try? I never give a thing up till I have turned it over in every sense."

It was Mrs. Burrage, however, who did most of the talking; Olive only inserted from time to time an inquiry, a protest, a correction, an ejaculation tinged with irony. None of these things checked or diverted her hostess; Olive saw more and more that she wished to please her, to win her over, to smooth matters down, to place them in a new and original light. She was very clever and (little by little Olive said to herself), absolutely unscrupulous, but she didn't think she was clever enough for what she had undertaken. This was neither more nor less, in the first place, than to persuade Miss Chancellor that she and her son were consumed with sympathy for the movement to which Miss Chancellor had dedicated her life. But how could Olive believe that, when she saw the type to which Mrs. Burrage belonged—a type into which nature herself had inserted a face turned in the very opposite way from all earnest and improving things? People like Mrs. Burrage lived and fattened on abuses, prejudices, privileges, on the petrified, cruel fashions of the past. It must be added, however, that if her hostess was a humbug, Olive had never met one who provoked her less; she was such a brilliant, genial, artistic one, with such a recklessness of perfidy, such a willingness to bribe you if she couldn't deceive you. She seemed to be offering Olive all the kingdoms of the earth if she would only exert herself to bring about a state of feeling on Verena Tarrant's part which would lead the girl to accept Henry Burrage.

"We know it's you—the whole business; that you can do what you please. You could decide it tomorrow with a word."

She had hesitated at first, and spoken of her hesitation, and it might have appeared that she would need all her courage to say to Olive, that way, face to face, that Verena was in such subjection to her. But she didn't look afraid; she only looked as if it were an infinite pity Miss Chancellor couldn't understand what immense advantages and rewards there would be for her in striking an alliance with the house of Burrage. Olive was so impressed with this, so occupied, even, in wondering what these mystic benefits might be, and whether after all there might not be a protection in them (from something worse), a fund of some sort that she and Verena might convert to a large use, setting aside the mother and son when once they had got what they had to give—she was so arrested with the vague daze of this vision, the sense of Mrs. Burrage's full hands, her eagerness, her thinking it worth-while to flatter and conciliate, whatever her pretexts and pretentions might be, that she was almost insensible, for the time, to the strangeness of such a woman's coming round to a positive desire for a connection with the Tarrants. Mrs. Burrage had indeed explained this partly by saying that her son's condition was wearing her out, and that she would enter into anything that would make him happier, make him better. She was fonder of him than of the whole world beside, and it was an anguish to her to see him yearning for Miss Tarrant only to lose her. She made that charge about Olive's power in the matter in such a way that it seemed at the same time a tribute to her force of character.

"I don't know on what terms you suppose me to be with my friend," Olive returned, with considerable majesty. "She will do exactly as she likes, in such a case as the one you allude to. She is absolutely free; you speak as if I were her keeper!"

Then Mrs. Burrage explained that of course she didn't mean that Miss Chancellor exercised a conscious tyranny; but only that Verena had a boundless admiration for her, saw through her eyes, took the impress of all her opinions, preferences. She was sure that if Olive would only take a favorable view of her son Miss Tarrant would instantly throw herself into it. "It's very true that you may ask me," added Mrs. Burrage, smiling, "how you can take a favorable view of a young man who wants to marry the very person in the world you want most to keep unmarried!"

This description of Verena was of course perfectly correct; but it was not agreeable to Olive to have the fact in question so clearly perceived, even by a person who expressed it with an air intimating that there was nothing in the world *she* couldn't understand.

"Did your son know that you were going to speak to me about this?" Olive asked, rather coldly, waiving the question of her influence on Verena and the state in which she wished her to remain.

"Oh yes, poor dear boy; we had a long talk yesterday, and I told him I would do what I could for him. Do you remember the little visit I paid to Cambridge last spring, when I saw you at his rooms? Then it was I began to perceive how the wind was setting; but yesterday we had a real

314

éclaircissement. I didn't like it at all, at first; I don't mind telling you that, now—now that I am really enthusiastic about it. When a girl is as charming, as original, as Miss Tarrant, it doesn't in the least matter who she is; she makes herself the standard by which you measure her; she makes her own position. And then Miss Tarrant has such a future!" Mrs. Burrage added, quickly, as if that were the last thing to be overlooked. "The whole question has come up again —the feeling that Henry tried to think dead, or at least dying, has revived, through the—I hardly know what to call it, but I really may say the unexpectedly great effect of her appearance here. She was really wonderful on Wednesday evening; prejudice, conventionality, every presumption there might be against her, had to fall to the ground. I expected a success, but I didn't expect what you gave us," Mrs. Burrage went on, smiling, while Olive noted her "you." "In short, my poor boy flamed up again; and now I see that he will never again care for any girl as he cares for that one. My dear Miss Chancellor, *j'en ai pris mon parti,* and perhaps you know my way of doing that sort of thing. I am not at all good at resigning myself, but I am excellent at taking up a craze. I haven't renounced, I have only changed sides. For or against, I must be a partisan. Don't you know that kind of nature? Henry has put the affair into my hands, and you see I put it into yours. Do help me; let us work together."

This was a long, explicit speech for Mrs. Burrage, who dealt, usually, in the cursory and allusive; and she may very well have expected that Miss Chancellor would recognize its importance. What Olive did, in fact, was simply to inquire, by way of rejoinder: "Why did you ask us to come on?"

If Mrs. Burrage hesitated now, it was only for twenty seconds. "Simply because we are so interested in your work."

"That surprises me," said Olive, thoughtfully.

"I daresay you don't believe it; but such a judgment is

315

superficial. I am sure we give proof in the offer we make," Mrs. Burrage remarked, with a good deal of point. "There are plenty of girls—without any views at all—who would be delighted to marry my son. He is very clever, and he has a large fortune. Add to that that he's an angel!"

That was very true, and Olive felt all the more that the attitude of these fortunate people, for whom the world was so well arranged just as it was, was very curious. But as she sat there it came over her that the human spirit has many variations, that the influence of the truth is great, and that there are such things in life as happy surprises, quite as well as disagreeable ones. Nothing, certainly, forced such people to fix their affections on the daughter of a "healer"; it would be very clumsy to pick her out of her generation only for the purpose of frustrating her. Moreover, her observation of their young host at Delmonico's and in the spacious box at the Academy of Music, where they had privacy and ease, and murmured words could pass without making neighbors more given up to the stage turn their heads—her consideration of Henry Burrage's manner, suggested to her that she had measured him rather scantily the year before, that he was as much in love as the feebler passions of the age permitted (for though Miss Chancellor believed in the amelioration of humanity, she thought there was too much water in the blood of all of us), that he prized Verena for her rarity, which was her genius, her gift, and would therefore have an interest in promoting it, and that he was of so soft and fine a paste that his wife might do what she liked with him. Of course there would be the mother-in-law to count with; but unless she was perjuring herself shamelessly Mrs. Burrage really had the wish to project herself into the new atmosphere, or at least to be generous personally; so that, oddly enough, the fear that most glanced before Olive was not that this high, free matron, slightly irritable with cleverness and at the same time good-natured with prosperity, would bully her son's bride, but rather that she might take too fond a possession of her. It was a fear which may be described as a presentiment of jealousy. It occurred, accordingly, to Miss Chancellor's quick conscience that, possibly, the proposal which presented itself in circumstances so complicated and anomalous was simply a magnificent chance, an improvement on the very best, even, that she had dreamed of for Verena. It meant a large command of money—much larger than her own; the association of a couple of clever people who simulated conviction very well, whether they felt it or not, and who had a hundred useful worldly ramifications, and a kind of social pedestal from which she might really shine afar. The conscience I have spoken of grew positively sick as it thought of having such a problem as that to consider, such an ordeal to traverse. In the presence of such a contingency the poor girl felt grim and helpless; she could only vaguely wonder whether she were called upon in the name of duty to lend a hand to the torture of her own spirit.

"And if she should marry him, how could I be sure that —afterwards—you would care so much about the question which has all our thoughts, hers and mine?" This inquiry evolved itself from Olive's rapid meditation; but even to herself it seemed a little rough.

Mrs. Burrage took it admirably. "You think we are feigning an interest, only to get hold of her? That's not very nice of you, Miss Chancellor; but of course you have to be tremendously careful. I assure you my son tells me he firmly believes your movement is the great question of the immediate future, that it has entered into a new phase; into what does he call it? the domain of practical politics. As for me, you don't suppose I don't want everything we poor women can get, or that I would refuse any privilege or advantage that's offered me? I don't rant or rave about anything, but I have—as I told you just now—my own quiet way of being zealous. If you had no worse partisan than I, you would do very well. My son has talked to me immensely about your ideas; and even if I should enter into them only because he does, I should do so quite enough. You may say you don't see Henry dangling about after a wife who gives public addresses; but I am convinced that a great many things are coming to pass—very soon, too—that we don't see in advance. Henry is a gentleman to his fingertips, and there is not a situation in which he will not conduct himself with tact."

Olive could see that they really wanted Verena immensely, and it was impossible for her to believe that if they were to get her they would not treat her well. It came to her that they would even over-indulge her, flatter her, spoil her; she was perfectly capable, for the moment, of assuming that Verena was susceptible of deterioration and that her own treatment of her had been discriminatingly severe. She had a hundred protests, objections, replies; her only embarrassment could be as to which she should use first.

"I think you have never seen Doctor Tarrant and his wife," she remarked, with a calmness which she felt to be very pregnant.

"You mean they are absolutely fearful? My son has told me they are quite impossible, and I am quite prepared for that. Do you ask how we should get on with them? My dear young lady, we should get on as you do!"

If Olive had answers, so had Mrs. Burrage; she had still an answer when her visitor, taking up the supposition that it was in her power to dispose in any manner whatsoever of Verena, declared that she didn't know why Mrs. Burrage addressed herself to *her,* that Miss Tarrant was free as air, that her future was in her own hands, that such a matter as this was a kind of thing with which it could never occur to one to interfere. "Dear Miss Chancellor, we don't ask you to interfere. The only thing we ask of you is simply *not* to interfere."

"And have you sent for me only for that?"

"For that, and for what I hinted at in my note; that you would really exercise your influence with Miss Tarrant to induce her to come to us now for a week or two. That is really, after all, the main thing I ask. Lend her to us, here, or a little while, and we will take care of the rest. That sounds conceited—but she *would* have a good time."

"She doesn't live for that," said Olive.

"What I mean is that she should deliver an address every night!" Mrs. Burrage returned, smiling

"I think you try to prove too much. You do believe—though you pretend you don't—that I control her actions, and as far as possible her desires, and that I am jealous of any other relations she may possibly form. I can imagine that we may perhaps have that air, though it only proves how little such an association as ours is understood, and how superficial is still"—Olive felt that her "still" was really historical—"the interpretation of many of the elements in the activity of women, how much the public conscience with regard to them needs to be educated. Your conviction with respect to my attitude being what I believe it to be," Miss Chancellor went on, "I am surprised at your not perceiving how little it is in my interest to deliver my—my victim up to you."

If we were this moment to take, in a single glance, an inside view of Mrs. Burrage (a liberty we have not yet ventured on), I suspect we should find that she was considerably exasperated at her visitor's superior tone, at seeing herself regarded by this dry, shy, obstinate, provincial young woman as superficial. If she liked Verena very nearly as much as she tried to convince Miss Chancellor, she was conscious of disliking Miss Chancellor more than she should probably ever be able to reveal to Verena. It was doubtless partly her irritation that found a voice as she said, after a self-administered pinch of caution not to say too much, "Of course it would be absurd in us to assume that Miss Tarrant would find my son irresistible, especially as she has already refused him. But even if she should remain obdurate, should you consider yourself quite safe as regards others?"

The manner in which Miss Chancellor rose from her chair on hearing these words showed her hostess that if she had wished to take a little revenge by frightening her, the ex-

319

periment was successful. "What others do you mean?" Olive asked, standing very straight, and turning down her eye as from a great height.

Mrs. Burrage—since we have begun to look into he mind we may continue the process—had not meant any one in particular; but a train of association was suddenl kindled in her thought by the flash of the girl's resentment She remembered the gentleman who had come up to he in the music-room, after Miss Tarrant's address, while sh was talking with Olive, and to whom that young lady ha given so cold a welcome. "I don't mean any one in particu lar; but, for instance, there is the young man to whom sh asked me to send an invitation to my party, and wh looked to me like a possible admirer." Mrs. Burrage als got up; then she stood a moment, closer to her visito "Don't you think it's a good deal to expect that, young pretty, attractive, clever, charming as she is, you should b able to keep her always, to exclude other affections, to cu off a whole side of life, to defend her against dangers—i you call them dangers—to which every young woman wh is not positively repulsive is exposed? My dear young lad I wonder if I might give you three words of advice?" Mr Burrage did not wait till Olive had answered this inquir she went on quickly, with her air of knowing exactly wh she wanted to say and feeling at the same time that, goo as it might be, the manner of saying it, like the manner o saying most other things, was not worth troubling muc about. "Don't attempt the impossible. You have got hold o a good thing; don't spoil it by trying to stretch it too far. you don't take the better, perhaps you will have to tak the worse; if it's safety you want I should think she wa much safer with my son—for with us you know the wor —than as a possible prey to adventurers, to exploiters, to people who, once they had got hold of her, would sh her up altogether."

Olive dropped her eyes; she couldn't endure Mrs. Bu rage's horrible expression of being near the mark, her loo of worldly cleverness, of a confidence born of much experience. She felt that nothing would be spared her, that she should have to go to the end, that this ordeal also must be faced, and that, in particular, there was a detestable wisdom in her hostess's advice. She was conscious, however, of no obligation to recognize it then and there; she wanted to get off, and even to carry Mrs. Burrage's sapient words along with her—to hurry to some place where she might be alone and think. "I don't know why you have thought it right to send for me only to say this. I take no interest whatever in your son—in his settling in life." And she gathered her mantle more closely about her, turning away.

"It is exceedingly kind of you to have come," said Mrs. Burrage, imperturbably. "Think of what I have said; I am sure you won't feel that you have wasted your hour."

"I have a great many things to think of!" Olive exclaimed, insincerely; for she knew that Mrs. Burrage's ideas would haunt her.

"And tell her that if she will make us the little visit, all New York shall sit at her feet!"

That was what Olive wanted, and yet it seemed a mockery to hear Mrs. Burrage say it. Miss Chancellor retreated, making no response even when her hostess declared again that she was under great obligations to her for coming. When she reached the street she found she was deeply agitated, but not with a sense of weakness; she hurried along excited and dismayed, feeling that her insufferable conscience was bristling like some irritated animal, that a magnificent offer had really been made to Verena, and that there was no way for her to persuade herself she might be silent about it. Of course, if Verena should be tempted by the idea of being made so much of by the Burrages, the danger of Basil Ransom getting any kind of hold on her would cease to be pressing. That was what was present to Olive as she walked along, and that was what made her nervous, conscious only of this problem that had suddenly turned the bright day to grayness, heedless of the sophisticated-looking people who passed her on the wide Fifth Avenue pavement. It had risen in her mind the day before, planted first by Mrs. Burrage's note; and then, as we know, she had vaguely entertained the conception, asking Verena whether she would make the visit if it were again to be pressed upon them. It had been pressed, certainly, and the terms of the problem were now so much sharper that they seemed cruel. What had been in her own mind was that if Verena should appear to lend herself to the Burrages Basil Ransom might be discouraged—might think that, shabby and poor, there was no chance for him as against people with every advantage of fortune and position. She didn't see him relax his purpose so easily; she knew she didn't believe he was of that pusillanimous fiber. Still, it was a chance, and any chance that might help her had been worth considering. At present she saw it was a question not of Verena's lending herself, but of a positive gift, or at least of a bargain in which the terms would be immensely liberal. It would be impossible to use the Burrages as a shelter on the assumption that they were not dangerous, for they became dangerous from the moment they set up as sympathizers, took the ground that what they offered the girl was simply a boundless opportunity. It came back to Olive, again and again, that this was, and could only be, fantastic and false; but it was always possible that Verena might not think it so, might trust them all the way. When Miss Chancellor had a pair of alternatives to consider, a question of duty to study, she put a kind of passion into it —felt, above all, that the matter must be settled that very hour, before anything in life could go on. It seemed to her at present that she couldn't re-enter the house in Tenth Street without having decided first whether she might trust the Burrages or not. By "trust" them, she meant trust them to fail in winning Verena over, while at the same time they put Basil Ransom on a false scent. Olive was able to say to herself that he probably wouldn't have the hardihood to push after her into those gilded salons, which, in any event, would be closed to him as soon as the mother and son should discover what he wanted. She even asked herself whether Verena would not be still better defended from the young Southerner in New York, amid complicated hospitalities, than in Boston with a cousin of the enemy. She continued to walk down the Fifth Avenue, without noticing the cross streets, and after a while became conscious that she was approaching Washington Square. By this time she had also definitely reasoned it out that Basil Ransom and Henry Burrage could not both capture Miss Tarrant, that therefore there could not be two dangers, but only one; that this was a good deal gained, and that it behooved her to determine which peril had most reality, in order that she might deal with that one only. She held her way to the Square, which, as all the world knows, is of great extent and open to the encircling street. The trees and grass-plats had begun to bud and sprout, the fountains plashed in the sunshine, the children of the quarter, both the dingier types from the south side, who played games that required much chalking of the paved walks, and much sprawling and crouching there, under the feet of passers, and the little curled and feathered people who drove their hoops under the eyes of French nursemaids—all the infant population filled the vernal air with small sounds which had a crude, tender quality, like the leaves and the thin herbage. Olive wandered through the place, and ended by sitting down on one of the continuous benches. It was a long time since she had done anything so vague, so wasteful. There were a dozen things which, as she was staying over in New York, she ought to do; but she forgot them, or, if she thought of them, felt that they were now of no moment. She remained in her place an hour, brooding, tremulous, turning over and over certain thoughts. It seemed to her that she was face to face with a crisis of her destiny, and that she must not shrink from seeing it exactly as it was. Before she rose to return to Tenth Street she had made up her mind that there was no menace so great as the menace of Basil Ransom; she had accepted in thought any arrangement which would deliver her from that. If the Burrages were to take Verena they would take her from Olive immeasurably less than he would do; it was from him, from him they would take her most. She walked back to her boarding house, and the servant who admitted her said, in answer to her inquiry as to whether Verena were at home, that Miss Tarrant had gone out with the gentleman who called in the morning, and had not yet come in. Olive stood staring; the clock in the hall marked three.

33

"Come out with me, Miss Tarrant; come out with me. *Do* come out with me." That was what Basil Ransom had been saying to Verena when they stood where Olive perceived them, in the embrasure of the window. It had of course taken considerable talk to lead up to this; for the tone, even more than the words, indicated a large increase of intimacy. Verena was mindful of this when he spoke; and it frightened her a little, made her uneasy, which was one of the reasons why she got up from her chair and went to the window— an inconsequent movement, inasmuch as her wish was to impress upon him that it was impossible she should comply with his request. It would have served this end much better for her to sit, very firmly, in her place. He made her nervous and restless; she was beginning to perceive that he produced a peculiar effect upon her. Certainly, she had been out with him at home the very first time he called upon her;

but it seemed to her to make an important difference that she herself should then have proposed the walk—simply because it was the easiest thing to do when a person came to see you in Monadnoc Place.

They had gone out that time because she wanted to, not because he did. And then it was one thing for her to stroll with him round Cambridge, where she knew every step and had the confidence and freedom which came from being on her own ground, and the pretext, which was perfectly natural, of wanting to show him the colleges, and quite another thing to go wandering with him through the streets of this great strange city, which, attractive, delightful as it was, had not the suitableness even of being his home, not his real one. He wanted to show her something, he wanted to show her everything; but she was not sure now—after an hour's talk—that she particularly wanted to see anything more that he could show her. He had shown her a great deal while he sat there, especially what balderdash he thought it —the whole idea of women's being equal to men. He seemed to have come only for that, for he was all the while revolving round it; she couldn't speak of anything but what he brought it back to the question of some new truth like that. He didn't say so in so many words; on the contrary, he was tremendously insinuating and satirical, and pretended to think she had proved all and a great deal more than she wanted to prove; but his exaggeration, and the way he rung all the changes on two or three of the points she had made at Mrs. Burrage's, were just the sign that he was a scoffer of scoffers. He wouldn't do anything but laugh; he seemed to think that he might laugh at her all day without her taking offense. Well, he might if it amused him; but she didn't see why she should ramble round New York with him to give him his opportunity.

She had told him, and she had told Olive, that she was determined to produce some effect on him; but now, suddenly, she felt differently about that—she ceased to care whether she produced any effect or not. She didn't see why she should take him so seriously, when he wouldn't take her so; that is, wouldn't take her ideas. She had guessed before that he didn't want to discuss them; this had been in her mind when she said to him at Cambridge that his interest in her was personal, not controversial. Then she had simply meant that, as an inquiring young Southerner, he had wanted to see what a bright New England girl was like; but since then it had become a little more clear to her—her short talk with Ransom at Mrs. Burrage's threw some light upon the question—what the personal interest of a young Southerner (however inquiring merely) might amount to. Did he too want to make love to her? This idea made Verena rather impatient, weary in advance. The thing she desired least in the world was to be put into the wrong with Olive; for she had certainly given her ground to believe (not only in their scene the night before, which was a simple repetition, but all along, from the very first), that she really had an interest which would transcend any attraction coming from such a source as that. If yesterday it seemed to her that she should like to struggle with Mr. Ransom, to refute and convince him, she had this morning gone into the parlor to receive him with the idea that, now they were alone together in a quiet, favorable place, he would perhaps take up the different points of her address one by one, as several gentlemen had done after hearing her on other occasions. There was nothing she liked so well as that, and Olive never had anything to say against it. But he hadn't taken up anything; he had simply laughed and chaffed, and unrolled a string of queer fancies about the delightful way women would fix things when, as she said in her address, they should get out of their box. He kept talking about the box; he seemed as if he wouldn't let go that simile. He said that he had come to look at her through the glass sides, and if he wasn't afraid of hurting her he would smash them in. He was determined to find the key that would open it, if he had to look for it all over the world; it was tantalizing only to be able to talk to her through the keyhole. If he didn't want to take up the subject, he at least wanted to take *her* up—to keep his hand upon her as long as he could. Verena had had no such sensation since the first day she went in to see Olive Chancellor, when she felt herself plucked from the earth and born aloft.

"It's the most lovely day, and I should like so much to show you New York, as you showed me your beautiful Harvard," Basil Ransom went on, pressing her to accede to his proposal. "You said that was the only thing you could do for me then, and so this is the only thing I can do for you here. It would be odious to see you go away, giving me nothing but this stiff little talk in a boardinghouse parlor."

"Mercy, if you call this stiff!" Verena exclaimed, laughing, while at that moment Olive passed out of the house and descended the steps before her eyes.

"My poor cousin's stiff; she won't turn her head a hair's breadth to look at us," said the young man. Olive's figure, as she went by, was, for Verena, full of a queer, touching, tragic expression, saying ever so many things, both familiar and strange; and Basil Ransom's companion privately remarked how little men knew about women, or indeed about what was really delicate, that he, without any cruel intention, should attach an idea of ridicule to such an incarnation of the pathetic, should speak rough, derisive words about it. Ransom, in truth, today, was not disposed to be very scrupulous, and he only wanted to get rid of Olive Chancellor, whose image, at last, decidedly bothered and bored him. He was glad to see her go out; but that was not sufficient, she would come back quick enough; the place itself contained her, expressed her. For today he wanted to take possession of Verena, to carry her to a distance, to reproduce a little the happy conditions they had enjoyed the day of his visit to Cambridge. And the fact that in the nature of things it could only be for today made his desire more keen, more full of purpose. He had thought over the whole question in the last forty-eight hours, and it was his belief that he saw things in their absolute reality. He took a greater interest in her than he had taken in any one yet, but he proposed, after today, not to let that accident make any difference. This was precisely what gave its high value to the present limited occasion. He was too shamefully poor, too shabbily and meagerly equipped, to have the right to talk of marriage to a girl in Verena's very peculiar position. He understood now how good that position was, from a worldly point of view; her address at Mrs. Burrage's gave him something definite to go upon, showed him what she could do, that people would flock in thousands to an exhibition so charming (and small blame to them); that she might easily have a big career, like that of a distinguished actress or singer, and that she would make money in quantities only slightly smaller than performers of that kind. Who wouldn't pay half a dollar for such an hour as he had passed at Mrs. Burrage's? The sort of thing she was able to do, to say, was an article for which there was more and more demand—fluent, pretty, third-rate palaver, conscious or unconscious perfected humbug; the stupid, gregarious, gullible public, the enlightened democracy of his native land, could swallow unlimited draughts of it. He was sure she could go, like that, for several years, with her portrait in the druggists' windows and her posters on the fences, and during that time would make a fortune sufficient to keep her in affluence forevermore. I shall perhaps expose our young man to the contempt of superior minds if I say that all this seemed to him an insuperable impediment to his making up to Verena. His scruples were doubtless begotten of a false pride, a sentiment in which there was a thread of moral tinsel, as there was in the Southern idea of chivalry; but he felt ashamed of his own poverty, the positive flatness of his situation, when he thought of the gilded nimbus that surrounded the protégée of Mrs. Burrage. This shame was possible to him even while he was conscious of what a mean business it was to practice upon human imbecility, how much better it was even to be seedy and obscure,

discouraged about one's self. He had been born to the prospect of a fortune, and in spite of the years of misery that
followed the war had never rid himself of the belief that a
gentleman who desired to unite himself to a charming girl
couldn't yet ask her to come and live with him in sordid
conditions. On the other hand it was no possible basis of
matrimony that Verena should continue for his advantage
the exercise of her remunerative profession; if he should
become her husband he should know a way to strike her
dumb. In the midst of this an irrepressible desire urged him
on to taste, for once, deeply, all that he was condemned
to lose, or at any rate forbidden to attempt to gain. To spend
a day with her and not to see her again—that presented
itself to him at once as the least and the most that was
possible. He did not need even to remind himself that
young Mr. Burrage was able to offer her everything *he*
lacked, including the most amiable adhesion to her views.

"It will be charming in the Park today. Why not take a
stroll with me there as I did with you in the little park at
Harvard?" he asked, when Olive had disappeared.

"Oh, I have seen it, very well, in every corner. A friend
of mine kindly took me to drive there yesterday," Verena
said.

"A friend?—do you mean Mr. Burrage?" And Ransom
stood looking at her with his extraordinary eyes. "Of course,
I haven't a vehicle to drive you in; but we can sit on a
bench and talk." She didn't say it was Mr. Burrage, but
she was unable to say it was not, and something in her
face showed him that he had guessed. So he went on:
"Is it only with him you can go out? Won't he like it, and
may you only do what he likes? Mrs. Luna told me he
wants to marry you, and I saw at his mother's how he
stuck to you. If you are going to marry him, you can drive
with him every day in the year, and that's just a reason
for your giving me an hour or two now, before it becomes
impossible." He didn't mind much what he said—it had
been his plan not to mind much today—and so long as he

made her do what he wanted he didn't care much how he did it. But he saw that his words brought the color to her face; she stared, surprised at his freedom and familiarity. He went on, dropping the hardness, the irony of which he was conscious, out of his tone. "I know it's no business of mine whom you marry, or even whom you drive with, and I beg your pardon if I seem indiscreet and obtrusive; but I would give anything just to detach you a little from your ties, your belongings, and feel for an hour or two, as if—as if——" And he paused.

"As if what?" she asked, very seriously.

"As if there were no such person as Mr. Burrage—as Miss Chancellor—in the whole place." This had not been what he was going to say; he used different words.

"I don't know what you mean, why you speak of other persons. I can do as I like, perfectly. But I don't know why you should take so for granted that *that* would be it!" Verena spoke these words not out of coquetry, or to make him beg her more for a favor, but because she was thinking, and she wanted to gain a moment. His allusion to Henry Burrage touched her, his belief that she had been in the Park under circumstances more agreeable than those he proposed. They were not; somehow, she wanted him to know that. To wander there with a companion, slowly stopping, lounging, looking at the animals as she had seen the people do the day before; to sit down in some out-of-the-way part where there were distant views, which she had noticed from her high perch beside Henry Burrage—she had to look down so, it made her feel unduly fine: that was much more to her taste, much more her idea of true enjoyment. It came over her that Mr. Ransom had given up his work to come to her at such an hour; people of his kind, in the morning, were always getting their living, and it was only for Mr. Burrage that it didn't matter, inasmuch as he had no profession. Mr. Ransom simply wanted to give up his whole day. That pressed upon her; she was, as the most good-natured girl in the world, too entirely tender not to feel any sacrifice that was made for her; she had always done everything that people asked. Then, if Olive should make that strange arrangement for her to go to Mrs. Burrage's he would take it as a proof that there was something serious between her and the gentleman of the house, in spite of anything she might say to the contrary; moreover, if she should go she wouldn't be able to receive Mr. Ransom there. Olive would trust her not to, and she must certainly, in future, not disappoint Olive nor keep anything back from her, whatever she might have done in the past. Besides, she didn't want to do that; she thought it much better not. It was this idea of the episode which was possibly in store for her in New York, and from which her present companion would be so completely excluded, that worked upon her now with a rapid transition, urging her to grant him what he asked, so that in advance she should have made up for what she might not do for him later. But most of all she disliked his thinking she was engaged to some one. She didn't know, it is true, why she should mind it; and indeed, at this moment, our young lady's feelings were not in any way clear to her. She did not see what was the use of letting her acquaintance with Mr. Ransom become much closer (since his interest did really seem personal); and yet she presently asked him why he wanted her to go out with him, and whether there was anything particular he wanted to say to her (there was no one like Verena for making speeches apparently flirtatious, with the best faith and the most innocent intention in the world); as if that would not be precisely a reason to make it well she should get rid of him altogether.

"Of course I have something particular to say to you—I have a tremendous lot to say to you!" the young man exclaimed. "Far more than I can say in this stuck-up, confined room, which is public, too, so that anyone may come in from one moment to another. Besides," he added, sophistically, "it isn't proper for me to pay a visit of three hours."

Verena did not take up the sophistry, nor ask him

whether it would be more proper for her to ramble about the city with him for an equal period; she only said, "Is it something that I shall care to hear, or that will do me any good?"

"Well, I hope it will do you good; but I don't suppose you will care much to hear it." Basil Ransom hesitated a moment, smiling at her; then he went on: "It's to tell you, once for all, how much I really do differ from you!" He said this at a venture, but it was a happy inspiration.

If it was only that, Verena thought she might go, for that was not personal. "Well, I'm glad you care so much," she answered, musingly. But she had another scruple still, and she expressed it in saying that she should like Olive very much to find her when she came in.

"That's all very well," Ransom returned; "but does she think that she only has a right to go out? Does she expect you to keep the house because she's abroad? If she stays out long enough, she will find you when she comes in."

"Her going out that way—it proves that she trusts me," Verena said, with a candor which alarmed her as soon as she had spoken.

Her alarm was just, for Basil Ransom instantly caught up her words, with a great mocking amazement. "Trusts you? and why shouldn't she trust you? Are you a little girl of ten and she your governess? Haven't you any liberty at all, and is she always watching you and holding you to an account? Have you such vagabond instincts that you are only thought safe when you are between four walls?" Ransom was going to speak, in the same tone, of her having felt it necessary to keep Olive in ignorance of his visit to Cambridge—a fact they had touched on, by implication, in their short talk at Mrs. Burrage's; but in a moment he saw that he had said enough. As for Verena, she had said more than she meant, and the simplest way to unsay it was to go and get her bonnet and jacket and let him take her where he liked. Five minutes later he was walking up and down the parlor, waiting while she prepared herself to go out.

They went up to the Central Park by the elevated railway, and Verena reflected, as they proceeded, that anyway Olive was probably disposing of her somehow at Mrs. Burrage's, and that therefore there wasn't much harm in her just taking this little run on her own responsibility, especially as she should only be out an hour—which would be just the duration of Olive's absence. The beauty of the "elevated" was that it took you up to the Park and brought you back in a few minutes, and you had all the rest of the hour to walk about and see the place. It was so pleasant now that one was glad to see it twice over. The long, narrow inclosure, across which the houses in the streets that border it look at each other with their glittering windows, bristled with the raw delicacy of April, and, in spite of its rockwork grottos and tunnels, its pavilions and statues, its too numerous paths and pavements, lakes too big for the landscape and bridges too big for the lakes, expressed all the fragrance and freshness of the most charming moment of the year. Once Verena was fairly launched the spirit of the day took possession of her; she was glad to have come, she forgot about Olive, enjoyed the sense of wandering in the great city with a remarkable young man who would take beautiful care of her, while no one else in the world knew where she was. It was very different from her drive yesterday with Mr. Burrage, but it was more free, more intense, more full of amusing incident and opportunity. She could stop and look at everything now, and indulge all her curiosities, even the most childish; she could feel as if she were out for the day, though she was not really—as she had not done since she was a little girl, when in the country, once or twice, when her father and mother had drifted into summer quarters, gone out of town like people of fashion, she had, with a chance companion, strayed far from home, spent hours in the woods and fields, looking for raspberries and playing she was a gypsy. Basil Ransom had begun with proposing, strenuously, that she should come somewhere and have luncheon; he had brought her out half an hour before that meal was served in West Tenth Street, and he maintained that he owed her the compensation of seeing that she was properly fed; he knew a very quiet, luxurious French restaurant, near the top of the Fifth Avenue: he didn't tell her that he knew it through having once lunched there in company with Mrs. Luna. Verena for the present declined his hospitality—said she was going to be out so short a time that it wasn't worth the trouble; she should not be hungry, luncheon to her was nothing, she would eat when she went home. When he pressed her she said she would see later, perhaps, if she should find she wanted something. She would have liked immensely to go with him to an eating-house, and yet, with this, she was afraid, just as she was rather afraid, at bottom, and in the intervals of her quick pulsations of amusement, of the whole expedition, not knowing why she had come, though it made her happy, and reflecting that there was really nothing Mr. Ransom could have to say to her that would concern her closely enough. He knew what he intended about her sharing the noonday repast with him somehow; it had been part of his plan that she should sit opposite him at a little table, taking her napkin out of its curious folds—sit there smiling back at him while he said to her certain things that hummed, like memories of tunes, in his fancy, and they waited till something extremely good, and a little vague, chosen out of a French *carte,* was brought them. That was not at all compatible with her going home at the end of half an hour, as she seemed to expect to. They visited the animals in the little zoological garden which forms one of the attractions of the Central Park; they observed the swans in the ornamental water, and they even considered the question of taking a boat for half an hour, Ransom saying that they needed this to make their visit complete. Verena replied that she didn't see why it should be complete, and after having threaded the devious ways of the Ramble, lost themselves in the Maze, and admired all the statues and busts of great men with which the grounds are decorated, they contented themselves with resting on a sequestered bench, where, however, there was a pretty glimpse of the distance and an occasional stroller creaked by on the asphalt walk.

They had had by this time a great deal of talk, none of which, nevertheless, had been serious to Verena's view. Mr. Ransom continued to joke about everything, including the emancipation of women; Verena, who had always lived with people who took the world very earnestly, had never encountered such a power of disparagement or heard so much sarcasm leveled at the institutions of her country and the tendencies of the age. At first she replied to him, contradicted, showed a high spirit of retort, turning his irreverence against himself; she was too quick and ingenious not to be able to think of something to oppose—talking in a fanciful strain—to almost everything he said. But little by little she grew weary and rather sad; brought up, as she had been, to admire new ideas, to criticize the social arrangements that one met almost everywhere, and to disapprove of a great many things, she had yet never dreamed of such a wholesale arrangement as Mr. Ransom's, so much bitterness as she saw lurking beneath his exaggerations, his misrepresentations. She knew he was an intense conservative, but she didn't know that being a conservative could make a person so aggressive and unmerciful. She thought conservatives were only smug and stubborn and self-complacent, satisfied with what actually existed; but Mr. Ransom didn't seem any more satisfied with what existed than with what she wanted to exist, and he was ready to say worse things about some of those whom she would have supposed to be on his own side than she thought it right to say about almost anyone. She ceased after a while to care to argue with him, and wondered what could have happened to him to make him so perverse. Probably something had gone wrong in his life—he

335

had had some misfortune that colored his whole view of the world. He was a cynic; she had often heard about that state of mind, though she had never encountered it, for all the people she had seen only cared, if possible, too much. Of Basil Ransom's personal history she knew only what Olive had told her, and that was but a general outline, which left plenty of room for private dramas, secret disappointments and sufferings. As she sat there beside him she thought of some of these things, asked herself whether they were what he was thinking of when he said, for instance, that he was sick of all the modern cant about freedom and had no sympathy with those who wanted an extension of it. What was needed for the good of the world was that people should make a better use of the liberty they possessed. Such declarations as this took Verena's breath away; she didn't suppose you could hear anyone say such a thing as that in the nineteenth century, even the least advanced. It was of a piece with his denouncing the spread of education; he thought the spread of education a gigantic farce—people stuffing their heads with a lot of empty catchwords that prevented them from doing their work quietly and honestly. You had a right to an education only if you had an intelligence, and if you looked at the matter with any desire to see things as they are you soon perceived that an intelligence was a very rare luxury, the attribute of one person in a hundred. He seemed to take a pretty low view of humanity, anyway. Verena hoped that something really bad had happened to him— not by way of gratifying any resentment he aroused in her nature, but to help herself to forgive him for so much contempt and brutality. She wanted to forgive him, for after they had sat on their bench half an hour and his jesting mood had abated a little, so that he talked with more consideration (as it seemed), and more sincerity, a strange feeling came over her, a perfect willingness not to keep insisting on her own side and a desire not to part from him with a mere accentuation of their differences. Strange I call the nature of her reflections, for they softly battled with each other as she listened, in the warm, still air, touched with the faraway hum of the immense city, to his deep, sweet, distinct voice, expressing monstrous opinions with exotic cadences and mild, familiar laughs, which, as he leaned toward her, almost tickled her cheek and ear. It seemed to her strangely harsh, almost cruel, to have brought her out only to say to her things which, after all, free as she was to contradict them and tolerant as she always tried to be, could only give her pain; yet there was a spell upon her as she listened; it was in her nature to be easily submissive, to like being overborne. She could be silent when people insisted, and silent without acrimony. Her whole relation to Olive was a kind of tacit, tender assent to passionate insistence, and if this had ended by being easy and agreeable to her (and indeed had never been anything else), it may be supposed that the struggle of yielding to a will which she felt to be stronger even than Olive's was not of long duration. Ransom's will had the effect of making her linger even while she knew the afternoon was going on, that Olive would have come back and found her still absent, and would have been submerged again in the bitter waves of anxiety. She saw her, in fact, as she must be at that moment, posted at the window of her room in Tenth Street, watching for some sign of her return, listening for her step on the staircase, her voice in the hall. Verena looked at this image as at a painted picture, perceived all it represented, every detail. If it didn't move her more, make her start to her feet, dart away from Basil Ransom and hurry back to her friend, this was because the very torment to which she was conscious of subjecting that friend made her say to herself that it must be the very last. This was the last time she could ever sit by Mr. Ransom and hear him express himself in a manner that interfered so with her life; the ordeal had been so personal and so complete that she forgot, for the moment, it was also the first time it had occurred. It might have been going on for months. She was perfectly aware that it could bring them to nothing, for one must lead one's own life; it was impossible to lead the life of another, especially when that other was so different, so arbitrary and unscrupulous.

34

"I presume you are the only person in this country who feels as you do," she observed at last.

"Not the only person who feels so, but very possibly the only person who thinks so. I have an idea that my convictions exist in a vague, unformulated state in the minds of a great many of my fellow-citizens. If I should succeed some day in giving them adequate expression I should simply put into shape the slumbering instincts of an important minority."

"I am glad you admit it's a minority!" Verena exclaimed. "That's fortunate for us poor creatures. And what do you call adequate expression? I presume you would like to be President of the United States?"

"And breathe forth my views in glowing messages to a palpitating Senate? That is exactly what I should like to be; you read my aspirations wonderfully well."

"Well, do you consider that you have advanced far in that direction, as yet?" Verena asked.

This question, with the tone in which it happened to be uttered, seemed to the young man to project rather an ironical light upon his present beggarly condition, so that for a moment he said nothing; a moment during which if his neighbor had glanced round at his face she would have seen it ornamented by an incipient blush. Her words had for him

said; I have lunched on abominations. And now you want me to dine with you? Thank you; I think you're cool!" Verena cried, with a laugh which her chronicler knows to have been expressive of some embarrassment, though Basil Ransom did not.

"You must remember that I have, on two different occasions, listened to you for an hour, in speechless, submissive attention, and that I shall probably do it a great many times more."

"Why should you ever listen to me again, when you loathe my ideas?"

"I don't listen to your ideas; I listen to your voice."

"Ah, I told Olive!" said Verena, quickly, as if his words had confirmed an old fear; which was general, however, and did not relate particularly to him.

Ransom still had an impression that he was not making love to her, especially when he could observe, with all the superiority of a man—"I wonder whether you have understood ten words I have said to you?"

"I should think you had made it clear enough—you had rubbed it in!"

"What have you understood, then?"

"Why, that you want to put us back further than we have been at any period."

"I have been joking; I have been piling it up," Ransom said, making that concession unexpectedly to the girl. Every now and then he had an air of relaxing himself, becoming absent, ceasing to care to discuss.

She was capable of noticing this, and in a moment she asked—"Why don't you write out your ideas?"

This touched again upon the matter of his failure; it was curious how she couldn't keep off it, hit it every time. "Do you mean for the public? I have written many things, but I can't get them printed."

"Then it would seem that there are not so many people —so many as you said just now—who agree with you."

"Well," said Basil Ransom, "editors are a mean, timorous lot, always saying they want something original, but deadly afraid of it when it comes."

"Is it for papers, magazines?" As it sank into Verena's mind more deeply that the contributions of this remarkable young man had been rejected—contributions in which, apparently, everything she held dear was riddled with scorn —she felt a strange pity and sadness, a sense of injustice. "I am very sorry you can't get published," she said, so simply that he looked up at her, from the figure he was scratching on the asphalt with his stick, to see whether such a tone as that, in relation to such a fact, were not "put on." But it was evidently genuine, and Verena added that she supposed getting published was very difficult always; she remembered, though she didn't mention, how little success her father had when he tried. She hoped Mr. Ransom would keep on; he would be sure to succeed at last. Then she continued, smiling, with more irony: "You may denounce me by name if you like. Only please don't say anything about Olive Chancellor."

"How little you understand what I want to achieve!" Basil Ransom exclaimed. "There you are—you women— all over; always meaning yourselves, something personal, and always thinking it is meant by others!"

"Yes, that's the charge they make," said Verena, gaily.

"I don't want to touch you, or Miss Chancellor, or Mrs. Farrinder, or Miss Birdseye, or the shade of Eliza P. Moseley, or any other gifted and celebrated being on earth—or in heaven."

"Oh, I suppose you want to destroy us by neglect, by silence!" Verena exclaimed, with the same brightness.

"No, I don't want to destroy you, any more than I want to save you. There has been far too much talk about you, and I want to leave you alone altogether. My interest is in my own sex; yours evidently can look after itself. That's what I want to save."

Verena saw that he was more serious now than he had

been before, that he was not piling it up satirically, but saying really and a trifle wearily, as if suddenly he were tired of much talk, what he meant. "To save it from what?" she asked.

"From the most damnable feminization! I am so far from thinking, as you set forth the other night, that there is not enough woman in our general life, that it has long been pressed home to me that there is a great deal too much. The whole generation is womanized; the masculine tone is passing out of the world; it's a feminine, a nervous, hysterical, chattering, canting age, an age of hollow phrases and false delicacy and exaggerated solicitudes and coddled sensibilities, which, if we don't soon look out, will usher in the reign of mediocrity, of the feeblest and flattest and the most pretentious that has ever been. The masculine character, the ability to dare and endure, to know and yet not fear reality, to look the world in the face and take it for what it is—a very queer and partly very base mixture—that is what I want to preserve, or rather, as I may say, to recover; and I must tell you that I don't in the least care what becomes of you ladies while I make the attempt!"

The poor fellow delivered himself of these narrow notions (the rejection of which by leading periodicals was certainly not a matter for surprise), with low, soft earnestness, bending toward her so as to give out his whole idea, yet apparently forgetting for the moment how offensive it must be to her now that it was articulated in that calm, severe way, in which no allowance was to be made for hyperbole. Verena did not remind herself of this; she was too much impressed by his manner and by the novelty of a man taking that sort of religious tone about such a cause. It told her on the spot, from one minute to the other and once for all, that the man who could give her that impression would never come round. She felt cold, slightly sick, though she replied that now he summed up his creed in such a distinct, lucid way, it was much more comfortable—one knew with what one was dealing; a declaration much at variance with the fact, for Verena had never felt less gratified in her life. The ugliness of her companion's profession of faith made her shiver; it would have been difficult to her to imagine anything more crudely profane. She was determined, however, not to betray any shudder that could suggest weakness, and the best way she could think of to disguise her emotion was to remark in a tone which, although not assumed for that purpose, was really the most effective revenge, inasmuch as it always produced on Ransom's part (it was not peculiar, among women, to Verena), an angry helplessness —"Mr. Ransom, I assure you this is an age of conscience."

"That's a part of your cant. It's an age of unspeakable shams, as Carlyle says."

"Well," returned Verena, "it's all very comfortable for you to say that you wish to leave us alone. But you can't leave us alone. We are here, and we have got to be disposed of. You have got to put us somewhere. It's a remarkable social system that has no place for *us!*" the girl went on, with her most charming laugh.

"No place in public. My plan is to keep you at home and have a better time with you there than ever."

"I'm glad it's to be better; there's room for it. Woe to American womanhood when you start a movement for being more—what you like to be—at home!"

"Lord, how you're perverted; you, the very genius!" Basil Ransom murmured, looking at her with the kindest eyes.

She paid no attention to this, she went on, "And those who have got no home (there are millions, you know), what are you going to do with *them?* You must remember that women marry—are given in marriage—less and less; that isn't their career, as a matter of course, any more. You can't tell them to go and mind their husband and children, when they have no husband and children to mind."

"Oh," said Ransom, "that's a detail! And for myself, I confess, I have such a boundless appreciation of your sex in private life that I am perfectly ready to advocate a man's having a half a dozen wives."

344

"The civilization of the Turks, then, strikes you as the highest?"

"The Turks have a second-rate religion; they are fatalists, and that keeps them down. Besides, their women are not nearly so charming as ours—or as ours would be if this modern pestilence were eradicated. Think what a confession you make when you say that women are less and less sought in marriage; what a testimony that is to the pernicious effect on their manners, their person, their nature, of this fatuous agitation."

"That's very complimentary to me!" Verena broke in, lightly.

But Ransom was carried over her interruption by the current of his argument. "There are a thousand ways in which any woman, all women, married or single, may find occupation. They may find it in making society agreeable."

"Agreeable to men, of course."

"To whom else, pray? Dear Miss Tarrant, what is most agreeable to women is to be agreeable to men! That is a truth as old as the human race, and don't let Olive Chancellor persuade you that she and Mrs. Farrinder have invented any that can take its place, or that is more profound, more durable."

Verena waived this point of the discussion; she only said: "Well, I am glad to hear you are prepared to see the place all choked up with old maids!"

"I don't object to the *old* old maids; they were delightful; they had always plenty to do, and didn't wander about the world crying out for a vocation. It is the new old maid that you have invented from whom I pray to be delivered." He didn't say he meant Olive Chancellor, but Verena looked at him as if she suspected him of doing so; and to put her off that scent he went on, taking up what she had said a moment before: "As for its not being complimentary to you, my remark about the effect on the women themselves of this pernicious craze, my dear Miss Tarrant, you may be quite at your ease. You stand apart, you are unique, extraordinary; you constitute a category by yourself. In you the elements have been mixed in a manner so felicitous that I regard you as quite incorruptible. I don't know where you come from nor how you come to be what you are, but you are outside and above all vulgarizing influences. Besides, you ought to know," the young man proceeded, in the same cool, mild, deliberate tone, as if he were demonstrating a mathematical solution, "you ought to know that your connection with all these rantings and ravings is the most unreal, accidental, illusory thing in the world. You think you care about them, but you don't at all. They were imposed upon you by circumstances, by unfortunate associations, and you accepted them as you would have accepted any other burden, on account of the sweetness of your nature. You always want to please someone, and now you go lecturing about the country, and trying to provoke demonstrations, in order to please Miss Chancellor, just as you did it before to please your father and mother. It isn't *you*, the least in the world, but an inflated little figure (very remarkable in its way too), whom you have invented and set on its feet, pulling strings, behind it, to make it move and speak, while you try to conceal and efface yourself there. Ah, Miss Tarrant, if it's a question of pleasing, how much you might please someone else by tipping your preposterous puppet over and standing forth in your freedom as well as in your loveliness!"

While Basil Ransom spoke—and he had not spoken just that way yet—Verena sat there deeply attentive, with her eyes on the ground; but as soon as he ceased she sprang to her feet—something made her feel that their association had already lasted quite too long. She turned away from him as if she wished to leave him, and indeed were about to attempt to do so. She didn't desire to look at him now, or even to have much more conversation with him. "Something," I say, made her feel so, but it was partly his curious manner —so serene and explicit, as if he knew the whole thing to an absolute certainty—which partly scared her and partly

346

made her feel angry. She began to move along the path to one of the gates, as if it were settled that they should immediately leave the place. He laid it all out so clearly; if he had had a revelation he couldn't speak otherwise. That description of herself as something different from what she was trying to be, the charge of want of reality, made her heart beat with pain; she was sure, at any rate, it was her real self that was there with him now, where she oughtn't to be. In a moment he was at her side again, going with her; and as they walked it came over her that some of the things he had said to her were far beyond what Olive could have imagined as the very worst possible. What would be her state now, poor forsaken friend, if some of them had been borne to her in the voices of the air? Verena had been affected by her companion's speech (his manner had changed so; it seemed to express something quite different), in a way that pushed her to throw up the discussion and determine that as soon as they should get out of the park she would go off by herself; but she still had her wits about her sufficiently to think it important she should give no sign of discomposure, of confessing that she was driven from the field. She appeared to herself to notice and reply to his extraordinary observations enough, without taking them up too much, when she said, tossing the words over her shoulder at Ransom, while she moved quickly: "I presume, from what you say, that you don't think I have much ability."

He hesitated before answering, while his long legs easily kept pace with her rapid step—her charming, touching, hurrying step, which expressed all the trepidation she was anxious to conceal. "Immense ability, but not in the line in which you most try to have it. In a very different line, Miss Tarrant! Ability is no word for it; it's genius!"

She felt his eyes on her face—ever so close and fixed there—after he had chosen to reply to her question that way. She was beginning to blush; if he had kept them longer, and on the part of anyone else, she would have called such a stare impertinent. Verena had been commended of old by

Olive for her serenity "while exposed to the gaze of hundreds"; but a change had taken place, and she was now unable to endure the contemplation of an individual. She wished to detach him, to lead him off again into the general; and for this purpose, at the end of a moment, she made another inquiry: "I am to understand, then, as your last word that you regard us as quite inferior?"

"For public, civic uses, absolutely—perfectly weak and second-rate. I know nothing more indicative of the muddled sentiment of the time than that any number of men should be found to pretend that they regard you in any other light. But privately, personally, it's another affair. In the realm of family life and the domestic affections——"

At this Verena broke in, with a nervous laugh, "Don't say that; it's only a phrase!"

"Well, it's a better one than any of yours," said Basil Ransom, turning with her out of one of the smaller gates—the first they had come to. They emerged into the species of *plaza* formed by the numbered street which constitutes the southern extremity of the park and the termination of the Sixth Avenue. The glow of the splendid afternoon was over everything, and the day seemed to Ransom still in its youth. The bowers and boskages stretched behind them, the artificial lakes and cockneyfied landscapes, making all the region bright with the sense of air and space, and raw natural tints, and vegetation too diminutive to overshadow. The chocolate-colored houses, in tall, new rows, surveyed the expanse; the streetcars rattled in the foreground, changing horses while the horses steamed, and absorbing and emitting passengers; and the beer-saloons, with exposed shoulders and sides, which in New York do a good deal toward representing the picturesque, the "bit" appreciated by painters, announced themselves in signs of large lettering to the sky. Groups of the unemployed, the children of disappointment from beyond the seas, propped themselves against the low, sunny wall of the park; and on the other side the commercial vista of the Sixth Avenue stretched away with a remarkable absence of aerial perspective.

"I must go home; good-by," Verena said, abruptly, to her companion.

"Go home? You won't come and dine, then?"

Verena knew people who dined at midday and others who dined in the evening, and others still who never dined at all; but she knew no one who dined at half-past three. Ransom's attachment to this idea therefore struck her as queer and infelicitous, and she supposed it betrayed the habits of Mississippi. But that couldn't make it any more acceptable to her, in spite of his looking so disappointed—with his dimly-glowing eyes—that he was heedless for the moment that the main fact connected with her return to Tenth Street was that she wished to go alone.

"I must leave you, right away," she said. "Please don't ask me to stay; you wouldn't if you knew how little I want to!" Her manner was different now, and her face as well, and though she smiled more than ever she had never seemed to him more serious.

"Alone, do you mean? Really I can't let you do that," Ransom replied, extremely shocked at this sacrifice being asked of him. "I have brought you this immense distance, I am responsible for you, and I must place you where I found you."

"Mr. Ransom, I must, I will!" she exclaimed, in a tone he had not yet heard her use; so that, a good deal amazed, puzzled and pained, he saw that he should make a mistake if he were to insist. He had known that their expedition must end in a separation which could not be sweet, but he had counted on making some of the terms of it himself. When he expressed the hope that she would at least allow him to put her into a car, she replied that she wished no car; she wanted to walk. This image of her "streaking off" by herself, as he figured it, did not mend the matter; but in the presence of her sudden nervous impatience he felt that here was a feminine mystery which must be allowed to take its course.

"It costs me more than you probably suspect, but I submit. Heaven guard you and bless you, Miss Tarrant!"

She turned her face away from him as if she were straining at a leash; then she rejoined, in the most unexpected manner: "I hope very much you *will* get printed."

"Get my articles published?" He stared, and broke out: "Oh, you delightful being!"

"Good-by," she repeated; and now she gave him her hand. As he held it a moment, and asked her if she were really leaving the city so soon that she mightn't see him again, she answered: "If I stay it will be at a place to which you mustn't come. They wouldn't let you see me."

He had not intended to put that question to her; he had set himself a limit. But the limit had suddenly moved on. "Do you mean at that house where I heard you speak?"

"I may go there for a few days."

"If it's forbidden to me to go and see you there, why did you send me a card?"

"Because I wanted to convert you then."

"And now you give me up?"

"No, no; I want you to remain as you are!"

She looked strange, with her more mechanical smile, as she said this, and he didn't know what idea was in her head. She had already left him, but he called after her, "If you do stay, I will come!" She neither turned nor made an answer, and all that was left to him was to watch her till she passed out of sight. Her back, with its charming young form, seemed to repeat that last puzzle, which was almost a challenge.

For this, however, Verena Tarrant had not meant it. She wanted, in spite of the greater delay and the way Olive would wonder, to walk home, because it gave her time to think, and think again, how glad she was (really, positively, *now*), that Mr. Ransom was on the wrong side. If he had been on the right——! She did not finish this proposition.

She found Olive waiting for her in exactly the manner she had foreseen; she turned to her, as she came in, a face sufficiently terrible. Verena instantly explained herself, related exactly what she had been doing; then went on, without giving her friend time for question or comment: "And you—you paid your visit to Mrs. Burrage?"

"Yes, I went through that."

"And did she press the question of my coming there?"

"Very much indeed."

"And what did you say?"

"I said very little, but she gave me such assurances——"

"That you thought I ought to go?"

Olive was silent a moment; then she said: "She declares they are devoted to the cause, and that New York will be at your feet."

Verena took Miss Chancellor's shoulders in each of her hands, and gave her back, for an instant, her gaze, her silence. Then she broke out, with a kind of passion: "I don't care for her assurances—I don't care for New York! I won't go to them—I won't—do you understand?" Suddenly her voice changed, she passed her arms round her friend and buried her face in her neck. "Olive Chancellor, take me away, take me away!" she went on. In a moment Olive felt that she was sobbing and that the question was settled, the question she herself had debated in anguish a couple of hours before.

Book Third

35

The August night had gathered by the time Basil Ransom, having finished his supper, stepped out upon the piazza of the little hotel. It was a very little hotel and of a very slight and loose construction; the tread of a tall Mississippian made the staircase groan and the windows rattle in their frames. He was very hungry when he arrived, having not had a moment, in Boston, on his way through, to eat even the frugal morsel with which he was accustomed to sustain nature between a breakfast that consisted of a cup of coffee and a dinner that consisted of a cup of tea. He had had his cup of tea now, and very bad it was, brought him by a pale, round-backed young lady, with auburn ringlets, a fancy belt, and an expression of limited tolerance for a gentleman who could not choose quickly between fried fish, fried steak, and baked beans. The train for Marmion left Boston at four o'clock in the afternoon, and rambled fitfully toward the southern cape, while the shadows grew long in the stony pastures and the slanting light gilded the straggling, shabby woods, and painted the ponds and marshes with yellow gleams. The ripeness of summer lay upon the land, and yet there was nothing in the country Basil Ransom traversed that seemed susceptible of maturity; nothing but the apples in the little tough, dense orchards, which gave a suggestion of sour fruition here and there, and the tall, bright goldenrod at the bottom of the bare stone dykes. There were no fields of yellow grain; only here and there a crop of brown hay. But there was a kind of soft scrubbiness in the landscape, and a sweetness begotten of low horizons, of mild air, with a possibility of summer haze, of unregarded inlets where on August mornings the water must be brightly blue. Ransom had heard that the Cape was the Italy, so to speak, of Massachusetts; it had been described to him as the drowsy Cape, the languid Cape, the Cape not of storms, but of eternal peace. He knew that the Bostonians had been drawn thither, for the hot weeks, by its sedative influence, by the conviction that its toneless air would minister to perfect rest. In a career in which there was so much nervous excitement as in theirs they had no wish to be wound up when they went out of town; they were sufficiently wound up at all times by the sense of all their sex had been through. They wanted to live idly, to unbend and lie in hammocks, and also to keep out of the crowd, the rush of the watering-place. Ransom could see there was no crowd at Marmion, as soon as he got there, though indeed there was a rush, which directed itself to the only vehicle in waiting outside of the small, lonely, hut-like station, so distant from the village that, as far as one looked along the sandy, sketchy road which was supposed to lead to it, one saw only an empty land on either side. Six or eight men, in "dusters," carrying parcels and handbags, projected themselves upon the solitary, rickety carryall, so that Ransom could read his own fate, while the ruminating conductor of the vehicle, a lean, shambling citizen, with a long neck and a tuft on his chin, guessed that if he wanted to get to the hotel before dusk he would have to strike out. His valise was attached in a precarious manner to the rear of the carryall. "Well, I'll chance it," the driver remarked, sadly, when Ransom protested against its insecure position. He recognized the southern quality of that picturesque fatalism—judged that Miss Chancellor and Verena Tarrant must be pretty thoroughly relaxed if they had given themselves up to the genius of the place. This was what he hoped for and counted on, as he took his way, the sole pedestrian in the group that had quitted the train, in the wake of the over-laden carryall. It helped him to enjoy the first country walk he had had for many months, for more than months, for years, that the reflection was forced upon him as he went (the mild, vague scenery, just beginning to be dim with twilight, suggested it at every step), that the two young women who constituted, at Marmion, his whole prefigurement of a social circle, must, in such a locality as that, be taking a regular holiday. The sense of all the wrongs they had still to redress must be lighter there than it was in Boston; the ardent young man had, for the hour, an ingenuous hope that they had left their opinions in the city. He liked the very smell of the soil as he wandered along; cool, soft whiffs of evening met him at bends of the road which disclosed very little more—unless it might be a band of straight-stemmed woodland, keeping, a little, the red glow from the west, or (as he went further) an old house, shingled all over, gray and slightly collapsing, which looked down at him from a steep bank, at the top of wooden steps. He was already refreshed; he had tasted the breath of nature, measured his long grind in New York, without a vacation, with the repetition of the daily movement up and down the long, straight, maddening city, like a bucket in a well or a shuttle in a loom.

He lit his cigar in the office of the hotel—a small room on the right of the door, where a "register," meagerly inscribed,

357

led a terribly public life on the little bare desk, and got its pages dog-eared before they were covered. Local worthies, of a vague identity, used to lounge there, as Ransom perceived the next day, by the hour. They tipped back their chairs against the wall, seldom spoke, and might have been supposed, with their converging vision, to be watching something out of the window, if there had been anything at Marmion to watch. Sometimes one of them got up and went to the desk, on which he leaned his elbows, hunching a pair of sloping shoulders to an uncollared neck. For the fiftieth time he perused the flyblown page of the recording volume, where the names followed each other with such jumps of date. The others watched him while he did so—or contemplated in silence some "guest" of the hostelry, when such a personage entered the place with an air of appealing from the general irresponsibility of the establishment and found no one but the village-philosophers to address himself to. It was an establishment conducted by invisible, elusive agencies; they had a kind of stronghold in the dining room, which was kept locked at all but sacramental hours. There was a tradition that a "boy" exercised some tutelary function as regards the crumpled register; but when he was inquired about, it was usually elicited from the impartial circle in the office either that he was somewhere round or that he had gone a-fishing. Except the haughty waitress who has just been mentioned as giving Ransom his supper, and who only emerged at mealtimes from her mystic seclusion, this impalpable youth was the single person on the premises who represented domestic service. Anxious lady-boarders, wrapped in shawls, were seen waiting for him, as if he had been the doctor, on horsehair rockingchairs, in the little public parlor; others peered vaguely out of back doors and windows, thinking that if he were somewhere round they might see him. Sometimes people went to the door of the dining room and tried it, shaking it a little, timidly, to see if it would yield; then, finding it fast, came away, looking, if they had been observed, shy and snubbed, at their fellows.

Some of them went so far as to say that they didn't think it was a very good hotel.

Ransom, however, didn't much care whether it were good or not; he hadn't come to Marmion for the love of the hotel. Now that he had got there, however, he didn't know exactly what to do; his course seemed rather less easy than it had done when, suddenly, the night before, tired, sick of the city air, and hungry for a holiday, he decided to take the next morning's train to Boston, and there take another to the shores of Buzzard's Bay. The hotel itself offered few resources; the inmates were not numerous; they moved about a little outside, on the small piazza and in the rough yard which interposed between the house and the road, and then they dropped off into the unmitigated dusk. This element, touched only in two or three places by a faraway dim glimmer, presented itself to Ransom as his sole entertainment. Though it was pervaded by that curious, pure, earthy smell which in New England, in summer, hangs in the nocturnal air, Ransom bethought himself that the place might be a little dull for persons who had not come to it, as he had, to take possession of Verena Tarrant. The unfriendly inn, which suggested dreadfully to Ransom (he despised the practice), an early bedtime, seemed to have no relation to anything, not even to itself; but a fellow-tenant of whom he made an inquiry told him the village was sprinkled round. Basil presently walked along the road in search of it, under the stars, smoking one of the good cigars which constituted his only tribute to luxury. He reflected that it would hardly do to begin his attack that night; he ought to give the Bostonians a certain amount of notice of his appearance on the scene. He thought it very possible, indeed, that they might be addicted to the vile habit of "retiring" with the cocks and hens. He was sure that was one of the things Olive Chancellor would do so long as he should stay —on purpose to spite him; she would make Verena Tarrant go to bed at unnatural hours, just to deprive him of his evenings. He walked some distance without encountering a creature or discerning an habitation; but he enjoyed the splendid starlight, the stillness, the shrill melancholy of the crickets, which seemed to make all the vague forms of the country pulsate around him; the whole impression was a bath of freshness after the long strain of the preceding two years, and his recent sweltering weeks in New York. At the end of ten minutes (his stroll had been slow), a figure drew near him, at first indistinct, but presently defining itself as that of a woman. She was walking apparently without purpose, like himself, or without other purpose than that of looking at the stars, which she paused for an instant, throwing back her head, to contemplate, as he drew nearer to her. In a moment he was very close; he saw her look at him, through the clear gloom, as they passed each other. She was small and slim; he made out her head and face, saw that her hair was cropped; had an impression of having seen her before. He noticed that as she went by she turned as well as himself, and that there was a sort of recognition in her movement. Then he felt sure that he had seen her elsewhere, and before she had added to the distance that separated them he stopped short, looking after her. She noticed his halt, paused equally, and for a moment they stood there face to face, at a certain interval, in the darkness.

"I beg your pardon—is it Doctor Prance?" he found himself demanding.

For a minute there was no answer; then came the voice of the little lady:

"Yes, sir; I am Doctor Prance. Any one sick at the hotel?"

"I hope not; I don't know," Ransom said, laughing.

Then he took a few steps, mentioned his name, recalled his having met her at Miss Birdseye's, ever so long before (nearly two years), and expressed the hope that she had not forgotten that.

She thought it over a little—she was evidently addicted neither to empty phrases nor to unconsidered assertions. "I presume you mean that night Miss Tarrant launched out so."

360

"That very night. We had a very interesting conversation."

"Well, I remember I lost a good deal," said Doctor Prance.

"Well, I don't know; I have an idea you made it up in other ways," Ransom returned, laughing still.

He saw her bright little eyes engage with his own. Staying, apparently, in the village, she had come out, bareheaded, for an evening walk, and if it had been possible to imagine Doctor Prance bored and in want of recreation, the way she lingered there as if she were quite willing to have another talk might have suggested to Basil Ransom this condition. "Why, don't you consider her career very remarkable?"

"Oh yes; everything is remarkable nowadays; we live in an age of wonders!" the young man replied, much amused to find himself discussing the object of his adoration in this casual way, in the dark, on a lonely country-road, with a short-haired female physician. It was astonishing how quickly Doctor Prance and he had made friends again. "I suppose, by the way, you know Miss Tarrant and Miss Chancellor are staying down here?" he went on.

"Well, yes, I suppose I know it. I am visiting Miss Chancellor," the dry little woman added.

"Oh indeed? I am delighted to hear it!" Ransom exclaimed, feeling that he might have a friend in the camp. "Then you can inform me where those ladies have their house."

"Yes, I guess I can tell it in the dark. I will show you round now, if you like."

"I shall be glad to see it, though I am not sure I shall go in immediately. I must reconnoiter a little first. That makes me so very happy to have met you. I think it's very wonderful—your knowing me."

Doctor Prance did not repudiate this compliment, but she presently observed: "You didn't pass out of my mind entirely, because I have heard about you since, from Miss Birdseye."

"Ah yes, I saw her in the spring. I hope she is in health and happiness."

"She is always in happiness, but she can't be said to be in health. She is very weak; she is failing."

"I am very sorry for that."

"She is also visiting Miss Chancellor," Doctor Prance observed, after a pause which was an illustration of an appearance she had of thinking that certain things didn't at all imply some others.

"Why, my cousin has got all the distinguished women!" Basil Ransom exclaimed.

"Is Miss Chancellor your cousin? There isn't much family resemblance. Miss Birdseye came down for the benefit of the country air, and I came down to see if I could help her to get some good from it. She wouldn't much, if she were left to herself. Miss Birdseye has a very fine character, but she hasn't much idea of hygiene." Doctor Prance was evidently more and more disposed to be chatty. Ransom appreciated this fact, and said he hoped she, too, was getting some good from the country-air—he was afraid she was very much confined to her profession, in Boston; to which she replied—"Well, I was just taking a little exercise along the road. I presume you don't realize what it is to be one of four ladies grouped together in a small frame-house."

Ransom remembered how he had liked her before, and he felt that, as the phrase was, he was going to like her again. He wanted to express his good will to her, and would greatly have enjoyed being at liberty to offer her a cigar. He didn't know what to offer her or what to do, unless he should invite her to sit with him on a fence. He did realize perfectly what the situation in the small frame-house must be, and entered with instant sympathy into the feelings which had led Doctor Prance to detach herself from the circle and wander forth under the constellations, all of which he was sure she knew. He asked her permission to accompany her on her walk, but she said she was not going much further in that direction; she was going to turn round. He turned round with her, and they went back together to the village, in which he at last began to discover a certain consistency, signs of habitation, houses disposed with a rough resemblance to a plan. The road wandered among them with a kind of accommodating sinuosity, and there were even cross-streets, and an oil-lamp on a corner, and here and there the small sign of a closed shop, with an indistinctly countrified lettering. There were lights now in the windows of some of the houses, and Doctor Prance mentioned to her companion several of the inhabitants of the little town, who appeared all to rejoice in the prefix of captain. They were retired shipmasters; there was quite a little nest of these worthies, two or three of whom might be seen lingering in their dim doorways, as if they were conscious of a want of encouragement to sit up, and yet remembered the nights in faraway waters when they would not have thought of turning in at all. Marmion called itself a town, but it was a good deal shrunken since the decline in the shipbuilding interest; it turned out a good many vessels every year, in the palmy days, before the war. There were shipyards still, where you could almost pick up the old shavings, the old nails and rivets, but they were grass-grown now, and the water lapped them without anything to interfere. There was a kind of arm of the sea put in; it went up some way, it wasn't the real sea, but very quiet, like a river; that was more attractive to some. Doctor Prance didn't say the place was picturesque, or quaint, or weird; but he could see that was what she meant when she said it was mouldering away. Even under the mantle of night he himself gathered the impression that it had had a larger life, seen better days. Doctor Prance made no remark designed to elicit from him an account of his motives in coming to Marmion; she asked him neither when he had arrived nor how long he intended to stay. His allusion to his cousinship with Miss Chancellor might have served to her mind as a reason; yet, on the other hand, it would have been open to her to wonder why, if he had come to see the young ladies from Charles Street, he was not in more of a hurry to present himself. It was plain Doctor Prance didn't go into that kind of analysis. If Ransom had complained to her of a sore throat she would have inquired with precision about his symptoms; but she was incapable of asking him any question with a social bearing. Sociably enough, however, they continued to wander through the principal street of the little town, darkened in places by immense old elms, which made a blackness overhead. There was a salt smell in the air, as if they were nearer the water; Doctor Prance said that Olive's house was at the other end.

"I shall take it as a kindness if, for this evening, you don't mention that you have happened to meet me," Ransom remarked, after a little. He had changed his mind about giving notice.

"Well, I wouldn't," his companion replied; as if she didn't need any caution in regard to making vain statements.

"I want to keep my arrival a little surprise for tomorrow. It will be a great pleasure to me to see Miss Birdseye," he went on, rather hypocritically, as if that at bottom had been to his mind the main attraction of Marmion.

Doctor Prance did not reveal her private comment, whatever it was, on this intimation; she only said, after some hesitation—"Well, I presume the old lady will take quite an interest in your being here."

"I have no doubt she is capable even of that degree of philanthropy."

"Well, she has charity for all, but she does—even she—prefer her own side. She regards you as quite an acquisition."

Ransom could not but feel flattered at the idea that he had been a subject of conversation—as this implied—in the little circle at Miss Chancellor's; but he was at a loss, for the moment, to perceive what he had done up to this time to gratify the senior member of the group. "I hope she will find me an acquisition after I have been here a few days," he said, laughing.

"Well, she thinks you are one of the most important converts yet," Doctor Prance replied, in a colorless way, as if she would not have pretended to explain why.

"A convert—me? Do you mean of Miss Tarrant's?" It had come over him that Miss Birdseye, in fact, when he was parting with her after their meeting in Boston, had assented to his request for secrecy (which at first had struck her as somewhat unholy), on the ground that Verena would bring him into the fold. He wondered whether that young lady had been telling her old friend that she had succeeded with him. He thought this improbable; but it didn't matter, and he said, gaily, "Well, I can easily let her suppose so!"

It was evident that it would be no easier for Doctor Prance to subscribe to a deception than it had been for her venerable patient; but she went so far as to reply, "Well, I hope you won't let her suppose you are where you were that time I conversed with you. I could see where you were then!"

"It was in about the same place you were, wasn't it?"

"Well," said Doctor Prance, with a small sigh, "I am afraid I have moved back, if anything!" Her sigh told him a good deal; it seemed a thin, self-controlled protest against the tone of Miss Chancellor's interior, of which it was her present fortune to form a part: and the way she hovered round, indistinct in the gloom, as if she were rather loath to resume her place there, completed his impression that the little doctress had a line of her own.

"That, at least, must distress Miss Birdseye," he said, reproachfully.

"Not much, because I am not of importance. They think women the equals of men; but they are a great deal more pleased when a man joins than when a woman does."

Ransom complimented Doctor Prance on the lucidity of her mind, and then he said: "Is Miss Birdseye really sick? Is her condition very precarious?"

"Well, she is very old, and very—very gentle," Doctor Prance answered, hesitating a moment for her adjective. "Under those circumstances a person may flicker out."

"We must trim the lamp," said Ransom; "I will take my turn, with pleasure, in watching the sacred flame."

"It will be a pity if she doesn't live to hear Miss Tarrant's great effort," his companion went on.

"Miss Tarrant's? What's that?"

"Well, it's the principal interest, in there." And Doctor Prance now vaguely indicated, with a movement of her head, a small white house, much detached from its neighbors, which stood on their left, with its back to the water, at a little distance from the road. It exhibited more signs of animation than any of its fellows; several windows, notably those of the ground floor, were open to the warm evening, and a large shaft of light was projected upon the grassy wayside in front of it. Ransom, in his determination to be discreet, checked the advance of his companion, who added presently, with a short, suppressed laugh—"You can see it is, from that!" He listened, to ascertain what she meant, and after an instant a sound came to his ear—a sound he knew already well, which carried the accents of Verena Tarrant, in ample periods and cadences, out into the stillness of the August night.

"Murder, what a lovely voice!" he exclaimed, involuntarily.

Doctor Prance's eye gleamed toward him a moment, and she observed, humorously (she was relaxing immensely), "Perhaps Miss Birdseye is right!" Then, as he made no rejoinder, only listening to the vocal inflections that floated out of the house, she went on—"She's practicing her speech."

"Her speech? Is she going to deliver one here?"

"No, as soon as they go back to town—at the Music Hall."

Ransom's attention was now transferred to his companion. "Is that why you call it her great effort?"

366

"Well, so they think it, I believe. She practices that way every night; she reads portions of it aloud to Miss Chancellor and Miss Birdseye."

"And that's the time you choose for your walk?" Ransom said, smiling.

"Well, it's the time my old lady has least need of me; she's too absorbed."

Doctor Prance dealt in facts; Ransom had already discovered that; and some of her facts were very interesting.

"The Music Hall—isn't that your great building?" he asked.

"Well, it's the biggest we've got; it's pretty big, but it isn't so big as Miss Chancellor's ideas," added Doctor Prance. "She has taken it to bring out Miss Tarrant before the general public—she has never appeared that way in Boston—on a great scale. She expects her to make a big sensation. It will be a great night, and they are preparing for it. They consider it her real beginning."

"And this is the preparation?" Basil Ransom said.

"Yes; as I say, it's their principal interest."

Ransom listened, and while he listened he meditated. He had thought it possible Verena's principles might have been shaken by the profession of faith to which he treated her in New York; but this hardly looked like it. For some moments Doctor Prance and he stood together in silence.

"You don't hear the words," the doctor remarked, with a smile which, in the dark, looked Mephistophelean.

"Oh, I know the words!" the young man exclaimed, with rather a groan, as he offered her his hand for good night.

36

A certain prudence had determined him to put off his visit till the morning; he thought it more probable that at that time he should be able to see Verena alone, whereas in the evening the two young women would be sure to be sitting together. When the morrow dawned, however, Basil Ransom felt none of the trepidation of the procrastinator; he knew nothing of the reception that awaited him, but he took his way to the cottage designated to him overnight by Doctor Prance, with the step of a man much more conscious of his own purpose than of possible obstacles. He made the reflection, as he went, that to see a place for the first time at night is like reading a foreign author in a translation. At the present hour—it was getting toward eleven o'clock— he felt that he was dealing with the original. The little strag- gling, loosely-clustered town lay along the edge of a blue inlet, on the other side of which was a low, wooded shore, with a gleam of white sand where it touched the water. The narrow bay carried the vision outward to a picture that seemed at once bright and dim—a shining, slumbering summer-sea, and a far-off, circling line of coast, which, un- der the August sun, was hazy and delicate. Ransom re- garded the place as a town because Doctor Prance had called it one; but it was a town where you smelt the breath of the hay in the streets and you might gather blackberries in the principal square. The houses looked at each other across the grass—low, rusty, crooked, distended houses, with dry, cracked faces and the dim eyes of small-paned, stiffly-sliding windows. Their little dooryards bristled with rank, old-fashioned flowers, mostly yellow; and on the quarter that stood back from the sea the fields sloped upward, and the woods in which they presently lost themselves looked down over the roofs. Bolts and bars were not a part of the domestic machinery of Marmion, and the responsive menial, receiving the visitor on the threshold, was a creature rather desired than definitely possessed; so that Basil Ransom found Miss Chancellor's house-door gaping wide (as he had seen it the night before), and destitute even of a knocker or a bell-handle. From where he stood in the porch he could see the whole of the little sitting room on the left of the hall —see that it stretched straight through to the back windows; that it was garnished with photographs of foreign works of art, pinned upon the walls, and enriched with a piano and other little extemporized embellishments, such as ingenious women lavish upon the houses they hire for a few weeks. Verena told him afterwards that Olive had taken her cottage furnished, but that the paucity of chairs and tables and bedsteads was such that their little party used almost to sit down, to lie down, in turn. On the other hand they had all George Eliot's writings, and two photographs of the Sistine Madonna. Ransom rapped with his stick on the lintel of the door, but no one came to receive him; so he made his way into the parlor, where he observed that his cousin Olive had as many German books as ever lying about. He dipped into this literature, momentarily, according to his wont, and then remembered that this was not what he had come for and that as he waited at the door he had seen, through another door, opening at the opposite end of the hall, signs of a small veranda attached to the other face of the house. Thinking the ladies might be assembled there in the shade, he pushed aside the muslin curtain of the back window, and saw that the advantages of Miss Chancellor's summer residence were in this quarter. There was a veranda, in fact, to which a wide, horizontal trellis, covered with an ancient vine, formed a kind of extension. Beyond the trellis was a small, lonely garden; beyond the garden was a large, vague, woody space, where a few piles of old timber were disposed, and which he afterwards learned to be a relic of the ship-building era described to him by Doctor Prance; and still beyond this again was the charming lake-like estuary he had already admired. His eyes did not rest upon the distance; they were attracted by a figure seated under the trellis, where the checkers of sun, in the interstices of the vine-leaves, fell upon a bright-colored rug spread out on the ground. The floor of the roughly-constructed veranda was so low that there was virtually no difference in the level. It took Ransom only a moment to recognize Miss Birdseye, though her back was turned to the house. She was alone; she sat there motionless (she had a newspaper in her lap, but her attitude was not that of a reader), looking at the shimmering bay. She might be asleep; that was why Ransom moderated the process of his long legs as he came round through the house to join her. This precaution represented his only scruple. He stepped across the veranda and stood close to her, but she did not appear to notice him. Visibly, she was dozing, or presumably, rather, for her head was enveloped in an old faded straw hat, which concealed the upper part of her face. There were two or three other chairs near her, and a table on which were half a dozen books and periodicals, together with a glass containing a colorless liquid, on the top of which a spoon was laid. Ransom desired only to respect her repose, so he sat down in one of the chairs and waited till she should become aware of his presence. He thought Miss Chancellor's back garden a delightful spot, and his jaded senses tasted the breeze— the idle, wandering summer wind—that stirred the vine-leaves over his head. The hazy shores on the other side of the water, which had tints more delicate than the street-vistas of New York (they seemed powdered with silver, a sort of midsummer light), suggested to him a land of dreams, a country in a picture. Basil Ransom had seen very few pictures, there were none in Mississippi; but he had a vision at times of something that would be more refined than the real world, and the situation in which he now found himself pleased him almost as much as if it had been a striking work of art. He was unable to see, as I have said, whether Miss Birdseye were taking in the prospect through open or only, imagination aiding (she had plenty of that), through closed, tired, dazzled eyes. She appeared to him, as the minutes elapsed and he sat beside her, the incarnation of well-earned rest, of patient, submissive superannuation. At the end of her long day's work she might have been placed there to enjoy this dim prevision of the peaceful river, the gleaming shores, of the paradise her unselfish life had certainly qualified her to enter, and which, apparently, would so soon be opened to her. After a while she said, placidly, without turning:

"I suppose it's about time I should take my remedy again. It does seem as if she had found the right thing; don't you think so?"

"Do you mean the contents of that tumbler? I shall be delighted to give it to you, and you must tell me how much you take." And Basil Ransom, getting up, possessed himself of the glass on the table.

At the sound of his voice Miss Birdseye pushed back her straw hat by a movement that was familiar to her, and twisting about her muffled figure a little (even in August she felt the cold, and had to be much covered up to sit out), directed at him a speculative, unastonished gaze.

"One spoonful—two?" Ransom asked, stirring the dose and smiling.

"Well, I guess I'll take two this time."

"Certainly, Doctor Prance couldn't help finding the right thing," Ransom said, as he administered the medicine; while the movement with which she extended her face to take it made her seem doubly childlike.

He put down the glass, and she relapsed into her position; she seemed to be considering. "It's homœopathic," she remarked, in a moment.

"Oh, I have no doubt of that; I presume you wouldn't take anything else."

"Well, it's generally admitted now to be the true system."

Ransom moved closer to her, placed himself where she could see him better. "It's a great thing to have the true system," he said, bending toward her in a friendly way; "I'm sure you have it in everything." He was not often hypocritical; but when he was he went all lengths.

"Well, I don't know that any one has a right to say that. I thought you were Verena," she added in a moment, taking him in again with her mild, deliberate vision.

"I have been waiting for you to recognize me; of course you didn't know I was here—I only arrived last night."

"Well, I'm glad you have come to see Olive now."

"You remember that I wouldn't do that when I met you last?"

"You asked me not to mention to her that I had met you; that's what I principally recall."

"And don't you remember what I told you I wanted to do? I wanted to go out to Cambridge and see Miss Tarrant. Thanks to the information that you were so good as to give me, I was able to do so."

"Yes, she gave me quite a little description of your visit," said Miss Birdseye, with a smile and a vague sound in her throat—a sort of pensive, private reference to the idea of laughter—of which Ransom never learned the exact significance, though he retained for a long time afterwards a kindly memory of the old lady's manner at the moment.

"I don't know how much she enjoyed it, but it was an immense pleasure to me; so great a one that, as you see, I have come to call upon her again."

"Then, I presume, she *has* shaken you?"

"She has shaken me tremendously!" said Ransom, laughing.

"Well, you'll be a great addition," Miss Birdseye returned. "And this time your visit is also for Miss Chancellor?"

"That depends on whether she will receive me."

"Well, if she knows you are shaken, that will go a great way," said Miss Birdseye, a little musingly, as if even to her unsophisticated mind it had been manifested that one's relations with Miss Chancellor might be ticklish. "But she can't receive you now—can she?—because she's out. She has gone to the post office for the Boston letters, and they get so many every day that she had to take Verena with her to help her carry them home. One of them wanted to stay with me, because Doctor Prance has gone fishing, but I said I presumed I could be left alone for about seven minutes. I know how they love to be together; it seems as if one *couldn't* go out without the other. That's what they came down here for, because it's quiet, and it didn't look as if there was anyone else they would be much drawn to. So it would be a pity for me to come down after them just to spoil it!"

"I am afraid I shall spoil it, Miss Birdseye."

"Oh, well, a gentleman," murmured the ancient woman.

"Yes, what can you expect of a gentleman? I certainly shall spoil it if I can."

"You had better go fishing with Doctor Prance," said Miss Birdseye, with a serenity which showed that she was far from measuring the sinister quality of the announcement he had just made.

"I shan't object to that at all. The days here must be very long—very full of hours. Have you got the doctor with you?" Ransom inquired, as if he knew nothing at all about her.

"Yes, Miss Chancellor invited us both; she is very thoughtful. She is not merely a theoretic philanthropist—she goes into details," said Miss Birdseye, presenting her large person, in her chair, as if she herself were only an item. "It seems as if we were not so much wanted in Boston, just in August."

"And here you sit and enjoy the breeze, and admire the view," the young man remarked, wondering when the two messengers, whose seven minutes must long since have expired, would return from the post office.

"Yes, I enjoy everything in this little old-world place; I didn't suppose I should be satisfied to be so passive. It's a great contrast to my former exertions. But somehow it doesn't seem as if there were any trouble or any wrong round here; and if there should be, there are Miss Chancellor and Miss Tarrant to look after it. They seem to think I had better fold my hands. Besides, when helpful, generous minds begin to flock in from *your* part of the country," Miss Birdseye continued, looking at him from under the distorted and discolored canopy of her hat with a benignity which completed the idea in any cheerful sense he chose.

He felt by this time that he was committed to rather a dishonest part; he was pledged not to give a shock to her optimism. This might cost him, in the coming days, a good deal of dissimulation, but he was now saved from any further expenditure of ingenuity by certain warning sounds which admonished him that he must keep his wits about him for a purpose more urgent. There were voices in the hall of the house, voices he knew, which came nearer, quickly; so that before he had time to rise one of the speakers had come out with the exclamation—"Dear Miss Birdseye, here are seven letters for you!" The words fell to the ground, indeed, before they were fairly spoken, and when Ransom got up, turning, he saw Olive Chancellor standing there, with the parcel from the post office in her hand. She stared at him in sudden horror; for the moment her self-possession completely deserted her. There was so little of any greeting in her face save the greeting of dismay, that he felt there was nothing for him to say to her, nothing that could mitigate the odious fact of his being there. He could only let her take it in, let her divine that, this time, he was not to be got rid off. In an instant—to ease off the situation—he held out his hand for Miss Birdseye's letters, and it was a proof of Olive's having turned rather faint and weak that she gave them up to him. He delivered the packet to the old lady, and now Verena had appeared in the doorway of the house. As soon as she saw him, she blushed crimson; but she did not, like Olive, stand voiceless.

"Why, Mr. Ransom," she cried out, "where in the world were *you* washed ashore?" Miss Birdseye, meanwhile, taking her letters, had no appearance of observing that the encounter between Olive and her visitor was a kind of concussion.

It was Verena who eased off the situation; her gay challenge rose to her lips as promptly as if she had had no cause for embarrassment. She was not confused even when she blushed, and her alertness may perhaps be explained by the habit of public speaking. Ransom smiled at her while she came forward, but he spoke first to Olive, who had already turned her eyes away from him and gazed at the blue sea-view as if she were wondering what was going to happen to her at last.

"Of course you are very much surprised to see me; but I hope to be able to induce you to regard me not absolutely in the light of an intruder. I found your door open, and I walked in, and Miss Birdseye seemed to think I might stay. Miss Birdseye, I put myself under your protection; I invoke you; I appeal to you," the young man went on. "Adopt me, answer for me, cover me with the mantle of your charity!"

Miss Birdseye looked up from her letters, as if at first she had only faintly heard his appeal. She turned her eyes from Olive to Verena; then she said, "Doesn't it seem as if we had room for all? When I remember what I have seen in the South, Mr. Ransom's being here strikes me as a great triumph."

Olive evidently failed to understand, and Verena broke in with eagerness, "It was by my letter, of course, that you knew we were here. The one I wrote just before we came, Olive," she went on. "Don't you remember I showed it to you?"

At the mention of this act of submission on her friend's part Olive started, flashing her a strange look; then she said to Basil that she didn't see why he should explain so much about his coming; everyone had a right to come. It was a very charming place; it ought to do anyone good. "But it will have one defect for you," she added; "three-quarters of the summer residents are women!"

This attempted pleasantry on Miss Chancellor's part, so unexpected, so incongruous, uttered with white lips and cold eyes, struck Ransom to that degree by its oddity that he could not resist exchanging a glance of wonder with Verena, who, if she had had the opportunity, could probably have explained to him the phenomenon. Olive had recovered herself, reminded herself that she was safe, that her companion in New York had repudiated, denounced her pursuer; and, as a proof to her own sense of her security, as well as a touching mark to Verena that now, after what had passed, she had no fear, she felt that a certain light mockery would be effective.

"Ah, Miss Olive, don't pretend to think I love your sex so little, when you know that what you really object to in me is that I love it too much!" Ransom was not brazen, he was not impudent, he was really a very modest man; but he was aware that whatever he said or did he was condemned to seem impudent now, and he argued within himself that if he was to have the dishonor of being thought brazen he might as well have the comfort. He didn't care a straw, in truth, how he was judged or how he might offend; he had a purpose which swallowed up such inanities as that, and he was so full of it that it kept him firm, balanced him, gave him assurance that might easily have been confounded with a cold detachment. "This place will do me good," he pursued; "I haven't had a holiday for more than two years, I couldn't have gone another day; I was finished. I would have written to you beforehand that I was coming, but I only started at a few hours' notice. It occurred to me that this would be just what I wanted; I remembered what Miss

Tarrant had said in her note, that it was a place where people could lie on the ground and wear their old clothes. I delight to lie on the ground, and all my clothes are old. I hope to be able to stay three or four weeks."

Olive listened till he had done speaking; she stood a single moment longer, and then, without a word, a glance, she rushed into the house. Ransom saw that Miss Birdseye was immersed in her letters; so he went straight to Verena and stood before her, looking far into her eyes. He was not smiling now, as he had been in speaking to Olive. "Will you come somewhere apart, where I can speak to you alone?"

"Why have you done this? It was not right in you to come!" Verena looked still as if she were blushing, but Ransom perceived he must allow for her having been delicately scorched by the sun.

"I have come because it is necessary—because I have something very important to say to you. A great number of things."

"The same things you said in New York? I don't want to hear them again—they were horrible!"

"No, not the same—different ones. I want you to come out with me, away from here."

"You always want me to come out! We can't go out here; we *are* out, as much as we can be!" Verena laughed. She tried to turn it off—feeling that something really impended.

"Come down into the garden, and out beyond there—to the water, where we can speak. It's what I have come for; it was not for what I told Miss Olive!"

He had lowered his voice, as if Miss Olive might still hear them, and there was something strangely grave—altogether solemn, indeed—in its tone. Verena looked around her, at the splendid summer day, at the much-swathed, formless figure of Miss Birdseye, holding her letter inside her hat. "Mr. Ransom!" she articulated then, simply; and as her eyes met his again they showed him a couple of tears.

"It's not to make you suffer, I honestly believe. I don't want to say anything that will hurt you. How can I possibly hurt you, when I feel to you as I do?" he went on, with suppressed force.

She said no more, but all her face entreated him to let her off, to spare her; and as this look deepened, a quick sense of elation and success began to throb in his heart, for it told him exactly what he wanted to know. It told him that she was afraid of him, that she had ceased to trust herself, that the way he had read her nature was the right way (she was tremendously open to attack, she was meant for love, she was meant for him), and that his arriving at the point at which he wished to arrive was only a question of time. This happy consciousness made him extraordinarily tender to her; he couldn't put enough reassurance into his smile, his low murmur, as he said: "Only give me ten minutes; don't receive me by turning me away. It's my holiday—my poor little holiday; don't spoil it."

Three minutes later Miss Birdseye, looking up from her letter, saw them move together through the bristling garden and traverse a gap in the old fence which enclosed the further side of it. They passed into the ancient shipyard which lay beyond, and which was now a mere vague, grass-grown approach to the waterside, bestrewn with a few remnants of supererogatory timber. She saw them stroll forward to the edge of the bay and stand there, taking the soft breeze in their faces. She watched them a little, and it warmed her heart to see the stiff-necked young Southerner led captive by a daughter of New England trained in the right school, who would impose her opinions in their integrity. Considering how prejudiced he must have been he was certainly behaving very well; even at that distance Miss Birdseye dimly made out that there was something positively humble in the way he invited Verena Tarrant to seat herself on a low pile of weather-blackened planks, which constituted the principal furniture of the place, and something, perhaps, just a trifle too expressive of righteous triumph in the manner in which the girl put the suggestion by and stood where she liked, a little proudly, turning a good deal away from him. Miss Birdseye could see as much as this, but she couldn't hear, so that she didn't know what it was that made Verena turn suddenly back to him, at something he said. If she had known, perhaps his observation would have struck her as less singular—under the circumstances in which these two young persons met—than it may appear to the reader.

"They have accepted one of my articles; I think it's the best." These were the first words that passed Basil Ransom's lips after the pair had withdrawn as far as it was possible to withdraw (in that direction) from the house.

"Oh, is it printed—when does it appear?" Verena asked that question instantly; it sprang from her lips in a manner that completely belied the air of keeping herself at a distance from him which she had worn a few moments before.

He didn't tell her again this time, as he had told her when, on the occasion of their walk together in New York, she expressed an inconsequent hope that his fortune as a rejected contributor would take a turn—he didn't remark to her once more that she was a delightful being; he only went on (as if her revulsion were a matter of course), to explain everything he could, so that she might as soon as possible know him better and see how completely she could trust him. "That was, at bottom, the reason I came here. The essay in question is the most important thing I have done in the way of a literary attempt, and I determined to give up the game or to persist, according as I should be able to bring it to the light or not. The other day I got a letter from the editor of the 'Rational Review,' telling me that he should be very happy to print it, that he thought it very remarkable, and that he should be glad to hear from me again. He shall hear from me again—he needn't be afraid! It contained a good many of the opinions I have expressed to you, and a good many more besides. I really believe it will attract some attention. At any rate, the simple fact that it is to be published makes an era in my life. This will seem pitiful to you, no doubt, who publish yourself, have been before the world these several years, and are flushed with every kind of triumph; but to me it's simply a tremendous affair. It makes me believe I may do something; it has changed the whole way I look at my future. I have been building castles in the air, and I have put you in the biggest and fairest of them. That's a great change, and, as I say, it's really why I came on."

Verena lost not a word of this gentle, conciliatory, explicit statement; it was full of surprises for her, and as soon as Ransom had stopped speaking she inquired: "Why, didn't you feel satisfied about your future before?"

Her tone made him feel how little she had suspected he could have the weakness of a discouragement, how little of a question it must have seemed to her that he would one day triumph on his own erratic line. It was the sweetest tribute he had yet received to the idea that he might have ability; the letter of the editor of the "Rational Review" was nothing to it. "No, I felt very blue; it didn't seem to me at all clear that there was a place for me in the world."

"Gracious!" said Verena Tarrant.

A quarter of an hour later Miss Birdseye, who had returned to her letters (she had a correspondent at Framingham who usually wrote fifteen pages), became aware that Verena, who was now alone, was re-entering the house. She stopped her on her way, and said she hoped she hadn't pushed Mr. Ransom overboard.

"Oh no; he has gone off—round the other way."

"Well, I hope he is going to speak for us soon."

Verena hesitated a moment. "He speaks with the pen. He has written a very fine article—for the 'Rational Review.' "

Miss Birdseye gazed at her young friend complacently; the sheets of her interminable letter fluttered in the breeze. "Well, it's delightful to see the way it goes on, isn't it?"

Verena scarcely knew what to say; then, remembering that Doctor Prance had told her that they might lose their dear old companion any day, and confronting it with something Basil Ransom had just said—that the "Rational Review" was a quarterly and the editor had notified him that his article would appear only in the number after the next —she reflected that perhaps Miss Birdseye wouldn't be there, so many months later, to see how it was her supposed consort had spoken. She might, therefore, be left to believe what she liked to believe, without fear of a day of reckoning. Verena committed herself to nothing more confirmatory than a kiss, however, which the old lady's displaced head-gear enabled her to imprint upon her forehead and which caused Miss Birdseye to exclaim, "Why, Verena Tarrant, how cold your lips are!" It was not surprising to Verena to hear that her lips were cold; a mortal chill had crept over her, for she knew that this time she should have a tremendous scene with Olive.

She found her in her room, to which she had fled on quitting Mr. Ransom's presence; she sat in the window, having evidently sunk into a chair the moment she came in, a position from which she must have seen Verena walk through the garden and down to the water with the intruder. She remained as she had collapsed, quite prostrate; her attitude was the same as that other time Verena had found her waiting, in New York. What Olive was likely to say to her first the girl scarcely knew; her mind, at any rate, was full of an intention of her own. She went straight to her and fell on her knees before her, taking hold of the hands which were clasped together, with nervous intensity, in Miss Chancellor's lap. Verena remained a moment, looking up at her, and then said:

"There is something I want to tell you now, without a moment's delay; something I didn't tell you at the time it happened, nor afterwards. Mr. Ransom came out to see me once, at Cambridge, a little while before we went to New York. He spent a couple of hours with me; we took a walk together and saw the colleges. It was after that that he wrote to me—when I answered his letter, as I told you in New York. I didn't tell you then of his visit. We had a great deal of talk about him, and I kept that back. I did so on purpose; I can't explain why, except that I didn't like to tell you, and that I thought it better. But now I want you to know everything; when you know that, you *will* know everything. It was only one visit—about two hours. I enjoyed it very much—he seemed so much interested. One reason I didn't tell you was that I didn't want you to know that he had come on to Boston, and called on me in Cambridge, without going to see you. I thought it might affect you disagreeably. I suppose you will think I deceived you; certainly I left you with a wrong impression. But now I want you to know all—all!"

Verena spoke with breathless haste and eagerness; there was a kind of passion in the way she tried to expiate her former want of candor. Olive listened, staring; at first she seemed scarcely to understand. But Verena perceived that she understood sufficiently when she broke out: "You deceived me—you deceived me! Well, I must say I like your deceit better than such dreadful revelations! And what does anything matter when he has come after you now? What does he want—what has he come for?"

"He has come to ask me to be his wife."

Verena said this with the same eagerness, with as determined an air of not incurring any reproach this time. But as soon as she had spoken she buried her head in Olive's lap.

Olive made no attempt to raise it again, and returned none of the pressure of her hands; she only sat silent for a time, during which Verena wondered that the idea of the episode at Cambridge, laid bare only after so many months, should not have struck her more deeply. Presently she saw it was because the horror of what had just happened drew her off from it. At last Olive asked: "Is that what he told you, off there by the water?"

"Yes"—and Verena looked up—"he wanted me to know it right away. He says it's only fair to you that he should give notice of his intentions. He wants to try and make me like him—so he says. He wants to see more of me, and he wants me to know him better."

Olive lay back in her chair, with dilated eyes and parted lips. "Verena Tarrant, what *is* there between you? what *can* I hold on to, what *can* I believe? Two hours, in Cambridge, before we went to New York?" The sense that Verena had been perfidious there—perfidious in her reticence—now began to roll over her. "Mercy of heaven, how you did act!"

"Olive, it was to spare you."

"To spare me? if you really wished to spare me he wouldn't be here now!"

Miss Chancellor flashed this out with a sudden violence, a spasm which threw Verena off and made her rise to her feet. For an instant the two young women stood confronted, and a person who had seen them at that moment might have taken them for enemies rather than friends. But any such opposition could last but a few seconds. Verena replied, with a tremor in her voice which was not that of passion, but of charity: "Do you mean that I expected him, that I brought him? I never in my life was more surprised at anything than when I saw him there."

"Hasn't he the delicacy of one of his own slave-drivers? Doesn't he know you loathe him?"

Verena looked at her friend with a degree of majesty which, with her, was rare. "I don't loathe him—I only dislike his opinions."

"Dislike! Oh, misery!" And Olive turned away to the open window, leaning her forehead against the lifted sash.

Verena hesitated, then went to her, passing her arm round her. "Don't scold me! help me—help me!" she murmured.

Olive gave her a sidelong look; then, catching her up and facing her again—"Will you come away, now, by the next train?"

"Flee from him again, as I did in New York? No, no,

Olive Chancellor, that's not the way," Verena went on, reasoningly, as if all the wisdom of the ages were seated on her lips. "Then how can we leave Miss Birdseye, in her state? We must stay here—we must fight it out here."

"Why not be honest, if you have been false—really honest, not only half so? Why not tell him plainly that you love him?"

"Love him, Olive? why, I scarcely know him."

"You'll have a chance, if he stays a month!"

"I don't dislike him, certainly, as you do. But how can I love him when he tells me he wants me to give up everything, all our work, our faith, our future, never to give another address, to open my lips in public? How can I consent to that?" Verena went on, smiling strangely.

"He asks you that, just that way?"

"No; it's not that way. It's very kindly."

"Kindly?" Heaven help you, don't grovel! Doesn't he know its my house?" Olive added, in a moment.

"Of course he won't come into it, if you forbid him."

"So that you may meet him in other places—on the shore, in the country?"

"I certainly shan't avoid him, hide away from him," said Verena, proudly. "I thought I made you believe, in New York, that I really cared for our aspirations. The way for me then is to meet him, feeling conscious of my strength. What if I do like him? what does it matter? I like my work in the world, I like everything I believe in, better."

Olive listened to this, and the memory of how, in the house in Tenth Street, Verena had rebuked her doubts, professed her own faith anew, came back to her with a force which made the present situation appear slightly less terrific. Nevertheless, she gave no assent to the girl's logic; she only replied: "But you didn't meet him there; you hurried away from New York, after I was willing you should stay. He affected you very much there; you were not so calm when you came back to me from your expedition to

384

the park as you pretend to be now. To get away from him you gave up all the rest."

"I know I wasn't so calm. But now I have had three months to think about it—about the way he affected me there. I take it very quietly."

"No, you don't; you are not calm now!"

Verena was silent a moment, while Olive's eyes continued to search her, accuse her, condemn her. "It's all the more reason you shouldn't give me stab after stab," she replied, with a gentleness which was infinitely touching.

It had an instant effect upon Olive; she burst into tears, threw herself on her friend's bosom. "Oh, don't desert me—don't desert me, or you'll kill me in torture," she moaned, shuddering.

"You must help me—you must help me!" cried Verena, imploringly too.

37

Basil Ransom spent nearly a month at Marmion; in announcing this fact I am very conscious of its extraordinary character. Poor Olive may well have been thrown back into her alarms by his presenting himself there; for after her return from New York she took to her soul the conviction that she had really done with him. Not only did the impulse of revulsion under which Verena had demanded that their departure from Tenth Street should be immediate appear to her a proof that it had been sufficient for her young friend to touch Mr. Ransom's moral texture with her finger, as it were, in order to draw back forever; but what she had learned from her companion of his own manifestations, his apparent disposition to throw up the game, added to her feeling of security. He had spoken to Verena of their little excursion as his last opportunity, let her know that he regarded it not as the beginning of a more intimate acquaintance but as the end even of such relations as already existed between them. He gave her up, for reasons best known to himself; if he wanted to frighten Olive he judged that he had frightened her enough: his Southern chivalry suggested to him perhaps that he ought to let her off before he had worried her to death. Doubtless, too, he had perceived how vain it was to hope to make Verena abjure a faith so solidly founded; and though he admired her enough to wish to possess her on his own terms, he shrank from the mortification which the future would have in keeping for him—that of finding that, after six months of courting and in spite of all her sympathy, her desire to do what people expected of her, she despised his opinions as much as the first day. Olive Chancellor was able to a certain extent to believe what she wished to believe, and that was one reason why she had twisted Verena's flight from New York, just after she let her friend see how much she should like to drink deeper of the cup, into a warrant for living in a fool's paradise. If she had been less afraid, she would have read things more clearly; she would have seen that we don't run away from people unless we fear them and that we don't fear them unless we know that we are unarmed. Verena feared Basil Ransom now (though this time she declined to run); but now she had taken up her weapons, she had told Olive she was exposed, she had asked *her* to be her defense. Poor Olive was stricken as she had never been before, but the extremity of her danger gave her a desperate energy. The only comfort in her situation was that this time Verena had confessed her peril, had thrown herself into her hands. "I like him—I can't help it—I do like him. I don't want to

386

marry him, I don't want to embrace his ideas, which are unspeakably false and horrible; but I like him better than any gentleman I have seen." So much as this the girl announced to her friend as soon as the conversation of which I have just given a sketch was resumed, as it was very soon, you may be sure, and very often, in the course of the next few days. That was her way of saying that a great crisis had arrived in her life, and the statement needed very little amplification to stand as a shy avowal that she too had succumbed to the universal passion. Olive had had her suspicions, her terrors, before; but she perceived now how idle and foolish they had been, and that this was a different affair from any of the "phases" of which she had hitherto anxiously watched the development. As I say, she felt it to be a considerable mercy that Verena's attitude was frank, for it gave her something to take hold of; she could no longer be put off with sophistries about receiving visits from handsome and unscrupulous young men for the sake of the opportunities it gave one to convert them. She took hold, accordingly, with passion, with fury; after the shock of Ransom's arrival had passed away she determined that he should not find her chilled into dumb submission. Verena had told her that she wanted her to hold her tight, to rescue her; and there was no fear that, for an instant, she should sleep at her post.

"I like him—I like him; but I want to hate——"

"You want to hate him!" Olive broke in.

"No, I want to hate my liking. I want you to keep before me all the reasons why I should—many of them so fearfully important. Don't let me lose sight of anything! Don't be afraid I shall not be grateful when you remind me."

That was one of the singular speeches that Verena made in the course of their constant discussion of the terrible question, and it must be confessed that she made a great many. The strangest of all was when she protested, as she did again and again to Olive, against the idea of their seeking safety in retreat. She said there was a want of dignity in it—

that she had been ashamed, afterwards, of what she had done in rushing away from New York. This care for her moral appearance was, on Verena's part, something new; inasmuch as, though she had struck that note on previous occasions—had insisted on its being her duty to face the accidents and alarms of life—she had never erected such a standard in the face of a disaster so sharply possible. It was not her habit either to talk or to think about her dignity, and when Olive found her taking that tone she felt more than ever that the dreadful, ominous, fatal part of the situation was simply that now, for the first time in all the history of their sacred friendship, Verena was not sincere. She was not sincere when she told her that she wanted to be helped against Mr. Ransom—when she exhorted her, that way, to keep everything that was salutary and fortifying before her eyes. Olive did not go so far as to believe that she was playing a part and putting her off with words which, glossing over her treachery, only made it more cruel; she would have admitted that that treachery was as yet unwitting, that Verena deceived herself first of all, thinking she really wished to be saved. Her phrases about her dignity were insincere, as well as her pretext that they must stay to look after Miss Birdseye: as if Doctor Prance were not abundantly able to discharge that function and would not be enchanted to get them out of the house! Olive had perfectly divined by this time that Doctor Prance had no sympathy with their movement, no general ideas; that she was simply shut up to petty questions of physiological science and of her own professional activity. She would never have invited her down if she had realized this in advance so much as the doctor's dry detachment from all their discussions, their readings and practicings, her constant expeditions to fish and botanize, subsequently enabled her to do. She was very narrow, but it did seem as if she knew more about Miss Birdseye's peculiar physical conditions—they were *very* peculiar—than anyone else, and this was a comfort at a time when that admirable woman seemed to be suffering a loss of vitality.

"The great point is that it must be met some time, and it will be a tremendous relief to have it over. He is determined to have it out with me, and if the battle doesn't come off today we shall have to fight it tomorrow. I don't see why this isn't as good a time as any other. My lecture for the Music Hall is as good as finished, and I haven't got anything else to do; so I can give all my attention to our personal struggle. It requires a good deal, you would admit, if you knew how wonderfully he can talk. If we should leave this place tomorrow he would come after us to the very next one. He would follow us everywhere. A little while ago we could have escaped him, because he says that then he had no money. He hasn't got much now, but he has got enough to pay his way. He is so encouraged by the reception of his article by the editor of the 'Rational Review,' that he is sure that in future his pen will be a resource."

These remarks were uttered by Verena after Basil Ransom had been three days at Marmion, and when she reached this point her companion interrupted her with the inquiry, "Is that what he proposes to support you with—his pen?"

"Oh yes; of course he admits we should be terribly poor."

"And this vision of a literary career is based entirely upon an article that hasn't yet seen the light? I don't see how a man of any refinement can approach a woman with so beggarly an account of his position in life."

"He says he wouldn't—he would have been ashamed—three months ago; that was why, when we were in New York, and he felt, even then—well (so he says) all he feels now, he made up his mind not to persist, to let me go. But just lately a change has taken place; his state of mind altered completely, in the course of a week, in consequence of the letter that editor wrote him about his contribution, and his paying for it right off. It was a remarkably flattering letter. He says he believes in his future now; he has before him a vision of distinction, of influence, and of fortune, not great, perhaps, but sufficient to make life tolerable. He doesn't think life is very delightful, in the nature of things; but one of the best things a man can do with it is to get hold of some woman (of course, she must please him very much, to make it worth while), whom he may draw close to him."

"And couldn't he get hold of anyone but you—among all the exposed millions of our sex?" poor Olive groaned. "Why must he pick you out, when everything he knew about you showed you to be, exactly, the very last?"

"That's just what I have asked him, and he only remarks that there is no reasoning about such things. He fell in love with me that first evening, at Miss Birdseye's. So you see there was some ground for that mystic apprehension of yours. It seems as if I pleased him more than anyone."

Olive flung herself over on the couch, burying her face in the cushions, which she tumbled in her despair, and moaning out that he didn't love Verena, he never had loved her, it was only his hatred of their cause that made him pretend it; he wanted to do that an injury, to do it the worst he could think of. He didn't love her, he hated her, he only wanted to smother her, to crush her, to kill her—as she would infallibly see that he would if she listened to him. It was because he knew that her voice had magic in it, and from the moment he caught its first note he had determined to destroy it. It was not tenderness that moved him—it was devilish malignity; tenderness would be incapable of requiring the horrible sacrifice that he was not ashamed to ask, of requiring her to commit perjury and blasphemy, to desert a work, an interest, with which her very heart-strings were interlaced, to give the lie to her whole young past, to her purest, holiest ambitions. Olive put forward no claim of her own, breathed, at first, at least, not a word of remonstrance in the name of her personal loss, of their blighted union; she only dwelt upon the unspeakable tragedy of a defection from their standard, of a failure on Verena's part to carry out what she had undertaken, of the horror of seeing her bright career blotted out with darkness and tears, of the joy and elation that would fill the breast of all their adversaries at this illustrious, consummate proof of the fickleness, the futility, the predestined servility, of women. A man had only to whistle for her, and she who had pretended most was delighted to come and kneel at his feet. Olive's most passionate protest was summed up in her saying that if Verena were to forsake them it would put back the emancipation of women a hundred years. She did not, during these dreadful days, talk continuously; she had long periods of pale, intensely anxious, watchful silence, interrupted by outbreaks of passionate argument, entreaty, invocation. It was Verena who talked incessantly, Verena who was in a state entirely new to her, and, as anyone could see, in an attitude entirely unnatural and overdone. If she was deceiving herself, as Olive said, there was something very affecting in her effort, her ingenuity. If she tried to appear to Olive impartial, coldly judicious, in her attitude with regard to Basil Ransom, and only anxious to see, for the moral satisfaction of the thing, how good a case, as a lover, he might make out for himself and how much he might touch her susceptibilities, she endeavored, still more earnestly, to practice this fraud upon her own imagination. She abounded in every proof that she should be in despair if she should be overborne, and she thought of arguments even more convincing, if possible, than Olive's, why she should hold on to her old faith, why she should resist even at the cost of acute temporary suffering. She was voluble, fluent, feverish; she was perpetually bringing up the subject, as if to encourage her friend, to show how she kept possession of her judgment, how independent she remained.

No stranger situation can be imagined than that of these extraordinary young women at this juncture; it was so singular on Verena's part, in particular, that I despair of presenting it to the reader with the air of reality. To understand it, one must bear in mind her peculiar frankness, natural and acquired, her habit of discussing questions, sentiments, moralities, her education, in the atmosphere of lecture-rooms, of *séances,* her familiarity with the vocabulary of emotion, the mysteries of "the spiritual life." She had learned to breathe and move in a rarefied air, as she would have learned to speak Chinese if her success in life had depended upon it; but this dazzling trick, and all her artlessly artful facilities, were not a part of her essence, an expression of her innermost preferences. What *was* a part of her essence was the extraordinary generosity with which she could expose herself, give herself away, turn herself inside out, for the satisfaction of a person who made demands of her. Olive, as we know, had made the reflection that no one was naturally less preoccupied with the idea of her dignity, and though Verena put it forward as an excuse for remaining where they were, it must be admitted that in reality she was very deficient in the desire to be consistent with herself. Olive had contributed with all her zeal to the development of Verena's gift; but I scarcely venture to think now, what she may have said to herself, in the secrecy of deep meditation, about the consequences of cultivating an abundant eloquence. Did she say that Verena was attempting to smother her now in her own phrases? did she view with dismay the fatal effect of trying to have an answer for everything? From Olive's condition during these lamentable weeks there is a certain propriety—a delicacy enjoined by the respect for misfortune—in averting our head. She neither ate nor slept; she could scarcely speak without bursting into tears; she felt so implacably, insidiously baffled. She remembered the magnanimity with which she had declined (the winter before the last) to receive the vow of eternal maidenhood which she had at first demanded and then put by as too crude a test, but which Verena, for a precious hour, forever flown, would *then* have been willing to take. She repented of it with bitterness and rage; and then she asked herself, more desperately still, whether even if she held that pledge she should be brave enough to enforce it in the face of actual complications. She believed that if it were in her power to say, "No, I won't let you off; I have your solemn word, and I won't!" Verena would bow to that degree and remain with her; but the magic would have passed out of her spirit forever, the sweetness out of their friendship, the efficacy out of their work. She said to her again and again that she had utterly changed since that hour she came to her, in New York, after her morning with Mr. Ransom, and sobbed out that they must hurry away. Then she had been wounded, outraged, sickened, and in the interval nothing had happened, nothing but that one exchange of letters, which she knew about, to bring her round to a shameless tolerance. Shameless Verena admitted it to be; she assented over and over to this proposition, and explained, as eagerly each time as if it were the first, what it was that had come to pass, what it was that had brought her round. It had simply come over her that she liked him, that this was the true point of view, the only one from which one could consider the situation in a way that would lead to what she called a *real* solution—a permanent rest. On this particular point Verena never responded, in the liberal way I have mentioned, without asseverating at the same time that what she desired most in the world was to prove (the picture Olive had held up from the first), that a woman *could* live on persistently, clinging to a great, vivifying, redemptory idea, without the help of a man. To testify to the end against the stale superstition—mother of every misery—that those gentry were as indispensable as they had proclaimed themselves on the house-tops—that, she passionately protested, was as inspiring a thought in the present poignant crisis as it had ever been.

The one grain of comfort that Olive extracted from the terrors that pressed upon her was that now she knew the worst; she knew it since Verena had told her, after so long and so ominous a reticence, of the detestable episode at Cambridge. That seemed to her the worst, because it had been thunder in a clear sky; the incident had sprung from a quarter from which, months before, all symptoms appeared to have vanished. Though Verena had now done all she could to make up for her perfidious silence by repeating everything that passed between them as she sat with Mr. Ransom in Monadnoc Place or strolled with him through the colleges, it imposed itself upon Olive that that occasion was the key of all that had happened since, that he had then obtained an irremediable hold upon her. If Verena had spoken at the time, she would never have let her go to New York; the sole compensation for that hideous mistake was that the girl, recognizing it to the full, evidently deemed now that she couldn't be communicative enough. There were certain afternoons in August, long, beautiful and terrible, when one felt that the summer was rounding its curve, and the rustle of the full-leaved trees in the slanting golden light, in the breeze that ought to be delicious, seemed the voice of the coming autumn, of the warnings and dangers of life—portentous, insufferable hours when, as she sat under the softly swaying vine-leaves of the trellis with Miss Birdseye and tried, in order to still her nerves, to read something aloud to her guest, the sound of her own quavering voice made her think more of that baleful day at Cambridge than even of the fact that at that very moment Verena was "off" with Mr. Ransom—had gone to take the little daily walk with him to which it had been arranged that their enjoyment of each other's society should be reduced. Arranged, I say; but that is not exactly the word to describe the compromise arrived at by a kind of tacit exchange of tearful entreaty and tightened grasp, after Ransom had made it definite to Verena that he was indeed going to stay a month and she had promised that she would not resort to base evasions, to fight (which would avail her nothing, he notified her), but would give him a chance, would listen to him a few minutes every day. He had insisted that the few minutes should be an hour, and the way to spend it was obvious. They wandered along the waterside to a rocky, shrub-covered point, which made a walk of just the right duration. Here all the homely languor of the region, the mild, fragrant Cape

quality, the sweetness of white sands, quiet waters, low
promontories where there were paths among the barber-
ries and tidal pools gleamed in the sunset—here all the
spirit of a ripe summer afternoon seemed to hang in the air.
There were wood-walks too; they sometimes followed
bosky uplands, where accident had grouped the trees with
odd effects of "style," and where in grassy intervals and
fragrant nooks of rest they came out upon sudden patches of
Arcady. In such places Verena listened to her companion
with her watch in her hand, and she wondered, very sincerely, how he could care for a girl who made the conditions
of courtship so odious. He had recognized, of course, at the
very first, that he could not inflict himself again upon Miss
Chancellor, and after that awkward morning call I have
described he did not again, for the first three weeks of his
stay at Marmion, penetrate into the cottage whose back
windows overlooked the deserted shipyard. Olive, as may
be imagined, made, on this occasion, no protest for the sake
of being ladylike or of preventing him from putting her
apparently in the wrong. The situation between them was
too grim; it was war to the knife, it was a question of which
should pull hardest. So Verena took a tryst with the young
man as if she had been a maid-servant and Basil Ransom a
"follower." They met a little way from the house; beyond it,
outside the village.

38

Olive thought she knew the worst, as we have perceived;
but the worst was really something she could not know, in-

asmuch as up to this time Verena chose as little to confide to her on that one point as she was careful to expatiate with her on every other. The change that had taken place in the object of Basil Ransom's merciless devotion since the episode in New York was, briefly, just this change—that the words he had spoken to her there about her genuine vocation, as distinguished from the hollow and factitious ideal with which her family and her association with Olive Chancellor had saddled her—these words, the most effective and penetrating he had uttered, had sunk into her soul and worked and fermented there. She had come at last to believe them, and that was the alteration, the transformation. They had kindled a light in which she saw herself afresh and, strange to say, liked herself better than in the old exaggerated glamour of the lecture-lamps. She could not tell Olive this yet, for it struck at the root of everything, and the dreadful, delightful sensation filled her with a kind of awe at all that it implied and portended. She was to burn everything she had adored; she was to adore everything she had burned. The extraordinary part of it was that though she felt the situation to be, as I say, tremendously serious, she was not ashamed of the treachery which she—yes, decidedly, by this time she must admit it to herself—she meditated. It was simply that the truth had changed sides; that radiant image began to look at her from Basil Ransom's expressive eyes. She loved, she was in love—she felt it in every throb of her being. Instead of being constituted by nature for entertaining that sentiment in an exceptionally small degree (which had been the implication of her whole crusade, the warrant for her offer of old to Olive to renounce), she was framed, apparently, to allow it the largest range, the highest intensity. It was always passion, in fact; but now the object was other. Formerly she had been convinced that the fire of her spirit was a kind of double flame, one half of which was responsive friendship for a most extraordinary person, and the other pity for the sufferings of women in general. Verena gazed aghast at the colorless

396

dust into which, in three short months (counting from the episode in New York), such a conviction as that could crumble; she felt it must be a magical touch that could bring about such a cataclysm. Why Basil Ransom had been deputed by fate to exercise this spell was more than she could say—poor Verena, who up to so lately had flattered herself that she had a wizard's wand in her own pocket.

When she saw him a little way off, about five o'clock—the hour she usually went out to meet him—waiting for her at a bend of the road which lost itself, after a winding, straggling mile or two, in the indented, insulated "point," where the wandering bee droned through the hot hours with a vague, misguided flight, she felt that his tall, watching figure, with the low horizon behind, represented well the importance, the towering eminence he had in her mind—the fact that he was just now, to her vision, the most definite and upright, the most incomparable, object in the world. If he had not been at his post when she expected him she would have had to stop and lean against something, for weakness; her whole being would have throbbed more painfully than it throbbed at present, though finding him there made her nervous enough. And who was he, what was he? she asked herself. What did he offer her besides a chance (in which there was no compensation of brilliancy or fashion), to falsify, in a conspicuous manner, every hope and pledge she had hitherto given? He allowed her, certainly, no illusion on the subject of the fate she should meet as his wife; he flung over it no rosiness of promised ease; he let her know that she should be poor, withdrawn from view, a partner of his struggle, of his severe, hard, unique stoicism. When he spoke of such things as these, and bent his eyes on her, she could not keep the tears from her own; she felt that to throw herself into his life (bare and arid as for the time it was), was the condition of happiness for her, and yet that the obstacles were terrible, cruel. It must not be thought that the revolution which was taking place in her was unaccompanied with suffering. She suffered less than Olive certainly, for her bent was not, like her friend's, in that direction; but as the wheel of her experience went round she had the sensation of being ground very small indeed. With her light, bright texture, her complacent responsiveness, her genial, graceful, ornamental cast, her desire to keep on pleasing others at the time when a force she had never felt before was pushing her to please herself, poor Verena lived in these days in a state of moral tension—with a sense of being strained and aching—which she didn't betray more only because it was absolutely not in her power to look desperate. An immense pity for Olive sat in her heart, and she asked herself how far it was necessary to go in the path of self-sacrifice. Nothing was wanting to make the wrong she should do her complete; she had deceived her up to the very last; only three months earlier she had reasserted her vows, given her word, with every show of fidelity and enthusiasm. There were hours when it seemed to Verena that she must really push her inquiry no further, but content herself with the conclusion that she loved as deeply as a woman could love and that it didn't make any difference. She felt Olive's grasp too clinching, too terrible. She said to herself that she should never dare, that she might as well give up early as late; that the scene, at the end, would be something she couldn't face; that she had no right to blast the poor creature's whole future. She had a vision of those dreadful years; she knew that Olive would never get over the disappointment. It would touch her in the point where she felt everything most keenly; she would be incurably lonely and eternally humiliated. It was a very peculiar thing, their friendship; it had elements which made it probably as complete as any (between women) that had ever existed. Of course it had been more on Olive's side than on hers, she had always known that; but that, again, didn't make any difference. It was of no use for her to tell herself that Olive had begun it entirely and she had only responded out of a kind of charmed politeness, at first, to a tremendous appeal. She had lent herself, given herself, utterly, and she ought to have known better if she didn't mean to abide by it. At the end of three weeks she felt that her inquiry was complete, but that after all nothing was gained except an immense interest in Basil Ransom's views and the prospect of an eternal heartache. He had told her he wanted her to know him, and now she knew him pretty thoroughly. She knew him and she adored him, but it didn't make any difference. To give him up or to give Olive up—this effort would be the greater of the two.

If Basil Ransom had the advantage, as far back as that day in New York, of having struck a note which was to reverberate, it may easily be imagined that he did not fail to follow it up. If he had projected a new light into Verena's mind, and made the idea of giving herself to a man more agreeable to her than that of giving herself to a movement, he found means to deepen this illumination, to drag her former standard in the dust. He was in a very odd situation indeed, carrying on his siege with his hands tied. As he had to do everything in an hour a day, he perceived that he must confine himself to the essential. The essential was to show her how much he loved her, and then to press, to press, always to press. His hovering about Miss Chancellor's habitation without going in was a strange regimen to be subjected to, and he was sorry not to see more of Miss Birdseye, besides often not knowing what to do with himself in the mornings and evenings. Fortunately he had brought plenty of books (volumes of rusty aspect, picked up at New York bookstalls), and in such an affair as this he could take the less when the more was forbidden him. For the mornings, sometimes, he had the resource of Doctor Prance, with whom he made a great many excursions on the water. She was devoted to boating and an ardent fisherwoman, and they used to pull out into the bay together, cast their lines, and talk a prodigious amount of heresy. She met him, as Verena met him, "in the environs," but in a different spirit. He was immensely amused at her attitude, and saw that nothing in the world could, as he expressed it, make her wink. She would never blench nor show surprise; she had an air of taking everything abnormal for granted; betrayed no consciousness of the oddity of Ransom's situation; said nothing to indicate she had noticed that Miss Chancellor was in a frenzy or that Verena had a daily appointment. You might have supposed from her manner that it was as natural for Ransom to sit on a fence half a mile off as in one of the red rocking chairs, of the so-called "Shaker" species, which adorned Miss Chancellor's back veranda. The only thing our young man didn't like about Doctor Prance was the impression she gave him (out of the crevices of her reticence he hardly knew how it leaked), that she thought Verena rather slim. She took an ironical view of almost any kind of courtship, and he could see she didn't wonder women were such featherheads, so long as, whatever brittle follies they cultivated, they could get men to come and sit on fences for them. Doctor Prance told him Miss Birdseye noticed nothing; she had sunk, within a few days, into a kind of transfigured torpor; she didn't seem to know whether Mr. Ransom were anywhere round or not. She guessed she thought he had just come down for a day and gone off again; she probably supposed he just wanted to get toned up a little by Miss Tarrant. Sometimes, out in the boat, when she looked at him in vague, sociable silence, while she waited for a bite (she delighted in a bite), she had an expression of diabolical shrewdness. When Ransom was not scorching there beside her (he didn't mind the sun of Massachusetts), he lounged about in the pastoral land which hung (at a very moderate elevation), above the shore. He always had a book in his pocket, and he lay under whispering trees and kicked his heels and made up his mind on what side he should take Verena the next time. At the end of a fortnight he had succeeded (so he believed, at least), far better than he had hoped, in this sense, that the girl had now the air of making much more light of her "gift." He was indeed quite appalled at the facility with which she threw it over, gave up the idea that it was useful and precious. That had been what he wanted her to do, and the fact of the sacrifice (once she had fairly looked at it), costing her so little only proved his contention, only made it clear that it was not necessary to her happiness to spend half her life ranting (no matter how prettily), in public. All the same he said to himself that, to make up for the loss of whatever was sweet in the reputation of the thing, he should have to be tremendously nice to her in all the coming years. During the first week he was at Marmion she made of him an inquiry which touched on this point.

"Well, if it's all a mere delusion, why should this facility have been given me—why should I have been saddled with a superfluous talent? I don't care much about it—I don't mind telling you that; but I confess I should like to know what is to become of all that part of me, if I retire into private life, and live, as you say, simply to be charming for you. I shall be like a singer with a beautiful voice (you have told me yourself my voice is beautiful), who has accepted some decree of never raising a note. Isn't that a great waste, a great violation of nature? Were not our talents given us to use, and have we any right to smother them and deprive our fellow-creatures of such pleasure as they may confer? In the arrangement you propose" (that was Verena's way of speaking of the question of their marriage), "I don't see what provision is made for the poor faithful, dismissed servant. It is all very well to be charming to you, but there are people who have told me that once I get on a platform I am charming to all the world. There is no harm in my speaking of that, because you have told me so yourself. Perhaps you intend to have a platform erected in our front parlor, where I can address you every evening, and put you to sleep after your work. I say our *front* parlor, as if it were certain we should have two! It doesn't look as if our means would permit that—and we must have some place to dine, if there is to be a platform in our sitting room."

"My dear young woman, it will be easy to solve the difficulty: the dining-table itself shall be our platform, and you

401

shall mount on top of that." This was Basil Ransom's sportive reply to his companion's very natural appeal for light, and the reader will remark that if it led her to push her investigation no further, she was very easily satisfied. There was more reason, however, as well as more appreciation of a very considerable mystery, in what he went on to say. "Charming to me, charming to all the world? What will become of your charm?—is that what you want to know? It will be about five thousand times greater than it is now; that's what will become of it. We shall find plenty of room for your facility; it will lubricate our whole existence. Believe me, Miss Tarrant, these things will take care of themselves. You won't sing in the Music Hall, but you will sing to me; you will sing to every one who knows you and approaches you. Your gift is indestructible; don't talk as if I either wanted to wipe it out or should be able to make it a particle less divine. I want to give it another direction, certainly; but I don't want to stop your activity. Your gift is the gift of expression, and there is nothing I can do for you that will make you less expressive. It won't gush out at a fixed hour and on a fixed day, but it will irrigate, it will fertilize, it will brilliantly adorn your conversation. Think how delightful it will be when your influence becomes really social. Your facility, as you call it, will simply make you, in conversation, the most charming woman in America."

It is to be feared, indeed, that Verena was easily satisfied (convinced, I mean, not that she ought to succumb to him, but that there were lovely, neglected, almost unsuspected truths on his side); and there is further evidence on the same head in the fact that after the first once or twice she found nothing to say to him (much as she was always saying to herself), about the cruel effect her apostasy would have upon Olive. She forbore to plead that reason after she had seen how angry it made him, and with how almost savage a contempt he denounced so flimsy a pretext. He wanted to know since when it was more becoming to take up with a morbid old maid than with an honorable young man; and when Verena pronounced the sacred name of friendship he inquired what fanatical sophistry excluded him from a similar privilege. She had told him, in a moment of expansion (Verena believed she was immensely on her guard, but her guard was very apt to be lowered), that his visits to Marmion cast in Olive's view a remarkable light upon his chivalry; she chose to regard his resolute pursuit of Verena as a covert persecution of herself. Verena repented, as soon as she had spoken, of having given further currency to this taunt; but she perceived the next moment no harm was done, Basil Ransom taking in perfectly good part Miss Chancellor's reflections on his delicacy, and making them the subject of much free laughter. She could not know, for in the midst of his hilarity the young man did not compose himself to tell her, that he had made up his mind on this question before he left New York—as long ago as when he wrote her the note (subsequent to her departure from that city), to which allusion has already been made, and which was simply the fellow of the letter addressed to her after his visit to Cambridge: a friendly, respectful, yet rather pregnant sign that, decidedly, on second thoughts, separation didn't imply for him the intention of silence. We know a little about his second thoughts, as much as is essential, and especially how the occasion of their springing up had been the windfall of an editor's encouragement. The importance of that encouragement, to Basil's imagination, was doubtless much augmented by his desire for an excuse to take up again a line of behavior which he had forsworn (small as had, as yet, been his opportunity to indulge in it), very much less than he supposed; still, it worked an appreciable revolution in his view of his case, and made him ask himself what amount of consideration he should (from the most refined Southern point of view), owe Miss Chancellor in the event of his deciding to go after Verena Tarrant in earnest. He was not slow to decide that he owed her none. Chivalry had to do with one's relations with people one hated, not with those one loved. He didn't hate poor Miss

Olive, though she might make him yet; and even if he did, any chivalry was all moonshine which should require him to give up the girl he adored in order that this third cousin should see he could be gallant. Chivalry was forbearance and generosity with regard to the weak; and there was nothing weak about Miss Olive, she was a fighting woman, and she would fight him to the death, giving him not an inch of odds. He felt that she was fighting there all day long, in her cottage-fortress; her resistance was in the air he breathed, and Verena came out to him sometimes quite limp and pale from the tussle.

It was in the same jocose spirit with which he regarded Olive's view of the sort of standard a Mississippian should live up to that he talked to Verena about the lecture she was preparing for her great exhibition at the Music Hall. He learned from her that she was to take the field in the manner of Mrs. Farrinder, for a winter campaign, carrying with her a tremendous big gun. Her engagements were all made, her route was marked out; she expected to repeat her lecture in about fifty different places. It was to be called "A Woman's Reason," and both Olive and Miss Birdseye thought it, so far as they could tell in advance, her most promising effort. She wasn't going to trust to inspiration this time; she didn't want to meet a big Boston audience without knowing where she was. Inspiration, moreover, seemed rather to have faded away; in consequence of Olive's influence she had read and studied so much that it seemed now as if everything must take form beforehand. Olive was a splendid critic, whether he liked her or not, and she had made her go over every word of her lecture twenty times. There wasn't an intonation she hadn't made her practice; it was very different from the old system, when her father had worked her up. If Basil considered women superficial, it was a pity he couldn't see what Olive's standard of preparation was, or be present at their rehearsals, in the evening, in their little parlor. Ransom's state of mind in regard to the affair at the Music Hall was simply this—that he was determined to circumvent it if he could. He covered it with ridicule, in talking of it to Verena, and the shafts he leveled at it went so far that he could see she thought he exaggerated his dislike to it. In point of fact he could not have overstated that; so odious did the idea seem to him that she was soon to be launched in a more infatuated career. He vowed to himself that she should never take that fresh start which would commit her irretrievably if she should succeed (and she would succeed—he had not the slightest doubt of her power to produce a sensation in the Music Hall), to the acclamations of the newspapers. He didn't care for her engagements, her campaigns, or all the expectancy of her friends; to "squelch" all that, at a stroke, was the dearest wish of his heart. It would represent to him his own success, it would symbolize his victory. It became a fixed idea with him, and he warned her again and again. When she laughed and said she didn't see how he could stop her unless he kidnapped her, he really pitied her for not perceiving, beneath his ominous pleasantries, the firmness of his resolution. He felt almost capable of kidnapping her. It was palpably in the air that she would become "widely popular," and that idea simply sickened him. He felt as differently as possible about it from Mr. Matthias Pardon.

One afternoon, as he returned with Verena from a walk which had been accomplished completely within the prescribed conditions, he saw, from a distance, Doctor Prance, who had emerged bareheaded from the cottage, and, shading her eyes from the red, declining sun, was looking up and down the road. It was part of the regulation that Ransom should separate from Verena before reaching the house, and they had just paused to exchange their last words (which every day promoted the situation more than any others), when Doctor Prance began to beckon to them with much animation. They hurried forward, Verena pressing her hand to her heart, for she had instantly guessed that something terrible had happened to Olive—she had given out, fainted away, perhaps fallen dead, with the cruelty of the strain. Doctor Prance watched them come, with a curious look in her face; it was not a smile, but a kind of exaggerated intimation that she noticed nothing. In an instant she had told them what was the matter. Miss Birdseye had had a sudden weakness; she had remarked abruptly that she was dying, and her pulse, sure enough, had fallen to nothing. She was down on the piazza with Miss Chancellor and herself, and they had tried to get her up to bed. But she wouldn't let them move her; she was passing away, and she wanted to pass away just there, in such a pleasant place, in her customary chair, looking at the sunset. She asked for Miss Tarrant, and Miss Chancellor told her she was out—walking with Mr. Ransom. Then she wanted to know if Mr. Ransom was still there—she supposed he had gone. (Basil knew, by Verena, apart from this, that his name had not been mentioned to the old lady since the morning he saw her.) She expressed a wish to see him—she had something to say to him; and Miss Chancellor told her that he would be back soon, with Verena, and that they would bring him in. Miss Birdseye said she hoped they wouldn't be long, because she was sinking; and Doctor Prance now added, like a person who knew what she was talking about, that it was, in fact, the end. She had darted out two or three times to look for them, and they must step right in. Verena had scarcely given her time to tell her story; she had already rushed into the house. Ransom followed with Doctor Prance, conscious that for him the occasion was doubly solemn; inasmuch as if he was to see poor Miss Birdseye yield up her philanthropic soul, he was on the other hand doubtless to receive from Miss Chancellor a reminder that *she* had no intention of quitting the game.

By the time he had made this reflection he stood in the presence of his kinswoman and her venerable guest, who was sitting just as he had seen her before, muffled and bonneted, on the back piazza of the cottage. Olive Chancellor was on one side of her, holding one of her hands, and on the other was Verena, who had dropped on her knees, close to her, bending over those of the old lady. "Did you ask for me—did you want me?" the girl said, tenderly. "I will never leave you again."

"Oh, I won't keep you long. I only wanted to see you once more." Miss Birdseye's voice was very low, like that of a person breathing with difficulty; but it had no painful nor querulous note—it expressed only the cheerful weariness which had marked all this last period of her life, and which seemed to make it now as blissful as it was suitable that she should pass away. Her head was thrown back against the top of the chair, the ribbon which confined her ancient hat hung loose, and the late afternoon light covered her octoge-narian face and gave it a kind of fairness, a double placid-ity. There was, to Ransom, something almost august in the trustful renunciation of her countenance; something in it seemed to say that she had been ready long before, but as the time was not ripe she had waited, with her usual faith that all was for the best; only, at present, since the right conditions met, she couldn't help feeling that it was quite a luxury, the greatest she had ever tasted. Ransom knew why it was that Verena had tears in her eyes as she looked up at her patient old friend; she had spoken to him, often, during the last three weeks, of the stories Miss Birdseye had told her of the great work of her life, her mission, repeated year after year, among the Southern blacks. She had gone among them with every precaution, to teach them to read and write; she had carried them Bibles and told them of the friends they had in the North who prayed for their deliver-ance. Ransom knew that Verena didn't reproduce these legends with a view to making him ashamed of his Southern origin, his connection with people who, in a past not yet re-mote, had made that kind of apostleship necessary; he knew this because she had heard what he thought of all that chapter himself; he had given her a kind of historical summary of the slavery-question which left her no room to say that he was more tender to that particular example of human imbecility than he was to any other. But she had told him that this was what *she* would have liked to do—to wander, alone, with her life in her hand, on an errand of mercy, through a country in which society was arrayed against her; she would have liked it much better than simply talking about the right from the gaslighted vantage of the New England platform. Ransom had replied simply "Balderdash!" it being his theory, as we have perceived, that he knew much more about Verena's native bent than the young lady herself. This did not, however, as he was perfectly aware, prevent her feeling that she had come too late for the heroic age of New England life, and regarding Miss Birdseye as a battered, immemorial monument of it. Ransom could share such an admiration as that, especially at this moment; he had said to Verena, more than once, that he wished he might have met the old lady in Carolina or Georgia before the war—shown her round among the negroes and talked over New England ideas with her; there were a good many he didn't care much about now, but at that time they would have been tremendously refreshing. Miss Birdseye had given herself away so lavishly all her life that it was rather odd there was anything left of her for the supreme surrender. When he looked at Olive he saw that she meant to ignore him; and during the few minutes he remained on the spot his kinswoman never met his eye. She turned away, indeed, as soon as Doctor Prance said, leaning over Miss Birdseye, "I have brought Mr. Ransom to you. Don't you remember you asked for him?"

"I am very glad to see you again," Ransom remarked. "It was very good of you to think of me." At the sound of his voice Olive rose and left her place; she sank into a chair at the other end of the piazza, turning round to rest her arms on the back and bury her head in them.

Miss Birdseye looked at the young man still more dimly than she had ever done before. "I thought you were gone. You never came back."

"He spends all his time in long walks; he enjoys the country so much," Verena said.

"Well, it's very beautiful, what I see from here. I haven't been strong enough to move round since the first days. But I am going to move now." She smiled when Ransom made a gesture as if to help her, and added: "Oh, I don't mean I am going to move out of my chair."

"Mr. Ransom has been out in a boat with me several times. I have been showing him how to cast a line," said Doctor Prance, who appeared to deprecate a sentimental tendency.

"Oh, well, then, you have been one of our party; there seems to be every reason why you should feel that you belong to us." Miss Birdseye looked at the visitor with a sort of misty earnestness, as if she wished to communicate with him further; then her glance turned slightly aside; she tried to see what had become of Olive. She perceived that Miss Chancellor had withdrawn herself, and, closing her eyes, she mused, ineffectually, on the mystery she had not grasped, the peculiarity of Basil Ransom's relations with her hostess. She was visibly too weak to concern herself with it very actively; she only felt, now that she seemed really to be going, a desire to reconcile and harmonize. But she presently exhaled a low, soft sigh—a kind of confession that it was too mixed, that she gave it up. Ransom had feared for a moment that she was about to indulge in some appeal to Olive, some attempt to make him join hands with that young lady, as a supreme satisfaction to herself. But he saw that her strength failed her, and that, besides, things were getting less clear to her; to his considerable relief, inasmuch as, though he would not have objected to joining hands, the expression of Miss Chancellor's figure and her averted face, with their desperate collapse, showed him well enough how *she* would have met such a proposal. What Miss Birdseye clung to, with benignant perversity, was the idea that, in spite of his exclusion from the house, which was perhaps only the result of a certain high-strung jealousy on Olive's part of her friend's other personal ties, Verena had drawn him in, had made him sympathize with the great reform and desire to work for it. Ransom saw no reason why such an illusion should be dear to Miss Birdseye; his contact with her in the past had been so momentary that he could not account for her taking an interest in his views, in his throwing his weight into the right scale. It was part of the general desire for justice that fermented within her, the passion for progress; and it was also in some degree her interest in Verena—a suspicion, innocent and idyllic, as any such suspicion on Miss Birdseye's part must be, that there was something between them, that the closest of all unions (as Miss Birdseye at least supposed it was), was preparing itself. Then his being a Southerner gave a point to the whole thing; to bring round a Southerner would be a real encouragement for one who had seen, even at a time when she was already an old woman, what was the tone of opinion in the cotton States. Ransom had no wish to discourage her, and he bore well in mind the caution Doctor Prance had given him about destroying her last theory. He only bowed his head very humbly, not knowing what he had done to earn the honor of being the subject of it. His eyes met Verena's as she looked up at him from her place at Miss Birdseye's feet, and he saw she was following his thought, throwing herself into it, and trying to communicate to him a wish. The wish touched him immensely; she was dreadfully afraid he would betray her to Miss Birdseye—let her know how she had cooled off. Verena was ashamed of that now, and trembled at the danger of exposure; her eyes adjured him to be careful of what he said. Her tremor made him glow a little in return, for it seemed to him the fullest confession of his influence she had yet made.

"We have been a very happy little party," she said to the old lady. "It is delightful that you should have been able to be with us all these weeks."

"It has been a great rest. I am very tired. I can't speak

much. It has been a lovely time. I have done so much—so many things."

"I guess I wouldn't talk much, Miss Birdseye," said Doctor Prance, who had now knelt down on the other side of her. "We know how much you have done. Don't you suppose every one knows *your* life?"

"It isn't much—only I tried to take hold. When I look back from here, from where we've sat, I can measure the progress. That's what I wanted to say to you and Mr. Ransom—because I'm going fast. Hold on to me, that right; but you can't keep me. I don't want to stay now; I presume I shall join some of the others that we lost long ago. Their faces come back to me now, quite fresh. It seems as if they might be waiting; as if they were all there; as if they wanted to hear. You mustn't think there's no progress because you don't see it all right off; that's what I wanted to say. It isn't till you have gone a long way that you can feel what's been done. That's what I see when I look back from here; I see that the community wasn't half waked up when I was young."

"It is you that have waked it up more than anyone else, and it's for that we honor you, Miss Birdseye!" Verena cried, with a sudden violence of emotion. "If you were to live for a thousand years, you would think only of others—you would think only of helping on humanity. You are our heroine, you are our saint, and there has never been anyone like you!" Verena had no glance for Ransom now, and there was neither deprecation nor entreaty in her face. A wave of contrition, of shame, had swept over her—a quick desire to atone for her secret swerving by a renewed recognition of the nobleness of such a life as Miss Birdseye's.

"Oh, I haven't effected very much; I have only cared and hoped. You will do more than I have ever done—you and Olive Chancellor, because you are young and bright, brighter than I ever was; and besides, everything has got started."

"Well, you've got started, Miss Birdseye," Doctor Prance

remarked, with raised eyebrows, protesting drily but kindly, and putting forward, with an air as if, after all, it didn't matter much, an authority that had been superseded. The manner in which this competent little woman indulged her patient showed sufficiently that the good lady was sinking fast.

"We will think of you always, and your name will be sacred to us, and that will teach us singleness and devotion," Verena went on, in the same tone, still not meeting Ransom's eyes again, and speaking as if she were trying now to stop herself, to tie herself by a vow.

"Well, it's the thing you and Olive have given your lives to that has absorbed me most, of late years. I did want to see justice done—to us. I haven't seen it, but you will. And Olive will. Where is she—why isn't she near me, to bid me farewell? And Mr. Ransom will—and he will be proud to have helped."

"Oh, mercy, mercy!" cried Verena, burying her head in Miss Birdseye's lap.

"You are not mistaken if you think I desire above all things that your weakness, your generosity, should be protected," Ransom said, rather ambiguously, but with pointed respectfulness. "I shall remember you as an example of what women are capable of," he added; and he had no subsequent compunctions for the speech, for he thought poor Miss Birdseye, for all her absence of profile, essentially feminine.

A kind of frantic moan from Olive Chancellor responded to these words, which had evidently struck her as an insolent sarcasm; and at the same moment Doctor Prance sent Ransom a glance which was an adjuration to depart.

"Good-by, Olive Chancellor," Miss Birdseye murmured. "I don't want to stay, though I should like to see what you will see."

"I shall see nothing but shame and ruin!" Olive shrieked, rushing across to her old friend, while Ransom discreetly quitted the scene.

39

He met Doctor Prance in the village the next morning, and
as soon as he looked at her he saw that the event which had
been impending at Miss Chancellor's had taken place. It
was not that her aspect was funereal; but it contained,
somehow, an announcement that she had, for the present,
no more thought to give to casting a line. Miss Birdseye
had quietly passed away, in the evening, an hour or two after
Ransom's visit. They had wheeled her chair into the house;
there had been nothing to do but wait for complete extinc-
tion. Miss Chancellor and Miss Tarrant had sat by her
there, without moving, each of her hands in theirs, and she
had just melted away, toward eight o'clock. It was a lovely
death; Doctor Prance intimated that she had never seen any
that she thought more seasonable. She added that she was a
good woman—one of the old sort; and that was the only
funeral oration that Basil Ransom was destined to hear pronounced upon Miss Birdseye. The impression of the simplicity and humility of her end remained with him, and he
reflected more than once, during the days that followed,
that the absence of pomp and circumstance which had
marked her career marked also the consecration of her
memory. She had been almost celebrated, she had been active, earnest, ubiquitous beyond anyone else, she had
given herself utterly to charities and creeds and causes; and
yet the only persons, apparently, to whom her death made
a real difference were three young women in a small

"frame-house" on Cape Cod. Ransom learned from Doctor Prance that her mortal remains were to be committed to their rest in the little cemetery at Marmion, in sight of the pretty sea-view she loved to gaze at, among old mossy headstones of mariners and fisher-folk. She had seen the place when she first came down, when she was able to drive out a little, and she had said she thought it must be pleasant to lie there. It was not an injuction, a definite request; it had not occurred to Miss Birdseye, at the end of her days, to take an exacting line or to make, for the first time in eighty years, a personal claim. But Olive Chancellor and Verena had put their construction on her appreciation of the quietest corner of the striving, suffering world so weary a pilgrim of philanthropy had ever beheld.

In the course of the day Ransom received a note of five lines from Verena, the purport of which was to tell him that he must not expect to see her again for the present; she wished to be very quiet and think things over. She added the recommendation that he should leave the neighborhood for three or four days; there were plenty of strange old places to see in that part of the country. Ransom meditated deeply on this missive, and perceived that he should be guilty of very bad taste in not immediately absenting himself. He knew that to Olive Chancellor's vision his conduct already wore that stain, and it was useless, therefore, for him to consider how he could displease her either less or more. But he wished to convey to Verena the impression that he would do anything in the wide world to gratify *her* except give her up, and as he packed his valise he had an idea that he was both behaving beautifully and showing the finest diplomatic sense. To go away proved to himself how secure he felt, what a conviction he had that however she might turn and twist in his grasp he held her fast. The emotion she had expressed as he stood there before poor Miss Birdseye was only one of her instinctive contortions; he had taken due note of that—said to himself that a good many more would probably occur before she would be quiet. A woman that listens is lost, the old proverb says; and what had Verena done for the last three weeks but listen?—not very long each day, but with a degree of attention of which her not withdrawing from Marmion was the measure. She had not told him that Olive wanted to whisk her away, but he had not needed this confidence to know that if she stayed on the field it was because she preferred to. She probably had an idea she was fighting, but if she should fight no harder than she had fought up to now he should continue to take the same view of his success. She meant her request that he should go away for a few days as something combative; but, decidedly, he scarcely felt the blow. He liked to think that he had great tact with women, and he was sure Verena would be struck with this quality in reading, in the note he presently addressed her in reply to her own, that he had determined to take a little run to Provincetown. As there was no one under the rather ineffectual roof which sheltered him to whose hand he could intrust the billet—at the Marmion hotel one had to be one's own messenger—he walked to the village post office to request that his note should be put into Miss Chancellor's box. Here he met Doctor Prance, for a second time that day; she had come to deposit the letters by which Olive notified a few of Miss Birdseye's friends of the time and place of her obsequies. This young lady was shut up with Verena, and Doctor Prance was transacting all their business for them. Ransom felt that he made no admission that would impugn his estimate of the sex to which she in a manner belonged, in reflecting that she would acquit herself of these delegated duties with the greatest rapidity and accuracy. He told her he was going to absent himself for a few days, and expressed a friendly hope that he should find her at Marmion on his return.

Her keen eye gauged him a moment, to see if he were joking; then she said, "Well, I presume you think I can do as I like. But I can't."

"You mean you have got to go back to work?"

"Well, yes; my place is empty in the city."

"So is every other place. You had better remain till the end of the season."

"It's all one season to me. I want to see my office-slate. I wouldn't have stayed so long for anyone but her."

"Well, then, good-by," Ransom said. "I shall always remember our little expeditions. And I wish you every professional distinction."

"That's why I want to go back," Doctor Prance replied with her flat, limited manner. He kept her a moment; he wanted to ask her about Verena. While he was hesitating how to form his question she remarked, evidently wishing to leave him a little memento of her sympathy, "Well, I hope you will be able to follow up your views."

"My views, Miss Prance? I am sure I have never mentioned them to you!" Then Ransom added, "How is Miss Tarrant today? is she more calm?"

"Oh no, she isn't calm at all," Doctor Prance answered, very definitely.

"Do you mean she's excited, emotional?"

"Well, she doesn't talk, she's perfectly still, and so is Miss Chancellor. They're as still as two watchers—they don't speak. But you can hear the silence vibrate."

"Vibrate?"

"Well, they are very nervous."

Ransom was confident, as I say, yet the effort that he made to extract a good omen from this characterization of the two ladies at the cottage was not altogether successful. He would have liked to ask Doctor Prance whether she didn't think he might count on Verena in the end; but he was too shy for this, the subject of his relations with Miss Tarrant never yet having been touched upon between them; and, besides, he didn't care to hear himself put a question which was more or less an implication of a doubt. So he compromised, with a sort of oblique and general inquiry about Olive; that might draw some light. "What do you think of Miss Chancellor—how does she strike you?"

Doctor Prance reflected a little, with an apparent consciousness that he meant more than he asked. "Well, she's losing flesh," she presently replied; and Ransom turned away, not encouraged, and feeling that, no doubt, the little doctress had better go back to her office-slate.

He did the thing handsomely, remained at Provincetown a week, inhaling the delicious air, smoking innumerable cigars, and lounging among the ancient wharves, where the grass grew thick and the impression of fallen greatness was still stronger than at Marmion. Like his friends the Bostonians he was very nervous; there were days when he felt that he must rush back to the margin of that mild inlet; the voices of the air whispered to him that in his absence he was being outwitted. Nevertheless he stayed the time he had determined to stay; quieting himself with the reflection that there was nothing they could do to elude him unless, perhaps, they should start again for Europe, which they were not likely to do. If Miss Olive tried to hide Verena away in the United States he would undertake to find her—though he was obliged to confess that a flight to Europe would baffle him, owing to his want to cash for pursuit. Nothing, however, was less probable than that they would cross the Atlantic on the eve of Verena's projected *début* at the Music Hall. Before he went back to Marmion he wrote to this young lady, to announce his reappearance there and let her know that he expected she would come out to meet him the morning after. This conveyed the assurance that he intended to take as much of the day as he could get; he had had enough of the system of dragging through all the hours till a mere fraction of time was left before night, and he couldn't wait so long, at any rate, the day after his return. It was the afternoon-train that had brought him back from Provincetown, and in the evening he ascertained that the Bostonians had not deserted the field. There were lights in the windows of the house under the elms, and he stood where he had stood that evening with Doctor Prance and listened to the waves of Verena's voice, as she rehearsed her

417

lecture. There were no waves this time, no sounds, and no sign of life but the lamps; the place had apparently not ceased to be given over to the conscious silence described by Doctor Prance. Ransom felt that he gave an immense proof of chivalry in not calling upon Verena to grant him an interview on the spot. She had not answered his last note, but the next day she kept the tryst, at the hour he had proposed; he saw her advance along the road, in a white dress, under a big parasol, and again he found himself liking immensely the way she walked. He was dismayed, however, at her face and what it portended; pale, with red eyes, graver than she had ever been before, she appeared to have spent the period of his absence in violent weeping. Yet that it was not for him she had been crying was proved by the very first words she spoke.

"I only came out to tell you definitely it's impossible! I have thought over everything, taking plenty of time—over and over; and that is my answer, finally, positively. You must take it—you shall have no other."

Basil Ransom gazed, frowning fearfully. "And why not, pray?"

"Because I can't, I can't, I can't, I can't!" she repeated, passionately, with her altered, distorted face.

"Damnation!" murmured the young man. He seized her hand, drew it into his arm, forcing her to walk with him along the road.

That afternoon Olive Chancellor came out of her house and wandered for a long time upon the shore. She looked up and down the bay, at the sails that gleamed on the blue water, shifting in the breeze and the light; they were a source of interest to her that they had never been before. It was a day she was destined never to forget; she felt it to be the saddest, the most wounding of her life. Unrest and haunting fear had not possession of her now, as they had held her in New York when Basil Ransom carried off Verena, to mark her for his own, in the park. But an immeasurable load of misery seemed to sit upon her soul; she ached with the bitterness of her melancholy, she was dumb and cold with despair. She had spent the violence of her terror, the eagerness of her grief, and now she was too weary to struggle with fate. She appeared to herself almost to have accepted it, as she wandered forth in the beautiful afternoon with the knowledge that the "ten minutes" which Verena had told her she meant to devote to Mr. Ransom that morning had developed suddenly into an embarkation for the day. They had gone out in a boat together; one of the village-worthies, from whom small craft were to be hired, had, at Verena's request, sent his little son to Miss Chancellor's cottage with that information. She had not understood whether they had taken the boatman with them. Even when the information came (and it came at a moment of considerable reassurance), Olive's nerves were not ploughed up by it as they had been, for instance, by the other expedition, in New York; and she could measure the distance she had traversed since then. It had not driven her away on the instant to pace the shore in frenzy, to challenge every boat that passed, and beg that the young lady who was sailing somewhere in the bay with a dark gentleman with long hair, should be entreated immediately to return. On the contrary, after the first quiver of pain inflicted by the news she had been able to occupy herself, to look after her house, to write her morning's letters, to go into her accounts, which she had had some time on her mind. She had wanted to put off thinking, for she knew to what hideous recognitions that would bring her round again. These were summed up in the fact that Verena was now not to be trusted for an hour. She had sworn to her the night before, with a face like a lacerated angel's, that her choice was made, that their union and their work were more to her than any other life could ever be, and that she deeply believed that should she forswear these holy things she should simply waste away, in the end, with remorse and shame. She would see Mr. Ransom just once more, for ten minutes, to utter one or two supreme truths to him, and then they would take up their old, happy, active, fruitful days again, would throw themselves more than ever into their splendid effort. Olive had seen how Verena was moved by Miss Birdseye's death, how at the sight of that unique woman's majestically simple withdrawal from a scene in which she had held every vulgar aspiration, every worldly standard and lure, so cheap, the girl had been touched again with the spirit of their most confident hours, had flamed up with the faith that no narrow personal joy could compare in sweetness with the idea of doing something for those who had always suffered and who waited still. This helped Olive to believe that she might begin to count upon her again, conscious as she was at the same time that Verena had been strangely weakened and strained by her odious ordeal. Oh, Olive knew that she loved him—knew what the passion was with which the wretched girl had to struggle; and she did her the justice to believe that her professions were sincere, her effort was real. Harassed and embittered as she was, Olive Chancellor still proposed to herself to be rigidly just, and that is why she pitied Verena now with an unspeakable pity, regarded her as the victim of an atrocious spell, and reserved all her execration and contempt for the author of their common misery. If Verena had stepped into a boat with him half an hour after declaring that she would give him his dismissal in twenty words, that was because he had ways, known to himself and other men, of creating situations without an issue, of forcing her to do things she could do only with sharp repugnance, under the menace of pain that would be sharper still. But all the same, what actually stared her in the face was that Verena was not to be trusted, even after rallying again as passionately as she had done during the days that followed Miss Birdseye's death. Olive would have liked to know the pang of penance that *she* would have been afraid, in her place, to incur; to see the locked door which *she* would not have managed to force open!

This inexpressibly mournful sense that, after all, Verena, in her exquisite delicacy and generosity, was appointed only to show how women had from the beginning of time been the sport of men's selfishness and avidity, this dismal conviction accompanied Olive on her walk, which lasted all the afternoon, and in which she found a kind of tragic relief. She went very far, keeping in the lonely places, unveiling her face to the splendid light, which seemed to make a mock of the darkness and bitterness of her spirit. There were little sandy coves, where the rocks were clean, where she made long stations, sinking down in them as if she hoped she should never rise again. It was the first time she had been out since Miss Birdseye's death, except the hour when, with the dozen sympathizers who came from Boston, she stood by the tired old woman's grave. Since then, for three days, she had been writing letters, narrating, describing to those who hadn't come; there were some, she thought, who might have managed to do so, instead of despatching her pages of diffuse reminiscence and asking her for all particulars in return. Selah Tarrant and his wife had come, obtrusively, as she thought, for they never had had very much intercourse with Miss Birdseye; and if it was for Verena's sake, Verena was there to pay every tribute herself. Mrs. Tarrant had evidently hoped Miss Chancellor would ask her to stay on at Marmion, but Olive felt how little she was in a state for such heroics of hospitality. It was precisely in order that she should not have to do that sort of thing that she had given Selah such considerable sums, on two occasions, at a year's interval. If the Tarrants wanted a change of air they could travel all over the country—their present means permitted it; they could go to Saratoga or Newport if they liked. Their appearance showed that they could put their hands into their pockets (or into hers); at least Mrs. Tarrant's did. Selah still sported (on a hot day in August), his immemorial waterproof; but his wife rustled over the low tombstones at Marmion in garments of which (little as she was versed in such inquiries), Olive could see that the cost had been large. Besides, after Doctor Prance had gone (when all was over), she felt what a relief it was that

Verena and she could be just together—together with the monstrous wedge of a question that had come up between them. That was company enough, great heaven! and she had not got rid of such an inmate as Doctor Prance only to put Mrs. Tarrant in her place.

Did Verena's strange aberration, on this particular day, suggest to Olive that it was no use striving, that the world was all a great trap or trick, of which women were ever the punctual dupes, so that it was the worst of the curse that rested upon them that they must most humiliate those who had most their cause at heart? Did she say to herself that their weakness was not only lamentable but hideous— hideous their predestined subjection to man's larger and grosser insistence? Did she ask herself why she should give up her life to save a sex which, after all, didn't wish to be saved, and which rejected the truth even after it had bathed them with its auroral light and they had pretended to be fed and fortified? These are mysteries into which I shall not attempt to enter, speculations with which I have no concern; it is sufficient for us to know that all human effort had never seemed to her so barren and thankless as on that fatal afternoon. Her eyes rested on the boats she saw in the distance, and she wondered if in one of them Verena were floating to her fate; but so far from straining forward to beckon her home she almost wished that she might glide away forever, that *she* might never see her again, never undergo the horrible details of a more deliberate separation. Olive lived over, in her miserable musings, her life for the last two years; she knew, again, how noble and beautiful her scheme had been, but how it had all rested on an illusion of which the very thought made her feel faint and sick. What was before her now was reality, with the beautiful, indifferent sky pouring down its complacent rays upon it. The reality was simply that Verena had been more to her than she ever was to Verena, and that, with her exquisite natural art, the girl had cared for their cause only because, for the time, no interest, no fascination, was greater. Her talent, the talent which was to achieve such wonders, was nothing to her; it was too easy, she could leave it alone, as she might close her piano, for months; it was only to Olive that it was everything. Verena had submitted, she had responded, she had lent herself to Olive's incitement and exhortation, because she was sympathetic and young and abundant and fanciful; but it had been a kind of hothouse loyalty, the mere contagion of example, and a sentiment springing up from within had easily breathed a chill upon it. Did Olive ask herself whether, for so many months, her companion had been only the most unconscious and most successful of humbugs? Here again I must plead a certain incompetence to give an answer. Positive it is that she spared herself none of the inductions of a reverie that seemed to dry up the mists and ambiguities of life. These hours of backward clearness come to all men and women, once at least, when they read the past in the light of the present, with the reasons of things, like unobserved finger-posts, protruding where they never saw them before. The journey behind them is mapped out and figured, with its false steps, its wrong observations, all its infatuated, deluded geography. They understand as Olive understood, but it is probable that they rarely suffer as she suffered. The sense of regret for her baffled calculations burned within her like a fire, and the splendor of the vision over which the curtain of mourning now was dropped brought to her eyes slow, still tears, tears that came one by one, neither easing her nerves nor lightening her load of pain. She thought of her innumerable talks with Verena, of the pledges they had exchanged, of their earnest studies, their faithful work, their certain reward, the winter nights under the lamp, when they thrilled with previsions as just and a passion as high as had ever found shelter in a pair of human hearts. The pity of it, the misery of such a fall after such a flight, could express itself only, as the poor girl prolonged the vague pauses of her unnoticed ramble, in a low, inarticulate murmur of anguish.

The afternoon waned, bringing with it the slight chill which, at the summer's end, begins to mark the shortening days. She turned her face homeward, and by this time became conscious that if Verena's companion had not yet brought her back there might be ground for uneasiness as to what had happened to them. It seemed to her that no sail-boat could have put into the town without passing more or less before her eyes and showing her whom it carried; she had seen a dozen, freighted only with the figures of men. An accident was perfectly possible (what could Ransom, with his plantation habits, know about the management of a sail?), and once that danger loomed before her—the signal loveliness of the weather had prevented its striking her before—Olive's imagination hurried, with a bound, to the worst. She saw the boat overturned and drifting out to sea, and (after a week of nameless horror) the body of an unknown young woman, defaced beyond recognition, but with long auburn hair and in a white dress, washed up in some faraway cove. An hour before, her mind had rested with a sort of relief on the idea that Verena should sink for ever beneath the horizon, so that their tremendous trouble might never be; but now, with the lateness of the hour, a sharp, immediate anxiety took the place of that intended resignation; and she quickened her step, with a heart that galloped too as she went. Then it was, above all, that she felt how *she* had understood friendship, and how never again to see the face of the creature she had taken to her soul would be for her as the stroke of blindness. The twilight had become thick by the time she reached Marmion and paused for an instant in front of her house, over which the elms that stood on the grassy wayside appeared to her to hang a blacker curtain than ever before.

There was no candle in any window, and when she pushed in and stood in the hall, listening a moment, her step awakened no answering sound. Her heart failed her; Verena's staying out in a boat from ten o'clock in the morning till nightfall was too unnatural, and she gave a cry, as she rushed into the low, dim parlor (darkened on one side, at that hour, by the wide-armed foliage, and on the other by the veranda and trellis), which expressed only a wild personal passion, a desire to take her friend in her arms again on any terms, even the most cruel to herself. The next moment she started back, with another and a different exclamation, for Verena was in the room, motionless, in a corner—the first place in which she had seated herself on re-entering the house—looking at her with a silent face which seemed strange, unnatural, in the dusk. Olive stopped short, and for a minute the two women remained as they were, gazing at each other in the dimness. After that, too, Olive still said nothing; she only went to Verena and sat down beside her. She didn't know what to make of her manner; she had never been like that before. She was unwilling to speak; she seemed crushed and humbled. This was almost the worst—if anything could be worse than what had gone before; and Olive took her hand with an irresistible impulse of compassion and reassurance. From the way it lay in her own she guessed her whole feeling—saw it was a kind of shame, shame for her weakness, her swift surrender, her insane gyration, in the morning. Verena expressed it by no protest and no explanation; she appeared not even to wish to hear the sound of her own voice. Her silence itself was an appeal—an appeal to Olive to ask no questions (she could trust her to inflict no spoken reproach); only to wait till she could lift up her head again. Olive understood, or thought she understood, and the woefulness of it all only seemed the deeper. She would just sit there and hold her hand; that was all she could do; they were beyond each other's help in any other way now. Verena leaned her head back and closed her eyes, and for an hour, as nightfall settled in the room, neither of the young women spoke. Distinctly, it was a kind of shame. After a while the parlor-maid, very casual, in the manner of the servants at Marmion, appeared on the threshold with a lamp; but Olive motioned her frantically away. She wished to keep the darkness. It was a kind of shame.

The next morning Basil Ransom rapped loudly with his walking-stick on the lintel of Miss Chancellor's house-door, which, as usual on fine days, stood open. There was no need he should wait till the servant had answered his summons; for Olive, who had reason to believe he would come, and who had been lurking in the sitting room for a purpose of her own, stepped forth into the little hall.

"I am sorry to disturb you; I had the hope that—for a moment—I might see Miss Tarrant." That was the speech with which (and a measured salutation), he greeted his advancing kinswoman. She faced him an instant, and her strange green eyes caught the light.

"It's impossible. You may believe that when I say it."

"Why is it impossible?" he asked, smiling in spite of an inward displeasure. And as Olive gave him no answer, only gazing at him with a cold audacity which he had not hitherto observed in her, he added a little explanation. "It is simply to have seen her before I go—to have said five words to her. I want her to know that I have made up my mind—since yesterday—to leave this place; I shall take the train at noon."

It was not to gratify Olive Chancellor that he had determined to go away, or even that he told her this; yet he was surprised that his words brought no expression of pleasure to her face. "I don't think it is of much importance whether you go away or not. Miss Tarrant herself has gone away."

"Miss Tarrant—gone away?" This announcement was so much at variance with Verena's apparent intentions the night before that his ejaculation expressed chagrin as well as surprise, and in doing so it gave Olive a momentary advantage. It was the only one she had ever had, and the poor girl may be excused for having enjoyed it—so far as enjoyment was possible to her. Basil Ransom's visible discomfiture was more agreeable to her than anything had been for a long time.

"I went with her myself to the early train; and I saw it leave the station." And Olive kept her eyes unaverted, for the satisfaction of seeing how he took it.

It must be confessed that he took it rather ill. He had decided it was best he should retire, but Verena's retiring was another matter. "And where is she gone?" he asked, with a frown.

"I don't think I am obliged to tell you."

"Of course not! Excuse my asking. It is much better that I should find it out for myself, because if I owed the information to you I should perhaps feel a certain delicacy as regards profiting by it."

"Gracious heaven!" cried Miss Chancellor, at the idea of Ransom's delicacy. Then she added more deliberately: "You will not find out for yourself."

"You think not?"

"I am sure of it!" And her enjoyment of the situation becoming acute there broke from her lips a shrill, unfamiliar, troubled sound, which performed the office of a laugh, a laugh of triumph, but which, at a distance, might have passed almost as well for a wail of despair. It rang in Ransom's ears as he quickly turned away.

40

It was Mrs. Luna who received him, as she had received him on the occasion of his first visit to Charles Street; by which I do not mean quite in the same way. She had known very little about him then, but she knew too much for her happiness today, and she had with him now a little invidious, contemptuous manner, as if everything he should say or do could be a proof only of abominable duplicity and perversity. She had a theory that he had treated her shamefully; and he knew it—I do not mean the fact, but the theory: which led him to reflect that her resentments were as shallow as her opinions, inasmuch as if she really believed in her grievance, or if it had had any dignity, she would not have consented to see him. He had not presented himself at Miss Chancellor's door without a very good reason, and having done so he could not turn away so long as there was anyone in the house of whom he might have speech. He had sent up his name to Mrs. Luna, after being told that she was staying there, on the mere chance that she would see him; for he thought a refusal a very possible sequel to the letters she had written him during the past four or five months—letters he had scarcely read, full of allusions of the most cutting sort to proceedings of his, in the past, of which he had no recollection whatever. They bored him, for he had quite other matters in his mind.

"I don't wonder you have the bad taste, the crudity," she said, as soon as he came into the room, looking at him more sternly than he would have believed possible to her.

He saw that this was an allusion to his not having been to see her since the period of her sister's visit to New York; he having conceived for her, the evening of Mrs. Burrage's party, a sentiment of aversion which put an end to such attentions. He didn't laugh, he was too worried and preoccupied; but he replied, in a tone which apparently annoyed her as much as any indecent mirth: "I thought it very possible you wouldn't see me."

"Why shouldn't I see you, if I should take it into my head? Do you suppose I care whether I see you or not?"

"I supposed you wanted to, from your letters."

"Then why did you think I would refuse?"

"Because that's the sort of thing women do."

"Women—women! You know much about them!"

"I am learning something every day."

"You haven't learned yet, apparently, to answer their letters. It's rather a surprise to me that you don't pretend not to have received mine."

Ransom could smile now; the opportunity to vent the exasperation that had been consuming him almost restored his good humor. "What could I say? You overwhelmed me. Besides, I did answer one of them."

"One of them? You speak as if I had written you a dozen!" Mrs. Luna cried.

"I thought that was your contention—that you had done me the honor to address me so many. They were crushing, and when a man's crushed, it's all over."

"Yes, you look as if you were in very small pieces! I am glad I shall never see you again."

"I can see now why you received me—to tell me that," Ransom said.

"It is a kind of pleasure. I am going back to Europe."

"Really? for Newton's education?"

"Ah, I wonder you can have the face to speak of that—after the way you deserted him!"

"Let us abandon the subject, then, and I will tell you what I want."

"I don't in the least care what you want," Mrs. Luna remarked. "And you haven't even the grace to ask me where I am going—over there."

"What difference does that make to me—once you leave these shores?"

Mrs. Luna rose to her feet. "Ah, chivalry, chivalry!" she exclaimed. And she walked away to the window—one of the windows from which Ransom had first enjoyed, at Olive's solicitation, the view of the Back Bay. Mrs. Luna looked forth at it with little of the air of a person who was sorry to be about to lose it. "I am determined you shall know where I am going," she said in a moment. "I am going to Florence."

"Don't be afraid!" he replied. "I shall go to Rome."

"And you'll carry there more impertinence than has been seen there since the old emperors."

"Were the emperors impertinent, in addition to their other vices? I am determined, on my side, that you shall know what I have come for," Ransom said. "I wouldn't ask you if I could ask any one else; but I am very hard pressed, and I don't know who can help me."

Mrs. Luna turned on him a face of the frankest derision. "Help you? Do you remember the last time I asked you to help me?"

"That evening at Mrs. Burrage's? Surely I wasn't wanting then; I remember urging on your acceptance a chair, so that you might stand on it, to see and to hear."

"To see and to hear what, please? Your disgusting infatuation!"

"It's just about that I want to speak to you," Ransom pursued. "As you already know all about it, you have no new shock to receive, and I therefore venture to ask you——"

"Where tickets for her lecture tonight can be obtained? Is it possible she hasn't sent you one?"

"I assure you I didn't come to Boston to hear it," said Ransom, with a sadness which Mrs. Luna evidently regarded as a refinement of outrage. "What I should like to ascertain is where Miss Tarrant may be found at the present moment."

"And do you think that's a delicate inquiry to make of *me*?"

"I don't see why it shouldn't be, but I know you don't think it is, and that is why, as I say, I mention the matter to you only because I can imagine absolutely no one else who is in a position to assist me. I have been to the house of

430

Miss Tarrant's parents, in Cambridge, but it is closed and empty, destitute of any sign of life. I went there first, on arriving this morning, and rang at this door only when my journey to Monadnoc Place had proved fruitless. Your sister's servant told me that Miss Tarrant was not staying here, but she added that Mrs. Luna was. No doubt you won't be pleased at having been spoken of as a sort of equivalent; and I didn't say to myself—or to the servant—that you would do as well; I only reflected that I could at least try you. I didn't even ask for Miss Chancellor, as I am sure she would give me no information whatever."

Mrs. Luna listened to this candid account of the young man's proceedings with her head turned a little over her shoulder at him, and her eyes fixed as unsympathetically as possible upon his own. "What you propose, then, as I understand it," she said in a moment, "is that I should betray my sister to you."

"Worse than that; I propose that you should betray Miss Tarrant herself."

"What do I care about Miss Tarrant? I don't know what you are talking about."

"Haven't you really any idea where she is living? Haven't you seen her here? Are Miss Olive and she not constantly together?"

Mrs. Luna, at this, turned full round upon him, and, with folded arms and her head tossed back, exclaimed: "Look here, Basil Ransom, I never thought you were a fool, but it strikes me that since we last met you have lost your wits!"

"There is no doubt of that," Ransom answered, smiling.

"Do you mean to tell me you don't know everything about Miss Tarrant that can be known?"

"I have neither seen her nor heard of her for the last ten weeks; Miss Chancellor has hidden her away."

"Hidden her away, with all the walls and fences of Boston flaming today with her name?"

"Oh yes, I have noticed that, and I have no doubt that

431

by waiting till this evening I shall be able to see her. But I don't want to wait till this evening; I want to see her now, and not in public—in private."

"Do you indeed?—how interesting!" cried Mrs. Luna, with rippling laughter. "And pray what do you want to do with her?"

Ransom hesitated a little. "I think I would rather not tell you."

"Your charming frankness, then, has its limits! My poor cousin, you are really too *naïf*. Do you suppose it matters a straw to me?"

Ransom made no answer to this appeal, but after an instant he broke out: "Honestly, Mrs. Luna, can you give me no clue?"

"Lord, what terrible eyes you make, and what terrible words you use! 'Honestly,' quoth me! Do you think I am so fond of the creature that I want to keep her all to myself?"

"I don't know; I don't understand," said Ransom, slowly and softly, but still with his terrible eyes.

"And do you think I understand any better? You are not a very edifying young man," Mrs. Luna went on; "but I really think you have deserved a better fate than to be jilted and thrown over by a girl of that class."

"I haven't been jilted. I like her very much, but she never encouraged me."

At this Mrs. Luna broke again into articulate scoffing. "It is very odd that at your age you should be so little a man of the world!"

Ransom made her no other answer than to remark, thoughtfully and rather absently: "Your sister is really very clever."

"By which you mean, I suppose, that I am not!" Mrs. Luna suddenly changed her tone, and said, with the greatest sweetness and humility: "God knows, I have never pretended to be!"

Ransom looked at her a moment, and guessed the meaning of this altered note. It had suddenly come over her that with her portrait in half the shop-fronts, her advertisement on all the fences, and the great occasion on which she was to reveal herself to the country at large close at hand, Verena had become so conscious of high destinies that her dear friend's Southern kinsman really appeared to her very small game, and she might therefore be regarded as having cast him off. If this were the case, it would perhaps be well for Mrs. Luna still to hold on. Basil's induction was very rapid, but it gave him time to decide that the best thing to say to his interlocutress was: "On what day do you sail for Europe?"

"Perhaps I shall not sail at all," Mrs. Luna replied, looking out of the window.

"And in that case—poor Newton's education?"

"I should try to content myself with a country which has given you yours."

"Don't you want him, then, to be a man of the world?"

"Ah, the world, the world!" she murmured, while she watched, in the deepening dusk, the lights of the town begin to reflect themselves in the Back Bay. "Has it been such a source of happiness to me that I belong to it?"

"Perhaps, after all, I shall be able to go to Florence!" said Ransom, laughing.

She faced him once more, this time slowly, and declared that she had never known anything so strange as his state of mind—she would be so glad to have an explanation of it. With the opinions he professed (it was for them she had liked him—she didn't like his character), why on earth should he be running after a little fifth-rate *poseuse,* and in such a frenzy to get hold of her? He might say it was none of her business, and of course she would have no answer to that; therefore she admitted that she asked simply out of intellectual curiosity, and because one always was tormented at the sight of a painful contradiction. With the things she had heard him say about his convictions and theories, his view of life and the great questions of the

433

future, she should have thought he would find Miss Tarrant's attitudinizing absolutely nauseous. Were not her views the same as Olive's, and hadn't Olive and he signally failed to hit it off together? Mrs. Luna only asked because she was really quite puzzled. "Don't you know that some minds, when they see a mystery, can't rest till they clear it up?"

"You can't be more puzzled than I am," said Ransom. "Apparently the explanation is to be found in a sort of reversal of the formula you were so good, just now, as to apply to me. You like my opinions, but you entertain a different sentiment for my character. I deplore Miss Tarrant's opinions, but her character—well, her character pleases me."

Mrs. Luna stared, as if she were waiting, the explanation surely not being complete. "But as much as that?" she inquired.

"As much as what?" said Ransom, smiling. Then he added, "Your sister has beaten me."

"I thought she had beaten someone of late; she has seemed so gay and happy. I didn't suppose it was *all* because I was going away."

"Has she seemed very gay?" Ransom inquired, with a sinking of the heart. He wore such a long face, as he asked this question, that Mrs. Luna was again moved to audible mirth, after which she explained:

"Of course I mean gay for her. Everything is relative. With her impatience for this lecture of her friend's tonight, she's in an unspeakable state! She can't sit still for three minutes, she goes out fifteen times a day, and there has been enough arranging and interviewing, and discussing and telegraphing and advertising, enough wire-pulling and rushing about, to put an army in the field. What is it they are always doing to the armies in Europe?—mobilizing them? Well, Verena has been mobilized, and this has been headquarters."

"And shall you go to the Music Hall tonight?"

"For what do you take me? I have no desire to be shrieked at for an hour."

"No doubt, no doubt, Miss Olive must be in a state," Ransom went on, rather absently. Then he said, with abruptness, in a different tone: "If this house has been, as you say, headquarters, how comes it you haven't seen her?"

"Seen Olive? I have seen nothing else!"

"I mean Miss Tarrant. She must be somewhere—in the place—if she's to speak tonight."

"Should you like me to go out and look for her? *Il ne manquerait plus que cela!*" cried Mrs. Luna. "What's the matter with you, Basil Ransom, and what are you after?" she demanded, with considerable sharpness. She had tried haughtiness and she had tried humility, but they brought her equally face to face with a competitor whom she couldn't take seriously, yet who was none the less objectionable for that.

I know not whether Ransom would have attempted to answer her question had an obstacle not presented itself; at any rate, at the moment she spoke, the curtain in the doorway was pushed aside, and a visitor crossed the threshold. "Mercy! how provoking!" Mrs. Luna exclaimed, audibly enough; and without moving from her place she bent an uncharitable eye upon the invader, a gentleman whom Ransom had the sense of having met before. He was a young man with a fresh face and abundant locks, prematurely white; he stood smiling at Mrs. Luna, quite undaunted by the absence of any demonstration in his favor. She looked as if she didn't know him, while Ransom prepared to depart, leaving them to settle it together.

"I'm afraid you don't remember me, though I have seen you before," said the young man, very amiably. "I was here a week ago, and Miss Chancellor presented me to you."

"Oh yes; she's not at home now," Mrs. Luna returned, vaguely.

"So I was told—but I didn't let that prevent me." And

435

the young man included Basil Ransom in the smile with which he made himself more welcome than Mrs. Luna appeared disposed to make him, and by which he seemed to call attention to his superiority. "There is a matter on which I want very much to obtain some information, and I have no doubt you will be so good as to give it to me."

"It comes back to me—you have something to do with the newspapers," said Mrs. Luna; and Ransom too, by this time, had placed the young man among his reminiscences. He had been at Miss Birdseye's famous party, and Doctor Prance had there described him as a brilliant journalist.

It was quite with the air of such a personage that he accepted Mrs. Luna's definition, and he continued to radiate toward Ransom (as if, in return, he remembered *his* face), while he dropped, confidentially, the word that expressed everything—" 'The Vesper,' don't you know?" Then he went on: "Now, Mrs. Luna, I don't care, I'm not going to let you off! We want the last news about Miss Verena, and it has got to come out of this house."

"Oh murder!" Ransom muttered, beneath his breath, taking up his hat.

"Miss Chancellor has hidden her away; I have been scouring the city in search of her, and her own father hasn't seen her for a week. We have got his ideas; they are very easy to get, but that isn't what we want."

"And what do you want?" Ransom was now impelled to inquire, as Mr. Pardon (even the name at present came back to him), appeared sufficiently to have introduced himself.

"We want to know how she feels about tonight; what report she makes of her nerves, her anticipations; how she looked, what she had on, up to six o'clock. Gracious! if I could see her I should know what I wanted, and so would she, I guess!" Mr. Pardon exclaimed. "You must know something, Mrs. Luna; it isn't natural you shouldn't. I won't inquire any further where she is, because that might seem a

436

little pushing, if she does wish to withdraw herself—though I am bound to say I think she makes a mistake; we could work up these last hours for her! But can't you tell me any little personal items—the sort of thing the people like? What is she going to have for supper? or is she going to speak—a—without previous nourishment?"

"Really, sir, I don't know, and I don't in the least care; I have nothing to do with the business!" Mrs. Luna cried, angrily.

The reporter stared; then, eagerly, "You have nothing to do with it—you take an unfavorable view, you protest?" And he was already feeling in a side-pocket for his notebook.

"Mercy on us! are you going to put *that* in the paper?" Mrs. Luna exclaimed; and in spite of the sense, detestable to him, that everything he wished most to avert was fast closing over the girl, Ransom broke into cynical laughter.

"Ah, but do protest, madam; let us at least have that fragment!" Mr. Pardon went on. "A protest from this house would be a charming note. We *must* have it—we've got nothing else! The public are almost as much interested in your sister as they are in Miss Verena; they know to what extent she has backed her: and I should be so delighted (I see the heading, from here, so attractive!) just to take down 'What Miss Chancellor's Family Think about It!' "

Mrs. Luna sank into the nearest chair, with a groan, covering her face with her hands. "Heaven help me, I am glad I am going to Europe!"

"That is another little item—everything counts," said Matthias Pardon, making a rapid entry in his tablets. "May I inquire whether you are going to Europe in consequence of your disapproval of your sister's views?"

Mrs. Luna sprang up again, almost snatching the memoranda out of his hand. "If you have the impertinence to publish a word about me, or to mention my name in print, I will come to your office and make such a scene!"

"Dearest lady, that would be a godsend!" Mr. Pardon cried, enthusiastically; but he put his notebook back into his pocket.

"Have you made an exhaustive search for Miss Tarrant?" Basil Ransom asked of him. Mr. Pardon, at this inquiry, eyed him with a sudden, familiar archness, expressive of the idea of competition; so that Ransom added: "You needn't be afraid, I'm not a reporter."

"I didn't know but what you had come on from New York."

"So I have—but not as the representative of a newspaper."

"Fancy his taking you——" Mrs. Luna murmured, with indignation.

"Well, I have been everywhere I could think of," Mr. Pardon remarked. "I have been hunting round after your sister's agent, but I haven't been able to catch up with him; I suppose he has been hunting on his side. Miss Chancellor told me—Mrs. Luna may remember it—that she shouldn't be here at all during the week, and that she preferred not to tell me either where or how she was to spend her time until the momentous evening. Of course I let her know that I should find out if I could, and you may remember," he said to Mrs. Luna, "the conversation we had on the subject. I remarked, candidly, that if they didn't look out they would overdo the quietness. Doctor Tarrant has felt very low about it. However, I have done what I could with the material at my command, and the 'Vesper' has let the public know that her whereabouts was the biggest mystery of the season. It's difficult to get round the 'Vesper.' "

"I am almost afraid to open my lips in your presence." Mrs. Luna broke in, "but I must say that I think my sister was strangely communicative. She told you ever so much that I wouldn't have breathed."

"I should like to try you with something you know!" Matthias Pardon returned, imperturbably. "This isn't a fair

trial, because you don't know. Miss Chancellor came round
—came round considerably, there's no doubt of that; because a year or two ago she was terribly unapproachable.
If I have mollified her, madam, why shouldn't I mollify
you? She realizes that I can help her now, and as I ain't
rancorous I am willing to help her all she'll let me. The
trouble is, she won't let me enough, yet; it seems as if she
couldn't believe it of me. At any rate," he pursued, addressing himself more particularly to Ransom, "half an hour ago,
at the Hall, they knew nothing whatever about Miss Tarrant,
beyond the fact that about a month ago she came there,
with Miss Chancellor, to try her voice, which rang all over
the place, like silver, and that Miss Chancellor guaranteed
her absolute punctuality tonight."

"Well, that's all that is required," said Ransom, at hazard;
and he put out his hand, in farewell, to Mrs. Luna.

"Do you desert me already?" she demanded, giving him
a glance which would have embarrassed any spectator but
a reporter of the "Vesper."

"I have fifty things to do; you must excuse me." He
was nervous, restless, his heart was beating much faster
than usual; he couldn't stand still, and he had no com-
punction whatever about leaving her to get rid, by herself,
of Mr. Pardon.

This gentleman continued to mix in the conversation,
possibly from the hope that if he should linger either Miss
Tarrant or Miss Chancellor would make her appearance.
"Every seat in the Hall is sold; the crowd is expected to
be immense. When our Boston public *does* take an idea!"
Mr. Pardon exclaimed.

Ransom only wanted to get away, and in order to facili-
tate his release by implying that in such a case he should
see her again, he said to Mrs. Luna, rather hypocritically,
from the threshold, "You had really better come tonight."

"I am not like the Boston public—I don't take an idea!"
she replied.

"Do you mean to say you are not going?" cried Mr.

Pardon, with widely open eyes, clapping his hand again to his pocket. "Don't you regard her as a wonderful genius?"

Mrs. Luna was sorely tried, and the vexation of seeing Ransom slip away from her with his thoughts visibly on Verena, leaving her face to face with the odious newspaperman, whose presence made passionate protest impossible—the annoyance of seeing everything and everyone mock at her and fail to compensate her was such that she lost her head, while rashness leaped to her lips and jerked out the answer—"No indeed; I think her a vulgar idiot!"

"Ah, madam, I should never permit myself to print that!" Ransom heard Mr. Pardon rejoin, reproachfully, as he dropped the *portière* of the drawing room.

41

He walked about for the next two hours, walked all over Boston, heedless of his course, and conscious only of an unwillingness to return to his hotel and an inability to eat his dinner or rest his weary legs. He had been roaming in very much the same desperate fashion, at once eager and purposeless, for many days before he left New York, and he knew that his agitation and suspense must wear themselves out. At present they pressed him more than ever; they had become tremendously acute. The early dusk of the last half of November had gathered thick, but the evening was fine and the lighted streets had the animation and variety of a winter that had begun with brilliancy. The shop-fronts glowed through frosty panes, the passers bustled on the pavement, the bells of the streetcars jangled in the cold air, the newsboys hawked the evening-papers, the vestibules of the theatres, illuminated and flanked with colored posters and the photographs of actresses, exhibited seductively their swinging doors of red leather or baize, spotted with little brass nails. Behind great plates of glass the interior of the hotels became visible, with marble-paved lobbies, white with electric lamps, and columns, and Westerners on divans stretching their legs, while behind a counter, set apart and covered with an array of periodicals and novels in paper covers, little boys, with the faces of old men, showing plans of the playhouses and offering librettos, sold orchestra-chairs at a premium. When from time to time Ransom paused at a corner, hesitating which way to drift, he looked up and saw the stars, sharp and near, scintillating over the town. Boston seemed to him big and full of nocturnal life, very much awake and preparing for an evening of pleasure.

He passed and repassed the Music Hall, saw Verena immensely advertised, gazed down the vista, the approach for pedestrians, which leads out of School Street, and thought it looked expectant and ominous. People had not begun to enter yet, but the place was ready, lighted and open, and the interval would be only too short. So it appeared to Ransom, while at the same time he wished immensely the crisis were over. Everything that surrounded him referred itself to the idea with which his mind was palpitating, the question whether he might not still intervene as against the girl's jump into the abyss. He believed that all Boston was going to hear her, or that at least everyone was whom he saw in the streets; and there was a kind of incentive and inspiration in this thought. The vision of wresting her from the mighty multitude set him off again, to stride through the population that would fight for her. It was not too late, for he felt strong; it would not be too late even if she should already stand there before thousands of converging eyes. He had had his ticket since the morning, and now the time was going on. He went back to his hotel at last for ten

minutes, and refreshed himself by dressing a little and by
drinking a glass of wine. Then he took his way once more
to the Music Hall, and saw that people were beginning to
go in—the first drops of the great stream, among whom there
were many women. Since seven o'clock the minutes had
moved fast—before that they had dragged—and now there
was only half an hour. Ransom passed in with the others;
he knew just where his seat was; he had chosen it, on
reaching Boston, from the few that were left, with what he
believed to be care. But now, as he stood beneath the faraway paneled roof, stretching above the line of little tongues
of flame which marked its junction with the walls, he felt
that this didn't matter much, since he certainly was not
going to subside into his place. He was not one of the
audience; he was apart, unique, and had come on a business
altogether special. It wouldn't have mattered if, in advance,
he had got no place at all and had just left himself to pay
for standing-room at the last. The people came pouring in,
and in a very short time there would only be standing-room
left. Ransom had no definite plan; he had mainly wanted
to get inside of the building, so that, on a view of the field,
he might make up his mind. He had never been in the
Music Hall before, and its lofty vaults and rows of overhanging balconies made it to his imagination immense and
impressive. There were two or three moments during which
he felt as he could imagine a young man to feel who, waiting in a public place, has made up his mind, for reasons
of his own, to discharge a pistol at the king or the president.

The place struck him with a kind of Roman vastness;
the doors which opened out of the upper balconies, high
aloft, and which were constantly swinging to and fro with
the passage of spectators and ushers, reminded him of the
vomitoria that he had read about in descriptions of the
Colosseum. The huge organ, the background of the stage
—a stage occupied with tiers of seats for choruses and civic
worthies—lifted to the dome its shining pipes and sculptured
pinnacles, and some genius of music or oratory erected him-

elf in monumental bronze at the base. The hall was so capacious and serious, and the audience increased so rapidly without filling it, giving Ransom a sense of the numbers it would contain when it was packed, that the courage of the two young women, face to face with so tremendous an ordeal, hovered before him as really sublime, especially the conscious tension of poor Olive, who would have been spared none of the anxieties and tremors, none of the previsions of accident or calculations of failure. In the front of the stage was a slim, high desk, like a music-stand, with a cover of red velvet, and near it was a light ornamental chair, on which he was sure Verena would not seat herself, though he could fancy her leaning at moments on the back. Behind this was a kind of semicircle of a dozen armchairs, which had evidently been arranged for the friends of the speaker, her sponsors and patrons. The hall was more and more full of premonitory sounds; people making a noise as they unfolded, on hinges, their seats, and itinerant boys, whose voices as they cried out "Photographs of Miss Tarrant —sketch of her life!" or "Portraits of the Speaker—story of her career!" sounded small and piping in the general immensity. Before Ransom was aware of it several of the armchairs, in the row behind the lecturer's desk, were occupied, with gaps, and in a moment he recognized, even across the interval, three of the persons who had appeared. The straight-featured woman with bands of glossy hair and eyebrows that told at a distance, could only be Mrs. Farrinder, just as the gentleman beside her, in a white overcoat, with an umbrella and a vague face, was probably her husband Amariah. At the opposite end of the row were another pair, whom Ransom, unacquainted with certain chapters of Verena's history, perceived without surprise to be Mrs. Burrage and her insinuating son. Apparently their interest in Miss Tarrant was more than a momentary fad, since—like himself—they had made the journey from New York to hear her. There were other figures, unknown to our young man, here and there, in the semicircle; but several

places were still empty (one of which was of course reserved
for Olive), and it occurred to Ransom, even in his preoccupation, that one of them ought to remain so—ought to be
left to symbolize the presence, in the spirit, of Miss Birdseye.

He bought one of the photographs of Verena, and thought
it shockingly bad, and bought also the sketch of her life
which many people seemed to be reading, but crumpled it
up in his pocket for future consideration. Verena was not
in the least present to him in connection with this exhibition
of enterprise and puffery; what he saw was Olive, struggling
and yielding, making every sacrifice of taste for the sake of
the largest hearing, and conforming herself to a great popular system. Whether she had struggled or not, there was a
catchpenny effect about the whole thing which added to
the fever in his cheek and made him wish he had money
to buy up the stock of the vociferous little boys. Suddenly
the notes of the organ rolled out into the hall, and he became aware that the overture or prelude had begun. This,
too, seemed to him a piece of claptrap, but he didn't wait
to think of it; he instantly edged out of his place, which he
had chosen near the end of a row, and reached one of the
numerous doors. If he had had no definite plan he now had
at least an irresistible impulse, and he felt the prick of
shame at having faltered for a moment. It had been his
tacit calculation that Verena, still enshrined in mystery by
her companion, would not have reached the scene of her
performance till within a few minutes of the time at which
she was to come forth; so that he had lost nothing by
waiting, up to this moment, before the platform. But now
he must overtake his opportunity. Before passing out of the
hall into the lobby he paused, and with his back to the
stage, gave a look at the gathered auditory. It had become
densely numerous, and, suffused with the evenly distributed
gaslight, which fell from a great elevation, and the thick
atmosphere that hangs forever in such places, it appeared
to pile itself high and to look dimly expectant and formid-
able. He had a throb of uneasiness at his private purpose of

balking it of its entertainment, its victim—a glimpse of the ferocity that lurks in a disappointed mob. But the thought of that danger only made him pass more quickly through the ugly corridors; he felt that his plan was definite enough now, and he found that he had no need even of asking the way to a certain small door (one or more of them), which he meant to push open. In taking his place in the morning he had assured himself as to the side of the house on which (with its approach to the platform), the withdrawing room of singers and speakers was situated; he had chosen his seat in that quarter, and he now had not far to go before he reached it. No one heeded or challenged him; Miss Tarrant's auditors were still pouring in (the occasion was evidently to have been an unprecedented success of curiosity), and had all the attention of the ushers. Ransom opened a door at the end of a passage, and it admitted him into a sort of vestibule, quite bare save that at a second door, opposite to him, stood a figure at the sight of which he paused for a moment in his advance.

The figure was simply that of a robust policeman, in his helmet and brass buttons—a policeman who was expecting him—Ransom could see that in a twinkling. He judged in the same space of time that Olive Chancellor had heard of his having arrived and had applied for the protection of this functionary, who was now simply guarding the ingress and was prepared to defend it against all comers. There was a slight element of surprise in this, as he had reasoned that his nervous kinswoman was absent from her house for the day—had been spending it all in Verena's retreat, wherever that was. The surprise was not great enough, however, to interrupt his course for more than an instant, and he crossed the room and stood before the belted sentinel. For a moment neither spoke; they looked at each other very hard in the eyes, and Ransom heard the organ, beyond partitions, launching its waves of sound through the hall. They seemed to be very near it, and the whole place vibrated. The policeman was a tall, lean-faced, sallow man, with a stoop of the shoulders, a small, steady eye, and something in his mouth which made a protuberance in his cheek. Ransom could see that he was very strong, but he believed that he himself was not materially less so. However, he had not come there to show physical fight—a public tussle about Verena was not an attractive idea, except perhaps, after all, if he should get the worst of it, from the point of view of Olive's new system of advertising; and, moreover, it would not be in the least necessary. Still he said nothing, and still the policeman remained dumb, and there was something in the way the moments elapsed and in our young man's consciousness that Verena was separated from him only by a couple of thin planks, which made him feel that she too expected him, but in another sense; that she had nothing to do with this parade of resistance, that she would know in a moment, by quick intuition, that he was there, and that she was only praying to be rescued, to be saved. Face to face with Olive she hadn't the courage, but she would have it with her hand in his. It came to him that there was no one in the world less sure of her business just at that moment than Olive Chancellor; it was as if he could see, through the door, the terrible way her eyes fixed on Verena while she held her watch in her hand and Verena looked away from her. Olive would have been so thankful that she should begin before the hour, but of course that was impossible. Ransom asked no questions —that seemed a waste of time; he only said, after a minute, to the policeman:

"I should like very much to see Miss Tarrant, if you will be so good as to take in my card."

The guardian of order, well planted just between him and the handle of the door, took from Ransom the morsel of pasteboard which he held out to him, read slowly the name inscribed on it, turned it over and looked at the back, then returned it to his interlocutor. "Well, I guess it ain't much use," he remarked.

"How can you know that? You have no business to decline my request."

"Well, I guess I have about as much business as you have to make it." Then he added, "You are just the very man she wants to keep out."

"I don't think Miss Tarrant wants to keep me out," Ransom returned.

"I don't know much about her, she hasn't hired the hall. It's the other one—Miss Chancellor; it's her that runs this lecture."

"And she has asked you to keep me out? How absurd!" exclaimed Ransom, ingeniously.

"She tells me you're none too fit to be round alone; you have got this thing on the brain. I guess you'd better be quiet," said the policeman.

"Quiet? Is it possible to be more quiet than I am?"

"Well, I've seen crazy folks that were a good deal like you. If you want to see the speaker why don't you go and set round in the hall, with the rest of the public?" And the policeman waited, in an immovable, ruminating, reasonable manner, for an answer to this inquiry.

Ransom had one, on the instant, at his service. "Because I don't want simply to see her; I want also to speak to her —in private."

"Yes—it's always intensely private," said the policeman. "Now I wouldnt lose the lecture if I was you. I guess it will do you good."

"The lecture?" Ransom repeated, laughing. "It won't take place."

"Yes it will—as quick as the organ stops." Then the policeman added, as to himself, "Why the devil don't it?"

"Because Miss Tarrant has sent up to the organist to tell him to keep on."

"Who has she sent, do you s'pose?" And Ransom's new acquaintance entered into his humor. "I guess Miss Chancellor isn't her nigger.

"She has sent her father, or perhaps even her mother. They are in there too."

"How do you know that?" asked the policeman, consideringly.

"Oh, I know everything," Ransom answered, smiling.

"Well, I guess they didn't come here to listen to that organ. We'll hear something else before long, if he doesn't stop."

"You will hear a good deal, very soon," Ransom remarked.

The serenity of his self-confidence appeared at last to make an impression on his antagonist, who lowered his head a little, like some butting animal, and looked at the young man from beneath bushy eyebrows. "Well, I *have* heard a good deal, since I've been in Boston."

"Oh, Boston's a great place," Ransom rejoined, inattentively. He was not listening to the policeman or to the organ now, for the sound of voices had reached him from the other side of the door. The policeman took no further notice of it than to lean back against the panels, with folded arms; and there was another pause, between them, during which the playing of the organ ceased.

"I will just wait here, with your permission," said Ransom, "and presently I shall be called."

"Who do you s'pose will call you?"

"Well, Miss Tarrant, I hope."

"She'll have to square the other one first."

Ransom took out his watch, which he had adapted, on purpose, several hours before, to Boston time, and saw that the minutes had sped with increasing velocity during this interview, and that it now marked five minutes past eight. "Miss Chancellor will have to square the public," he said in a moment; and the words were far from being an empty profession of security, for the conviction already in possession of him, that a drama in which he, though cut off, was an actor, had been going on for some time in the apartment he was prevented from entering, that the situation was extraordinarily strained there, and that it could not come to an end without an appeal to him—this transcendental assumption acquired an infinitely greater force the instant he perceived that Verena was even now keeping her audience waiting. Why didn't she go on? Why, except that she knew he was there, and was gaining time?

"Well, I guess she has shown herself," said the doorkeeper, whose discussion with Ransom now appeared to have passed, on his own part, and without the slightest prejudice to his firmness, into a sociable, gossiping phase.

"If she had shown herself, we should hear the reception, the applause."

"Well, there they air; they are going to give it to her," the policeman announced.

He had an odious appearance of being in the right, for there indeed they seemed to be—they were giving it to her. A general hubbub rose from the floor and the galleries of the hall—the sound of several thousand people stamping with their feet and rapping with their umbrellas and sticks. Ransom felt faint, and for a little while he stood with his gaze interlocked with that of the policeman. Then suddenly a wave of coolness seemed to break over him, and he exclaimed: "My dear fellow, that isn't applause—it's impatience. It isn't a reception, it's a call!"

The policeman neither assented to this proposition nor denied it; he only transferred the protuberance in his cheek to the other side, and observed:

"I guess she's sick."

"Oh, I hope not!" said Ransom, very gently. The stamping and rapping swelled and swelled for a minute, and then it subsided; but before it had done so Ransom's definition of it had plainly become the true one. The tone of the manifestation was good-humored, but it was not gratulatory. He looked at his watch again, and saw that five minutes more had elapsed, and he remembered what the newspaperman in Charles Street had said about Olive's guaranteeing Verena's punctuality. Oddly enough, at the moment the image of this gentleman recurred to him, the gentleman himself burst through the other door, in a state of the liveliest agitation.

"Why in the name of goodness don't she go on? If she wants to make them call her, they've done it about enough!" Mr. Pardon turned, pressingly, from Ransom to the policeman and back again, and in his preoccupation gave no sign of having met the Mississippian before.

"I guess she's sick," said the policeman.

"The public'll be sick!" cried the distressed reporter. "If she's sick, why doesn't she send for a doctor? All Boston is packed into this house, and she has got to talk to it. I want to go in and see."

"You can't go in," said the policeman, drily.

"Why can't I go in, I should like to know? I want to go in for the 'Vesper'!"

"You can't go in for anything. I'm keeping this man out, too," the policeman added genially, as if to make Mr. Pardon's exclusion appear less invidious.

"Why, they'd ought to let *you* in," said Matthias, staring a moment at Ransom.

"Maybe they'd ought, but they won't," the policeman remarked.

"Gracious me!" panted Mr. Pardon; "I knew from the first Miss Chancellor would make a mess of it! Where's Mr. Filer?" he went on, eagerly, addressing himself apparently to either of the others, or to both.

"I guess he's at the door, counting the money," said the policeman.

"Well, he'll have to give it back if he don't look out!"

"Maybe he will. I'll let *him* in if he comes, but he's the only one. She is on now," the policeman added, without emotion.

His ear had caught the first faint murmur of another explosion of sound. This time, unmistakably, it was applause—the clapping of multitudinous hands, mingled with the noise of many throats. The demonstration, however, though considerable, was not what might have been expected, and it died away quickly. Mr. Pardon stood listening, with an expression of some alarm. "Merciful fathers! can't they give her more than that?" he cried. "I'll just fly round and see!"

When he had hurried away again, Ransom said to the policeman—"Who is Mr. Filer?"

"Oh, he's an old friend of mine. He's the man that runs Miss Chancellor."

"That runs her?"

"Just the same as she runs Miss Tarrant. He runs the pair, as you might say. He's in the lecture-business."

"Then he had better talk to the public himself."

"Oh, *he* can't talk; he can only boss!"

The opposite door at this moment was pushed open again, and a large, heated-looking man, with a little stiff beard on the end of his chin and his overcoat flying behind him, strode forward with an imprecation. "What the h——are they doing in the parlor? This sort of thing's about played out!"

"Ain't she up there now?" the policeman asked.

"It's not Miss Tarrant," Ransom said, as if he knew all about it. He perceived in a moment that this was Mr. Filer, Olive Chancellor's agent; an inference instantly followed by the reflection that such a personage would have been warned against him by his kinswoman and would doubtless attempt to hold him, or his influence, accountable for Verena's unexpected delay. Mr. Filer only glanced at him, however, and to Ransom's surprise appeared to have no theory of his identity; a fact implying that Miss Chancellor had considered that the greater discretion was (except to the policeman) to hold her tongue about him altogether.

"Up there? It's her jackass of a father that's up there!" cried Mr. Filer, with his hand on the latch of the door, which the policeman had allowed him to approach.

"Is he asking for a doctor?" the latter inquired, dispassionately.

"You're the sort of doctor he'll want, if he doesn't produce the girl! You don't mean to say they've locked themselves in? What the plague are they after?"

"They've got the key on that side," said the policeman, while Mr. Filer discharged at the door a volley of sharp knocks, at the same time violently shaking the handle.

"If the door was locked, what was the good of your standing before it?" Ransom inquired.

"So as you couldn't do that"; and the policeman nodded at Mr. Filer.

"You see your interference has done very little good."

"I dunno; she has got to come out yet."

Mr. Filer meanwhile had continued to thump and shake, demanding instant admission and inquiring if they were going to let the audience pull the house down. Another round of applause had broken out, directed perceptibly to some apology, some solemn circumlocution, of Selah Tarrant's; this covered the sound of the agent's voice, as well as that of a confused and divided response, proceeding from the parlor. For a minute nothing definite was audible; the door remained closed, and Matthias Pardon reappeared in the vestibule.

"He says she's just a little faint—from nervousness. She'll be all ready in about three minutes." This announcement was Mr. Pardon's contribution to the crisis; and he added that the crowd was a lovely crowd, it was a real Boston crowd, it was perfectly good-humored.

"There's a lovely crowd, and a real Boston one too, I guess, in here!" cried Mr. Filer, now banging very hard. "I've handled prima donnas, and I've handled natural curiosities, but I've never seen anything up to this. Mind what I say, ladies; if you don't let me in, I'll smash down the door!"

"Don't seem as if *you* could make it much worse, does it?" the policeman observed to Ransom, strolling aside a little, with the air of being superseded.

42

Ransom made no reply; he was watching the door, which at that moment gave way from within. Verena stood there —it was she, evidently, who had opened it—and her eyes went straight to his. She was dressed in white, and her face was whiter than her garment; above it her hair seemed to shine like fire. She took a step forward; but before she could take another he had come down to her, on the threshold of the room. Her face was full of suffering, and he did not attempt—before all those eyes—to take her hand; he only said in a low tone, "I have been waiting for you—a long time!"

"I know it—I saw you in your seat—I want to speak to you."

"Well, Miss Tarrant, don't you think you'd better be on the platform?" cried Mr. Filer, making with both his arms a movement as if to sweep her before him, through the waiting room, up into the presence of the public.

"In a moment I shall be ready. My father is making that all right." And, to Ransom's surprise, she smiled, with all her sweetness, at the irrepressible agent; appeared to wish genuinely to reassure him.

The three had moved together into the waiting room, and there at the farther end of it, beyond the vulgar, perfunctory chairs and tables, under the flaring gas, he saw Mrs. Tarrant sitting upright on a sofa, with immense rigidity, and a large flushed visage, full of suppressed distortion, and beside her prostrate, fallen over, her head buried in the lap of Verena's mother, the tragic figure of Olive Chancellor. Ransom could scarcely know how much Olive's having flung herself upon Mrs. Tarrant's bosom testified to the convulsive scene that had just taken place behind the locked door. He closed it again, sharply, in the face of the reporter and the policeman, and at the same moment Selah Tarrant descended, through the aperture leading to the platform, from his brief communion with the public. On seeing Ransom he stopped short, and, gathering his waterproof about him, measured the young man from head to foot.

"Well, sir, perhaps *you* would like to go and explain our hitch," he remarked, indulging in a smile so comprehensive that the corners of his mouth seemed almost to meet behind. "I presume that you, better than anyone else, can give them an insight into our difficulties!"

"Father, be still; father, it will come out all right in a moment!" cried Verena, below her breath, panting like an emergent diver.

"There's one thing I want to know: are we going to spend half an hour talking over our domestic affairs?" Mr. Filer demanded, wiping his indignant countenance. "Is Miss Tarrant going to lecture, or ain't she going to lecture? If she ain't, she'll please to show cause why. Is she aware that every quarter of a second, at the present instant, is worth about five hundred dollars?"

"I know that—I know that, Mr. Filer; I will begin in a moment!" Verena went on. "I only want to speak to Mr. Ransom—just three words. They are perfectly quiet—don't you see how quiet they are? They trust me, they trust me, don't they, father? I only want to speak to Mr. Ransom."

"Who the devil is Mr. Ransom?" cried the exasperated, bewildered Filer.

Verena spoke to the others, but she looked at her lover, and the expression of her eyes was ineffably touching and beseeching. She trembled with nervous passion, there were sobs and supplications in her voice, and Ransom felt himself flushing with pure pity for her pain—her inevitable agony. But at the same moment he had another perception, which brushed aside remorse; he saw that he could do what he wanted, that she begged him, with all her being, to spare her, but that so long as he should protest she was submissive, helpless. What he wanted, in this light, flamed before him and challenged all his manhood, tossing his determination to a height from which not only Doctor Tarrant, and Mr. Filer, and Olive, over there, in her sightless, soundless shame, but the great expectant hall as well, and the mighty multitude, in suspense, keeping quiet from minute to minute and holding the breath of its anger—from which all these things looked small, surmountable, and of the moment only. He didn't quite understand, as yet, however; he saw that Verena had not refused, but temporized, that the spell upon her—thanks to which he should still be able to rescue her—had been the knowledge that he was near.

"Come away, come away," he murmured, quickly, putting out his two hands to her.

She took one of them, as if to plead, not to consent. "Oh, let me off, let me off—for *her,* for the others! It's too terrible, it's impossible!"

"What I want to know is why Mr. Ransom isn't in the hands of the police!" wailed Mrs. Tarrant, from her sofa.

"I have been, madam, for the last quarter of an hour." Ransom felt more and more that he could manage it, if he only kept cool. He bent over Verena with a tenderness in which he was careless, now, of observation. "Dearest, I told you, I warned you. I left you alone for ten weeks; but could that make you doubt it was coming? Not for worlds, not for millions, shall you give yourself to that roaring crowd. Don't ask me to care for them, or for anyone! What do they care for you but to gape and grin and babble? You are mine, you are not theirs."

"What under the sun is the man talking about? With

the most magnificent audience ever brought together! The city of Boston is under this roof!" Mr. Filer gaspingly interposed.

"The city of Boston be damned!" said Ransom.

"Mr. Ransom is very much interested in my daughter. He doesn't approve of our views," Selah Tarrant explained.

"It's the most horrible, wicked, immoral selfishness I ever heard in my life!" roared Mrs. Tarrant.

"Selfishness! Mrs. Tarrant, do you suppose I pretend not to be selfish?"

"Do you want us all murdered by the mob, then?"

"They can have their money—can't you give them back their money?" cried Verena, turning frantically round the circle.

"Verena Tarrant, you don't mean to say you are going to back down?" her mother shrieked.

"Good God! that I should make her suffer like this!" said Ransom to himself; and to put an end to the odious scene he would have seized Verena in his arms and broken away into the outer world, if Olive, who at Mrs. Tarrant's last loud challenge had sprung to her feet, had not at the same time thrown herself between them with a force which made the girl relinquish her grasp of Ransom's hand. To his astonishment, the eyes that looked at him out of her scared, haggard face were, like Verena's, eyes of tremendous entreaty. There was a moment during which she would have been ready to go down on her knees to him, in order that the lecture should go on.

"If you don't agree with her, take her up on the platform, and have it out there; the public would like that, first-rate!" Mr. Filer said to Ransom, as if he thought this suggestion practical.

"She had prepared a lovely address!" Selah remarked, mournfully, as if to the company in general.

No one appeared to heed the observation, but his wife broke out again. "Verena Tarrant, I should like to slap you!

Do you call such a man as that a gentleman? I don't know where your father's spirit is, to let him stay!"

Olive, meanwhile, was literally praying to her kinsman. "Let her appear this once, just this once: not to ruin, not to shame! Haven't you any pity; do you want me to be hooted? It's only for an hour. Haven't you any soul?"

Her face and voice were terrible to Ransom; she had flung herself upon Verena and was holding her close, and he could see that her friend's suffering was faint in comparison to her own. "Why for an hour, when it's all false and damnable? An hour is as bad as ten years! She's mine or she isn't, and if she's mine, she's all mine!"

"Yours! Yours! Verena, think, think what you're doing!" Olive moaned, bending over her.

Mr. Filer was now pouring forth his nature in objurgations and oaths, and brandishing before the culprits—Verena and Ransom—the extreme penalty of the law. Mrs. Tarrant had burst into violent hysterics, while Selah revolved vaguely about the room and declared that it seemed as if the better day was going to be put off for quite a while. "Don't you see how good, how sweet they are—giving us all this time? Don't you think that when they behave like that—without a sound, for five minutes—they ought to be rewarded?" Verena asked, smiling divinely, at Ransom. Nothing could have been more tender, more exquisite, than the way she put her appeal upon the ground of simple charity, kindness to the great good-natured, childish public.

"Miss Chancellor may reward them in any way she likes. Give them back their money and a little present to each."

"Money and presents? I should like to shoot you, sir!" yelled Mr. Filer. The audience had really been very patient, and up to this point deserved Verena's praise; but it was now long past eight o'clock, and symptoms of irritation—cries and groans and hisses—began again to proceed from the hall. Mr. Filer launched himself into the passage leading to the stage, and Selah rushed after him. Mrs. Tarrant extended herself, sobbing, on the sofa, and Olive, quivering in the storm, inquired of Ransom what he wanted her to do, what humiliation, what degradation, what sacrifice he imposed.

"I'll do anything—I'll be abject—I'll be vile—I'll go down in the dust!"

"I ask nothing of you, and I have nothing to do with you," Ransom said. "That is, I ask, at the most, that you shouldn't expect that, wishing to make Verena my wife, I should say to her, 'Oh, yes, you can take an hour or two out of it!' Verena," he went on, "all this is out of it—dreadfully, odiously—and it's a great deal too much! Come, come as far away from here as possible, and we'll settle the rest!"

The combined effort of Mr. Filer and Selah Tarrant to pacify the public had not, apparently, the success it deserved; the house continued in uproar and the volume of sound increased. "Leave us alone, leave us alone for a single minute!" cried Verena; "just let me speak to him, and it will be all right!" She rushed over to her mother, drew her, dragged her from the sofa, led her to the door of the room. Mrs. Tarrant, on the way, reunited herself with Olive (the horror of the situation had at least that compensation for her), and, clinging and staggering together, the distracted women, pushed by Verena, passed into the vestibule, now, as Ransom saw, deserted by the policeman and the reporter, who had rushed round to where the battle was thickest.

"Oh, why did you come—why, why?" And Verena, turning back, threw herself upon him with a protest which was all, and more than all, a surrender. She had never yet given herself to him so much as in that movement of reproach.

"Didn't you expect me, and weren't you sure?" he asked, smiling at her and standing there till she arrived.

"I didn't know—it was terrible—it's awful! I saw you in your place, in the house, when you came. As soon as we got here I went out to those steps that go up to the stage and I looked out, with my father—from behind him —and saw you in a minute. Then I felt too nervous to speak! I could never, never, if you were there! My father didn't know you, and I said nothing, but Olive guessed as soon as I came back. She rushed at me, and she looked at me—oh, how she looked! and she guessed. She didn't need to go out to see for herself, and when she saw how I was trembling she began to tremble herself, to believe, as I believed, we were lost. Listen to them, listen to them, in the house! Now I want you to go away—I will see you tomorrow, as long as you wish. That's all I want now; if you will only go away it's not too late, and everything will be all right!"

Preoccupied as Ransom was with the simple purpose of getting her bodily out of the place, he could yet notice her strange, touching tone, and her air of believing that she might really persuade him. She had evidently given up everything now—every pretense of a different conviction and of loyalty to her cause; all this had fallen from her as soon as she felt him near, and she asked him to go away just as any plighted maiden might have asked any favor of her lover. But it was the poor girl's misfortune that, whatever she did or said, or left unsaid, only had the effect of making her dearer to him and making the people who were clamoring for her seem more and more a raving rabble.

He indulged not in the smallest recognition of her request, and simply said, "Surely Olive must have believed, must have known, I would come."

"She would have been sure if you hadn't become so unexpectedly quiet after I left Marmion. You seemed to concur, to be willing to wait."

"So I was, for a few weeks. But they ended yesterday. I was furious that morning, when I learned your flight, and during the week that followed I made two or three attempts to find you. Then I stopped—I thought it better. I saw you were very well hidden; I determined not even to write. I felt I *could* wait—with that last day at Marmion to think of. Besides, to leave you with her awhile, for the last, seemed more decent. Perhaps you'll tell me now where you were."

"I was with father and mother. She sent me to them that morning, with a letter. I don't know what was in it. Perhaps there was money," said Verena, who evidently now would tell him everything.

"And where did they take you?"

"I don't know—to places. I was in Boston once, for a day; but only in a carriage. They were as frightened as Olive; they were bound to save me!"

"They shouldn't have brought you here tonight then. How could you possibly doubt of my coming?"

"I don't know what I thought, and I didn't know, till I saw you, that all the strength I had hoped for would leave me in a flash, and that if I attempted to speak—with you sitting there—I should make the most shameful failure. We had a sickening scene here—I begged for delay, for time to recover. We waited and waited, and when I heard you at the door talking to the policeman, it seemed to me everything was gone. But it will still come back, if you will leave me. They are quiet again—father must be interesting them."

"I hope he is!" Ransom exclaimed. "If Miss Chancellor ordered the policeman, she must have expected me."

"That was only after she knew you were in the house. She flew out into the lobby with father, and they seized him and posted him there. She locked the door; she seemed to think they would break it down. I didn't wait for that, but from the moment I knew you were on the other side of it I couldn't go on—I was paralyzed. It has made me feel better to talk to you—and now I could appear," Verena added.

"My darling child, haven't you a shawl or a mantle?" Ransom returned, for all answer, looking about him. He perceived, tossed upon a chair, a long, furred cloak, which he caught up, and, before she could resist, threw over her. She even let him arrange it and, standing there, draped from head to foot in it, contented herself with saying, after a moment:

"I don't understand—where shall we go? Where will you take me?"

"We shall catch the night-train for New York, and the first thing in the morning we shall be married."

Verena remained gazing at him, with swimming eyes. "And what will the people do? Listen, listen!"

"Your father is ceasing to interest them. They'll howl and thump, according to their nature."

"Ah, their nature's fine!" Verena pleaded.

"Dearest, that's one of the fallacies I shall have to woo you from. Hear them, the senseless brutes!" The storm was now raging in the hall, and it deepened to such a point that Verena turned to him in a supreme appeal.

"I could soothe them with a word!"

"Keep your soothing words for me—you will have need of them all, in our coming time," Ransom said, laughing. He pulled open the door again, which led into the lobby, but he was driven back, with Verena, by a furious onset from Mrs. Tarrant. Seeing her daughter fairly arrayed for departure, she hurled herself upon her, half in indignation, half in a blind impulse to cling, and with an outpouring of tears, reproaches, prayers, strange scraps of argument and iterations of farewell, closed her about with an embrace which was partly a supreme caress, partly the salutary castigation she had, three minutes before, expressed the wish to administer, and altogether for the moment a check upon the girl's flight.

"Mother, dearest, it's all for the best, I can't help it, I love you just the same; let me go, let me go!" Verena stammered, kissing her again, struggling to free herself, and holding out her hand to Ransom. He saw now that she only wanted to get away, to leave everything behind her. Olive was close at hand, on the threshold of the room, and as soon as Ransom looked at her he became aware that the weakness she had just shown had passed away. She had straightened herself again, and she was upright in her desolation. The expression of her face was a thing to remain with him forever; it was impossible to imagine a more vivid presentment of blighted hope and wounded pride. Dry, desperate, rigid, she yet wavered and seemed uncertain; her pale, glittering eyes straining forward, as if they were looking for death. Ransom had a vision, even at that crowded moment, that if she could have met it there and then, bristling with steel or lurid with fire, she would have rushed on it without a tremor, like the heroine that she was. All this while the great agitation in the hall rose and fell, in waves and surges, as if Selah Tarrant and the agent were talking to the multitude, trying to calm them, succeeding for the moment, and then letting them loose again. Whirled down by one of the fitful gusts, a lady and a gentleman issued from the passage, and Ransom, glancing at them, recognized Mrs. Farrinder and her husband.

"Well, Miss Chancellor," said that more successful woman, with considerable asperity, "if this is the way you're going to reinstate our sex!" She passed rapidly through the room, followed by Amariah, who remarked in his transit that it seemed as if there had been a want of organization, and the two retreated expeditiously, without the lady's having taken the smallest notice of Verena, whose conflict with her mother prolonged itself. Ransom, striving, with all needful consideration for Mrs. Tarrant, to separate these two, addressed not a word to Olive; it was the last of her, for him, and he neither saw how her livid face suddenly glowed, as if Mrs. Farrinder's words had been a lash, nor how, as if with a sudden inspiration, she rushed to the approach to the platform. If he had observed her, it might have seemed to him that she hoped to find the fierce expiration she sought for in exposure to the thousands she had disappointed and deceived, in offering herself to be trampled to death and torn to pieces. She might have suggested to him some feminine firebrand of Paris revolutions, erect on a barricade, or even the sacrificial figure of Hypatia, whirled through the furious mob of Alexandria. She was arrested an instant by the arrival of Mrs. Burrage and her son, who had quitted the stage on observing the withdrawal of the Farrinders, and who swept into the room in the manner of people seeking shelter from a thunderstorm. The mother's face expressed the well-bred surprise of a person who should have been asked out to dinner and seen the cloth pulled off the table; the young man, who supported her on his arm, instantly lost himself in the spectacle of Verena disengaging herself from Mrs. Tarrant, only to be again overwhelmed, and in the unexpected presence of the Mississippian. His handsome blue eyes turned from one to the other, and he looked infinitely annoyed and bewildered. It even seemed to occur to him that he might, perhaps, interpose with effect, and he evidently would have liked to say that, without really bragging, *he w*ould at least have kept the affair from turning into a row. But Verena, muffled and escaping, was deaf to him, and Ransom didn't look the right person to address such a remark as that to. Mrs. Burrage and Olive, as the latter shot past, exchanged a glance which represented quick irony on one side and indiscriminating defiance on the other.

"Oh, are *you* going to speak?" the lady from New York inquired, with her cursory laugh.

Olive had already disappeared; but Ransom heard her answer flung behind her into the room. "I am going to be hissed and hooted and insulted!"

"Olive, Olive!" Verena suddenly shrieked; and her piercing cry might have reached the front. But Ransom had already, by muscular force, wrenched her away, and was hurrying her out, leaving Mrs. Tarrant to heave herself into the arms of Mrs. Burrage, who, he was sure, would, within the minute, loom upon her attractively through her tears, and supply her with a reminiscence, destined to be valuable, of aristocratic support and clever composure. In the outer labyrinth hasty groups, a little scared, were leaving the hall, giving up the game. Ransom, as he went, thrust the hood of Verena's long cloak over her head, to conceal her face and her identity. It quite prevented recognition, and as they mingled in the issuing crowd he perceived the quick, complete, tremendous silence which, in the hall, had greeted Olive Chancellor's rush to the front. Every sound instantly dropped, the hush was respectful, the great public waited, and whatever she should say to them (and he thought she might indeed be rather embarrassed), it was not apparent that they were likely to hurl the benches at her. Ransom, palpitating with his victory, felt now a little sorry for her, and was relieved to know that, even when exasperated, a Boston audience is not ungenerous. "Ah, now I am glad!" said Verena, when they reached the street. But though she was glad, he presently discovered that, beneath her hood, she was in tears. It is to be feared that with the union, so far from brilliant, into which she was about to enter, these were not the last she was destined to shed.

The Best of the World's Best Books
COMPLETE LIST OF TITLES IN
THE MODERN LIBRARY

A series of handsome, cloth-bound books, formerly available only in expensive editions.

MISCELLANEOUS

MODERN LIBRARY GIANTS

A series of sturdily bound and handsomely printed, full-sized library editions of books formerly available only in expensive sets. These volumes contain from 600 to 1,400 pages each.

THE MODERN LIBRARY GIANTS REPRESENT A
SELECTION OF THE WORLD'S GREATEST BOOKS